WitchBorn

MM GAY PARANORMAL ROMANCE

A KITSUNE CHRONICLES STORY
BOOK FIVE

LISSA KASEY

CRAFTY FOX, LLC

WitchBorn : A Kitsune Chronicles Story
Copyright © 2024 Lissa Kasey
All rights reserved
Cover Art by Doelle Designs
Editing: Christy Duke
Published by Lissa Kasey
http://www.lissakasey.com

Please Be Advised

This is a work of fiction. Names, characters, businesses, places, events and incidents are either the products of the author's imagination or used in a fictitious manner. Any resemblance to actual persons, living or dead, or actual events is purely coincidental.

If you enjoyed this book, please post a review.

Trigger Warning

Listed below are the trigger warnings for this book. If any of these things bother you, please proceed with caution:

- References to past sexual assault and coercion
- Memories of child abuse/neglect
- Mental illnesses including Anxiety, Depression, SI
- Violence and gore

Prologue

FINN

The sun dipped below the horizon, casting the vast expanse of the woods in an eerie glow. I adjusted my backpack as I got out of the car, glancing at Luke and Jason, friends and fellow ghost hunters. The rumors of a ghostly wolf prowling the woods drove me to arrange the trip, and tonight, I was desperate to find it.

"Want to do the intro now?" Luke asked.

I shook my head. "Tomorrow. If we find something. You got the gear?"

"I'm grabbing the night cam," Jason said. He tugged on a pack of supplies and Luke picked up the pop-up tent.

"I've marked a few GPS points on our map. Let's head for the first one," I said. My phone had a half dozen apps that helped with our investigations. The actual audio and camera equipment had a habit of malfunctioning when I touched them, which meant I left that stuff to the guys.

"I've got audio," Luke said. He tucked the spare battery block in his pocket. "Stay close," he glared at me. "No running after shit, Finn."

"No kidding," Jason added. "Mr. I-Get-Lost-in-the-Grocery-Store."

"I do not." Well, sometimes. My phone was fully charged, and I opted for the regular camera as anything else would raise questions of legitimacy. "Let's do this."

We set off into the woods, the peaceful calm of them stretching high overhead easing my anxiety. The deeper we walked, the more shadows stretched into wells of overwhelming darkness. If I stared at them too long they moved, but then I'd blink and it would go back to being long shadows. I tried a few videos and Jason kept the camera going. Luke asked questions as he held an audio recorder out in front of him.

We'd been walking almost two hours when Jason asked, "Isn't it weirdly quiet?"

We all froze. The crunch of leaves beneath our feet faded and with it every other sound.

"Is someone here with us?" Luke whispered.

I raised my phone and turned on the video, scanning the area in a wide arc, but nothing showed up on the feed. "Nothing."

We stood in the silence for another few minutes. My gaze drawn to the far side of the area we stood. Was it getting darker? Night had set, but the headlamps the guys wore illuminated a couple dozen yards.

"Do you feel that?" Jason asked.

A chill filled the air, sharp, and biting. My breath puffed out in visible clouds, while my heart raced with both fear and anticipation. A flicker of movement caught my eye, and I lifted my phone, flipping on the video as I scanned the area. The height of the trees added layers of shadow and a cast of darkness around us, adding to the creepy sensation of being watched. If I stared too long at the shadows, I could almost feel them moving, slinking forward like some sort of dark ooze.

"I've never been more creeped out in my life," Luke said.

"Me either," Jason agreed.

I tiptoed toward the darkest of shadows, never one to be afraid of the dark.

"Fuck, Finn, why you gotta pick the spookiest of places?" Jason complained.

"You see something?" Luke asked.

I kept my phone focused on the dark. The closer I got the more I felt something lingered. "Nothing yet." I gazed into the brush, crouching to focus. "Hello? Anyone there?"

A pair of glowing eyes appeared in the depths of the shadows and I gasped for air as if I'd been sucker punched. Jason and Luke yelped beside me, so I knew they saw it too. I tried to zoom the video in, still heading for the darkness.

"Stop, Finn. It could be a bear or something."

"Bears don't have glowing eyes, dumbass," Luke griped.

The edges of it materialized as I got closer, still too far to capture a solid view of more than a hint of shadow and shape. Was it the ghost wolf?

I reached out a hand, wondering if I could get close enough to touch it. A shuddering icy cold pooled up from the ground around me, as though trying to stop my forward movement, and the glowing eyes suddenly lunged. We all screamed.

I flipped backward, half rolling as I found my feet and ran. We scattered, racing away with no real direction in mind. I clung to my phone, heart pounding, but tripped over something that sent me sprawling face first into a well of shadows.

My gut swirled and spiraled for a half second as though I'd fallen a thousand feet instead of a handful. I landed in a heap, on my back, staring up at the sky, trees overhead tinted with reds and golds in thick streams of moonlight. The scent of rain and freshly fallen leaves filled my senses and I sighed, heart slowing as the eerie sensation of being watched faded.

I got up and realized Luke and Jason were nowhere in sight. Neither was the crazy dark shadow wolf or unnatural movement of the darkness. The chill seeped away and aches arose in a dozen places. A skinned knee, a twinge in my back, something hot ran down my elbow and I suspected I'd been cut on something. But the chaotic and disturbing ambiance of the woods had vanished.

What the hell? I turned off the video and opened the GPS. No service.

"Guys?" I called. Which way had I come from?

My voice echoed, but beyond a fluttering of leaves on the wind, nothing else made a sound. Okay, that was a little creepy. I gazed upward trying to find the moon, but realizing there was sunlight. Had I been out long enough for it to be morning? The pale sky covered in clouds hovered above the trees, hiding the direction of the sun or any indication of which way I'd come.

Maybe that's why I smelled rain? A storm coming? If I'd knocked myself out, shouldn't I hurt more? Or maybe I was remembering wrong and it hadn't been dark yet when we entered the woods. Forests could breed darkness as the canopies snuffed out anything above, so maybe that's why I'd thought it was night.

I turned in a slow circle, trying to catch a sense of where I was, but it all looked the same, towering trees in every direction. And Jason had the pack of supplies.

"Fuck," I cursed, checking my phone again, wandering a few feet and finding no matter which way I went, I had no service, and my battery was quickly running low. I watched back the video I took, wondering if the wolf really appeared, but there it was, plain as day, captured on my phone camera. "Stuck in the woods with no way to show the world. Debunk this, assholes!" I shouted as if someone could hear.

But my voice faded away, leaving me with nothing but silence, trees, and rising anxiety.

Wesley

One

WESLEY

Where are you, Wesley? A voice asked a dozen times in my dreams. I often sat at a table with honeyed bread and fresh tea like I waited for someone while listening for the voice.

The scent of the tea reminded me of last days at the Autumn court with the last of the summer breeze blowing through the dying flora as the nights cooled before I'd been old enough to know the realm was collapsing.

A chill trickled through the dream, unrelenting with an icy bite, startling me out of the pleasant memories and back into reality.

I gasped for breath, air burning my lungs with crystalline cold. My skin stiff, half frozen to the ground, lashes coated in frost, freezing my eyes shut. A blessing, perhaps because they stung from the temperature.

The thick chain clenched tightly around my throat kept me from filling my lungs. It wouldn't kill me, neither the cold nor the lack of air. Being part fae was a curse rather than a blessing. That I blended, and could be mistaken for true fae, extended my life. Why had I bothered if this was to be my fate?

The zombie remains of the court sat in silence like an early winter morning when the temperature dropped below artic levels, wind dying away to leave only the barest rippling crackle of ice forming. Winter had fled with the tattered bits of her realm, saving a handful from Spring's wrath. But fae abandoned the last court in droves, realizing as I did that the walls, thin frozen illusions of castles and a prosperous realm, crumbled. Many slowly disintegrating, others crackling in a web of interlaced lines wriggling through the very core of the space waiting for a strong wind to unravel it all.

Winter was coming to an end. The Hag raged about lack of foes and the weakness of the rising kings. Always demanding a battle between courts despite their need to co-exist if they wanted to retain power at all. Winter warred hard rather than stepping down to let a new power rise. They clung to the threads of dying magic and tried to destroy the buds of new power, threatening to take all life with it.

The Fates were bitter bitches, winding the lives of mortals together in unbreakable ways. Demanding the rise and fall of courts, and death and destruction of species.

Were they losing power, as the modern world descended into chaos, or simply letting all the madness free to further tangle the weave in the fabric of reality? They weren't benevolent despite what many followers claimed. The few remaining gods with power to change the world, they were as corrupt as the darkest of courts. Could the Fates change hands? I'd given up hope of ever knowing.

It was strange to be visionless. A lifetime of waking nightmares of other people's fate falling silent should have been a blessing, but it worried me. What was I missing? Had the little King embraced his power? I hid him as long as I could, but his few years offered the barest of armor to help him stand his ground as the new Summer. Fate tied the wolf to him, but a blessing or a curse? Love could deliver both.

The crackling ice continued in a popping orchestra of sound around me. The lack of life and my ear pressed to the floor, made it louder than it probably was. I forced my eyes open, the cold stinging them instantly, but the sight of *him* comforting as usual.

Bound in stone like some science fiction movie, he screamed out the raging madness of a partial change into a beast of lore. Not unlike many lost creatures of Underhill, as he'd been long corrupted by the dark waves of ice and pain. One of the first witch-blood mutts lost inside the mortal world after the veil opened.

Summer warmed him for a while, delaying his fall into this frozen madness. I wondered if he was meant to be Winter. His pain said no. Winter would never fight the cold as he had. Winter would revel in the chill, finding the crisp bite comforting. The beast bound by magic wasn't Winter.

A rare comfort as I knew he was mine. Tied to me in some way. Life or death, whatever that was meant to be. Our paths crossed and my vision stopped.

A finger-wide crack crawled along the floor to his feet, slow at first, the break barely noticeable. I'd been watching it for weeks, or what felt like centuries. When it touched his toes, I feared he'd crack with it, chiseling away whatever remained of the terrifying thing held back by dying magic.

But the stone encasing his legs whittled away. Tiny slivers of rock crumbling like dust, unnoticed by all but me. The fissure widening, a swirl of wriggling energy inside rather than a person. A corrupt king?

I watched it for endless hours, days, and weeks, until my vision blurred and I could stay awake no longer, losing myself in dreams for a short time until the cold jolted me back. Parts of his wings were freed from the stone, a stretch of leather skin between bony juts of darkness. I waited for them to move, my breath catching for long minutes as I prayed for an eruption that would end my suffering even if it was a swift death.

He stood immobile. The stone near his face cracked like a shattered mirror, a net of shards cascading outward.

Another thick break freed his fingertips. They moved. I

gasped, blinked, thinking I'd been mistaken. But he moved again, hand clenching, fist forcing the arm to flex and more of the stone crumbled. Audible now with a cracking that couldn't be mistaken for ice.

He ripped his arm free, shards of rock ricocheting in a dozen directions, hitting the walls like tiny missiles, which exploded the thin layers of ice.

Someone screamed, followed by a dozen more, that shifted into a deafening roar that shook the realm with earthquake ferocity. His face morphed from semi-human, to the elongated snout and sharp fangs of a dragon. Many of the *WitchBorn* could take this form, though few had ever attempted to learn to control it.

Enormous, like the storybooks, with a crown of horns ringing his brow, he erupted from the stone, body completing its change, part serpentine, a chaos of legends. His tail smashed free of the remaining stone, releasing the monster from the crackling remnant of broken ice magic. The beast snapped at the movement around him, latching onto a few remaining fae, piercing them with fang and claw.

He devoured fae whole, biting some into pieces, the others swallowed in a single gulp as everyone ran and the beast jolted toward the screaming chaos, claws as large as my head paused inches from my face. Once changed like this, the beast rarely stopped, the hunger driving them to madness. The prince had consumed legions of fae before he'd been entombed in ice and saved by the mortals fated to ground him and give Spring life.

The end it was to be then, wasn't it? That was okay. It explained a lot. A payback by the Fates of sorts for meddling with their design.

Did he kill the Winter Queen?

I hoped so. That bitch needed to end; it was time for a fresh Winter to rise.

Closing my eyes, I breathed, ignoring the shaking and painful shrieks of the dying. I sank into the comfort that the end was coming. Freedom could come in a lot of ways. Enslaved to the courts, the expectation of death had been my only hope to find it.

The shrieking terror trickled away, leaving only the sound of my breathing in the barren space. Had I been the only one to survive? Cursed to remain bound here motionless in endless torture? That sounded a thousand times worse.

I opened my eyes to find the dragon gazing at me with glazed eyes, its hot breath close enough to warm my face. I couldn't help the tears. The human form, forced into by the magic binding chains, added weaknesses and lack of control when emotions over-whelmed me. My father's genes cursed my existence with tainted blood much as the Summer and Spring kings.

A sharp talon traced the chains binding me to the floor. I couldn't tear my gaze away from his, and wondered if he saw me at all. His clouded eyes feverish, perhaps maddened by the magic that had kept him bound or the thorns of corruption they'd dug into his soul?

I swallowed; the dagger-like claws close to my skin. A sharp tip slid beneath the tight link around my neck. The metal parted as though the talon sliced through butter rather than thick magic coated silver. The chain slipped off my throat.

I gasped, chilled air half-choking me as I breathed deeply for the first time in ages.

The beast snuffled, pressing its face to my chest, his head easily as large as half my body. It tilted its head. Did it expect me to run? A coughing fit seized control of me for several long minutes, but a dozen other chains locked me to the floor.

It snarled, mouth opening in a gaping maw of rage and heated breath, screaming again. I flinched, ears aching as the sound shat-tered the remaining stone. The bonds slipped away, Winter's power broken, though I didn't move.

Lying beneath the beast, I thought he'd take a bite, or devour me as he had the other fae, but a careful talon-tipped hand wrapped around my core and lifted me.

I couldn't stifle my scream as skin ripped away in a dozen places where the ice had fused me to the floor, pain sharp and white hot. My vision blacked out as I envisioned myself eaten by the beast and prayed for a quieter ever after.

Two

WESLEY

Sweat dripped from my brow, heat warming my bones as I waded out of the dark thinking I'd find myself back in the realm of the Summer King again. The heat of his temper a melting blaze, though rare. He preferred the gentle warmth of sunny days in the shade, or a cup of hot tea in the winter.

Wesley?

I blinked open my eyes at the call of my name, expecting the dream to fade, but finding myself in a patch of sun-filled grass. Was Sebastian here?

Trees towered around me, but I basked in a thick ray of sunlight, burning away the lingering chill. Everything hurt. The mortal body far too fragile, I'd learned to manage the weaknesses, drawing close to power, and hiding among both mortals and fae.

My skin ached, healing, a tingling mesh of magic like bee stings wriggling over my flesh. But my lungs filled easily, air warm and soothing. If it were a dream, it was a good one.

I rolled over, forcing my body to shift from human to beast, and rose to unsteady legs. My stag form wobbly after months of inactivity. The rack of horns on my head weighed more than I remembered, and I sank back to the thick layer of grass, thirsty, hungry, but too joyous over the warmth to leave yet.

Had Summer finally solidified his realm? Had he rescued me from the dragon?

I sucked in a thick breath of air searching for the scents of him and his mate: honey and clover, icing and fresh baked bread, but all I smelled was lush grass, and the hint of changing leaves. I nibbled at the grass, desperate to ease the gnawing hunger gaping inside, and even that small amount of energy was more than I had. The warm waves of the sun on my skin lulled me back to sleep, dreamless for a time, a true rest I expected to be interrupted by the daggered reach of cold which always ripped me back into reality.

But the trickling sound of water dragged me from sleep rather than pain. First with a few broken dreams of drinking my fill, and then with a need to empty my bladder. Human shortcomings, my own witchblood ever a curse.

I struggled to my feet, the sun absent as night had fallen, but the moon stretched overhead large and full, beautiful as I couldn't recall it ever being. The glowing orb hung huge and close, like I could leap toward it and land on the surface with one mighty jump. Perhaps when my strength returned.

My wobbling legs steadied as I emptied my bladder then followed the sound of water to a stream, studied it for several minutes, my heart racing, and throat clenching to drink. The fae could corrupt anything. I took a few hesitant steps toward the shore, expecting it to lunge at me, but it tinkled and danced as a normal stream should.

I couldn't wait any longer and bowed my head to drink, the water tasting clean and fresh, slightly cool. The gentle breeze blew through the trees a soft caress rather than biting cold or stifling heat. I drank my fill and sank into the water, letting it pool around me, washing away the filth with the memories.

Had I found my way back to the mortal realm? It couldn't be part of Winter; it was too warm. But the trees, a mix of oak, pine, and fir, were common to the mortal world and without blight. Layers of green moss crawled up the trunks of the thick trees and the grass grew tall enough to sway in the wind. The leaves high up danced with a soothing rustle, but the dark made it hard to define their color.

Movement caught my gaze, and my attention snapped toward a distant bush. Shadows hid a slinking darkness. It stilled, trying to blend, but in this form, I saw the outline of the beast. Too small to be the dragon. Was it the Hunt? I had thought Spring took control of those monsters, stealing them from Winter.

I got to my feet, ready to run. Another curse or blessing, perhaps, as none could catch me unless I allowed myself to be caught. Even tired as I was, I'd run until my heart gave out and the wild magic between worlds took back my soul to birth another White Stag.

The beast slid from the bush, muzzle darkened, wet with crimson in the bright moonlight, and dropped something at the shore's edge a dozen yards from where I stood. Our gaze met for several seconds, but it slipped back into the shadows and vanished. I hesitantly inched forward to see what it had left.

A rabbit. Fresh kill.

I sighed, my mortal mind reminding me of meals that included the flesh of creatures. Not all bad, but the Stag hated it. We would be happier with mushrooms, or soft moss. Was this some sort of courting dance? The dragon turned to a wolf-like creature? Or something else?

I wandered away from the kill, determined to find a place to settle for the night that wouldn't leave my back exposed, nibbling moss until a spread of clover sprouting between trees drew me in.

Gorging on the clover, I couldn't help but settle into the thick spread of it and roll around. If this was a dream, it felt real.

The trees towered overhead, a canopy to case the glowing light of the over-sized moon. Clover, a thick mat beneath me, and the distant sound of the stream, I lay down to rest. Would the beast return? Fed and warm for the first time in ages, I didn't care. I'd have bowed to the Summer King and promised him anything for this moment, as fleeting as it might be.

Only the absence of bird chatter hinted where I was. Not the mortal realm, even though I'd been brought a rabbit and saw fish in the stream. The stretching silence, a lack of bugs, birds, or any movement beyond the water, made me search the trees for a sign of the spirits that haunted the mortal world.

There were two possibilities, either I had fallen into the purview of the earth spirit, or Green Man, as the mortals called him, or this was a fae realm. The presence of the beast, meant likely the latter, but I'd worry about it when I woke in the morning and found myself still curled up in the clover instead of chained to the floor of the Winter court.

Three

WESLEY

Days of wandering and searching for a way out left me frustrated. The realm spread wide, but repeated. A new realm with an unestablished king. Not the little King and his sorcerer wolf mate with their growing Summer court as I had hoped, and not Spring with his sarcasm and wit, which drew the remaining fae to him, not because of his power, but because his servants helped him craft a welcoming home of wakening buds and wild energy storms to recharge their fading power.

After exploring in long circles led back to the stream, I wondered if any other beings existed in this realm. The dark beast hadn't returned, nor had I glimpsed the dragon, though twice I'd been left fresh kills of small creatures, various offerings of fish or fowl, which I ignored in favor of clover and moss.

Often when I slept, I'd feel watched. Uneasy, but also protected.

The silence added to my loneliness. Long years of learning to be independent from other fae meant great survival skills, but survival didn't equal joy or even peace. I'd rest a few hours, then get up to wander again, looking for a change, finding boundless forest and a stream that meandered in replicating bends, but never had a beginning or an end.

I followed the water, drenching my hooves in it as if defiant, petty and willing to ruin the pretty peace of the landscape. The evenings got cold enough to force me to seek shelter in a thicket of trees, which often magically appeared as though my wish were tied to the realm. During the day, the warmth of the sun on my back and cool touch of water at my feet kept me moving.

Circles, only never truly around. Fae realms were maddening places. I'd come to love the material comforts of the mortal world, wealth, shelter, and the fine couture. Fae simplicity, and how their magic warred with the mere idea of modern items, drove my irritation, much like the ever-flowing stream.

The water never got past my knees, and I longed to soak in the cool spread. I traveled the stream until the sky colored with the painted pink, orange, and gray of dusk.

A small pond emerged as I rounded a bend thinking I'd stop for the night to eat and rest. That pond had not been there, though I'd passed that annoying stretch of birch trees a dozen times, having nibbled at the moss near the roots.

With a heavy bit of apprehension, I approached the pond. The gurgle of water soft and soothing, still silent of bugs, birds, or frogs. I gazed into the pool from a respectable distance, waiting for movement, or a sign of danger. Fae traps and bodies of water went hand in hand. Even with Underhill destroyed, the last threads of power scattered among the mortal world as seeds to be gathered and grown within new realms, my anxiety over being eaten by some wild selkie or brazen water nymph kept me from moving closer.

I kicked a few stones into the water, watching them skip a time or two and sink, the water resettling, and looking... normal.

My Stag form could outrun anything that might pop up from the depths, though my human side begged for a soaking bath.

The sun vanished behind the trees, leaving the sky washed in pretty colors as the moon rose, the remix in the sky worthy of a painting. Was a bath worth death? An end was an end, wasn't it?

I stepped into the pool, carefully letting my hooves find purchase in the sandy bottom. Nothing moved as I climbed deeper, soaking all the way over my back, and until I had to lift my head nothing moved beyond me in the small pool. Though I waited a long while before shifting into my human form and finding a spot to sit that left me neck deep.

I could wish for a heated spring, but the soothing chill of the water helped ease some of the ache of still healing flesh, my mortal body slower to repair itself than the Stag.

I washed, gaze half-blinded by the brightness of the moon, still a perfect orb of blazing brightness above after days inside the realm. I could feel my ribs, and the lack of muscle tone was concerning. How long had I been in locked in Winter? Sometimes the realms ate years, though it seemed less and less so as the modern world merged with the magic remains of Underhill.

Would there be anything to return to? Had the little King taken his throne? I would have liked to have been there to watch him finally ascend. He'd arrive in a mighty storm of winds, pelting rain, and dangerously green skies. I had seen it, long before my vision had been defined enough to know what the Fates showed.

I sighed and dove beneath the water to scrub at my hair, finding it too long, and instantly annoyed. The cut had been expensive in mortal terms, and time without maintenance left it a rat's nest of tangled curls in need of a weedwacker.

The desire for air made me resurface, lungs still sensitive from the icy cold which had dug deep inside. I rose up to find myself face to face with the wolf of shadows. The true outline of his size was hard to define in the dark as he almost seemed to have wings tucked to his side, and more than four legs, but even the bright glowing moon couldn't pierce the ooze that coated him. The beast towered over me, easily three times the size of a normal beast and not the fluffy spread of fur I knew the little

King's mate to be. Rather this beast wriggled with dark slugs of magic.

Infected by Winter, perhaps?

I didn't run. The shift and the chase could begin in a heartbeat, but once it started, it wouldn't end until one of us was dead. Maybe even both.

It snarled at me, dripping viscous liquid from fetid breath while everything it touched died beneath the ooze of the dark shadows. The shore at its feet curdled and shrank away turning from sand to tar, and I couldn't help my flinch as a few drops landed in the water like floating turds writhing with worms.

I slid back, scrambling for the opposite shore, expecting chase, but it didn't leap for me. That showed resolve I had never met before. The human form didn't produce the same impulse of *prey* as the Stag did, but I'd had more than my fair share of unwanted encounters due to the lingering tease of pheromones and cursed fae magic.

The beast slid back from the water's edge, revealing a small shock of pure white fur. Had it killed another rabbit? I had yet to see a rabbit in the days of wandering, and he was somehow slaughtering them for me when I didn't eat meat unless the Stag took control and we were desperate for food.

"Thanks, but no thanks," I told it. "I'll stick with clover. Some berries would be nice, but this dance of slaughter is not going to win me over." I backed away slowly, finding myself near the trees I often rested, worried that the area wouldn't be safe anymore. Which brought an uncomfortable chuckle to my lips. It had *never* been safe. That was the point, right? Whatever pocket realm I'd become trapped in was another cage of sorts.

Did it belong to the *WitchBorn* dragon I'd witnessed rip itself from icy rock? Why send beasts to offer food? I had yet to encounter the dragon or the man I'd dreamt of a thousand times. Without another vision to tell me why I was here, or where *here* was, I was as blind as any other being.

Unsettling. I'd never loved my second sight, but a clue would have been nice.

I shifted to the Stag, needing the protection of speed, magic, and the lack of bare mortal flesh between us.

The beast inched away, sliding into the swelling darkness of the trees until nothing else moved again. The water burbled, spitting out the dark chunks. The ground regrew, overtaking the darkness with ease, burying it deep. Would it suffocate down there, or fester? I wasn't going to dig to find out.

The white fluff lingered on my mind, too bright in the glowing moonlight to be natural. What had the beast found in the strange world?

I stalked closer, gaze constantly searching the deep shadows for movement, and crossed the steam to approach the white fluff. Was it moving?

Breathing?

I inched toward it, rack forward, ready for it to leap at me with fang or claw. It blinked tiny eyes at me, yawned, baring tiny teeth, little ears, and a fluffy snow-white body.

A kitten?

It left me a kitten?

I blinked, and shifted, fearing for a few seconds it was all some trick, but as I sank to my knees in quickly growing moss, the kitten stumbled to tiny legs, and wobbled its way over.

The soft mew begging for adoration as it scrambled around my knee. I picked it up carefully, examining it, finding a fluffy baby. Was it old enough to be without its mom? I cradled it to my chest, trying to warm it as it snuggled close.

Could it hear my heartbeat?

We sat waiting together, watching the shadows in the thick growing moss. The stillness only minimally comforting.

"Never felt like Alice before," I said to the kitten. Though I had teased the little King with the remark. "Into a wonderland of clover, snow white kittens, and leering dark beasts."

The kitten meowed, a breathy high-pitched cry as it licked my hand.

"Yes, yes, what am I to do with you? What do kittens eat? Not moss for certain. Be happy I'm not turning you into a handbag or something hideous like that. I know many a fae who would out of spite."

I carried the kitten to the small nest of trees that had become my home, wishing for a cabin or a shelter of some kind if I was to be stuck in mortal flesh again. My Stag form might be safer for me, but what if it triggered the chase in the kitten? What if I accidentally stepped on it? Or it touched a tip on my rack and the poison made it wither and fade?

"Hardly a Hilton," I told it as I laid down in the moss and clover bed, grateful for the soft pallet as I set it down. The critter curled up against me, face pressed to my chest, its soft purr giving me a soothing vibration that helped me settle to rest. "Never got a kitten from the Hilton..."

Four

WESLEY

I slept hard, a dead sleep that only my bladder could bring me back with an abrupt and painful reminder of mortal needs. But I was insanely warm, covered in a fluffy weighted blanket, even while the sun pierced the back of my eyelids with incessant brightness.

When I tried to stretch, something wriggled against me. I startled, sitting up and pulling away, half terrified I was back in the Winter court forced to entertain others. Chained to the floor and their whims of torture.

The blazing light of the new day burned colored spots into my vision and I blinked tears to clear my sight, fearing attack, but none came. I held out a hand, a universal gesture for *stop, keep away,* half expecting something to bite it off, but it licked me.

I rubbed my eyes, color pops giving me only partial sight, much as the dreaded migraines I suffered after an actual vision, with wiggling lines of writhing brightness blotting out portions of the world.

A huge white shape lingered in front of me, easily as large as mortal canine, like a Great Dane.

The kitten?

I sucked in a deep gulp of air, willing my sensitive eyes to focus, even as I wove my hand into thick fur where it touched my palm. It pressed itself into my reach, as though it could force me to pet it that way. The blind floundering erupted into a slow throb at my temple. A migraine coming. Fuck. Sometimes it preceded a vision, though that was rare. Usually, they happened after I had one. The more chaotic and violent the vision, the worse the migraine.

Had I missed a vision? I'd never slept through them before. But I couldn't recall the last time I'd felt rested.

Something shifted above, clouds covered some of the blazing brightness, casting us in shade. I rubbed my forehead, though the throbbing only got worse, a sign that I would be incapacitated soon with pain turning my brain to mush.

The wiggling lines, like maggots of brightness, danced around the edge of my sight, and gave me the very center of my left eye to see with. I focused on the furry beast instead of looking overhead and chancing more light damage.

"Not a kitten," I said, staring at a thick coated leopard with white fur. It lounged at my feet as if it were a friendly housecat. Too big to be the real thing, though the shape of the face and spots reflected what I knew from mortal zoos and reference books. "You're not going to eat me, right?" I asked, frowning at the arm draped over my leg with a paw as large as my hand relaxed near my groin. "Keep the murder mittens tucked away, yeah?"

My head throbbed, and I couldn't help my wince. The cat slid up with a slow and careful grace, as though afraid to startle me, and pressed its face to mine, scenting my pain.

"What are you, some sort of supernatural service animal? I'm pretty sure I can't take you into the grocery store with me. Panic would ensue." And I was going crazy, talking to a white leopard while sitting naked in a field of clover on the verge of a massive migraine.

My stomach growled thinking of a grocery store and the common produce section I'd grown to love over the years. Seasonal fruits and veggies drew me like a fly to honey. Not caviar and lobster dreams like many mortals, but fresh apples, juicy berries, and even a thick squash.

I sighed. Mortal hunger outweighed the Stag's need. The Stag could eat the entire forest and my human gut would beg for more. Because the food was part of the magic of a realm and couldn't sustain a mortal? Or simply because a mortal needed more varied nutrients? I suspected the latter.

The cat nudged me, face shoving up my arm.

"Sorry, pussy cat. A migraine is about to make me useless. Normally I hide in a dark room until it passes. Don't suppose you can keep your scary wolf friend at bay until I'm feeling better?" The Stag could still run. Even blind it would evade the beast until one of us died. But I didn't look forward to the pain changing would cause, or losing myself in a chase.

The cat nudged me again, squirming until it seemed to be trying to lift me, or at least encourage me to my feet. I sighed and reluctantly got up. "Okay, Lassie. Is Timmy stuck in a well? If it's your oozing wolf friend, he can stay there."

The cat brushed itself along my outer thigh and walked a few feet in one direction, pausing to look back to check that I followed. "Yes, yes. I'm Alice now, aren't I? I'm coming. Let's not be late."

I found my way to a bush to relieve myself, glancing back a few times at the cat, who turned away as if giving me privacy. Strange. But I rinsed in the stream again, and then focused on the cat, waving at him to, "Lead the way."

The critter led me through a weave of thick clover and tightly knit trees, most looking the same as I'd seen in my wandering, though I couldn't recall the trees being that big, towering into the sky to ease the bright light of the day. The growing migraine slowed me down and brought a wobble to my step as I had to cover one eye completely with my hand as it eased the throbbing on that side of my skull.

We rounded another section of the stream, the trees widening, and suddenly a cabin stood there, like something out of a storybook, built out of logs and moss, tree limbs growing from the top, flowers decorating the base.

"Uh..." I froze a dozen yards away feeling like a witch should come charging out of the cute little hut to roast me and throw me in a soup pot.

The cat slunk forward, reaching the cabin and rubbing its side along the wood beneath the front window. It sat down in front of the door, expectant.

I stood there, struck half-stupid, half terrified. Too many stories, fae mixed with mortal retellings of misfortune. The longing to be inside, find darkness to ease the pain, and the sense of false safety that walls provided making my heart race. I could enact wards with physical barriers as a guide. Inside a realm, the effect may be minimal, but give me warning. I couldn't open a portal between worlds, realms, or even free myself from this place, as I'd already tried. The ability lost when the little King drank down the remains of Underhill and spit out a god.

The tiny cabin could be a sanctuary or a prison.

My head throbbed again, and my stomach rebelled, threatening a rash of vomiting if I didn't rest. I could lie down in the thick grass and hope for the best, or open the door and pray for darkness that would ease the ache chiseling its way through my brain.

I took a step toward the door, hesitant, but the cat slid to the side, watching me intently. "If you're the Cheshire cat, leading me to madness, you should know I've been there for years. Insanity is part of the fae lineage." I reached for the door handle, shoved it open, anticipating an attack, but found it empty; a small space with a narrow bed and bland walls, lifeless mostly, but the dark welcoming.

The cat shoved its way inside. Should I leave the door open? It waited, watching, perched a few feet away. I closed the door. The bed, though narrow, was piled in lush blankets, none fur, for which I was grateful. Sleeping under dead critters would guarantee nightmares and might trigger the Stag's bloodlust. Being part fae was a mixed bag of terrors.

Thick curtains covered the windows, blocking out the sun, only the barest glimpses of it trickling through at the edges to give me an idea where anything was in the darkness. I crawled into the bed, digging myself a cavern beneath the blankets and finding the pillow a soft cloud of comfort. Not the Hilton, or even a Days Inn, but it smelled clean, the blankets warming my cooled flesh, and the darkness eased my throbbing skull.

The cat leapt up beside me, squeezing me back toward the wall, and putting itself between the door and me. Protection? My mortal anxiety faded and I couldn't keep my eyes open as the beast began to purr. Could mortal leopards do that? I didn't think so, but warm, and feeling safe, I let my eyes close and hoped the headache would vanish without delivering me a vision I couldn't convey to anyone.

Five

WESLEY

The forest shriveled, rotting and tumbling into goopy puddles of ooze. The landscape filled like an oil spill, the rainbow-colored swirl coating everything, iridescent and pretty beneath the glow of the blazing sun while it destroyed everything it touched.

Trees melted, the fabric of their magic unraveling. The spread of thick pines fading into darkness became the night, a pool of unlit madness and twisting chaos. The touch of the growing monster inched forward in a painful progression all around.

I shivered, chilled to the bone, curled up into a ball in the center, watching it all approach and unable to stop it. A sign of the end coming, my end, the world's end, who knew. I'd never made it to the part of the dream in which it reached me, though I intrinsically knew when it did, I would unravel too, dissolving into the last remains of wild magic left to my line.

Would the destruction end all I was? The lineage of the White Stag extended from the beginning of sentient life, evolving as the world did. But with mortal blood, part witchborn, I was far from invincible. Could I be the end of the line? Or would the magic take new form?

The ooze reached the tip of my big toe, a touch so cold and searing with a bitter icy snap that I screamed, flailed, and ripped myself away.

A light appeared, the world coming back into focus as my heart pounded. I was inside the cabin, in the narrow bed, the kitten beside me on the pillow, and a lamp that hadn't been there before, lit to a soft yellow glow.

I sucked in air in gulping gasps, chest aching from the race of my heart, though all around everything sat in quiet stillness. The kitten stood up on tiny legs and stretched, opening its mouth to a breathy yawn. It reached up with a small fluffy paw and put it on my arm.

"You take up less of the bed this way," I grumbled at it, annoyed. Kitten or leopard, at least this way it was pocket sized.

Had the room changed or had I missed it all in my headache induced lack of focus? The light cast a soft glow off a tiny kitchen, an open door that appeared to lead to a bathroom, and a handful of furniture, like a kitchen table, a dressing stand, and a fabric coated chaise that I didn't recall being there when I went to sleep.

I eyed the kitten. It leapt off the bed with a floundering gait that looked completely kitten like, and waddled its tiny butt toward the kitchen. "I really feel like Alice," I said more to myself than the beast.

Was that a working kitchen faucet? In a realm? I stared at it another minute and eyed the dark shadow of the bathroom, which appeared to have a toilet. The thought *I would kill for a shower*, fierce in my mind. But realms... at least the fae created ones I'd existed in most of my life... didn't have modern conveniences.

I shoved off the blankets and rose to my feet, testing the strength of my legs as well as for any lingering pain in my head. A dull ache rested over my left brow, fading, but a reminder that it could flare again. I stalked to the kitchen and turned the faucet expecting nothing, but water poured out in a thick, clear stream. The temperature adjusted with the handle.

Was this a modern realm? The little King hadn't perfected the weave of magic with realism like this, at least not before I'd been captured by Winter. Spring perhaps? He had always adored the comforts of mortals, but I never imagined I'd be allowed in his realm. He hated all things fae with good reason as they spent his entire existence trying to destroy him.

I drank my fill from the tap and turned to the bathroom, drawing close and wondering if there was light. Stepping into the doorway did something to illuminate the room, which was far more spacious than I'd thought from the glimpse I'd caught from the bed. A huge soaking tub sat in one corner, a large, but open stone shower stall in the other, a toilet and a sink opposite it.

"This doesn't give the cabin in the woods vibe, thankfully, and I'll take it." I went to the shower, turning the silver handle and rewarded with a rainfall of warm drops. "If this is a dream, I'd like to stay," I told the kitten who sat itself down on a plush rug near the sink like a mini loaf of bread. "With minor additions of soap, towels, and maybe some clothes?" I said as I stepped under the water, letting it ease the ache in my muscles and wash away days of dust and the last remnant of the nightmare.

Months had passed since that dream plagued my sleep. Not a nightmare, but a vision. Something to come that I seemed unable to change. I thought it had been the end of Underhill as the dream stopped after the realm fell to the little King. Maybe it wasn't Underhill at all? Did it mean I'd failed to hasten the rise of the new courts? Would Spring and Summer fall before they could fully solidify?

I closed my eyes and let myself sink to the floor under the soothing rush of warm water. My racing heart, unusually fast since entering this new realm, let anxiety cling in my gut like a parasite.

Decades of suffering, planning, and manipulating, and I'd failed? Tears stung my eyes and I let them fall, mixing with the water, and ignoring the kitten even as it gave me tiny mewing cries at the edge of the shower.

The last of my glamour vanished with my resolve, leaving my physical form less perfect and not exactly human with small nubs at my brow where the horns would be, legs long and thin, more animal than human. The pretty façade and perfect grace I hid beneath to protect my mortal side vanished, leaving a cutesy mess of fawn-like cosplay. Not bulky or hairy enough to be a satyr, but not feminine enough for the pretty brethren of fawns I'd lived among in my early years.

This form required less magic, as it was made to absorb others and recharge a realm. The mortal form I spent years crafting to draw in others, like the little King and those around him, suppressed both the Stag and the Fawn sides of me. Natural yes, but always a low hum of energy required. Pretty privilege wasn't only a fae shortcoming. Mortals drew to beauty like bees to pollen. Even the Stag was a thing of beauty, perfection and strength. The Fawn was...weak, ordinary, and unlovable. That curse left me with far too many memories I wished to forget. I buried the Fawn deep, willing to die with that last bit of glamour in place. The last of wild magic could scatter my ashes to dust before I let anyone see.

Why let it go here with no one to see but some strange fae kitten? The failure weighed too much to hold it all. Wasn't it my calling to guide the rise of the new courts and rebalance magic? If not, then what was the point of all the pain?

I curled up into a ball and sobbed, leaving my back to the kitten, willing myself to drown in the flow of the gentle warm water, but deprived of even that. Perhaps I'd remain in this form and present myself to the shadow wolf. If I begged, maybe the beast would end my suffering.

None who knew this form existed anymore, except maybe the puck, but I avoided him easily. He clung to the little King with his own secrets and stayed out of mine. The Winter Queen had never seen this form, though knew it existed as she'd cast me into Zephyr's arms so he could use me to strengthen his power. But he'd been shorn in half by Spring's lover, and her curse had trapped me in ice, draining my strength, but never allowing the Fawn free. I suspected she hated it too, though none despised it as much as I did. Would the wolf use me, or end me? Did it matter? I sighed and let my melancholy thoughts pour out of me and into the water.

WESLEY

The water never ran cold, even while I huddled beneath the spray until long past my skin pruned from the damp. When I unfurled myself from the ground, my muscles groaned with stiffness. Part need to run, part tension. I stood, reinstating my human form and rubbed my hair, now shoulder length instead of the short cut I adored.

A bar of soap sat on a small stone shelf. I reached for it, knowing it hadn't been there when I entered the shower, but the solid cake smelled like lavender. I brought it to my nose, recalling the delicate bars the little King made from time to time with infusions of lemon grass, lavender, and occasionally a touch of blue bells. I'd been swiping them from him for over a decade. Soap, some tea, and once or twice, a slice of cake.

He either never noticed, or blamed the puck, or someone in his pack. Once he left the purview of the king of wolves, our connection had stretched more digitally. I'd gone from the deer he greeted from time to time near his garden, to a vague memory.

Glamour had its uses.

Where are you? The voice whispered softly. I couldn't tell if my imagination created it, or someone looked for me. Would Sebastian care? He didn't seem to like me much, though I'd tried to show him brotherly regard. Admittedly I had little skill in familial affection. Copying what had been done to me as a child was considered trauma to mortals. Rather I tried to remain aloof and protective. Was that wrong?

My stupid curse of visions offered no solution.

I lathered up with the soap and washed completely, feeling clean for the first time in ages, then set the soap down and turned off the water, hesitating to get out as the steam warmed my lungs. A stack of fluffy towels sat on a bench beside the exit of the shower. I knew neither had been there before, but the kitten had vanished too. He might have wandered out, growing bored with my long wash. Or this strange realm could have absorbed him back into some wild chaos of magic to create me towels.

I examined one, which felt like cotton and not fur. I dried off, trying to keep the idea of a kitten turned into a towel by magic and rubbing it all over my body out of my head. A breathy mew made me freeze, but a small bit of fluff rubbed over my ankle.

"Where did you go, pest?" I asked. "Did you report to your master that I'm finally clean?" I finished drying off as the kitten returned to its loaf position, and I went to the sink. A toothbrush, tube of paste, and a comb sat there. "I could use some lotion too," I told no one. Toiletries were more than I'd received anywhere else, and old routines comforted my racing anxiety. "Now I need something to wear, and maybe you can tell your boss that it would be okay to let me go home?"

Did I still have one? I rented an apartment near the little King's realm, with money from long years of planning to tie me close to him. If decades or centuries passed, it might all be ash by now. Drawing close to the monarchs of the courts had been both dangerous, and for safety. Everyone wanted a seer, even if that seer was considered volatile and incoherent most of the time.

I never told the little King or his mate what I was. Why? Fear? Worry they'd turn on me like all the other courts did with a demand for answers I didn't have? And now knowing that the destruction of magic hadn't been prevented... what was the point?

The kitten mewed, a long cry that made me look its way with the toothbrush in my mouth and foam everywhere. It sat beside the door next to a thin chair with a stack of clothing sitting on it.

I spit out the foam. "Um..." Was the kitten some sort of realm servant? Why make it helpless and sweet-looking? I put the brush down, rinsed and spit, washed my face, and reached for the stack of clothing.

Jeans, a T-shirt, a hoodie, loafers, and even boxers, the pile could have come from the little King's closet. I frowned at it, thinking I had better couture at home, but what the hell. Everything fit. More magic I assumed, though couldn't sense the ghost-like prickling that came from someone else's glamour touching my skin.

I paused to stare in the mirror, another thing that hadn't been there, and winced at my gaunt face and the troughs of discoloration around my eyes. The length of white-gold curls brushing my shoulders softened the hollowness of my long time without food or light. I picked up the brush, combing the strands back and securing it into a band that magically appeared on the vanity top. A man could get used to things appearing when called.

"How about a pretty man with a big dick who wants to kiss my feet and worship me instead of hurt me?" I asked my reflection, pausing a few seconds like someone would appear and somehow *not* scare the ever-living shit out of me. "He should be rich too. I have expensive taste."

No one showed, and that was okay. The kitten stood in the doorway, fluffy little face looking up at me with bright blue eyes. I reached down and picked it up, tucking it in the front pocket of the hoodie as I made my way back to the kitchen. It wriggled around, sticking its little nose out of the hole but settled down as though it were perfectly fine being my new pocket pet.

Seven

WESLEY

U nlike everything else, the kitchen sat bare. There wasn't a fridge or more than an old-style wood stove, and a handful of old pans, which meant if I wanted warm food, I'd have to collect both the food and the wood. "Reduced to manual labor," I grumbled as I opened the door, expecting a flood of bright light to pierce my skull and reignite the migraine, but the day was cloudy and cool, the breeze warning of an overnight chill to come.

I'd have to get wood for warmth, too. Outside the cabin I hoped to find a woodpile, but sadly other than the cabin itself and a spread of berry bushes filled with ripe fruit, there wasn't enough sticks to keep the stove lit long enough to warm the house. "Off to Narnia we go then, eh?" I told the kitten. "Or wonderland, pick your novel world of choice. Not certain either are more terrifying than reality. The human creative mind is a horrifying place to get lost."

I followed the stream, trying to gain direction, not looking forward to finding my way back. Had the cabin been there the whole time? Probably not. The realm shifting and changing meant it was awakening. Good or bad, yet to be determined.

The kitten rode along, without a peep, barely more than an

occasional wiggle in my front pocket, but a lot of warmth and comfort as it made biscuits against my stomach.

The comfort of having another living being close calmed the raging anxiety as the stream snaked around, the same as yesterday. Had the cat led me to the cabin? Maybe it could lead me out of here?

I tugged back the fabric to find it sleeping. "So helpful," I said.

The sound of something trickled through the trees, movement, voices, and I froze mid step. Was that a person or the shadow wolf again? I dropped to a crouch and waited, listening intently for the sound to come again.

"Hello?" the muffled call came from the distance to the north, opposite the cabin. A person? Had someone else wandered into the realm and gotten stuck?

I waited for the call again. Too irregular to be an animal, but the echo gave me a direction, and I snuck my way through the brush, tempted to change, but also aware that I had clothes and a kitten in my pocket, neither of which I wanted to lose. Friend or foe?

"Anyone?" he called. "Way to go, asshole. Get lost..."

His movement filtered through the trees easily a dozen yards away, and I plastered myself to a tree trunk, careful and waiting, studying him from a distance. He looked normal enough. Young like the Summer King, dressed in jeans and a college hoodie, hair cut short on the sides, slightly longer on the top, dark in color, eyes a rich deep brown. Attractive, but averagely so. He could claim pretty privilege, sure, but he was no Henry Cavill.

I didn't smell a weapon, or a concentration of magic, but the entire realm coated everything in magic. I knew the kitten in my pocket was a magic thing, but couldn't smell its magic either.

"Hello?" I called, keeping trees between us just in case the man turned into some sort of beast.

He paused and blinked, staring through the trees. "Hello? Someone there? I'm lost."

"Strange place to be lost, friend," I said.

He jolted, gaze searching the trees before landing on me, then turned and slowly walked in my direction. "Are you a ghost?"

"Why would I be a ghost?"

"My buddies and I were out here searching for ghosts. We have a YouTube channel that shows a lot of crazy stuff."

"That's far enough," I told him when he was about twenty feet away.

He put his hands up. "Okay. I'm not armed or anything."

"No camera either. Strange way to ghost hunt."

"I'm the host. My buddies and I were investigating. I was using my phone to film, but Jason had the night cam." He squinted in my direction. "Never seen hair that color before. You sure you're not a ghost?"

Was my hair off? If I spent too much time in my fawn form it often turned more a spun gold wheat, but I didn't think it all that unusual. My reflection in the mirror at the cabin hadn't been strange. Maybe what the reflection showed wasn't reality? I reached up to pull the length of my hair around, trying to make out the color. Was there a rose gold tint to it? Was the realm doing that?

"No ghosts here, friend. You've stumbled into a fae forest," I said wanting to gauge his reaction.

He blinked, confused. "Fae? Are ghosts fae? Wait, what?" He pulled a cell phone out of his pocket and stared at it a minute before cursing. "No service. You don't happen to have a phone with service?"

"No phone at all." Realms monkeyed with technology. Would the modern realms have that option? I hoped so as I'd become partial to streaming services. "Where were you ghost hunting?"

"Gifford Pinchot National Forest."

"Ghost hunting or bigfoot hunting?" I knew of the forest, most anyone who spent any time in small towns in Washington knew of the forest and the ban on weapons to hunt sasquatch. The little King's chosen town was four, almost five hours north by car, near the Canadian border, and I didn't think that was where we were at all.

"Both. I mean we are trying to document ghosts, but a bigfoot would get us views too." He squinted in my direction and took a few more steps forward. I backed away. "No harm, man. You said this is a fae forest? You mean like fairies? The little flying things?"

I snorted. "Fae are manipulators of magic powerful enough to move oceans or fry you with a thought. The *little flying* type you mention would sooner lead you to a bog to be eaten by a selkie than anything like storybooks of guidance and peace."

"Right." He looked around. "Fae forest... and you're like a wood nymph or something? I thought those were all supposed to be hot girls? Big boobs, no clothes, that sort of thing? No offense, you're pretty and all, for a guy."

"I asked for a guy with a big dick, not one who *is* a big dick," I muttered, hoping the realm would hear my complaint. A little louder, I said, "I'm lost here, too. Not a nymph, haven't seen any. They aren't all the legends claim they are. Not pretty and they are carnivorous. Probably not the ideal way to die. They would probably bite your dick off first. They are sadistic like that."

He stared at me as though the words I spoke were in another language, but made a move to protect his balls as his gaze scanned the forest. "Scary. Ah, okay. Any chance you can point me back to a road? I can wave down help? Once I get back to my friends, I can make sure you get home, too."

"You could go back the way you came."

"I've been wandering a while. Trying to figure out the direction by the sun. But it's behind the clouds and hard to tell. Also spent some time trying to get my phone to connect. Battery is almost dead. You don't have a charger and one of those portable power packs, do you?"

"No." I turned and headed back toward the river, and hopefully the cabin. I should have stayed in bed. The crunch of leaves behind me said he followed. "Don't follow me."

"Shouldn't we stick together? If we're both lost? Safety in numbers and all that."

"No," I said. "Haven't you heard of the man or the bear question? I'd choose the bear any day. Take your bro-self in the other direction, that's where you came from. I need to find food and wood as it gets cold at night. I don't need an idiot who gets himself lost in a fae forest while actively hunting ghosts. Who the fuck hunts ghosts in this day and age? They are everywhere. Why hunt them? The fuckers never shut up." I stomped away, frustrated, and didn't hear him following me.

Eight

WESLEY

I gathered an armful of sticks to burn, thankfully found the cabin easily enough and left several loads near the door. I filled a basket with elderberries, blueberries, though I ate more than I collected of those, wild onions and carrots, and even some dandelion greens. It wouldn't be a filling meal, but after searching the trees for nuts and bushes for any beans, I'd given up in favor of the ground cherries and salad options.

The wind picked up, adding a biting chill to the air as the sun slipped low.

My mortal friend vanished. Had the realm spit him out? I hoped so, and felt guilty for leaving him behind. But I couldn't help myself, how was I supposed to help a complete stranger? Why had the realm taken him anyway? I hadn't seen any other fae or mortals. Only the shadow wolf thing, the kitten, and myself.

"Don't suppose you have a lighter?" I asked the kitten as I stuffed the wood stove full of sticks. It stared back at me with nothing but cute wide eyes and kitten fluff. "Why do you have to be so damn cute? I'm used to being the cutest thing in the room. I don't like competition."

It tilted its little head at me. I sighed. "I guess I need to find stones to click together for a spark or something. Fire magic is not really my strength." I scooped up the kitten, stuffed it in my pocket and headed for the door.

Night had fallen, full dark hours away, but the woods eerie quiet and cast in a million shadows. The chill slid bone deep, and I wished for a coat heavier than the hoodie, but started searching the ground for rocks. Did it have to be special rocks?

The kitten pawed its way out of my pocket and leapt down, giving me a tiny mew.

"Rocks. For fire," I told it. "Unless you can do fire?"

It waddled a few feet away to examine a rock that was easily four times its size. "Not the brightest bulb are you?" I sighed. "Flint. I think it's supposed to be flint. What the fuck does flint look like?"

I picked up a few rocks examining them as though I knew what I was looking for, even tried clicking them together. Nothing. "Fuck," I cursed. The kitten gave me a tiny meow. "I won't freeze to death, but I'd like to be warm for a change. Maybe roast some onions and carrots. Warm food. You could give me some coffee or a nice cup of hot tea with milk."

It stared at me.

"Not your day with the brain cell?" I asked.

A masculine scream echoed through the woods followed by a growling snarl that made my stomach sink. I was running before I could comprehend what I was doing. Why was I running toward the sound?

Fuck. Stupid human. Had he gotten himself killed?

I raced through the trees, guided by instinct rather than the sound. Magic drawn to magic. The shadow wolf found the human male, that much I understood. Had it pulled him into the world just to devour him? I half flew through the vegetation, speed reminiscent of my other form though I still wore human skin. I wove around trees and bushes, racing as though pulled by a string.

The ground dropped out beneath me, brush and darkness

hiding a ravine. I slid, cursing the twigs and sharp edges that scratched me on the way down. I landed in a puddle of mud next to my human friend. His heartbeat racing and audible to my sensitive ears. The terror on his face made me fear looking up.

The shadow wolf eclipsed the entire other side of the ravine. A spread of darkness oozing from it to drip death and rot down over the land. We stood ankle deep in a pool of rising dark turds. The snarling snout of the beast easily as big as my entire body. Was this some Hunt beast left to corruption in this abandoned world?

I shoved the mortal behind me and bowed my head, giving in to a partial change. Not to my natural form, or even the full majesty of the Stag, but to a part human mix, with added bulk of muscle, and a giant rack of deadly horns. I'd never win an actual fight against a monster like this, but rarely had to in this form.

The display made my head ache, the weight of the horns warning of a headache to come. This form solely for intimidation rather than function, I prayed it worked as the horns dripped with poison, sharper than a sword, deadly and more useful than any magic shield. My bowed head presented not deference, but defense. A warning: advance and die.

The human hid behind me, his touch warm and light on my back, as if afraid to startle me. I paid him no mind as I waited for the shadow wolf to decide. The snarls stopped. Oozing darkness slipping backward into the swell of the forest. I continued to wait, fearing movement would trigger the hunt instinct. Was it gone, or watching? In this magic realm, I *always* felt watched.

I counted to a hundred, and focused my breathing on slowing my heart rate. The human male mimicked me, his forehead pressed to my back between my shoulder blades. Careful, though still using me as a shield. Maybe he wasn't completely stupid.

We waited in silence another handful of minutes before I opened my eyes and swept my gaze across the opposite ravine. No movement. No sign of shadows, and no wolf, only trees and the impossible stillness of an abandoned fae realm. Gone for now then, but who knew how far.

I shifted back to my mortal form, irritated by the ooze soaking my feet and turned to the human, ready to rage, but startled silent by his wide eyes.

"You had horns," he whispered.

"I'm fae, dumbass. I told you you're in a fae forest."

Nine

❧

WESLEY

I scrambled up the embankment, hoping to find my way back to the cabin though full dark left little light to illuminate my path. Blood dripped down my face. The previous shift more glamour than physical, hadn't healed the cuts from the fall. Everything hurt. Ankles, back, head, and my left elbow. Had I landed on it on the way down?

I'd need rest and food to heal, but since I was only partially human, infection wasn't something I'd ever worried about. My clothes were stained and wet, adding to the icy chill already expanding in my gut. Instinct demanded I change to my other form and abandon the weak mortal skin, but I wouldn't.

The man followed. I didn't tell him not to. I could have enacted the fae demand: a life for a life. I'd saved his, now he owed me eternal servitude. But I hated those old rules and hoped the new kings would break them.

I tripped over a log, missing the tip of it jutting from the ground. The mortal caught me, arm wrapped around my waist, holding me in a half hug. I steadied myself and pulled away.

"I could use some fucking light!" I shouted at the forest, fixing my hoodie which rode up at his touch.

"I have a lighter," the mortal said.

I gazed his way and saw him holding out a small cigarette lighter. He flicked it and the flame bounced to life. Tiny, useless to illuminate the dark, but exactly what I'd needed to light the damn twigs I'd stuffed in the wood stove.

"Follow me," I told him. "Save the lighter. We'll need to use it when we get to the cabin."

"You have a cabin here? Did you make it with magic?" He followed close behind. I watched my feet, trying not to focus on his warm body radiating heat inches from my back.

"I didn't make it. The world did. I told you I'm just as lost as you."

"But you're fae."

"Doesn't mean I'm meant to be here," I said.

"I was wondering about that."

"About what?" I asked. Were we going in the right direction? I tiptoed through a thick area of brush and found mushrooms glowing to light a path. "Fuck me," I growled at it. Nothing like the world rolling out the welcome mat.

"Why there are so few fae here. Since you said it's a fae world and all that. All I've seen here is you and the ghost wolf."

"I'm pretty certain that ghost wolf is some kind of fae."

He thought about that for a minute, following me through the glowing path. "Should we be following the creepy glowing mushrooms or running the other way?"

Observant fuck. "Sadly, this world seems to like me. It's been gifting me things, like the cabin, food, and now a way back to the cabin." I paused to glare at the path that screamed fae intervention. "I hope."

He stayed close, letting me lead and occasionally reaching out to touch the back of my hoodie. I don't know if he knew he was doing it, like he had to make certain over and over that I was real, but since he didn't hold on or pull me back, I let it go.

The cabin came into sight with a welcome wave of relief. It

looked the same, though the glow of mushrooms surrounded it like a beacon in the dark. Those hadn't been there. But the kitten vanished, too. Had it followed me into the woods and gotten lost?

I approached the door, praying it really was the same place and not some dupe filled with an otherworld witch wanting to cook a tasty stag up for an evening meal.

Something launched itself out of a tree above us. I caught the movement out of the corner of my eye and turned, throwing myself backward, but the mortal was the focus of the attack. The kitten, now back to its leopard self, landed with deadly precision on the mortal, knocking him on his ass and snarling in his face.

"Who are you?" I asked the man out loud, wondering just why everything in this world was out to get this particular mortal.

"Uh," the mortal gasped, frozen beneath the sharp claws and deadly fangs of the leopard.

"Come on, kitty," I called the cat. "Let the frat boy go. He's got a lighter. Remember I asked you for one of those?"

The cat glanced at me, then back at the mortal before bouncing off him and to my side to rub up against me and give that little rumbling growl of warning. I petted its head, and the cat leaned up into my touch to gain a good eyebrow scratch.

"I totally knew you were a Disney Princess."

"What the fuck?"

"You talk to animals."

I glared at him, but continued to pet the leopard.

"Is it your pet?" The mortal asked.

"Nope. Pretty sure it's some kind of fae. Like the cabin, it came to me."

"Seems protective." The mortal started to get up, but the leopard growled at him. He held out his hands. "Not doing anything bad, kitty. Not going to hurt your pretty friend."

Pretty friend? I tilted my head, wondering if he realized what he said.

"Anyway, my name is Finley, everyone calls me Finn. I already told you the rest of my story. I was ghost hunting with friends. Got separated, and somehow ended up here. What about you?"

"Did you walk through a portal?" I ignored his question, needing answers. Why him? Why in this vast empty world of wild magic, had it picked him? Fluke? Probably not.

"I don't think so. I mean I've heard people talk about portals, but never seen one." He stared at the cat, keeping still, but let his gaze flick to my face. "I was running," he admitted. "From the ghost wolf."

Ten

WESLEY

"The ghost wolf was in the mortal realm?" I opened the door to the cabin, relieved to find it the same as I'd left it, with a lamp lit in the corner. Though I knew it couldn't be plugged into anything, it glowed like it had a modern-day bulb rather than a flame of any sort. I stepped inside, and my new friend Finn tried to follow but the leopard stood between us.

"Let him in," I said. "I can keep track of him better once he's inside, and I'd like to warm up." The chill of the evening invaded my bones, plus wet clothes and the seeping of mud in between my toes made me desperately want to light the fire in the stove, eat a bit and curl up under the blankets until warmth seeped back in.

The leopard stalked by me, rubbing against my side as it slipped into the cabin. Finn trailed inside slower, keeping me between him and the cat. I closed the door.

"Lighter?" I held out my hand.

He dropped it in my palm, the heat of his touch making me wonder if he was cold at all. I still planned to light the fire, even if that meant he had to sleep outside because he would be too hot once I stoked the flames to remove the chill. I made my way to the wood stove and opened it. Decades of convenience couldn't over-

53

ride a century of experience, and soon the stove bloomed with fire and heat. I sank to the thick rug at the base of it to soak up the warmth.

"I have a video on my phone of the wolf," Finn said. "But not much battery life left."

I flicked my gaze his way.

He held out his phone and tapped the screen to show the video. The replay, while dark, showed some movement. If I had never encountered the shadow wolf before I might not have known what it was. A ghost, perhaps, or simply a trick of light, while there really was none. But it lunged at Finn. The video echoed the movement of him throwing himself backward and running in the opposite direction. Shaky camera and labored breathing.

He tapped the screen to turn off the replay, his face red with embarrassment, but running from something like that was smart. Maybe it was part of the Hunt. His instincts were good. Death or running away? I was a fan of living another day, it was part of what the Stag was.

I stood and stretched, the fire warming the space. "I'm going to shower off the mud. Don't touch anything." I glanced at the cat. "I'm sure my leopard friend will be watching." I made my way to the bathroom and closed the door. The shower beckoned. I forgot I had no other clothes for a few seconds until after I'd stepped beneath the warm spray of water, leaving the mess of them on the rug.

When I glanced back they were gone. Reabsorbed back into the world?

I put the open room behind me and closed my eyes to bask in the water. A cake of soap and a soft cloth waited on a ledge, untouched. I grabbed them and scrubbed, my skin tingling from the shadow beast's touch. None of its magic clung to me, and I searched for it, dropping and shifting my glamour in a dozen ways. My status as the Stag meant I generated fae magic, but had limited abilities to create things. This realm and all the magic inside, were beyond my skills, though the Summer King could have done it with ease. I really hoped he was learning to use his power rather than running from it as he had for years.

When I stepped out of the shower, a fresh set of towels and clothing sat on the stool beside the door. Rather than the jeans and a hoodie, it left me pajama pants and a sleep t-shirt. I studied them, as I'd never really used that sort of thing. Another gift of the world? Tiny cakes were printed on the fabric of the pants. Was this the Summer King's world? Was he messing with me? Cutting me off from everything and everyone to pay me back for working with Winter?

We all did shitty things for survival. Especially us half-breeds.

I tugged them on, the fit perfect, and thankful the world had given me underwear as the pants were too thin to give reasonable coverage.

The door opened and I prepared to rage at Finn, but it was the kitten, back to its tiny size, staring at me with big eyes. I sighed and picked it up. "Not Summer," I told it. Summer wouldn't have nights dropping near freezing.

I cupped the kitten in the crook of my arm, holding it like a football while it purred, and headed into the main part of the cabin. Finn stood in the kitchen mixing something in a bowl.

"You can use the shower," I told him. I wondered if the world would let him. I stared over his shoulder and found a bowl of some sort of bean salad, using some of the ingredients I'd gathered, and a lot of beans I knew I didn't have. "Where did you find the beans?"

He blinked wide eyes at me and opened the upper cupboard nearby. A display of perfectly lined up cans of beans filled all three shelves. "Not yours?"

I stared at them, glanced down at the cat in my grip and back to it. "Any nuts by chance?"

"Walnuts," Finn said, stirring the salad and lifting a spoon to show me some chopped up in it.

"Were those in the cupboard, too?"

"No, it was in the pile of berries and roots on the counter here," he pointed to the pile I'd left from foraging. There hadn't been any nuts when I set them there.

"I hope you didn't use all the carrots and onions. I wanted to cook them." The complaint sounded petty to my ears and I was the one who said it. But he glanced at the counter top, some carrots and onions remained, but not a lot. I sighed.

"Sorry," Finn said. He put the spoon in the bowl and took a step toward the shower. "I'll go clean up if that's okay with you."

I grabbed his face, searching it, while he gulped, eyes wide.

"You sure you're not fae?" I asked him.

"I thought you said *you* were fae. I'm nothing, just a guy looking for ghosts."

I couldn't sense any magic from him, but maybe he had really powerful glamour? I frowned at him, which he mirrored. "I'm going to search you for magic."

"Huh?" He asked a half second before I pressed my lips to his.

I expected him to jerk away, but he sank into my kiss, lips opening, which was exactly what I needed to unravel any glamour he might be using. I slid my magic into him with my tongue, exploring his mouth and his soul at the same time. He hesitated for a few seconds, but returned the kiss, careful, and sweet, which I hadn't expected at all from him. Sloppy would have fit his bro-persona, but I enjoyed the boy next door tentativeness as I searched for lingering spells, magic, or anything meant to fool me.

Finally, I pulled away, mind churning to continue to explore his lips, especially when he stared at me with wide eyes, flushed cheeks and smelling of desire.

"I thought you said you weren't a nymph?" he asked.

"I'm the farthest thing from a nymph you'll ever meet. But there's no magic on you." I took a step away, needing the distance else I'd jump him and pin him to the counter to discover just how far his desire went.

"I told you that already," Finn said. He touched his lips as if tracing our kiss.

"Don't worry. I won't tell anyone you kissed a boy and liked it."

"*You* kissed me," he protested.

I waved a hand at him, annoyed, and wondering if the world would spit him out when he stepped into the shower. Would it give him clothes? "Go clean up."

He hesitated, something needy in his gaze.

"What?" I asked.

He shook his head and darted around me, into the bathroom.

"Don't send him out naked," I told the world, wondering how much it listened. The cabin remained the same, set up like a studio apartment. One room that was the living room, bedroom, and kitchen, and the separate bathroom. I stared at the tiny twin-sized bed heaped with blankets. The chaise too small for anyone to sleep on without sitting up. "How about giving us another bed?"

The room remained unchanged. I sighed as I heard the water run in the bathroom and picked up a pan and the knife to heat some carrots and onions. I'd never done it before. Watched the Summer King a lot, and even had a favorite restaurant or two that would serve some delicious food. It couldn't be that hard, right?

Eleven

WESLEY

Okay, so cooking wasn't my forte. Who knew you could burn onions and carrots and that the smell would be repulsive enough to make my eyes water?

Finn stepped out of the bathroom in a t-shirt and sweatpants that left nothing to the imagination. Had the realm not given him underwear? Big dick indeed. His nose wrinkled at the smell and he stepped up close to me, staring over my shoulder. His body heat taking away the chill of the room with only a few inches separating us.

"Looks great," he said.

"I'm not a cook," I snapped, stepping away from him and instantly regretting it as the chill returned.

He studied me, but kept his distance. He picked up the pan of overcooked veggies and slid them onto the cutting board. I made my way to the bed, sorted through the blankets, picking a few for him, and regretting having to give them up as the chill etched up my spine. Cupboards opened and closed, Finn searching for something, and a few minutes later he appeared at my side, bowl and fork in hand.

"Eat," he commanded.

I took the bowl, but glared at him, expecting to have to choke down the stuff I burned. But the bean salad he had made filled the bowl. I poked it with the fork and found tiny bits of the onion and carrot in it, but when I brought the first taste to my lips, couldn't tell they were in there, or how badly I'd burned them.

Finn dished himself a bowl and perched on the only other chair in the room. Gaze on the food and not on me, though I felt his regard several times. He ate quickly and in silence. I stewed on the fact that he was not only good looking, had a big dick, he could cook, and was a great kisser. Had my request brought him here? Why? What did this realm want from me?

"There's more if you want," Finn offered, pointing to the bowl. He glanced toward the bathroom. "My other clothes vanished... phone, too."

"Maybe the world will spit them back out clean and charged." I motioned to the pile of blankets I'd made. "I trust you can make yourself a comfortable place to sleep."

"Sure," Finn said. "I've done a lot of camping in my life." He laid out the blankets, two on the bottom as a mattress in the center of the room, one folded as a pillow and one for an actual blanket. "I run pretty warm, so I may not need this," he offered it back.

"It's fine," I said. "Kitty will help keep me warm." The leopard sat by the door acting as a guard, tail twitching, but otherwise still. That the cat kept its leopard form when Finn was around made me wonder if it knew something about Finn that I didn't or was simply being cautious.

"Is that his name?"

"No idea. He doesn't talk."

"Shouldn't a fae cat talk?" Finn asked, not me, but the cat.

It glanced at him as if he was bothering it.

"You look more like one of those snow leopards than a kitty," Finn said as he lay down on his makeshift bed. "Do you want some bean salad?"

The cat didn't move. I hadn't seen it eat.

"I could probably try to hunt a squirrel or something tomorrow," Finn muttered. "Had a pocket knife and that's gone with my clothes. At least I left the lighter on the counter." It sat beside the wood stove.

"Anything you try to hunt in this world will eat you," I said.

"Yeah?"

"Yes."

"Scary." He sounded tired, but not all that frightened. "I'll call him, Snow."

"It's a little rude to assume someone's name," I said, turning my back to him and pulling up the blankets to burrow beneath and pray for warmth.

"Still don't know yours," Finn pointed out. "Only fair that you share it since you had your tongue in my mouth."

Silence stretched between us. Names had power, and mine was ordinary. Finally, I said, "My name is Wesley."

He didn't say anything for a while. I closed my eyes, the light in the corner dimmed. "Nice to meet you, Wesley."

I grunted at him. Faintly I heard, "Can you keep him warm, Snow?"

Was he talking to the cat? A few seconds later, the leopard leapt up onto the bed and slid itself into the narrow space at my back, warmth projecting from it and instantly sucking the lingering chill out of me. I sighed in relief, exhaustion hitting hard. Sleep sucked me down to dreams of pastries, warm fruity tea, and big dicks.

Twelve

WESLEY

The shriveling forest and oil slick ooze surrounded me. My heart pounded in terror. Death and destruction creeping in with a rising chill that made my breath mist and skin prickle with the pain of a thousand needles.

It had all been a dream, hadn't it? Escaping the Winter realm and finding a forest with cool nights and warm days, all a fantasy. My soul ached. I didn't want to run anymore. I didn't want to hurt anymore. I dropped to my knees, sinking to the ground to let the dark come. The end would be better than this nightmare continuing.

Decades of hiding myself, keeping close to power, no matter the consequences, hadn't ended the nightmare. The Summer King taught me running wouldn't work, and now I knew nothing would. My fate inescapable.

The slime inched forward, a gurgle of noise sounding like a stomach digesting bad burritos. Cold burned my skin. I covered my head, curling up into a ball like a child protecting itself from the boogeyman simply wanting it all to end, and too tired to fight anymore.

Someone cursed and it wasn't me. Arms wrapped around me,

picking me up, and for a half second I thought to struggle, fearing the world's ooze developed human features. But warmth projected through me where we touched, and heat draped itself over me, as though protecting me from the cold. The grip firm, but gentle, held me up and ran, as if we could outpace the slime through distance alone.

I blinked open my eyes, thinking I'd wake back in the ice palace, but found myself locked in the forest of ooze with Finn using his body to protect me. His back to the slime, he ran, but got nowhere, the dark curse too fast. He sucked in a deep, pained breath as it touched him, but kept himself between the ooze and me.

It couldn't be real. How was he in my dream?

"Finn?" I gasped out his name, horrified at the bubbling slime that crawled up his back as if to swallow him whole, while he kept himself between the nightmare and me. I flailed. The dream burst and the lamp in the corner lit up as I jolted up in bed, shivering with cold and terror, fearing Finn would be gone, eaten by the world.

He sat up on his makeshift mat, blinking wide eyes and staring at me. His heartbeat as rapid as mine.

"Sorry," I said, my hand pressed to my chest as though I could will my fear away, thinking my nightmare had woken him. "Bad dream."

"What was that?" Finn asked. "The world devoured by an oil slick?"

I blinked at him. He couldn't have... there was no way he would have... how could he have been in my dreams with me? "What?"

He got up and picked up his blankets, carefully spreading them out on top of me. "You're freezing. Take these."

"Finn," I said, clutching the edge of the blankets, terror still raw.

"Kitty friend has vanished," he remarked as he sat on the edge of the bed. Heat projected off of him as it often did the Summer King. I longed to wrap myself in the warmth and let the bite of ice fade.

"Tell me about your dream," I demanded.

"We were surrounded by dark goo that ate everything it touched. You stopped, sank to the ground and didn't move. At first, I thought you were hurt."

"You can't have the same dream I did."

"It's not a fae thing?" he asked. He glanced around the room. "Because we're in this place?"

Maybe. I hugged myself, pressing back in the bed until I touched the wall, unable to stop the shivering.

He lifted the blankets, making to slide in with me.

"What are you doing?" I demanded.

"You're freezing. I run hot, remember? Let me get you warm. It's the middle of the night. Your kitty friend isn't here to keep you warm."

"I can add more wood to the fire." Except I'd used all the sticks I'd gathered. I stared at him, heat radiating even from where he sat. No kidding about running warm. "Fine. But keep your hands to yourself."

He held up his hands in an 'I'm-harmless gesture,' then picked up the blanket edge and slid in. The warmth instantly soaked through the blankets and into me. I couldn't help my sigh. The bed was far too small for two grown men.

My heart pounded, though as he settled in, keeping barely an inch between us on the tiny bed, my terror dripped away. The memory of our kiss made me want to roll over and sample him again. It was all too simple. Finn appearing in this world. The two of us shoved together by fate. It was like some sort of twisted fairytale.

"Who are you?" I asked again, wondering why he'd been chosen. "Did your friends get stuck here too and we haven't found them?"

"I wandered for a while," Finn said. "You're the only other person I've seen."

I chewed on that thought for a while. "Straight guys don't sleep in the same bed," I muttered more to myself than him, thinking that felt off. A lot of things did. How could Finn be so accepting of the fae world? Of learning I was fae? Why wasn't he running terrified that maybe I was the ghost wolf in another form?

"Yeah? Guess that means you're not straight, eh?" He didn't open his eyes, and his heartbeat had returned to normal.

"I was talking about you."

"Never said I was straight, and *you* kissed me, remember?" Finn said. "Not like you asked. I consider myself an equal opportunity guy." He let out a long breath. "What I am, right this minute, is really sleepy. Are you warm enough? I can feel a chill coming off you." He scooted closer, but I pressed my hand to his stomach, keeping him away. His body radiated warmth I longed to soak up.

"You kissed me back," I said, hating the idea that I'd forced him to kiss me, and I sort of had.

"I did. It was nice."

"Nice..."

"More than nice. Not a lot of guys like to kiss. You kissed like you do."

I took that as consent and let the guilt seep away as sleep tugged at me. "No more nightmares," I whispered. Hoping for a break from the dark.

"I'm with you on that, Princess," he muttered.

I'd have argued his pet name but fell asleep before a coherent thought formed.

Thirteen

WESLEY

Tea. The soft fruity scent of a good strawberry green tea roused me. "If you'd tell me where you are, I can bring you some," Sebastian said as he poured a cup.

I blinked through a haze of half formed images. A dream, but not completely. Was the Summer king finally embracing his power?

"Trying. You're still mine, right?"

Not really. Simply waiting for my place. Serving power was a double-edged sword.

"You protected me when you could have served me up to Winter with ease. I want you to be happy and safe, Wesley. Can I help you achieve that?"

Why would he want to?

He stared at me, and I met his gaze, feeling mute, but also at peace. His stupid omega power eased the waves of unease I'd spent my entire life burying. "Kiran says you're a seer."

I sucked in a hard breath, terrified of what him knowing would mean.

"You protected me for a long time. I'm grateful. Liam is a little more conflicted, thinking you should have prevented all the things

I went through. But you're not a god and I needed to learn." He stared off into the distance. "We are all bound by fate. I understand that. You can't see your own fate, right? How would you know where you would end up?"

Other than the face I'd seen frozen in ice before he had shifted into a dragon of nightmares and dragged me into this world, generally yes. Fate hid my future from me. In fact, anyone I got too close to, or who would be woven directly with my own life often vanished to my second sight.

"Liam said you kept others away because it helps you see them. If we got too close, you'd be blind to mine as well, right? Can we fix that? I don't mind not knowing. I won't demand you tell me anything. Fate is rarely kind. Can I help you somehow face what's coming? Do you know? I think isolating yourself only to glimpse terrible futures sounds really lonely. Who does it help?"

He wasn't wrong, but I did what I thought was best anyway. People who knew me hurt me. Distance kept my eyes open. Would the little king really not demand his future foretold?

"Liam says you knew I was meant to be this." He waved his hand as if indicating him sitting at a table in a dream creation drinking tea and talking to a statue of me was something special.

King. He was the Summer king. Different from any legend or mythology ever written. Chaos and peace all in one. Ascended, as the heat radiated off of him, though still building because I could see the fluctuation of his power. Kitsunes, a species of magical half-breeds, part fae, part mortal, exuded wild magic in a structured world. Technically, I was among their kin.

Staring at him, I couldn't see anything beyond the dark forest. Not his future, nor the babe he'd created from spitting out Under-hill's corpse, or the touch of any of his people. Had we grown too close? Did our fates intertwine? When had that happened?

Sebastian sighed and slid the cup of tea over. A giant slice of strawberry shortcake appeared on a plate, heaped in glowing summer magic. "Liam thinks this might strengthen our bond to help me find you. But I give you the choice. Eat it only if you want to. I won't force you to serve me. You know that's never been my thing."

The little king's past created a lot of pain for him to work through. I stared at the cake, uncertain if I could reach for it even if I wanted to.

"I have been trying to find the forest god." He took a sip from his own cup of tea and stared off into the distance. "He's not answering. Either he doesn't know where you are, or..."

I was where he wanted me to be. The earth elementals were fickle beings. Liam, an alpha werewolf, had been chosen as mate to the Summer king by the elemental. It seemed like a bad deal for Liam at the time, as he was a stable and strong ruler, wise and organized, while Sebastian was chaos on a razor blade. Dangerous and wild. But the duo fit perfectly, an ebb and flow of magic, power, and emotion that I could never fathom would have been possible before meeting them.

What did that mean for me? If I was the stable one, did that mean madness was my other half? I prayed not.

The world faded. Sebastian's power eased away. "Your choice," he said as he left the cake and tea behind. I'd have reached for them if I could, but was too warm to move for the first time in ages, and let myself sink into restful dark, dreamless sleep for a short time.

When I woke, opening my eyes to the cabin, it was because the chill had returned and I found myself alone in bed, the door to the cabin open, a slight *chop chop* coming from outside. But a slice of cake and a teacup sat on the counter in the kitchen untouched.

I jolted out of bed. Was it real? I approached it with caution. Finn was no longer in bed, and the bathroom door was open, light off. Was he outside making that noise or had the world done something crazy like turned him into the cake and tea I longed for?

I turned to the open front door, the morning chill crisp as I stepped out and found Finn outside, cutting wood, shirt off, chest glistening with sweat. Frat boy had a nice body.

He glanced up. "Morning, princess," he said as he picked up the next log to split it.

"Not a princess," I said. "I hope you didn't cut down a tree. Fae trees are usually living beings of some sort."

He hesitated, then shook his head and brought the axe down to split the wood as though he'd spent his entire life doing it. "This one was fallen and rotting. Do living things rot in the fae world?"

"Sometimes, depends on the realm."

Finn examined the wood. I couldn't sense any life from it. I shivered and decided it was a good time for a hot shower. Small favors and all that.

"I'll stoke the fire in a few minutes," Finn said. "Get back inside and curl up in the blankets to keep warm. It's chilly out here."

"Says the man without a shirt," I remarked.

"Ha. I run hot."

"You are hot," I muttered.

A tiny smile lifted the corners of his lips as if he'd heard me. I hoped not. He bent to pick up another log and half turned his back to me. A dark blotch of discoloration painted his back as though he had a bruise nearly large enough to coat his spine.

I gasped.

"What?" he asked, turning my way.

"Your back." Maybe I was overreacting and it was a birthmark or something. My gut said it was from the nightmare, where the shadow ooze slunk up him trying to reach me.

"My back?" he turned around as if he could see his back. He set the axe down and tried to touch the spot. "What?"

I crossed the space, rocks digging into the sensitive bottoms of my feet, but my heart pounded in fear as I closed in on him to examine the mark. "You don't have some giant birthmark on your back, right? Something that would look like a bruise?"

"No."

The mark painted a long diagonal swatch of purple and blue

darkness up toward his right shoulder. I hovered my fingers over it, afraid to touch for a thousand reasons, but watching for any sign of movement.

"Does it hurt?" I asked.

"No. I feel a little chilled now that I'm not cutting the wood, but my back doesn't hurt."

I traced the edge of the mark with my fingertips, fearing it would stick to me, or hurt him. "Anything?" His skin, hot where it was unmarked, chilled my fingers where the dark blotch began.

He frowned.

"What?" I demanded.

"Touch my shoulder, please."

I hesitated, but after a few seconds rested my hand on his shoulder. He nodded.

"Now where you see this mark?"

I slid my hand back down, touch light.

"Are you touching it?" he asked.

"Yes."

"I can't feel it."

"What if I press harder?" I put my palm to the center of the mark, the chill adding a burning ache to my skin as if I stuck my hand in a freeze. "Fuck, that's cold."

"Can't feel it."

I pulled my hand away and he turned to face me, eyes wide.

"What does it mean?" he asked.

"I don't know." And I didn't, but I suspected it had to do with the dream we shared. Was it because of me? Had I cursed him? I backed away, heading back toward the cabin. Maybe it was still a dream... a nightmare even.

"Wesley?" Finn asked.

"I don't know," I said again and raced inside, heading into the bathroom to drown myself in the shower, or at least bury my fear.

Fourteen

WESLEY

When I exited the bathroom, clean and dressed, my stomach growling with hunger, I hoped to open the door to a place in the Summer realm, but it was the cabin. The fire blazed, radiating warmth, and Finn sat perched on the edge of the only chair, his shirt back on. The cake and tea, untouched. No sign of my kitten friend.

"You can have the shower," I said. Maybe I could make something else with all the beans that had appeared in the cupboard. I opened the door to study them, hoping for cans with recipes on them, only to find a brick wall where they had been. "What the fuck?"

"Yeah, they are gone," Finn said as he got up. "I thought I'd throw together something before I went outside to get wood for the fire, but all of the cabinets are like that now." He waved his hand at the row of storage. "I hoped maybe it was your magic that made them appear or something." His gaze wandered to the cake.

"We can share it," I offered, thinking maybe it would trigger a way back to Sebastian's court, or at least out of this world.

"I can't touch it," Finn admitted.

"What?" I reached for the plate and picked it up. The waves of magic pulsing off it a beacon of otherworldliness that made me salivate. Strange as I wasn't one who needed to eat magic to survive. I generated it, much to the bane of my existence.

"I wondered if it was real and tried to pick it up. But I can't." Finn carefully touched the tip of his finger to the plate, but it went right through, as if the plate wasn't there, or Finn was a ghost of some kind. "I can't touch it. Not the cake or the tea."

I set the plate down, mind churning through a thousand thoughts and worries. If it was a way out, it meant leaving Finn behind. Why did this world want him?

"It's okay," Finn said. "Eat. I'll go jump in the shower as long as the water still works for me. Maybe you can show me where you found some of that food from yesterday. We can forage."

Wait... "Did the food yesterday have a taste to you? The beans and carrots and stuff?"

"Yes. I mean the beans. The other stuff not so much."

"Did you still feel hungry after you ate?"

"No."

If only the beans had flavor...

"What?" he asked.

"You follow ghost lore, but did you ever read fae lore?"

"Outside of the occasional romance novel, no."

"You don't seem the romance novel type."

"Why?" Finn asked. "I do a lot of traveling. Reading is a good distraction. Romances are easy to find."

"I thought you'd be more of a travel guide or non-fiction how-to-become-a-millionaire guy."

"I do read travel guides. The millionaire stuff not so much. Why? What about fae don't I know?"

"Mortals can't eat food in a fae realm. Well, they can, it just won't satisfy their hunger. I suspect someone from outside the realm sent the beans." Mainly Sebastian or perhaps his wizard wolf mate. And now the realm had blocked the beans. Only the cake and tea left behind because it pulsed with otherworld magic. What about the kitten? From this world or outside influence?

Finn stared at me a few more seconds then said, "So we will starve if we stay here."

"I'm part fae, the food from here works fine for me." I felt bad admitting it, but he had to understand what it meant to be mortal in a fae realm.

"And you can't make outside food appear?" he asked.

"No. Someone sent the beans, maybe they will send more?" I could eat the cake and escape, maybe tell Sebastian about Finn and see if he had ideas. Not that the Summer king had reason to do anything for me. It was part of why I still hesitated to accept his help with the cake, if that's what it was. Why would he want to get me out? To punish me for helping Zephyr and capturing the wolf?

"But the world, realm, or whatever this is, is blocking it now. Why?" Finn folded his arms across his chest, frown deep on his handsome face. He looked tired, and I wondered if he had gotten any rest or simply suffered my nightmares. "You can touch the cake. Does that mean the world likes you?"

"I don't think the cake is from this world. I think it's some-one's outside interference. Does this world like me?" I shrugged. "It gave me this cabin. I've been able to find food in this world and escape the wolf each time I've seen it." Equating *like* to those things was a stretch, but I didn't seem as cursed as poor Finn. I refused to mention the wolf bringing me dead animals as though trying to woo me.

Finn lingered a few seconds more, a war of emotions on his face which made me think not only was he younger than I origi-nally thought, but also respect his willpower to not shout or scream about the unfairness of it all. He glanced once more at the cake, then headed to the bathroom, leaving the door open. I heard the shower turn on, and made my way to sit on the bed.

He popped his head out the doorway. "I'm going to leave the

door open..." He hesitated as if embarrassed. "I feel safer if I can hear you out here."

"I don't think the world is going to eat you while you're in the shower."

"Well, that's one of us," Finn grumbled vanishing back into the bathroom.

I had to work to not think about him naked a dozen feet away. My stomach grumbled with hunger, the cake tempting, the tea wafting with steam, somehow still hot after sitting there for who knows how long. The sounds of Finn in the bathroom, moving around under the water, and faintly, his heartbeat, added a level of comfort I couldn't recall experiencing in my long life. I wasn't alone.

It was a dumb thought. We were all alone. Everyday always until the very end of our life when we died praying we'd done something important only to find it didn't matter at all. The curse of a seer meant knowing too much and having little control over anything.

I sucked in a deep breath at the wave of melancholy, stronger than my normal depression, and wondered if it was the world adding to the darkness or the circumstances. The cake beckoned. Sweet tempting strawberries, plump and red, juicy like a siren song. A simple plate of spongy cake topped with delightful berries, no cream, which most would have found odd, but I thought maybe the Summer king might recall what I enjoyed. Or heard legend that eating things with animal products in it like eggs or real cream could trigger the Stag's bloodlust.

Did Sebastian have a sponge cake recipe without eggs?

The water turned off, and I stared at the doorway, watching for Finn, gaze drawn back to the cake, time and again. When he appeared, dressed again, still in sweatpants that were far too revealing, he followed my gaze to the cake.

"Eat it. It's fine. No reason for both of us to be hungry."

WESLEY

Maybe I could feed it to him. He wouldn't know to find Sebastian, and would likely wake up thinking it was all a fever dream, but he'd be safe. Did we have to eat the whole cake to escape? And why did I care about a mortal I'd only just met?

I picked up the cake and used the fork sitting on the plate beside it to slice a piece off and hold it out for Finn. "Try this."

"I can't touch it."

"You're not. That's why I'm trying to feed it to you. I want to see if the magic will recognize me, but let you eat it."

"You should try it first."

"I don't think it's poison or anything."

"But you don't know either," Finn said. He folded his arms across his chest. Would the cake turn bad if he *could* touch it?

"I think the cake is from a fae I committed to serve from outside the realm," I said.

"Committed to serve? Like slavery?"

"I know it sounds strange to an American, but it's normal among the fae."

"I'm actually from Canada," Finn said. "Committed to serve

sounds like some sort of ownership to royalty. Slavery or indentured servitude."

"It is. That's how being fae works. The other fae is the Summer king. I believe he or his mate sent the food to try to connect with me."

"Why?"

"Why what?"

"Why do you have to be a slave to this guy?"

"Because he's more powerful than I am."

Finn stared at me; eyes narrowed.

"Yes, it's archaic, but Sebastian is young and part human. I think he's a little more laid back as a leader."

"Okay, but they wouldn't know me at all." Finn pointed out.

"Sebastian is that sort of sickly-sweet type who tries to rescue everyone. He and his mate own a bakery and a tea shop. They have the most delicious teas," I said wistfully.

"A fae king owns a bakery?" He eyed the cake.

"I'm hoping if I feed it to you, you can eat it and maybe get pulled out of this world?"

"What about you?"

"I can drink the tea instead. You eat the cake."

"What if you need both to get out?"

Why did he have to ask so many questions? "Can you try it, please?" I asked, unable to hide my frustration. What was it about this man that made me impatient to save him? I'd watched plenty of mortals die. The fae were really good at killing the fragile things of the mortal world. "I still don't know if you can touch it, but I'm hopeful. As a mortal, you shouldn't be in this realm at all."

"Wait, mortal? Does that mean you're immortal?"

"No one is really immortal," I huffed. "Some things are just harder to kill. Like the fae..."

"Creepy."

"Please just try the fucking cake."

"Fine," Finn said and leaned in, opening his mouth.

I stared at him for a half second, then carefully slid the fork of cake toward his mouth.

The cabin trembled, a booming shake rippling through the walls and floor as though it were meant to shatter. The cake never made it to Finn's lips, and I dropped the cake and the fork, both of them landing together on the plate as though drawn by a magnet. Finn grabbed my arm to steady me as the entire cabin rolled and shook, noise deafening. The light flickered and vanished.

"What the fuck?"

The cabin crumbled, pieces of the ceiling tumbled around us in broken bits of logs and debris. Finn pulled me close, arm strong as a vise around me, warming me as he yanked me out of the path of a giant beam that landed where we'd been standing.

"Okay, maybe we angered your Summer king or something?" Finn said.

The tea sat on the counter, unmoved by the shaking, cake also perfectly still. But the wood stove opened, door swinging hard to the side and fire leapt upward, engulfing the cabinets in seconds.

"I don't think this is Sebastian's doing." Fire licked at the walls, exploding through the kitchen part of the cabin in seconds.

"Jesus, fuck," Finn said as he dragged me toward the door.

A giant beam fell over the door as if to block it. I knew there couldn't have been anything in the roof of the cabin that large. Did that mean it was an illusion?

Finn cursed, and reached for the beam, trying to lift it, but it wouldn't budge.

"Step back," I told him.

He hesitated only a half second, and I kicked the beam, expecting my leg to go through it like it was an illusion, only the wood splintered in half.

"That was helpful. Fae are super strong, eh?" He grabbed at the broken edge shoving it aside to push open the door.

A gust of wind slammed into the cabin, making the entire thing sway. Deep into the woods, surrounded by trees, I knew wind of that force wasn't scientifically possible, which meant only one thing. Fae magic.

Was this world trying to kill Finn? Why?

He shoved at the door until the narrow slit was barely wide enough to crawl through. "Come on," he shouted, the crackling fire, wailing wind, and popping of burning wood muting his words. "You first."

"Gentlemanly and all, but I think you better go first." A thousand fears of him getting trapped inside after I was already freed crossed my mind. I put my hand on my chest. "Fae, remember? Harder to kill."

"Are you fireproof?" he asked.

Another beam fell, this one a flaming stretch across the living space that left us only a few inches of space to move, heat rising, and smoke choking.

"Fuck, you better be right behind me," Finn cursed, crawling out the door and shoving at it as he went. He waited until I slid into the space too, shoving and holding the opening, then reached back to yank me out as he popped free.

We both tumbled a few steps from the door, a wave of fire and heat lapping at the open space we'd crawled through, the entire cabin engulfed and blazing. Finn swallowed hard enough for me to hear and gripped my arm, gaze upward. For a half second I thought the trees had caught flame too, but it was worse than that.

"Please tell me that's another form of our kitten friend," Finn said face inches from the snout of a dark dragon with more teeth than a shark, and shadows dripping from its scales.

Sixteen

WESLEY

This was the beast that had broken free from the Winter court ice and devoured the fae, ripping me free from that nightmare and into this one. I shoved Finn behind me and stared up at the dragon wondering if this was where it all ended. Other than the nightmare of the slime eating the forest, I hadn't had a vision in ages.

Where had the man the dragon had been gone, the werewolf king as Sebastian thought of him. Turned to darkness? I met the dragon's gaze with defiance, unwilling to become a slave again to another nightmare will not my own. The Summer king could make demands, but I learned to avoid him, which would negate any commands he wanted to give.

A trick of the modern fae or something more? Perhaps running from them would have always saved me from their madness.

"You brought me here," I told the beast. "Now you try to kill me? Why not end me in the Winter court like you did so many others? What do you want from me?"

The heat of its breath warmed my face like a late summer breeze, thankfully without any stench of death or rot. It could have opened its jaws and swallowed us both whole. I glared at it with defiance, tired of the cat and mouse game.

The dragon growled a nearly undistinguishable word, "Mine."

"Uh," Finn said. "Did that thing talk?"

"Fae," I said again. Maybe? My lifetime of visions fed me glimpses of this monster, and the man trapped in stone, but I couldn't recall anything specifically pointing to the beast being fae. "Are you fae?" I asked the dragon.

"Yesss," it hissed, and then "No."

"Well, that's clear as mud," I grumbled.

"Mine," the beast growled again.

"Articulate. The mortal is mine. Okay? How about you let us go and we'll all have a better day."

The beast narrowed its gaze, focus on Finn who huddled behind me. The cabin crackled and snapped with the fire eating away at it, heat blazing at our backs. Contained to the cabin, as none of the brush touching it caught.

"Mate..." A dark ripple of shadow slid free from the dark, a leathery wing with hooks on the edges reached for me. I flinched, taking a half step back, which made Finn stumble and wrap his arm around me from behind to steady us both. The dragon snarled, and I expected an attack, but it huffed and reared back, then vanished into a poof of shadows as if it had never existed.

My heart raced, the final word of the dragon weaving a thousand ideas, none of them good. Of course, fate sought to fuck with me. Centuries of doing their bidding and now they had mated me to the Autumn king?

"Bitches!" I screamed. "Heartless witches! Manipulating my life like this. I don't want it!" The forest stood in silent eeriness around us. The crackling fire of the fallen cabin snapped and popped in the otherwise soundless woods.

"Did that thing say you were its mate?" Finn asked.

"Yes," I said as I ripped myself out of his grasp, and stalked away from him. With the cabin gone, once again I'd have to find shelter or change forms. If there had been any glimpse of daylight or warmth, it vanished with the departure of the dragon, leaving the sky overcast with clouds. Rain spit down on us, landing in large fat droplets warning of a downpour. "Dammit!"

Finn followed close behind. I wanted to be away from everyone and everything. Cry in the rain or run from the nightmare, but it wasn't fair to him. This was my nightmare, my curse. Why was he even here?

"And why won't you fucking show me anything?" I shouted at the sky. Centuries of brutal visions, to now being blinded to my own future.

I found the stream as water began to rain sheets around us, the chill etching through my skin and deep into my core. "I'm going to change," I told him, pausing to glance back. His wide eyes made me freeze. The sound of his racing heart muffled beneath the rain. "It's fine. My other form generates more heat."

"Mate.... Not like the Australian mate?" Finn asked hesitantly.

"Like bound by the hags of fate to be tied to a monster!" I yelled at the woods, which didn't answer. Bad enough I'd served Winter for a time, survival forcing me to bow and simp for Zephyr who treated me like he preferred to have me shackled at his feet. My dreams of saving the Summer king and finding a final peaceful rest away from the nightmares had shattered.

The man in stone should have killed me. I wanted it, if I couldn't have peace and freedom, why stay? Why continue to run much as the Summer king had? At least he'd gotten his perfect match in the end. Was it too much to want a happy ending of my own?

That had been the elementals twisting his fate. Who had more power, the hags of eternity with their disastrous weaving or the elementals? Or did they work together?

"They cursed me to see everyone's future but mine, and then tied me to a nightmare. Is it too much to hope for freedom if I can't have love? Even if that freedom is an end to my life? Can't they saddle another poor bastard with the curse of the Stag and my fucking Vision and save me the trouble?"

Finn flinched at my shouting, the two of us drenched from the rain. "You can see the future? Like you saw we'd be here?"

"No. I never saw you at all." Ever. And wasn't that strange. The moment he'd entered this world and across my path I should have gotten some inkling vision of his fate, especially if it were meant to be short and gruesome. My sight specialized in that nasty nightmare. "The last vision I had, beyond that dream of the woods dissolving around us, was meeting the dragon, and that's already happened." I gazed at him, young and handsome, but ordinary to my sight, a thousand unanswered questions about him. "Who are you? Why does this world want you? I know why it wants me. That *thing* thinks I'm its mate."

"You don't get a choice?" Finn asked.

"About what?" I demanded. Did I ever have a choice about anything?

"The mate thing. Is it because you're fae? Can't you tell it no and walk away?"

"Since we're both trapped in this world, the answer seems to be no." I turned away from him and stripped off my shirt. "Don't look at me. I'm going to change and find us some shelter from the rain. Stay close if you want to keep warm."

When I glanced back, he had turned away, giving me the illusion of privacy, but a shiver ran through his lean form. I had to get us both someplace safe for a while. I shifted into my Stag form, pawed at the ground to bring attention back. He glanced my way and hesitantly approached.

He snatched up my discarded clothing, then reached careful fingertips to my flank, my back higher than his head, and sank his fingers into my fur. A soft breath slipped out of him as he pressed himself to my side. His chilled body ached like an ice cube, but I let him lean into my warmth, and guided us toward the spot I'd slept when I first arrived. The field of clover stretched between a thick canopy of trees, and a layer of moss above eased the flow of rain.

Finn said nothing as I guided him to a narrow opening in the root of a tree. He climbed in, and I blocked the opening with my body, settling down outside as a barrier and heater all at once. The blaze of my renewing fae energy would last for days as long as I munched on the clover around us. He would need food and water. Once the rain stopped, I'd search for another way to help him escape before the world killed him. There was no reason my nightmare end had to be his.

Seventeen

WESLEY

Finn climbed over me at some point, muttering something about having to go to the bathroom. But the rain had stopped and the sun returned, for which I was grateful. I nibbled on clover and stayed in my Stag form, ears focused on the sound of his movement and searching for the sound of anything else nearby.

When he returned it was only in the sweatpants. He crawled into the hole of the roots, pulled out our clothing, and spread them out in the sun to dry.

"I don't suppose this weird magic world will spit new ones out for us?" he asked as he returned to my side, immediately tangling his fingers in my fur. His stomach growled. "Sorry."

Was the spot on his back smaller? Maybe it had been a bruise. I nudged him with my nose. He looked up at me, a single brow raised, a hint of scruffiness coating his jawline. Okay, he was handsome, hair a mess of dark waves from sleep and the rain; Shirtless, and not sculpted like Henry Cavill from the *Witcher*, but fine. I'd have tapped that in my less troubled days.

I nudged him again, pressing my snout at his shoulder, careful of my antlers, to get him to turn. He stepped away and presented his back to me, looking over his shoulder.

The mark was smaller, only half the size of his back. I shifted to my human form thinking I'd glamour myself some clothes for modesty, but I wound up naked. Was the realm preventing that, too?

"Don't look at me," I instructed. He faced forward.

"Is it worse?"

I traced the edge of the mark from the chilling center around the edge where the skin looked fine, better, and naturally warm. He shivered under my touch, but focused his gaze forward.

"It's smaller," I told him. "Healing maybe?"

"Because we didn't have the same dream again?"

I hadn't slept. "I don't know why you had that vision. I've been having it since I was a child and have never shared a vision with anyone. It wasn't a dream, more a nightmare of the future to come."

He swallowed and looked up the sky. "Pleasant. This world is filled with so many wonderful things." His sarcasm biting deep. I pulled my hand away knowing I was one of the unpleasant things. "I didn't mean you."

"It's fine. The fae are a special type of monster. I'm well aware of what I am." I tried to change back to the Stag form, but couldn't. What the hell?

He began to turn my way.

"Don't," I commanded. He stopped. "I was going to change back into the Stag."

"Okay," he said, waiting as if I needed to hide from him to do it.

"But I can't."

"Why?"

"If I knew fucking why, I wouldn't be freaking out right now!" I shouted at him. Stupid fucking human. "Don't turn around!"

He stopped. "Okay. I'm going to grab your hoodie and walk backward to hand it to you. Okay?"

"Stop saying okay." I couldn't breathe, what the hell was

wrong with my power? I stared at my hands and legs, hoping I hadn't completely lost my other form. Finn might think the Stag a majestic beast, but he'd laugh at my fawn side. Everyone did. I'd hate to have to kill him when I'd fought to keep him alive.

He bounded forward, picking up the hoodie and patting it, then setting it back down and grabbing the other, which had been his, and picking that one. I would have protested, but he slowly walked backward, holding the hoodie over his shoulder. "This one's drier. They are both a little wet. Your pants are soaked." His stomach grumbled again. How long could a mortal live without food and water? A few days? Months?

I snatched the hoodie out of his hand and tugged it over my head. At least it landed mid-thigh. The one I'd been wearing wouldn't have covered much. Had he been thinking of that?

"I saw a bush with some berries when I was relieving myself," Finn said. "Fae world and all that, I didn't touch them, thinking they might eat me. But if you're hungry I can show you where they are."

How fair was that if *he* couldn't eat them? "We need to focus on getting you out of here."

"Can I look now?"

"There's nothing worth looking at, but whatever."

He turned, his gaze hesitant, but he didn't stare or gloat. "Do you have a plan to get us out?"

"Do I look like a guy with a plan?"

"Yeah, actually. I mean you know more about all of this," he waved his hand at the world. "More than I do. What can we do to get out? I know that dragon thing said it's your mate, but I don't buy the 'no choice' thing. Can't you ask your Summer king to help?"

"If we could get word to him, maybe. But this world is blocking the outside from leeching in, and us from getting out. I wandered for days before running into you, finding only circles of sameness."

Finn puffed out his cheeks as he blew a breath and put his hands in his hair as though that helped him think. He walked the clearing for a dozen or so paces, keeping his distance from any trees or brush. "You said something about wandering through a portal."

"Yes. Most mortals are drawn that way. Portals can look like anything. The Summer king called them buttholes to other realms, but they can be the back of a closet or a ring of mushrooms, or a section of the forest filled with weird flowers."

"Buttholes to other realms. I might like your Summer king."

"Most people do," I grumbled. "He can open doors. Summer always has that power."

Finn paused to stare at me.

"We are in the Autumn realm. The dragon is the Autumn king. His realm, his rules. He doesn't seem to want outside influence." But kept Finn here for some reason.

Finn nodded and resumed his pacing. "Is there anything special about Autumn we should know? Weaknesses?"

"Me."

"Mate, right. Is that a weakness? Like does he have to do what you say? If you walk up to him and say, 'Let us go,' what does he do?"

"Burn the cabin down."

"Point." He wandered in a careful line around the area, avoiding the thick lines of clover.

"The clover isn't dangerous."

"But your other form likes to eat it, right?"

"Yes."

"Then it's rude to walk in it." He continued his pacing while I pondered that he'd been thoughtful. "What power do the mates have to fae? You said the Summer king has a mate. Anything you know about them?"

"They are sickly sweet together. Chosen by the Elementals rather than the Weavers."

"Capital E and Capital W? Titles instead of people?"

Observant little shit. "Yes."

"What makes you think that the Weavers chose the Autumn king for you and the Elementals," he wriggled his hands in the air like he knew what it all meant, "chose the Summer king and his mate?"

"Because the fae tried to choose a mate for Summer and he rejected them for the one the Elemental picked."

"Are the Weavers fae?"

No one really knew. I suspected they were because they cursed so much of mortality with their tangled fates. "I don't know."

"Why do you think your mate was picked by the Weavers?"

"My Vision is a curse from the Weavers, and I've seen the Autumn king in my dreams for a long time."

"The dragon?"

"He has a human form."

"But you said you can't see your future."

"I didn't know he was my mate. Only that his fate was tied to mine somehow."

"Isn't that literally the meaning of mate? Tied together by fate?"

"I saw a man trapped in stone. When he turned into a giant dragon and devoured half the Winter court, I thought he'd end me too. Deaths are fate, too."

Finn froze, his expression a mask of confusion.

"What?"

"A man trapped in stone? Han Solo like? Sorry, don't know if you get the *Star Wars* reference, but there is this movie..."

"I've seen the damn movie, and yes, sort of Han Solo like. Why?"

"Because I've been having a nightmare since I was a kid that I got stuck in stone and couldn't breathe."

Eighteen

WESLEY

I stalked back to his side to capture his face again between my hands, searching for anything that meant he was fae or something more than the handsome young man he presented. He didn't flinch this time, rather stared back with curiosity.

"It's okay if you kiss me again," he said.

"Uh." Why did the thought of that short-circuit my brain?

"Search me for power or whatever? I don't have any, but whatever makes you feel better."

I let him go. He frowned. "Show me where these berries are," I said.

He shrugged and led the way. Eight thousand questions and I was still without answers. I tugged the berries off the bush, piling them into the hoodie pocket and wishing for something more substantial or to be able to change into my fucking Stag form.

Finn sat leaning against the roots of the tree we'd created as a shelter. Only one would fit at a time, and that hadn't been an issue until I couldn't shift. He looked tired, lips dry, stomach gurgling from time to time. Hungry and thirsty, still I'd pestered him until I was certain he didn't know.

"No idea how you got stuck in stone in these dreams?" I asked again as I stalked to his side and sat down, pulling the hoodie over my legs and a handful of berries out of the pocket to offer to him.

"Nope. Never remember that part." He hesitated to take the berries. "I can't eat them anyway, right?"

"The old legends said eating offerings of the fae made you their slave," I corrected. "Is being a slave to me better or worse than starving to death?"

"Is it true?"

"No idea. I'm not royalty. I didn't make these berries." Would they tie him tighter to the Autumn king, whatever their bond? "I don't have the power to manifest food."

"I ate the beans and the carrot stuff in the cabin. Wouldn't that already make me your slave?"

"Do a hundred jumping jacks," I commanded.

He stared at me in confusion.

"Obviously you're not my slave. You made the food at the cabin; I didn't even offer it to you."

"Oh, point." He nodded and took a berry from my hand, popping it in his mouth.

"Taste like anything?"

"Slightly sweet?"

"Do you feel the mindless need to do whatever I tell you?"

"No." He took another berry and ate it. "Slavery to the fae sounds bad. How many do you think it will take?"

"Does it feel like you're eating?"

He ate a half dozen more, expression changing a few times to unreadable. "Not really? Maybe I'm super hungry?"

I stewed on that. Could I make food for him appear? Generating magic and actually using it for useful things, were two very different skills, and my ability to turn back into a Stag or clothe myself with glamour had yet to return. Did the Autumn realm change things? My powers hadn't ever been limited by the court.

"How about water?" I asked and stuffed the berries back in the pocket. I tugged the hoodie down and made my way to the creek.

Finn followed, his eyes a bit glazed. Was that magic or hunger? I knelt to cup the water in my hands, drank a mouthful to test it was clear, then lifted it for him. He stared for a half-second, and I was ready to roast him for refusing to drink from my hand if it saved him, but he leaned in, and then yelped as suddenly something yanked his feet out from under him.

He slammed into the ground, dragged at a lightning speed into the water, no longer a narrow creek with a visible bottom, but a raging river. I grabbed his hand and tugged. His fingers slipped through mine and in a heartbeat, he vanished beneath the waves that had not been there minutes ago.

"Fucking world! Stop trying to kill him!" I screamed and dove into the waves halfway expecting it to turn back into a shallow creek bed and break my neck. The water, a slap of icy prickling pain, shoved me, trying to keep me out. My swimmer's build, sleek and strong with the muscles of the Stag always waiting beneath, propelled me through the water toward the twitching of Finn's panicked outstretched hand. I feared he'd be dead before I could save him. Had we missed a selkie or some water sprite? Other than us and the shadow wolf/dragon, the realm seemed barren.

Something dragged him deeper, snatching his fingers from mine twice before we could touch. A dark weave of shadows wrapped around his legs. Was it the dragon again? I hadn't sensed him at all. But the world was his, was he trying to prove a point? Total control and all of that asinine fae bullshit I hoped would die off with the old ways?

I caught Finn's hand and tugged, but the thing held strong. My heart flipped over in fear at his terrified expression. He was running out of time and air. I swam toward the shadows, determined to rip him free, but my fingers slid through them as though they weren't even there.

Fuck!

Finn thrashed furiously, but slowed, his hand over his mouth as he fought himself from running out of air. I jolted to the top, breaking the surface and gulping a huge mouthful of the chilled wind before flipping to rush back to Finn's side. His fighting stilled, eyes open, panic slowing, but he still held on, gaze pleading. Eventually he'd lose consciousness and be forced to drown.

I reached for him, his gaze only half focusing on me as I pressed my lips to his and forced air into his lungs. A kiss of need rather than intimacy, I gripped him around the waist, staring unashamed in his stunned eyes. The shadows would have to take us both. Did Autumn care?

The inky binding around his legs held firm, but I did too. I wrapped my legs around him, arms in a hug over his shoulders. Our kiss ended as I had nothing more to share and ached for air myself. Part fae, part mortal, always meant weak to the fae. Maybe the Autumn king would be happy to be rid of me.

I met Finn's fearful gaze, the bright light of the day far overhead the only source of miniscule light in our fading drag into the dark. Why die for him? I barely knew him. But, why not? I thought the dragon would kill me. I expected I'd die to free the Summer king and give him the chance to grow. I'd even thought Zephyr would eventually kill me because I refused to tell him what my Vision wouldn't show me.

My lungs burned and Finn relaxed against me, bubbles cascading through my hair. I wouldn't watch him die and feel like I'd failed. But least of all, I didn't want to be alone again.

Let the end take us both, I prayed, and closed my eyes unable to hold my breath any longer.

Nineteen

WESLEY

I blacked out for a half second, snagged into a dream that tilted and wobbled not unlike bobbing in the water. The dream, perhaps Vision, solidified in a haze of misty darkness around me.

A forest, dark and deep, but in the distance spanned a row of houses. Flickers of lights glowing in a beacon of hope.

Tired, and hungry, I lay with my cheek to the dirt staring at the houses, silently pleading, Save me.

Darkness enveloped me, like the shadows themselves wrapped me in a cloak of inky night. The tendrils of oozing black crept in a rippling shudder of endless movement, around me and from me. Was I made from the darkness? My breath visible in tiny puffs like smoke in the chilly evening air, too fast, but slowing as exhaustion tugged me to sleep.

A howl pierced the silence of the night. The chill intensified my shiver as the shadows shook with anxiety, though it wasn't them I feared. They sought to hide me from the chase. A dozen more cries pierced the night, a spooky primal wail of recognition. The Hunt had found me. How long had we been running?

The inky form of a wolf briefly solidifying to grip the back of my shirt with its teeth, willing me to my feet. Shadows dripped off him as he nudged and shoved me toward the scattered lights of houses, open backyards, and the gut-wrenching terror of humans.

Not my memory as I'd learned to fear the fae more than any human monster.

I locked eyes with the wolf, a glow of gold told me it too, had fae blood, but the sense of safety and home flooded me with a will to move. We crept through the brush, keeping low, the shadows oozing off the wolf to hide our tracks as we darted from hiding place to hiding place.

The silence of the late night emboldened my flight. No humans about and away from the Hunt, as though there were another option. The beast towered over me with an otherworldly dark fierceness.

Another eerie howl pierced the stillness. Too close.

Lights turned on. A row of spotlights popping up to try to ward off the unnatural darkness. People awakening to the horror that would just as soon take them as it would me. Unseen eyes watched from the fading tree line as I raced for the nearest light. The wolf around me as a silent guardian.

A door opened and my heart squeezed with terror, a thousand faded memories of humans fluttering through my mind without gaining purchase to clarify. A woman raced forward, short hair a mess, in pajama pants and bunny slippers, and a shotgun in her grip.

"It's a baby, Camille, there's a baby out here!"

Another howl, and it chilled me to the core. The ice ate up the ground, interlacing beneath my feet as though to grab me and drag me back into their nightmare. The Hunt close enough that my guardian turned to snarl and launch itself at them. I stumbled, slipped and fell, head over heels in a tangle of limbs.

The woman ran my way, another not far behind.

"Wolves!"

"I'll scare them off," the first one said. "Get the baby." She

paused to aim, and I wanted to scream, but the shot went over my head, over the shadow wolf and into the woods, the echo of it deafening. A boom of thundering noise as the ice climbed my flesh and reached for my heart.

The second woman reached me, ripping me off the ground and turning in a single breath to sprint back to the house. "He's freezing! Amber, get back to the house."

"Get him inside and warm," the first said, her gun pointed firmly at the dark. The grumble of other humans made my gut churn as I caught the glimpse of the shadow wolf melting into the trees. The Hunt with their icy silver glinting in the returning moonlight, chasing after it.

I gasped for air and reached for the wolf, an ache deep inside I couldn't articulate.

Torn. Came a stray thought, but the woman carried me inside and I lost consciousness to the panic. Dream ripped away and reality slammed me down into my physical body.

I opened my eyes and coughed, water wrenching from my lungs as I heaved the liquid shadows. The glare of the sun beamed overhead, warming me, and leaving me in a ray of brightness with shadows lingering inches away.

Finn rolled over and choked up water, his lungs sounding wet and pained. Relief slid through my gut. We made it.

The ground shuddered and growled as the waves crashed, spraying water like a geyser. Shivers slid down my spine as shadows dripped from the dark, growing, pool of obsidian water.

I tugged Finn away from the menacing waves eroding the shoreline, heart skipping a beat when the water dripped shadows, and the sunlight stuttered through the trees as though afraid to illuminate the nightmare. The outline of the dragon stretched itself over us.

"Not this again," I said and shoved myself to my feet and stood in front of Finn. "If you think we are going to be mates, you've got to stop trying to kill him." The dragon's scales gleamed obsidian in the sunlight, its eyes burning with an otherworldly fire tinted with gold.

"Mine," the dragon rumbled.

I glanced at Finn, the memory of the short dream churning in my head. Maybe I had read this all wrong. Weren't we tied by some fate bond? It had called me mate, what if it meant, "Finn is yours?" The shadow wolf in the dream and the dragon, one being? And the child? Had it been Finn?

"Mine."

"Not really into sharing," I said. "You should have sought the original fox." Kiran, the Spring king, had two mates, and that worked great for them. I wanted a relationship more like the Summer king and his alpha. A yin and yang. "If I'm your mate, how is he yours?"

If Finn belonged to the Autumn king, why did the realm keep trying to kill him?

The dragon towered over us, shadows twisting and dripping. Then it shrank, shifting and churning, darkness splitting and coloring until before me stood the man I'd seen the Summer king call *Apa*. Wolf King, Alpha of Alpha's, Monster in his own right. The wolves whispered of the terrifying thing he could be. Handsome and sculpted like male flesh in a fantasy novel, he'd left behind his will to hide what he was, not ordinary or in any way mortal. This was fae, power of a king, nightmare and angel all in one.

Too perfect. Wasn't that what Sebastian thought whenever he encountered the tempting forms of the divine? I could sculpt my glamour to show beauty and perfection like this, but it would be a lie. All glamour hid something, and this man, the wolf king, buried something beneath the perfection.

"Mate," he said, voice gruff, more like a wolf's howl than a man used to speaking. He reached for me, fingertips caressing my face, careful, yet rough, as if he'd forgotten what it was to touch another.

I fought to hide my flinch, but his touch brought a warmth of magic, and a pool of quick rising heat to my groin. He could take my will, force me to my knees in submission. I was a simple beast after all. The Stag blood would rise and demand either intimacy or death. My mortal soul could scream and flail in protest all it wanted. The magic made me little more than a slave. I expected him to lean in and overwhelm me with endless waves of lust. An easy way to mate, perhaps, but the swirl of his magic retreated, as Finn's arms wrapped around me from behind.

"Please don't hurt him," Finn asked, his body spooned against my back, cold and shivering from the water. A human shouldn't have the strength to stand before the power that lapped at me in waves of excruciating need. I longed to sink to my knees and bow in submission despite knowing the pain it would bring. "Don't make him, please," Finn begged, holding me up. He shivered at my back, a grounding touch of comfort as we stood before absolute power.

"Mate," the king said again.

"But does he want that?" Finn asked. "Doesn't he get a choice?"

The king snarled. His fingers slid over my throat, threatening and pulsing with scorching heat, but Finn held tight. I swallowed, uncertain, body betraying me with physical desire while my mind wove circles to justify my feelings. Fate left few choices. The Summer king made me hope love was necessary for that equation, but faced with fate myself, I suspected, like death, fated love would hardly be kind.

He could have choked me, caused pain, or added fear to his firm grip on my throat, but he caressed my jawline with his thumb as if studying me. His golden gaze blazed as our eyes met, and I sensed his desperation, but couldn't pinpoint why.

"Mate," he said again, more a whisper than a growl. His hand slipped away and the water swirled up around him in an enormous splash that carried him and all his darkness back to the depths of darkness.

Everything stilled except my pounding heart. The tiny creek returned, and Finn shivered at my back, holding tight, face pressed into my hair. The fear we shared added a sour unease to the air. I wanted to shove him away and pretend the last few minutes had all been a nightmare, but I knew if he let me go right then, I'd have unraveled.

Twenty

WESLEY

"Finn?" I asked, my heart still pounding, body confused with lingering lust and terror. Never a fun combination. He tugged me away from the creek's edge, until we stood in the last narrow band of sunlight.

The light blasted away the lingering desire, and the fear faded as the forest settled into familiar, though eerie stillness. I blinked back tears at the brightness as my head gave a warning throb.

Had the bit about the wolf and the child been a Vision? I rarely saw the past, but my mind churned with questions, desperate for answers, yet fearing them at the same time. Finn had shared the nightmare of the realm devoured by shadows, had he seen this Vision as well?

"Did you dream of the child and the shadow wolf, too?"

"Yes," Finn whispered hesitantly.

"Finn..."

"My moms..." Finn whispered. "Amber and Camille. I don't remember any of that, but I was adopted by them. They said I'd been wandering in the woods." He dropped into silence for a few seconds, arms strong around me, clinging as if he needed to hold me to keep himself upright.

I sucked in a narrow breath, heart squeezing. "The shadow wolf protected you from the Hunt." The familiar and terrifying wail of the icy monsters left a lifetime of bitter memories for any who survived crossing their path. I'd led them away from the Summer king. Ran until I thought I'd die with them chasing me through the unraveling chaos of Underhill, and I'd never forget their howl. "The fae fucking Hunt was after you as a kid?"

"I didn't know," he said. "Sometimes I dreamed of the wail, or of something lunging at me in the dark. As a kid, I had an unexplainable fear of the woods. It's one of the reasons I went into ghost hunting, to face my fears. I thought if I proved to myself none of it was real, I could overcome the trauma."

And still wound up yanked into a fae realm at the mercy of greater power. He was lucky he hadn't been caught by the Hunt. Why had the shadow wolf protected him? Why had the Hunt been after him? Thousands of stories of changelings, and I'd never met one. The idea that a fae would leave its child in the mortal realm and take a powerless mortal one in return, sounded crazy to me. Mortals stumbled themselves into slavery to the fae all the time without having to be taken as children. But maybe I was wrong.

And the Hunt didn't trade kids, they hunted to devour magic.

"They never found your parents? Or why you were in the woods?"

"No one claimed me," Finn said. "I had a couple of foster homes that lasted a few days, weeks at most. Had night terrors and a lot of other issues as a kid, but it was my moms who took me in the end and raised me. They had to fight for custody, but they loved me and accepted my weirdness."

"Do you recall what sort of weirdness? Other than the nightmares. Did you see ghosts as a kid?"

He hesitated.

"Finn." I tugged out of his grasp and turned to look at him. "That shadow thing thinks you belong to it."

"Why do you say that? You're its mate, not me."

"It said *mine*, and it wasn't referring to me. It thinks you belong to it. And if it's the same shadow wolf as in your dream..." He had been singled out by the Autumn king. Everyone recognized the power of Autumn as dark, moody, with unpredictable lows and highs, but it was Winter that stole lives with their cold grasp. Why did Autumn need this human?

"I don't know what that means," he said.

Neither did I. Why would the Hunt want a mortal child? All of my senses, magic and otherwise told me he was human. Ordinary.

Mostly.

In fact, most mortals weren't as ordinary as Finn. Many had a touch of magic, even if they ignored it. The weave of the mystical in the mortal world touched everything. But not Finn. I stared at him, searching for that familiar spark, but found nothing.

Ordinary. Unnoticeable or hidden?

"What?" Finn asked.

What had the wolf meant by 'torn'?

"Weirdness," I prompted again.

"I spoke in an unknown language as a kid, and talked to shadows," Finn said. "They thought I was autistic for a long time." He hugged himself and wouldn't meet my gaze. "I try really hard to fit in, but a lot of it is a performance. I've always been *weird*, and most people don't like weird. Many sense it before I can get close and avoid me."

"Do you still talk to shadows and speak in unknown languages?"

"No. Other than talking to that dragon thing. But you saw it too. I'm not imagining things."

"Anything else that would make you stand out? Powers? Like seeing dead people." My temple gave another warning throb. I was going to need to sleep someplace dark soon or risk the migraine making me immobile. Losing the cabin really hurt.

"I've always been drawn to the woods, and I think I can sense ghosts as we often catch something on camera wherever we go. It's how my vlog has gotten popular. We find unexplainable crap. Even got an offer to do a cable show, but I like having control too much to let some producer fake crap for views." He glanced my way, as though looking for disgust or disbelief on my face. "But you said ghosts are everywhere. That means it's not special to sense them, right?"

"For a human it would be." I covered my eyes as my head throbbed. "I'm not certain you're human anymore. Fuck," I cursed. "I've got to get someplace dark. My head is killing me."

"Did the dragon do something to you?"

"No. Any time I have a Vision, I'm *rewarded* with a terrible migraine. If I don't find a place to rest from the light soon, I'll start vomiting until I pass out."

"That sounds awful." Finn asked. "Close your eyes. I'll find us some place dark and safe." He wrapped his arms around me and guided me away from the creek and to somewhere safe and sheltered. "What about the shadows?"

"Are they moving?" I asked without opening my eyes. My stomach gave a warning lurch. If I didn't rest soon, I'd be upchucking air.

"Um... only normally, I think. Like when the sun vanishes behind the trees. Not dripping dragon like. And what do you mean you don't think I'm human?"

"Can we discuss it after I rest?"

"Yes. Though it's going to eat at me."

"Sorry. Pain is making my brain mush." All light and sound added to the growing pain. The air rustling bushes and leaves, and the sun shining through my eyelids rattled my resolve with every step. Finn led me in a solid path through thick grass, holding tight and keeping me upright even when I stumbled with each violent throb of my temple.

"Being fae doesn't sound all that great. Cursed with Visions that make you sick, mated to some dude who doesn't seem to understand boundaries, stuck in a world away from amazing things like coffee and chocolate chip bagels."

"Half fae," I corrected. "Other half is elemental."

"What is an elemental?"

"An earth spirit." I sighed. "Brain, hurt." A sharp spike jutted through my brow from left to right, smashing my eyesight to an array of colored squiggles. My gut flipped over, and I yanked myself away from him to vomit up bile and shadow-stained water. At least I passed out after less than a half dozen attempts to throw up my own stomach.

Twenty-One

WESLEY

The warmth of the sun eased me awake from a dreamless and finally restful sleep. I blinked several times to find a shirt draped over my face blocking out the bulk of the brightness. A cool breeze picked up and I could sense the sky beginning to darken. I must have slept the day away.

I lifted the shirt and gazed at a collection of sticks haphazardly thrown together to help ease the light. If I moved too much, I suspected the thing would fall. Why hadn't he gone back to the tree?

My magic swirled in strong waves, as if it were happy to be back. I slid my glamour around me in a thin protective shield as well as the illusion of clothing and climbed out of the tiny hut. Finn lay a dozen yards away, looking relaxed, spread out in the dying sunbeams as if he were a cat sunning himself.

"Hey," he said, sitting up. "You're awake."

"Where are we?"

"No idea. I wandered for a bit, trying to find the tree, but couldn't. Made do with what I could find. Sorry. I'm not a prepper or anything. I know hiking and basic camping, but surviving without any supplies is not my strength." He looked tired, bags under his eyes, lips chapped from lack of water, and shoulders hunched inward as if to hide the concave emptiness of his stomach. He was shirtless and the dark blotch of the mark on his back carved itself all the way over his shoulders and onto his chest, even wrapping around his throat.

I gasped at seeing the way the mark had grown. How? Why? I reached for him, but he cringed and I stopped. "Sorry. I was going to examine the mark."

"I can't feel it," Finn said. "Any of it. My skin where it touches me. Or anything really. I was really afraid for a while that when it moved over my neck I wouldn't be able to breathe. But it's fine. I feel okay. Chilled, numb, but okay."

"Hungry, thirsty and tired," I corrected. "You should have woken me when you saw it growing."

"Do you know how to fix it?" Finn asked.

"No."

"Then it was better that you slept." He studied me. "You look better. Not as pale." He waved his hand at my outfit. "Dressed in clean clothes."

"Glamour. It's a minor shield, not real physical clothes. It would keep out a drizzle or the subtle breeze blowing right now, but it won't help if it downpours or freezes." I sat down beside him, letting him have a solid personal bubble. "Thank you." I instantly cursed myself for uttering those words. Sebastian's lax court having unraveled my careful control over my tongue. But Finn was human and no sense of magic obligation rippled around me.

"I thought the fae weren't into thank yous?"

"Remember nothing else of the fae, but remember that?"

"It was in a romance where the fae took ownership of the MC for daring to thank him for saving her life."

"Romanticizing slavery is a trope that never seems to die," I said. "Sadly, slavery is never cute or romantic."

"As long as it's fiction, it's fine. That's why I asked. I'm smart enough to understand the difference." Finn said. "Am I your slave now?"

"You ate the berries I gave you and seem fine."

Finn shifted the way he sat, to turn in my direction, his pants leg riding up, and the dark blotch covered his ankle too.

"Fuck," I cursed and pushed up the fabric. "How bad is it?"

"Anywhere the shadow thing touched me," Finn said. "Growing up my legs where it yanked me into the water, and over my back, spreading from the dream..." He looked away, jaw clenched as if he had a something not nice to say, and I couldn't blame him for thinking it was my fault. "You said you don't think I'm human. Can you tell me why now?"

"You feel ordinary to my senses," I said. "Too ordinary." I reached out to hover my hand close enough to linger in the space of his aura, but not touch him. "Humans by nature are tainted with the weave of elemental magic. Most are disconnected from the earth, like those who live in big cities often have the least of it, but it touches everyone. With you, I sense nothing."

"And that means I'm not human?"

"I think someone, or something, is hiding your power."

"You mean the Autumn king? That shadow wolf-dragon, creepy dude?"

"Yes," I agreed. "I heard that the wolf king was really protective of his children. Maybe you are one of his?"

"Well, that makes him a shit dad then since I spent my whole life without one wondering why someone would abandon me in the fucking woods." He sounded bitter and I understood.

"Mine too, oddly enough," I said. "But elementals do that a lot. Pop out half-breeds they leave to fumble through life."

"You don't know your dad, either?"

"I know of him. Only ever spoken to him twice in my life. Elementals don't think the same way humans or fae do. Which in some ways is good, I suppose. Fae are very selfish, hoarding power and stabbing anyone in the back that would help their cause."

"Humans, too," Finn said. "I can't tell you the number of people I thought were friends who do shit that makes me wonder why I'm not evil. Like when I started my vlog, this dude was faking some ghost shit for views. Then got pissed when I cut his stuff out in editing. He claimed I was faking the stuff I saw, but that was real."

"Being selfish isn't inherently evil. Sometimes it's all we can do to survive." Like sleeping with the enemy and dancing around the corruption of Underhill. I stared at him, my gut churning with worry over the blotchy darkness spreading over his skin like some magical bruise. "Speaking of survival, we need to find a way to get food and water into you."

"Hm," he grunted.

"Very caveman of you. You said you couldn't find the tree, what about the cabin?"

"Nope. I wandered in circles. Finally gave up because I was too tired to keep going."

"Dragging my ass around, too."

He smirked. "Your ass isn't that heavy."

"How about I change into the Stag, and we can search for the cabin."

He sighed, his posture and half lidded eyes would have looked great in my bed, but the exhaustion on his face added to my anxiety. Why hadn't he rested when I had? "How about I wait here?" Finn offered.

"Every time I leave you alone the shadow wolf attacks."

"It attacks when you're with me, too," he pointed out. "Seems a strange thing to do when it thinks I belong to it. As if I'm its kid or something. What do we need at the cabin? It's not much use to us burned up."

"I'm hoping the realm restored it."

He stared at me.

"Don't look at me like I'm crazy. This whole world is created from a mix of fae and elemental magic. Weirder things can happen." I actually prayed the cabin returned to its former glory and inside the cake from Sebastian would still be waiting for me. I'd drag Finn with me somehow. Would Liam and Seb know how to save him? Since I was running out of ideas, I had to find hope somewhere.

Twenty-Two

WESLEY

"Does it hurt when you change?" Finn asked with his back to me while I dropped the illusion of clothing. "Like they say in all the books, bones breaking and all that."

"No. I'm witchborn, it's as easy as breathing for me." Witchborn and witchblood shared similar traits, part magic, the variation of the phrase coming from which side was dominant, human or fae. I was more fae than human, thus witchborn. Sebastian was more human than fae, thus witchblood. I'd always hated the terms as there was nothing witch-like about my species, but those of us who straddled the line between human and *other*, fit the title. As if created by witches, but witches weren't born, it was a religion. Some of them came with magic, others could try spells over a thousand lifetimes and never realize the power they craved. My chaos lingered in my blood and soul. Inseparable from who and what I was. "Werewolves are different. Cursed rather than born."

"Werewolves are real?"

I folded up the clothes from the little dwelling he had built, adding them to a careful pile though they were dirty. "Lots of shifters are real. The Summer king is a fox. Vampires are real, too."

"Holy shit. Vampires, shifters, and fae. Oh, my!"

"It's not sweet and sexy like romances make them out to be. They are all deadly." I pointed to my forehead. "Even my Stag. Don't touch my antlers, they are poisonous. The tiniest cut will grant you a slow and excruciating death."

"Scary." He didn't sound scared.

"And if I run, don't follow. You'll be forced to run until you die." I glanced his way, but his back was to me.

"I'm pretty sure if you're running from something, I should probably be running too," Finn said.

"Smart ass. Yes, you should run, but not the same direction as me."

He gazed over his shoulder with a thoughtful expression. "Run toward the scary thing chasing us. Okay. Am I bait? Crunchy and delicious with ketchup like a potato chip?"

I snorted. "If I run forward, you run at a three o'clock or nine o'clock angle. Whatever is chasing us will be caught in the Stag's magic. Run until it dies."

"Handy, but what about you?"

"I'll be fine. The Stag can outrun just about everything." Until my mortal half gave out. Which meant I wouldn't last as long as my full-blooded fae brethren, not that they cared.

"Does it work when you're human?"

"No."

"What about that other form you had?"

"Other form?"

"When you scared the wolf away the first time."

"Oh. That was mostly glamour adding the Stag's bulk to my human form. I only have three real forms."

"Three?"

"The Stag, this one, which is my human form, and my fae form."

"What's the fae form like?"

"Weak. I never use that form. It's useless." I changed into my Stag form, relieved by the easy change. Maybe this realm required me to rest more often to recharge. He stared at me with a frown on his face, but I hoped he understood my fae form wasn't up for discussion.

Finn gathered up the abandoned clothes, tugged his hoodie back on and held on to mine. Everything needed a wash but his hesitation to go near the water made sense. He wove his fingers through the side of my fur and we headed in toward the fading light of the day. Finn's grip grounded the churning anxiety in my gut. He was close and safe, and while his heart beat sluggishly in my heightened hearing, I knew I could head off the wolf again in this form if needed.

Twenty-Three

WESLEY

We walked a while. Not in circles, as I identified a few types of trees and plants, but helpful mushrooms or guiding kittens remained elusive. Finn stumbled twice. The first time I had thought maybe I'd missed a root as I led him, but the second time he leaned hard into me, breathing tight, one sleeve pushed up to reveal the mark extended all the way to his wrist.

His touch on my side ached with a growing chill, adding to my worry.

The longer we walked the more frustrated I got. The world around us was changing, but none of the old landmarks reappeared. Finn slowed until he only moved because I did, leaning into me as if I were the only thing keeping him upright. I stopped, fearing he'd fall over. He slid to the ground. The mark stretched up over the left side of his face, blending in with the heavy bags of exhaustion around his eyes.

I shifted to my human form, pulling him into my arms. "Hey," I said.

He fought to open his eyes, but they only fluttered.

"Fuck," I cursed.

"Sorry," Finn slurred. "Tired."

But with the sky overhead darkening to full night, and the pinprick of stars illuminating the barest of details, resting for the night was a bad idea. With little more than a handful of trees and distant bushes, we were too vulnerable. I needed to get him up and moving and to find something to put to our backs for safety.

"Hey," I shook him. "I'm going to change, and I'll need you to crawl up on my back."

"You're so pretty."

"And you're delusional. I'm not using any glamour right now. This is as ordinary human as I can be." I tried to lift him, but he sighed and stared at my face, hand lifting as if to reach my hair.

"It's like spun rose gold."

"In the dark?" I asked and pressed my fingers to his forehead. "You're not feverish."

"Cold," he said, shivering and pressing himself into my touch. "You're warm."

And since the mark sprawled over his skin, I worried.

"Mhmm. Oh, you're naked." He shut his eyes.

"Yeah, well pretty comes with all the parts. If I change into the Stag, can you climb on? I'll try to find us a safe place for the night."

"Sure, but you're really tall in that form."

"I'll crouch. Remember not to touch my antlers." I leaned him up against a tree and shifted. The air crackled with energy as the change slid over me, muscles rippling beneath my skin as I became the Stag.

When I bowed beside him, he didn't move. I waited, hoping he hadn't passed out. After a few seconds he slid one arm over and then the next. His movements painfully slow as he climbed on, my clothes grasped tightly in his arms as though he were afraid to lose them. Everywhere he touched ached with an icy bite, reminding me of the Winter court and the endless torture at the Queen's feet.

Finn settled onto my back, the weight of his exhaustion heavy, his breaths uneven and labored. The darkness of night cloaked the landscape, and the sound of the forest faded to chilling, ominous silence. I studied the darkest edges of shadows, searching for signs of the shadow beast, or any movement. The weight of being watched was heavy even though I saw no one. The longer I stared at the distant trees, the edges rippled with a trickle of movement. An illusion?

I cursed the realm for being tricksy, remembering how terrible Underhill had been, and headed toward the trees. Finn sprawled over my back like a pulse of living ice. I could feel him breathing, and the gentle grip of his fingers in my fur trying to keep himself steady. If he passed out and fell, I'd have no chance of catching him before he hit the ground.

Approaching the magic quiver of forest, the air shimmered with a faint otherworldly glow, casting strange shadows that danced on the forest floor. I hesitated, half worried stepping through the veil would bring me to the den of the shadow wolf, and half hopeful it would rip us free from the realm altogether. Would the mark vanish if Finn escaped? Or would it force him to remain in this madness, tearing him from my back?

As I stepped into the midst of the illusion, the world around us twisted, the familiar landscape morphed into something altogether unfamiliar. Mushrooms popped up in an array of color and sizes not typical to a part of the mortal world. Trees sprouted where none had stood before, their branches reaching out like twisted fingers grasping at the darkness. Faces carved from their bark with contorted expressions.

My heart flipped over with fear at the memory of Underhill before its collapse and how blighted the landscape had been. The mushrooms provided light, but cast squirming shadows over the gnarled faces making them appear alive.

Autumn as a king had been the first to be lost, and his chaos spread to Underhill in this sort of Halloween-esque nightmare. Was this the final sign that the new king was already beyond saving?

I stared at a nearby tree, feeling the carved face tug with a sense of familiarity. The longer I studied the carve of the face, the more real it felt. As if a person had been sucked into the tree and entombed there.

I took a few steps back, the ground beneath my hooves soft and unstable, like I walked on shifting sands rather than solid earth. The deafening silence chilled me to the core, making me wonder if I'd lost my hearing. I froze and listened, hearing Finn's sluggish heartbeat after a few seconds. I really needed to get him to safety.

Should I go back? The arch of surrounding trees filled with frozen and contorted faces loomed close. Finn's grip tightened. I steadied my breath hoping to give him the impression of calm confidence, though my anxiety rose as we wove through a dozen carved trees.

The gnarled growths of Underhill vibrated with magic. Their roots having eaten fae much as the kings could, though unable to weave the remains into anything other than a resonating nightmare of the past. The faces, trees, and even the brush surrounding us in the faint light of glowing mushrooms lacked any sense of life at all. More like statues than plants, or a carved area of the realm meant to reflect the living sense of a painting, only filled with the life the onlooker gave it.

"What is this place?" Finn whispered. He clung to my back, lying pressed against me, grip tight. "Are they people? Fae?"

An array of bright mushrooms surrounded a nearby tree, illuminating it to clarify the face with an uncomfortable familiarity. Not people, I realized, but perhaps a shrine to them. Parts of the Autumn king's past? This one lacked the contorted nightmare expression of the others, appearing with eyes closed, half turned away, and calm.

Sebastian.

Twenty-Four

WESLEY

Finn sat up on my back. "Do you know him?"

Since I couldn't answer in my shifted form, I kept walking. The carved trees and glowing mushrooms a distracting maze of confusion. The magic in this area had faded to a ripple. Finn's icy touch on my back ached, my muscles tired. Maybe I'd walked farther than I thought?

I paused at the edge of another contorted tree. The carving of something not human this time, and the mushrooms at its base wafted shadows rather than glowed. The bite of ice still touched the tree. Winter's curse.

Was that why Finn's touch hurt? Had he been cursed by Winter, too?

He slid off my back, landing firmly, grip strong on my side. "There's something about this one..." he didn't finish what he was trying to say, but reached for it.

I shifted to my human form, the change usually one heartbeat to the next, but taking a few seconds longer which made my heart turn over with anxiety. Finn paused, gaze on me. His face flushed as he glanced at me, then shoved the clothes my way. I tried for glamour, but it didn't happen. Maybe this world took more of my magical energy than I thought?

"Don't touch things," I said, annoyed, and grabbed the shirt from him and tugged it over my head. It caught for a half second in my hair, then fell over my shoulders. I reached up and found the nubs of antlers on my head. That wasn't right. "What the fuck?"

I held up my hand, fearing I'd shifted all the way to my fae form, but my hand and legs were human. The nubs remained.

"They're cute," Finn said.

"Don't patronize me."

"I'm not. You sort of look like what I thought a fae might look like now. Not that it's bad or anything," he rushed to say. "Are they deadly in this form?"

"No," I said. Because they weren't sharp. In fact, in my fae form they had a completely different use. Finn reached for them. "Don't touch," I snapped.

He yanked his hand away. "Sorry."

"You must be feeling better." I grabbed his wrist and shoved the sleeve back; the mark was gone. "Let's go to one of the lighted mushrooms. I need to look at you."

"You don't have super vision or something?" he asked.

"Other than the ability to see most people's gruesome deaths, no." We paused back at Sebastian's tree, the lights of the mushrooms blazing and I stared at Finn's face, his expression apprehensive. "I'm not going to hurt you."

"I didn't think you were."

"Can you take off your shirt?"

"Forward of you. If you want me naked, just say so."

"Smart ass. I want to look at the mark. It had spread up over your face, now I don't see it at all. Maybe it's gone? Entering this area removed it?"

He took a step back and lifted his shirt. The stretch of the blotchy purple and blue bruise-like mark covered his torso, but the shape was odd, as if where he'd lain against me while I walked, had removed the mark. "I still feel it. The cold, numbness on my back, half down my spine, and my sides. Couldn't feel one arm for a while. You were warm. I thought maybe that was helping. Your fae magic healing me or something."

"I don't have that kind of magic. I'm a battery for the kings, that's all."

"What does that mean?"

"I was meant to be used," I said without emotion. Accepting my role meant casting out hope for anything else, and I would fight that to the end of my days.

I studied Sebastian's tree, hoping for a way to contact him, or a sign that it was anything other than some elaborate carving in a long dead tree.

"Who is he?"

"The Summer king," I said. "I think all of these carvings are statues of people from the Autumn king's past. He raised the Summer king. Tried to keep him safe, even if he really sucked at it." The contorted monster-like carving I suspected had been Felix. Whatever remained of his humanity lost to the Autumn king's memory. I'd only ever seen the man once. Sebastian had been very young, and I kept my distance, trying to add a layer of safety to the wolf king's protection. I knew of the last living child of the Volkov, but not much about him. He'd appeared ordinary in that quick glimpse, like any other wolf.

I'd never actually met Xander, the Volkov himself. Would it have triggered a more detailed vision of how I was somehow meant to be his mate? The wolves spoke of him with fear and reverence, but he'd kept to his compound, and when Sebastian vanished inside the walls of the Volkov's space, he was eclipsed from my sight, too. The Autumn king's power? Or something more?

I took a step toward the tree, wondering if I could connect with Sebastian if I touched it. Would he sense me? But my left leg gave out, and I crumpled. Finn caught me, holding me tight to his chest.

"Are you okay?"

"I must be more tired than I thought I was. Maybe this world is draining my energy."

"I feel better than I did," Finn said. "Can we sit here by the Summer king's tree and rest a while? He won't mind, right?"

"It's just a statue," I said. "They are all statues. Lifeless memories. Like humans take pictures, it seems the Autumn king has created his own snapshots in time."

"Creepy," Finn said but found a spot near the base of the tree and curled himself around me. I sighed, too tired to pull away, and secretly enjoying his protective side. "Have you gotten smaller?"

"No," I said, checking my hands and feet again. Still human. I could only imagine Finn's horror if he saw the fae version of me. My flirty partner in survival would vanish in a heartbeat.

"Close your eyes and rest," Finn said tucking his legs around me as a shield. "I'll keep watch."

"We should keep moving. Nothing is safe."

"Sure," Finn said, but kept himself tight around me. "You took care of me. Let me take care of you for a while." I shivered and leaned into him. Maybe a short nap. If magic came at us, I'd sense it.

Twenty-Five

WESLEY

My cock ached, hard and desperate to be touched. Someone kissed along my throat, touch light and fleeting. I groaned, shoving my hips into them, the need racing through my veins like fire. I blinked open my eyes to see the Autumn king in his sculpted physical perfection leaning over me, hand gliding over my cock.

"Stop," I demanded. The pulsing waves of magic familiar and inescapable. Desire pooled over my skin drawing a gasp of need from my lips as my hips ground against him seeking friction.

He gripped my chin and pressed his lips to mine. I thought to break away but the desperate heat made me open to him. His kiss dove deep, exploring my lips with brutal, yet delicious precision. He nipped my lower lip as he drew away.

"I can show you endless pleasure," he growled.

"The desire isn't mine," I ground out, angry at my body's betrayal.

"Yet you cursed the Summer child with the same heat," he accused.

I'd once tried to seduce Sebastian in a dream pond with a sculpted form most men who loved men would fall for, but he'd ripped himself away. The idea of it made me sick, but I was following orders. He'd awakened to his mate, and been able to fill the heat in a much better way than I ever had.

"Zephyr demanded it, forced my hand. And it was only a dream," not real like this, only as I stared past him the space around us lacked clarity. This too was a dream. "No," I said. "Let me go."

"I've waited a long time, mate," he said, leaning back but continuing to stroke me with a firm and skilled hand. "Loved many to ensure I'd be ready for you."

"Didn't need to know that," I huffed.

The Summer king's mate had threatened me for daring to touch his love. At the time, explaining would have meant admitting betrayal in two ways. Playing both sides coming to a head. But Zephyr enhanced the dream, wrapped Sebastian in sexual desire for a glamoured version of me, thinking perhaps like would be drawn to like. When Sebastian rejected me, forcing the unnatural desire, a sort of incubus draw from others to me, to return, it had no outlet other than Zephyr's brutality. Thankfully I'd blacked out partway through, the beast too rough for the tiny fae form he loathed.

"Please don't," I begged. "If you care at all that I am your mate, you won't force me."

He frowned, but his touch eased away. "You are my mate. You do not desire me?"

"I don't know anything about you," I said.

"Human minds..." he growled and stood, his human male perfection shifting from man to wolf, the shadows sliding over his skin as if suctioned to him. That couldn't be good.

"Yes, us thinking folks are super complicated." I sighed at the absence of his touch, though my body pulsed with the fire of desire. "Can you undo the need?"

But he slipped into the shadows, and I blinked to focus on his departure, only to open my eyes to Finn holding me, his fingers tickling one of my antler nubs. I gasped, the lust raging forward in a terribly familiar way. A disturbing heat ached in my groin, fire pouring down my spine and into the betraying bit of flesh desperate for touch. That couldn't be. Only the fae form experienced a real heat.

"You're so tiny and cute," Finn remarked, seeing my eyes open.

I gasped, yanking myself out of his arms, though my body demanded his touch. The hoodie reached my knees, hiding my engorged cock, but baring the not quite human legs of my fawn form. I lifted my hands, staring in horror at the thick tan fuzz covering the backs. "No, no, no," I chanted, trying to will myself to my human or even Stag forms.

"What's wrong?" Finn asked. He stood, towering easily a half foot over me now.

I took a step back though everything in me wanted to throw myself at him and beg him to cool the heat.

"I'm not going to hurt you, Wesley," Finn said, his expression sad. He leaned against the tree, hands out as if to show he wouldn't press the issue.

"But I could hurt you," I said.

"Yep," Finn said. "Your Stag antlers are scary."

"I mean right now." A wave of need pulsed through me, part desperation to be touched, part hunger to create. This form had one use, and one use only. A fulfilled heat brought life to the forest as I cast off earthen magic each time I came. The fawn's curse gifted by my elemental sire.

"Wesley?"

I dropped to my knees and wrapped the hoodie around me as if it could shield me from everything my body demanded. Finn leapt to tug me into his arms as if I'd fallen.

"No," I whispered. His touch added an icy blast to chill the desperate heat, temporarily clearing my head.

"No what?" Finn asked. "You're not hurt? I can't help? Tell me what's wrong?"

"Look at me! This is my fae form. Weak, useless, the only purpose of it is to be fucked and create magic to grow things."

Finn blinked, his expression changing a few times as he processed my words, but he held firm.

"Run away," I told him. Would the pheromones of my heat turn whatever half-human mortal thing he was into the beast of desperation like Zephyr and every other of my lovers in the past had been? "Before the heat catches you."

"Heat?"

I gripped the hoodie, tugging it up, showing the backward bend of my knees, and my feet more hooves than feet. "I'm an animal, can't you tell?"

"Is this because I touched your antlers?"

"No. Yes. Maybe. I think the Autumn king triggered it. He tried before by the creek." This time the heat was too far aroused to be shoved back. Maybe I was overdue, or maybe he'd hoped for a way to claim me as his mate.

"What can I do to help?" Finn asked.

I wanted to demand he fuck me, but that wasn't fair. "Run away." I curled up in a ball, the pain of need ripping through every vein as it rolled through my blood.

"Will it go away if I leave?"

"No." An unserved heat could last for days, and nothing I could do alone would fulfill the demand of my body and the magic's desperation to grow.

"Then I'm not leaving." He folded his arms across his chest.

Stubborn man. "I can't promise I won't rape you!" I shouted at him, trying to make him afraid. He might claim he played both sides of the field, but screwing the pretty little fawn boy was a whole other ballgame. The longer the heat lasted, the more frantic for relief I would become, and my mind already clouded with the demand for release.

He stared at me for a moment, then unfolded his arms and lifted his hoodie up off his chest over his head and tossed it aside.

"What are you doing?" I demanded.

"Can't rape the willing," he said as he shoved down his sweatpants, baring his body and his hard cock. "If this is what helps…"

"You're not willing. It's the pheromones making you feel this way. You don't want me." No one did. I was a tool to be used.

He spread the pants and top out beneath him and sat down at the base of the tree, legs splayed to show me how *interested* he was. The fact that he wasn't jumping me, forcing me onto my stomach to shove himself inside, confused me. "I'm willing, but it's your choice."

"I have no choice!" He couldn't understand what the heat meant. The pain, the desire, the relief and how amazing it actually felt when I finally came, no matter how much I bleed from whomever used me.

"You do," Finn said. "I can't stop this thing from happening to you. I'm sorry if I caused it. But I'm not afraid of you, and I want you to have the choice." He remained at the base of the tree, rooted and waiting, his dick hard and leaking. He didn't touch it. I could imagine what it felt like inside. Thick and long, breaching me, slamming into me, filling me with his spend which would erupt from me in waves of magic.

I cried and rolled on the ground, rubbing myself in the grass as if it would help. It didn't. My ass ached for the stretch and the slamming glide of a cock tunneling into me. I rolled over to glare at him. Why wasn't he coming unglued at the pheromones and magic allure? He sat against the tree, shoulders tense, cock standing straight up, his eyes half lidded as he panted, hands gripped on his knees.

Control. I'd never met a male of any species with that level of control.

"You can't be real," I whispered.

"One hundred percent real," Finn said. "But it's your choice. I am here. Willing." He let out a long stuttering breath. "Hornier than I've ever felt in my life. Holy shit, but yeah, one hundred percent real."

Twenty-Six

WESLEY

I hesitated. Heart hammering in my chest, lungs tight, gaze glued to his cock. The idea that penises were ugly, shattered by the beauty of his. Long, thick, uncut, the hair surrounding it trimmed to frame it like the treat it was, a nearly otherworldly perfection.

"Fuck," I growled. A drop of liquid slid from the opening and my mouth watered, gut churning with the idea of a single drop of his seed lost when I could make magic from it. "You're not real," I repeated.

"I am," he insisted.

I tiptoed forward watching the precome glide over the wrinkle of his foreskin and pause as though ready to drip away. "Can I?" I licked my lips.

"Anything you want."

A guy never turned down a blow job, right? I glanced at his face and crept forward my gaze drawn back to that drip about to be lost. Before I realized what I'd done, I'd dropped to my knees and caught the escaping drop on my tongue. I licked up his dick, following the path to catch the salty trail, magic churning in me.

More, I needed more.

His lust-filled gaze made me want to skewer myself on him and ride hard until the forest around us shifted to a growing jungle of fae magic. Finn gripped his knees, hands white knuckled, the desire chipping away at his resolve.

I licked the tip of him, tongue teasing his foreskin and catching stray drops of his spend. Each sip added to the growing waves of magic building inside. I'd need release to set them free, but the heat would force that on me whether my lover saw to my needs or not.

I backed away, ass clenching with demand to be filled.

"Your eyes are like the grass after a few days of rain," Finn said. "Brilliant green. Glowing. Beautiful."

"It's the magic," I said.

"Okay," he agreed absently, his gaze focused on my face. "What would help you the most right now?"

"If you ran away."

"But you said this heat thing won't stop. Does it hurt?"

"I'll survive."

"Uh, that wasn't a no. *Does. It. Hurt*?"

"Unfulfilled, yes."

"Then not running. What else helps?" He wrapped his fingers around his cock and slid up and down the length. "Watching?"

"No!" I cried, desperate as his masturbation brought more spend to the tip.

He paused.

Would he run away if I told him all of it? Maybe he'd turn feral and fuck me until I bled. Was it sad that I craved that? Or simply the curse of this form?

"I need to be fucked," I said. "I need you to fill me with your spend until I'm dripping with it. And the mix of pheromones and magic will keep you hard. The heat won't end until I'm covered in your spend and erupting with magic all over this place. It could take hours, days even."

"Wow. Kinky. It sounds pretty good for me. But how do I make that good for you?"

"The heat will make it good for me."

He frowned.

"What?" I demanded.

His expression remained pensive. I ripped off the hoodie, casting it aside, and turned over to present him my ass.

Finn remained rooted to the base of the tree. I glanced back, waiting, my ass dripping lubricant to ease his way. This form begged for it. I adjusted my weight on my knees and pulled my ass cheeks open, holding them with firm hands. "See how bad I need you? I'm dripping for you. I was made for this."

He finally moved, inching forward. "Can I touch you?"

"I'm begging you to fuck me, of course you can touch me." Soon I'd be completely irrational, begging for him to grind his fine cock deep.

He carefully rested a palm on my spine, his skin adding a chill to the heat which made me shiver and press back into his touch. He traced the length of my spine with his fingertip, leaving me shivering and clenching.

"Fuck," I groaned.

"Eventually, maybe," Finn said.

"Maybe?" I squeaked, frustrated. Couldn't he see I was ready to be used?

"Let me clarify," Finn said.

"How much clarifying do you need to finally fuck me?"

"Bossy," Finn grumbled. "You create magic from my come?"

"Yes."

"And spread the magic to the forest how?"

"Every time I come."

"Well, that doesn't sound horrible. Us having a good time, making flowers grow."

I grunted.

He ran his fingers over my hip bone and down to my cheeks. "And we don't even need lube 'cause you make your own. That's handy."

"Only in this form. This body is meant to be fucked."

He circled the ring of my pucker with his thumb, teasing, maybe testing the slipperiness, but I needed him inside. "And this form is male? All the same triggers as a guy?"

"Uh, yeah. I thought you said you were equal opportunity. Please tell me you've screwed a guy before." Not that it would matter. He could be a clumsy oaf and still make me come with the heat raging like this.

He slipped a careful digit into my hole. My ass sucked it in desperately, the hard length too small to do much. "That's pretty hot," he said, twisting his finger to search for something.

I saw stars. My body jerked and I cried out as he tickled my prostate and I came unglued, spurting all over the ground. My hips jerked involuntarily fucking myself on his finger, needing more, even while I barely kept myself upright. He wrapped his arm around my stomach, holding me, body a cool anchor against the near painful fire of my skin.

"Flowers," Finn said as he kissed my shoulder gently, his gaze directed at my spend and the instant reward of greenery coming to life anywhere it touched. "Your orgasms make things grow. Not sure you really need my spunk."

"I do!" I insisted, hips grinding back onto his finger, wishing he'd just shove his dick in me and get started. "I need it to make magic. I'm meant to be a come dump," I said, hoping my nasty talk would inspire him to use me. "You could bring a dozen men to fuck me and I'd use their come to create a forest larger than half the globe." Begging for it the entire time, while mentally checked out.

"But you need to feel good, too," Finn insisted.

"The heat will make it good," I said again.

"You mean, even if I hurt you, you'll still come."

"Yes. But you can't hurt me. You're mostly human. I'm anything but."

He was silent for a minute, then he unwrapped his arm from around me. His touch slipped away, finger leaving my channel, and

I wanted to scream. But he cupped my ass, brushing away my hands. "You're fascinating."

"Not a science project," I snapped. But a second later something tickled my rim and I nearly came unglued again. "What are you doing?"

"Haven't eaten in days. Don't tell me you've never had someone eat your ass? It's delicious." He licked my rim again, tickling the sensitive outer edge, pressing his tongue into the opening for a half second to feel the resistance and returning to the slow torture of teasing my hole.

"Finn!" I cried.

"Hmm," Finn said. "I love the way you say my name."

"Fuck me already."

"Soon. I know as soon as I'm inside you, I won't want to stop."

"That's the point!"

"Ha, no, the point is making you feel good."

"It's not."

"It is. If you don't want me, say so, and I'll walk away. I hate leaving you in this heat thing, but I'm not going to force you."

"The heat won't let me say no." While it was the truth, I knew instantly it was the wrong thing to say.

Finn pulled away, and I whimpered with disappointment. "I won't be one of those guys, Wesley. You don't want me. I don't want you to suffer, but I'm not going to rape you because some weird fae magic has a hold on us."

I heard him move away and wanted to scream. He planted himself back at the base of the tree, knees closed and face turned away as though not looking at me would help his resolve. "It's not rape if I'm willing."

"You're not willing if you can't say no," Finn threw back.

I curled up into a ball in the dried grass cursing my luck to be stuck with the last truly noble man on the planet.

Twenty-Seven

WESLEY

I don't know how long I laid there, rubbing myself in the grass, finger fucking myself, searching for release and praying something I did triggered Finn to reconsider. He had balls of steel to keep from sliding home with how much I begged. I panted a half dozen meters away, staring at him and cursing his betrayal.

Finn refused to meet my gaze, but the tension in his shoulders and the bulging line of veins in his arms as he gripped his knees together, told me he still felt the pull. He leapt up, tugged the sweat pants back on, making me whine, but he stalked away, pacing.

"What if we summoned the Autumn king?" Finn finally asked. His hard cock bounced in the pants, outline clear, my mouth watering, as I focused on it and how desperate I was to feel it burrow its way inside me. "Wesley?"

"Hmm?"

"Are you listening to me?"

"Come stick your cock in me and you'll have my rapt attention."

He snorted. "Tempting as that may be, does this heat thing

have a lull? A break of any time in which you might be thinking rationally?"

"Once you fuck me, sure. Might even get a nap in-between sessions."

"What if we called for the Autumn king. Do you think he would come?"

"I could make him come." In a dozen ways. I imagined that sculpted body of male perfection that I knew was more glamour than reality, and how it could satisfy the heat no matter what it hid beneath.

"Right. Sex on the brain. Should I call him for you? Since you're mates and all?"

"He'd seal our mate bond," I said, briefly sobering and fearing what that meant for me. Would he lock me away? As my bound mate he'd have the ability to raise my heat as often as he'd like. The truth of mating a king, subject to his whims, might not have bothered Sebastian's wolf, but the pair loved each other.

"Is that a good or bad thing?"

"Rather you fuck me."

"That's what I mean. The king is your mate. I'm just some guy."

"I'd rather *you* fuck me."

"Uh..."

I rolled over onto my back, legs spread to show my engorged cock, unable to come by myself, no matter how I tried. Magic sucked in a lot of ways. Rules, checks and balances to follow else the entirety of all existence might erupt. The fae mixing with humans had never been a good idea. Would I choose Finn, the college bro ghost hunting nerd over a king of fae? Yeah, probably.

Why? If my mind weren't clogged with lust, I might have pinpointed some of his assets other than the fine cock he couldn't hide from me. But until the heat cooled, I was little more than walking desire.

"Please," I said, not above begging.

"I don't want you to hate me," he hesitated, gaze turned away. "Or myself for feeling like you don't have a choice."

"If it were the king or you," I said, "I'd choose you."

"You're only saying that cause I'm all you have right now."

"You are hot and that cock is very fine. If I'd met you in a bar, I probably would have gone home with you."

He sighed.

"I get it," I said. "This form doesn't do it for you. The fawn form is meant for sex, to submit and obey. But I can't even glamour to something better until the heat is over. Small and cute, not exactly human, all negative checkmarks."

"Not true," Finn said. "I'm into all your forms. The majestic stag, the hot twink, and even the little king. I just don't like taking advantage of you. Makes me sus, right? We are supposed to be all in over this sex thing." He let out a long sigh. "And I want to be."

Little king? "Hot twink?"

"Uh yeah. The regular human form? What else would you call it? Sex on legs? Never thought I was into blonds until I saw you."

"But that form isn't glamour at all."

"Okay, and that's bad, why?" Finn stared at me and absently rubbed himself through his pants. My mouth watered at the wet spot appearing near the tip.

"I can take care of that for you," I offered.

He groaned. "We've both got sex on the brain."

"Nothing wrong with that. I like sex."

"Even when this heat thing isn't making you feel it?"

"Uh, yeah. Guy, remember." I spread my thighs, desperate for him. "Slide tab A into slot B and let's ride this wave to the best orgasms you'll ever have in your life."

Still, he hesitated, gaze needy as it roamed over me in the way I wish his hands would.

"Please," I begged.

"You're evil," he said tiptoeing my way. I wanted to scream with joy that he was finally giving in, but he left his pants on.

Dammit. He knelt and leaned over me, sliding the cloth covered length of his hard dick over my sensitive hole. Finn panted, arms straining as he held himself up, his control waning as I ground my hips into his. "Can I kiss you?"

"You don't need to."

"Can. I. Kiss. You?" He ground out, lips hovering above mine.

"I guess. But it won't change how bad I want your cock."

"Okay," he agreed and pressed his lips to mine. Finn nipped at my lower lip, sucking on it for a few seconds before running his tongue over the plump flesh, then teasingly thrust his tongue inside my mouth, mimicking what I wanted our lower bodies to do. I opened for him, letting him slide his mouth against mine, surprised by the gentle exploration and skilled kiss that made me sigh and relax into him. How could he be so young and still an amazing kisser?

His closed eyes added comfort, and I shut mine, letting our bodies grind together as he explored my mouth. Who kissed like that? Like he could tongue fuck a pastry cream to gather all the gooeyness without disturbing the soft puff dough around it?

He eased away, forehead pressed to mine and I opened my eyes to meet his gaze.

"Who the fuck are you?" I demanded again. "No one kisses like that."

"Was it bad? I really like kissing. Not a lot of people do. But I do. I've tried to get a lot of practice. Would have been better the first time at the cabin, but you surprised me."

"Holy fuck."

Finn reached down to run a fingertip around my hole again. I shoved against him, wanting him inside. "I'd like to do that to this," he offered.

I blinked, processing his words and nearly coming unglued as I realized he meant he wanted to tongue fuck my asshole. "No."

"Why not?"

"'Cause I need your cock if this damn heat is ever going to end and if we do *that* I'd like to be more in control." The truth was that often I remembered little of my heats. And experiencing something as divine sounding as Finn eating my ass until I saw stars, I wanted to remember that. Especially since I was mated to the Autumn king and who knew what sort of lover he would be.

"Raincheck on ass eating then. Promises, promises."

I gaped at him. "Once your head is clear you won't want me."

"Okay," he said without agreement. "Can I kiss you more? Your mouth, I mean."

"If you put your cock in me."

He sighed. "I'm not sure I can retain control if I do that."

"That's what I want."

"Me to lose control?"

"Yes."

He bit his lip, concentration fierce in the tightness of his shoulders. "How about you top then?"

"What part of I need you *in* me do you not understand?" Top *him?* During a heat? Was he crazy?

"Right, I get that part. But I mean, you ride... control what you need... on top. Make sense?" He dragged himself to his feet and lifted me up to follow, tugging me back to the base of the tree. He settled back on the spread-out hoodies, both his and mine, and waved at his lap.

I stared at him a few seconds wondering how much control he was giving me and licked my lips recalling the tiny taste I had of him. Too much time had passed for that to satisfy me now. "Can I see it?"

Finn shoved his sweatpants down, his cock springing free. He bunched fabric under his balls, framing that beautiful dick as it stood in engorged glory, weeping with need.

"Holy fuck, your dick is fine," I said.

"You're good for my ego. I'm average at best."

Average. Ha. Above average at least. "I'm going to shove that in my ass until we both see stars."

He gulped. "Okay."

Finally!

"But I can still kiss you, right?"

"Weirdly obsessive, but sure." I knelt over him, focusing the angle to press his weeping head to my throbbing and needy hole. My body desperate to be filled and dripping lubricant of my heat, eased his entrance, and I sighed with relief as he slid home.

Finn wrapped his hand around the back of my neck and pulled me forward to meet his lips. His kiss as desperate as my body to fuck. I ground my hips down until he was fully sheathed, groaning against his lips as my ass stretched around him. I lifted up a half inch, testing the angle, resistance, and drag. Slow and calculating, knowing eventually we would devolve into rutting.

His kiss grew more intense, needy as I played with the rise, squeezing my ass around his cock, feeling the heat of his dripping spend coat my insides with building magic. This form experienced sensation a thousand times more intensely than my human one. Made for sex, made to be fucked, made to craft magic from pleasure.

Finn raised his knees, giving me a seat between them to sink into. He rested his other hand on my lower back, the one on my neck keeping my lips to his as the other one steadied my glide. He gasped, his lips breaking from mine to suck in air, eyes half lidded with lust as I bounced on him, every instinct screaming *'Yes, yes, yes!'*

"Has to be a dream," Finn grumbled, little sounds falling from his lips each time I met his groin and squeezed my ass as I slid back up.

Our connection only changed an inch or so, up and down, squeeze and release, a teasing dance, frustrating as I couldn't quite hit the right spot in this position. I grunted in irritation, shifting position slightly, seeking that hyperdrive button that would launch us into the thrall of the heat.

"What?" Finn asked, nipping my lower lip.

"Can't get the right angle," I complained. Was it because I was meant to be mated to the Autumn king? I'd never had an issue with anyone else, but I hadn't met the king before. Had fate changed something? This heat would last forever if I could ride Finn but never come.

Finn cradled me against him, leaning over me until our hips were sandwiched between his bent knees. He swung his hips in one direction, stabbing into me, then the other, shoving hard at the end, and finally pegging my prostate. I howled, thrusting against him, demanding more.

"Found it," Finn panted, doing it again. He caught my lips again as he ground his cock into me, swinging in a playful rotation of in most of the way, out, in and slid over my prostate, then shove hard and slip away. "Not gonna last much longer," Finn said. "Sorry."

I didn't need him to last. But his next thrust tickling over my prostate launched me into the stars, rare as he hadn't given me a full load of his spend yet, but I screamed, jerking against him as though I could drag him deeper, cock erupting between us, in a wave of lines to coat our stomachs.

Then he growled and released inside, digging his hip bones into mine as though his body knew it needed to deposit his seed as deep as it could go. Flowers, grass, and a thousand tiny little trees popped up around us. A ring of mushrooms sprouted around where we lay, the tops glowing in gold, orange, and red to combat the dreary area of the Autumn king's garden of statues.

I sucked in air, the magic churning through me in building waves. Finn caught my lips in a kiss again, our groins grinding together, orgasm cresting and falling in a few seconds of overstimulation before assaulting us with another orgasm.

"You weren't lying," Finn said lips hovering above mine. "And I wasn't wrong."

"About?" I asked as I wrapped my legs around him to keep him from pulling out.

"Best orgasm of my life. And not wanting to ever stop," Finn said as he thrust against me. "I think I'm going to die grinding into you. And that's okay. What a fucking way to go."

"Hmm," I muttered as he kissed me again. The man had skill with his mouth. Okay, his cock too. I came again, a fountain of come to match every ounce he gave me. But a heat could milk him for days, until we both had rubbed ourselves raw from the demand.

With flowers and life exploding around us from the growing waves of magic, the realm began to feel less like a prison, and more like a sanctuary.

"Don't stop," I demanded.

He teased my prostate again, making me grumble and beg. "Not planning to."

Twenty-Eight

WESLEY

I woke to a light rain drizzling in cooling droplets, and Finn curled around me. As with all previous heats, I'd blacked-out after the fourth-dozen or so time coming on Finn's cock. The ache lingered, muscles overworked, ass raw, but deep within my bones, magic and satisfaction radiated, well fed and well fucked.

Despite the rain, light assaulted the back of my eyelids, and I flinched away from opening them. Grumbling about needing more sleep.

"Rest as long as you need, but I have berries if you're hungry. I can eat them, and hope you can too," Finn said.

How did he have any energy left?

I squeezed open an eye, gazing at him sitting beside me, handful of ripe raspberries held out. He chose a single plump fruit and pressed it to my lips. I let it slide between my lips and unconsciously sucked on his thumb for a half second. The berry popped with sweet flavor in my mouth. His skin tasted warm and salty.

"I think your heat thing is over," Finn said. "I'm not hard and neither are you. Not sure I can get it up for a while."

I sucked in air and stretched. "Ow."

"You okay?"

"Sore."

"Did I hurt you?"

"Not really." Nothing felt torn or bleeding. I stared at him searching for any sign of the dark blight that had been slowly inching its way across his skin had vanished. He looked radiant, near glowing with health. I sat up, finding myself in my mortal form, which never happened after a heat. The light drizzle dripped in a cooling trickle to wash away some of the crustiness. Mushrooms glowed from the newly erupted growth around us, and the trees, waved from the gentle breeze and rain, sharing glimpses of the sky and muted sunlight of a cloudy day.

"Sorry about the ah..." Finn waved at me.

"Huh?" I glanced down, finding my chest and thighs covered with tiny marks. Bites? Hickies?

"Never done that before, but I couldn't get enough of your skin."

"Okay, Hannibal Lecter."

He laughed, which brought a smile to my lips as the sound was warm and comforting.

"How do you feel?"

"Fantastic," Finn said, stuffing more berries into his mouth. He chewed and swallowed. "Like I could run a marathon." His expression soured and he frowned, mirroring me, I realized. "Why, is that bad?"

"Proof you're not human. That heat would have killed an ordinary human."

"Fucked to death? Sounds like a great way to go."

"Hmm," I grumbled. "I told you to run away."

"Do you have some former lover you accidentally killed?"

"Anyone I've ever killed has been on purpose."

"Scary. Why does it make you hotter?"

"'Cause you're a masochist?"

"Maybe. Learn something new every day, I guess." Finn held out berries. "Want some? I think there are some carrots over there, too." He pointed a half dozen yards away. "But the trees are really sus'. I feel like their eyes are following me."

Sebastian's statue stood a sentinel of serene quiet a meter away. I hoped we hadn't fucked like bunnies at the base of it giving the Summer king dirty dreams or triggering his heat, though his mate never seemed to mind.

Rows of wispy wildflowers gathered rain drops, leading to a thin line of lavender plants. I stood up to peer over the new growth, startled to find Finn's perception fitting as creepy faces stared out of carved wood in our direction. Plants grew around them in an array of autumn colors, brush in gold and red, a handful of swatches of fall berries, the greenery of carrot stalks, and wriggling curl of pumpkin vines leading to giant orange gourds.

"This isn't right," I said, letting the rain rinse away the sweat and dried come. The cool drip chilled my skin with a gentle caress.

"What isn't?"

"The Autumn king is my mate."

Finn tensed. "Okay."

"Why are you tensing."

"Cause it's technically cheating, what we did. You belong to someone else."

"I *belong* to no one. I'm not property."

"I mean respect wise. Guy-code. Bro-code. We don't screw each other's lovers."

"Since when? Every man I've ever met would as happily screw their best friend's lover if they could. And you and the Autumn king aren't exactly cozy. Unless something happened after I blacked out?"

"Nope. Well, lots of snuggling between you and me, but that's all."

I squinted at him. He copied me.

"Snuggling?"

"I wasn't going to keep screwing your unconscious body,"

Finn defended. "Hugs are okay, right? Not creepy or rapey..." He coughed to clear his throat and looked away. "Anyway, explain the rest. Why do you think something is wrong?"

"My magic produces growth," I said and waved my hands at the chaos of plant-life around us.

"Yeah, you warned me your come would make flowers. How cool is that?"

"Cool isn't what I would call it. But all of this is autumn growth."

"Isn't that because we are in the Autumn king's realm?"

"No. I was born in the spring."

He opened his mouth, closed it, pointed, and then frowned before he said, "Explain it to me in crayon-eating terms."

I laughed, unable to ignore his earnest and curious expression. "You're too young for me. Too pure for a jaded old Stag like me."

Finn snorted. "Not what you were saying when I had my cock buried in you. And I still plan to eat your ass." He grimaced. "Maybe once we can bathe? I've never come that much in my life. As sexy as the pornos make it look, sucking my spend out of your ass sounds gross. Not that I didn't enjoy putting it there." He glanced down at his lap. "New meaning to limp dick. Over-worked." He sighed dreamily. "I'd do it again in a heartbeat."

My cock made a halfhearted attempt to rise at the image he planted in my head, but it too, was exhausted. "All the plants around us should be spring plants, not autumn. Not unless I had sealed my bond with the Autumn king. All of the kings," or queens if any of them other than Winter were left, "can use my power. But without them it should be spring." Had Autumn snuck in after I blacked out? "Was anyone else here when you woke up?"

"I never slept, and no. Just you, me, and all the creepy statues."

"You never passed out?" Meanwhile he sat there practically glowing with energy. "What about the spot on your back?"

Finn turned and the dark splotch had vanished. "I don't feel it."

"It's gone."

He threw me a radiant smile. "You healed me. Even if it took an insane amount of sex to get the job done. Should we need to do that again, I volunteer."

Boxes checked inside my head in a growing list of *not right* pieces coming together. Finn, not quite human, with strange memories of a shadow wolf as a child, healed by my touch, nearly strong enough to resist the pull of a true heat, and now glowing with magic.

"Why do you look like I kicked your dog?" Finn asked.

"You're bound to Autumn somehow, and through you, he's bound me."

Twenty-Nine

WESLEY

Finn stared at me, head tilted, expression troubled. "How? Is that a fae thing?"

"As much as I'd like to say I know everything about the fae, they are as different as humans. Crazy powerful, and often sociopaths, but varied and secretive bastards."

"Well..." He trailed off at a loss for what to say. He picked up his discarded sweatpants, but they were beyond dirty. "I guess one positive from all of this is I seem to be able to eat the food here?"

"Not dying of starvation is good," I agreed. "We should find some water." I peered out over the wild overgrowth of the forest around the statues and didn't see any pools of water, though the drizzle of rain continued, light and refreshing. I held my hand out to let the rain drip. "Maybe we can find a way to collect the rain?"

"Sure," Finn said. He reached for a big leaf growing from the swell of Sebastian's statue. But he miscalculated and stumbled, planting his palm against the tree to stabilize himself. His gasp was the first indication of something gone wrong.

As Finn's palm connected with the rough bark, a jolt of magic writhed in a visual surged through him. I watched his eyes turn white which meant he was having a vision of some kind. Had this realm somehow taken the ability from me and given it to Finn?

"Fucking chaotic shit realm," I cursed as I grabbed Finn around the waist intending to rip him away from the tree, but the vision wrapped around me, too. Dragging me into a memory that began as a swirling mist dissolved, and I found myself standing in a forest, the air thick with the scent of pine and earth. The trickle of running water, and birds singing, filled the area with a peaceful ambiance.

In the distance, a child darted through the brush. The child was small, with a face framed by red hair and dark, fearful eyes. As I watched, the boy shifted seamlessly into a fox, his fur a blaze of blood red against the green growth. Sebastian.

A growl rumbled through the forest, low and menacing. My heart flipped over in fear as a massive black wolf, its fur dark and glistening with shards of ice, raced to follow the fox. The wolf lunged, jaws snapping as if to devour the baby fox whole, but another wolf leapt into the fray, and collided with the shadow wolf. A shockwave of magic rippled through the forest, the ground shaking beneath their struggle. The new wolf took a tearing bite to its side, and a wide gash down its flank, distracting the dark beast from the fox.

The second wolf howled in pain. The tiny fox cowered in a bush, frozen in fear, yipping with terror. The second wolf, smaller and lighter in color, fought hard, bleeding and snarling, taking the brunt of the attack even if it meant its death.

The shadow wolf snapped at him, its eyes glowing with a malevolent light, dripping ice. I recognized the curse of Winter. The dark wolf was turning into a monster of the Wild Hunt, its hunger for magic would supersede all reason until any mortal presence it had died and left only the shell to become a puppet of death and destruction.

But the lighter wolf fought relentlessly with a ferocity that I could only describe as insane. The dark wolf tore into the lighter wolf's shoulder, ripping a gash of spraying blood, hitting something vital. The lighter one yelped and writhed, a signal of death throes more than the will to fight, but ice slid from the dark wolf to the other, coating the wound in a crystalizing film.

Fuck! Winter's curse spread to the second wolf, and I knew instantly what I was seeing. The vision of Sebastian's youth, when the Volkov had fought his son to keep Felix from killing Sebastian and devouring his magic.

I reacted without thinking, leaping as if I had physical form to break them apart. I hooked my arms around the lighter wolf and yanked, mind screaming *No!* as if that would stop the blight from spreading.

The vision shattered like glass the ripple of it cutting into my sensitive mind as the forest with the fight vanished and returned me to the chaos of the Autumn realm. A headache pulsed behind my eyes as I gasped for air, arms around Finn, who stared back with a haunted expression.

"What the hell just happened?" I demanded; my heart pounding as if I'd run a marathon.

Finn blinked, disoriented and panting. He reached up to touch his shoulder, gazing at it as though he expected to find an open wound spurting blood and ice, but it was untouched. "I saw a child change into a fox. He was running from a dark wolf." His gaze met mine in horror. "Did I have another one of those visions of yours?"

"Not mine," I said. "The vision started before I touched you."

Finn shook his head as if he could shake off the lingering fear. "I... I fought the wolf. As a wolf." He held out his hands, staring at them as though he could see the blood. "Are all your visions like that? Real?"

"Never," I said. "I'm never one of the participants in a vision, only an observer." I had never been able to touch any of them before, and yet my arms around the Volkov had turned into arms around Finn. "You were the Volkov."

"Who?"

"The Autumn king."

"Me?" His gaze rested on Sebastian's tree. "You said this one is the Summer king. Did I save him? As a child? Is that a memory from another life or something?"

"Sebastian is only a few years older than you."

"But he's the Summer king?"

"Newly anointed," I said releasing Finn and taking a step back. I glared at the dark blotch that reappeared on his back. "I don't suggest touching anymore of the statues."

"The cold spot is back," Finn said grimly.

"Yes." My gaze found one particular statue in the distance which I knew would be disaster to touch. Felix's nightmarish face nearly hidden in the overgrowth of wildflowers seeking their last gasp of warmth and rain.

Finn stared at Sebastian's tree, the drops of rain growing in size as they sluiced down his bare shoulders. "I really am tied to the Autumn king somehow?" He turned to meet my gaze; eyes wide. Finn looked really young in that moment and I didn't want to be the one to put more fear in his eyes by telling him what I suspected.

Torn, the shadow wolf had said. The human had been torn from the wolf. By memories or fate, I wasn't certain it mattered.

"Wesley?"

"Don't touch the trees," I said. How long would it take for all the memories to reawaken who he was? Tales of the Volkov's monster spread across the world, to the fae and beyond, leaving every supernatural being quaking with fear for centuries. The stories faded to a lull two decades ago, vanishing as the king of werewolves hid himself away in a compound raising a peculiar kitsune child.

Would the man Finn was, be lost beneath the weight of his past? I decided that we needed to get out of this creepy little garden.

"What aren't you telling me?" Finn asked.

"We should go," I said as the rain intensified, sky opening and dumping water on us as if a floodgate opened overhead. His lips moved, but the downpour made it impossible to hear him even though he was less than a step away. I reached for him, a distant rumble, a low, thunderous growl that seemed to rise from the depths of the ground itself.

The noise grew louder and more intense. A roar punctuated the deep, resonant boom of water slamming into solid surfaces. A wall of water slammed into the distant statues, swallowing them whole, splashing around them in a wave like an unleashed ocean. I gasped in horror, grabbed Finn's arm to drag him to run, but the water crashed into us with no other warning.

Thirty

WESLEY

The swell of water ripped through the sanctuary like a tidal wave, engulfing us in half a heartbeat. I gripped Finn's hand and sucked in a deep breath before the water and debris swirled around us, trying to tear us apart. The icy sea reminded me of the nightmares of the Winter court as it pounded against us, needles of cold inching itself beneath my skin as if shoving us deeper and deeper beneath the waves.

My lungs burned for air, and I gripped Finn's hand hard enough I feared breaking it. The water smashed into the stone figures and swirled around the dense vegetation. The glowing mushrooms swayed, while the brush and grass became dark blotches of seaweed ready to tangle.

Finn wrapped his arms around me and launched us upward in a diver's move, seeking the surface. I gasped as we found air, but sank again with a dozen waves smashing us back down like the worst game of Whac-A-Mole ever.

"Fuck," Finn cursed and I agreed, swallowing water between broken breaths, limbs freezing from the icy water. He turned us as if to use himself as a shield, gaze upward, his added curses lost in the noise.

I followed his line of sight to see the shadow wolf/dragon hovering.

"Double fuck," I shouted, the sound mostly lost beneath the roaring water.

The wolf lunged, dragging with it a tidal wave of water that soared into the sky. Jaws snapped as though to swallow us both whole as it dove toward the water in a graceful arch. The wave behind a menacing monster of strength.

We both sucked in a deep breath, and Finn yanked me beneath the surface as the wall of water smashed down with a stone mallet force. The current shoved us into a dizzying spin.

I scrabbled for a grip as the force of the water tore us apart. Finn vanished in a swirl of bubbles, his silhouette fading into the murky depths. The current caught me dead center and smashed into me. I slammed into a tree trunk with bone-jarring force, hitting mid-back. Pain exploded, vision darkening with pops of sparkles.

Disoriented, I struggled to stay conscious and hold my breath, the water pressing in from all sides. Where had Finn gone? The vegetation melded with shadows writhing like hands from a nightmare of the river Styx. I struggled to keep my eyes open, searching for the glowing mushrooms, Finn, or any way to escape.

Which way was up? Was there even an up?

My lungs burned for air as a dark shape skated through the water, sliding through the depths like a rocket. The shadow wolf, its dark fur rippling like liquid night, swam with terrifying speed, eyes glowing with malevolence, focused on me. The beast's jaws snapped open, ready to strike while I struggled to lift my head and stare death in the face.

A blur of movement caught my eye. Finn propelled himself from the darkness, arms outstretched. He blasted past the wolf aiming for me. The shadow wolf lunged, nipping at Finn, who slammed a fist into its snout and spun my way, colliding with me, but holding tight. Finn wrapped me in a protective grip. Body in front of mine as a shield while the wolf snarled at him.

I focused on his glowing form, clawing for consciousness as I lost the battle for air and sucked in water, ice filling me from the inside out. The weight of water filled my chest with an intense pain. Who knew fae could die by drowning? I never imagined it was the way I'd go. But I was part mortal after all.

My eyes wouldn't stay open, and the darkness slid in as Finn gripped me around the waist and dragged us downwards. A wriggle of magic tingled over my skin, and I glimpsed a dark swirl of a chaotic whirlpool, water and shadows churning that registered in half a fading heartbeat in my mind as a portal.

Was it freedom from this world? I had a half second to hope as the pain vanished with my consciousness. Darkness overwhelmed my senses as Finn yanked us through the portal.

I blacked out, rising for a few seconds to the feel of his lips on mine, familiar now, though strange as few ever cared to kiss me as he had. But it wasn't a kiss this time. He forced air into my lungs, which screamed in pain as they were overwhelmed with water.

"Breathe! Wesley! Don't die!" Finn begged. His hands on my chest hurting as he shoved the water out of me. I choked and sputtered, turning to upchuck water and bile, but losing my battle with consciousness again as the icy goo poured out of me.

Finn's warm body curled up behind me slowed my shivers as I came back to. I vomited more, a sick human sensation that I really hated. But Finn kept me from falling into the mess and held me tight despite the shivers. I thought he was growling, the muted sound coming from behind us, but as I glanced back I realized we had landed back in the clover field, but weren't alone.

"He's not going to touch you," Finn promised. "Just breathe, okay? You really scared me."

I coughed, the sound matching the pain, but nothing else came up.

"Release him," a deep voice growled.

"No," Finn said. "You tried to kill him."

"Should have snuffed you permanently," the wolf snarled. "Useless and weak."

"Whatever," Finn said, using himself as barrier between us. "You don't like either of us, let us go."

"Mine."

"Yeah, yeah," Finn said. "You'd make a shitty lover. Killing your mate and all that."

"Not me," the wolf growled. "You. Always you. Weak. Human mistakes."

Finn frowned, confusion crossing his face. He mouthed the word *me?*

But I understood, even as my heart raced, lungs ached, and sleep tugged at me. The wolf, dragon, shadow, or whatever remained of the Autumn king had torn itself apart.

I reached up to touch Finn's face, searching for the resemblance, finding only tiny traces of it. "You are the Autumn king's human soul," I said. Not some strange rescue or even a child the King had hidden away. "You are the Autumn king."

Thirty-One

WESLEY

"What? How is that possible?" Finn asked. The dark blotch of discolor had crept up his shoulder again, expanding from his back, and stretching around to crawl across the stretch of his chest. From gone to quickly growing, I recalled the wriggle of magic before the portal appeared.

"You opened a portal in the water. Holy shit."

"What? No, I didn't."

"Mate," the wolf growled.

"Yeah, yeah," I said. I rose shakily to my feet, clinging to Finn. He kept himself between me and the wolf. "What's your goal here, Mr. Wolf?" I asked. "You can't kill him because destroying your mortal soul would end you both. Am I the weak link here? 'Cause if so, send me back to the mortal realm. I didn't *choose* to be here. You brought me here. Why? You don't seem to like me much."

The wolf morphed into the human male form. Too perfect to be real, and now standing several steps from the wolf and Finn, more of the resemblance bled through. I cursed myself for not seeing it sooner, but Finn, the poor bastard, was in the thick of it. "Mate, mine, protect."

"Super, caveman. I get your wolfy brain doesn't work the same way, but you lived with a human half for a few centuries, right? You were old long before you met Sebastian. Shouldn't you have picked up more about humans?" I waved a hand at his physical form, meant to entice? Or did at one point in history Finn look like that?

He flinched when I said Sebastian. Was that a sore spot?

"Sebastian is looking for me," I tried. "And he's looking for his *Apa*."

"Pup is mine," the wolf snarled from human lips.

"Makes a lot of sense now," I said. "Sebastian being the way he is. Literally raised by wolves. No wonder he's half feral. Everyone wonders why Xander was such a piece of shit dad. But it's because there was no Xander, right? Just the wolf pretending to be human."

He stalked our way, shadows pooling around him, ice dripping like glass breaking with every step. Winter's touch clung to him, even though he still fought. Was it the curse that brought the madness, or simply the wolf dragged into the fallacy of human thinking?

Finn faced him, keeping me at his back and stared in the face of the snarling beast who paused only a hair's breath away. The cold slinked up Finn's back, chilling my fingers. I refused to let go. Did proximity to his other half make the curse grow?

The wolf reached for me, but Finn blocked his touch. "Don't touch him."

"Mine," the wolf said. The man's rage filled face focused on Finn. Mouth gaping wide and spittle flying as it spoke. "Weak."

"You can think whatever you want of me, but if you want to keep him safe, let him go," Finn demanded.

The wolf's human hand morphed into claw-tipped, blackened fingers, more like that of a bird and rose as if he would slit Finn's throat. The man's face shifted to a dark stretch of skin over bone, skeletal. A reflection of the curse, and I wondered how it had lasted this long with that nasty nightmare of Winter eating away at it.

Finn remained solid, jaw set in a firm line, shoulders tense and tight, shielding me first. "You can't kill me," he said, sounding certain. "Right?" Finn asked me.

"Spring's mate was split and each time his other half nearly died, so did the wolf," I offered, though in reality, I didn't know. The new fae court sought to break all the old rules. Sebastian had set the book on fire and thrown it off a cliff. Winter shouldn't have been able to curse any of the other sovereigns, and yet she'd infected them all. Spring and Summer had broken free, could Autumn?

I wrapped my arm around Finn's stomach from behind and rested my cheek on his shoulder. He relaxed as though my trust meant more than anything I could say.

"We done here?" Finn asked the wolf.

It growled and made to swipe, but vanished in a flurry of shadows, leaving us in the eerie silence of a dim morning of the clover field. I sucked in a deep breath, lungs still aching, chest tight from the water and the hit that shoved me into the tree.

Finn turned and I realized I was still shivering. "We need to get you warm."

"You're the Autumn king," I said.

"I guess. Whatever that means." He held me tight, forehead pressed to mine. "Your pupils are huge. Are you okay? Did you hit your head? Why is your skin like ice?"

"Almost died," I said. The wolf wanted me dead. Why? Because it couldn't kill Finn? And if Finn and I were bonded now, thanks to the undeniable heat that still made my ass ache, if the wolf killed me, it might very well end Finn. Mate bonds were tricky things. Did the wolf understand that?

"I need to get you warmed up," Finn said. "Your skin is like ice."

"Not ready for more foreplay, cowboy," I said, words suddenly slurred as the chill snaked up my spine. Was I infected with

Winter's curse too? "Ass still aches. But you can kiss me as much as you'd like."

His cheeks turned pink, but he tugged me into his arms, leading me, and taking my weight. "We're back in the regular part of the realm, right? Let me find that tree."

"Realms are a creation of the king's magic. You could make a tree," I said, but let him lead me until my feet wouldn't lift anymore. My energy sapped away as the adrenaline faded. That part of being human really sucked sometimes. "Why is the only stamina I have related to running from something as a Stag, or being fucked within an inch of my life as a fawn? Couldn't I have gotten marathon skills as a human, too?" I cursed fate.

"Not sure I caught all that," Finn said. "But I'll run a marathon with you when we get out of here."

"Would rather you fuck me again."

"That too," Finn said. He helped me sit near a tree, the long branches of a willow, the leaves gone yellow flowed around us. "Can you glamour a fire or something? Clothes? Warmth?"

"Glamour is an illusion."

"Fuck," Finn cursed. He pressed himself against me, chest to chest as if he could single-handedly ease my chill when his body heat waned too.

"You're king of this realm. Create a fire, or magic or something."

"Right..." Finn trailed off. "And how exactly do I do that?"

"Uh, wish to?" I knew Sebastian's magic had structure as most of the mortal realm required checks and balances. Kiran's magic, while wild and unstructured, needed Nicky and Toby to craft it into usable things. Within his own realm he could go a little crazy with the chaos of his unchecked magic, which spiraled him into an unending drain on his power. Before I'd been taken by Winter, Sebastian had yet to establish a set realm. Likely, as the alpha wolf was a wizard and his mate, it would be a crafted and very structured thing standing adjacent to the mortal realm.

Autumn so far chose a mix of structure and chaos. Touches reminiscent of Underhill with spreads of mortal forests, and simple structure laced within. Was that because the wolf built the realm? Or had they begun before the tear in their soul?

"Wishing isn't working," Finn said. "Wishing for blankets, or clothes or even the trees to let in some sun. If wishes were pennies…"

How much magic did the human half have? "I don't know," I said, answering him and myself. "Good news, though."

"Yeah?"

"You won't starve."

"There are no berries here."

"Ha, no. I mean I'm your mate. I feed you energy. Even without mortal food." Winter's curse had completely vanished after our heat, and Finn glowed. He'd been devouring the magic energy I generated. The entire point of my existence was to work as a battery for a sovereign. I thought to choose Sebastian. Winter took my power by force. And Fate mated me to Autumn. I was fucked coming or going, but at least I'd enjoyed my time with Finn. Was there any use in hoping some of his boyish charm would remain once he reunited with the wolf?

Hot tears warmed my shoulder. I turned to try to catch Finn's expression, but he wouldn't look at me.

"Why are you upset?"

"This is all my fault."

"How do you figure?"

"I am this Autumn king, right? The wolf brought you here."

"Yeah, the wolf. Not you."

"But I am the wolf."

"Yes and no." I captured his face between my hands and kissed the tip of his nose. The sorrow in his gaze unnerving.

"It wants you dead. Doesn't that mean, I…" he flinched.

"No."

He shook his head, breaking free from my grasp, but gathering me up to cradle me in his arms. "Is this okay?" he asked after a minute.

"Sure," I said, not certain what he was asking about.

"To hold you, I mean."

"Oh," I said. "Yes."

"And to cry. My moms always said it was okay to cry. Let it out. Don't bottle emotion as it would swell until it broke me." He took a deep breath. "And this is a lot."

"Your moms sound brilliant. I'd love to meet them someday."

"Yeah?" He let out a startled laugh. "Sometimes mom jokes are as bad as dad jokes."

"I wouldn't know."

"I'm sorry." Finn held me. For a thousand things and for nothing, I assumed rather than asking. But that was okay. The chill began to ease with his embrace, as did his tears. We both had dragons in our past, his more literal than mine. Maybe fate wasn't wrong about mating us. I couldn't help but enjoy the small kisses he peppered all over my face as he held me close and wondered if he really was meant to be mine.

Thirty-Two

WESLEY

I dozed in and out, the tightness in my chest making it hard to rest. Finn held me, his body warm. Absorbing my energy I realized, and was too sore and tired to care.

"Your tiny horns are back," Finn whispered, but nuzzled my cheek rather than teasing the hyper sensitive horns. "I'm draining you, aren't I?"

"It's okay," I said.

"I don't know how to stop. Will your fawn form return? Does that heat come with it every time?"

"Yes, and yes."

Finn cursed, and I flinched. "It's not that I don't want to do that... what I mean is it's not what we need right now. You're sick and hurt and we need to find a way out of here."

"Winter's curse is draining you, and you take from me to keep going. It's a vicious cycle."

"At least you're not slurring your words anymore. How do we break this curse thing?"

"True wuv," I said, then giggled. "Mawridge..."

"The Princess Bride?" Finn asked. "There weren't any fae in that. Can love fix this?"

I snorted. "No. I don't know. Maybe? Summer and Spring broke theirs, but I never really asked how. Whether it had to do with finding their mates or not," I shrugged.

"But if you're the wolf's mate, that means you're my mate, too," Finn said.

"Leave it to you to be rational."

"That's me... rational."

I stared at him, memorizing the lines of his face. "You could kiss me."

"I could, yes, but is that likely to get us out of here? Won't it trigger your heat?"

"Eventually. But you created a portal in the water when you were all charged up. Maybe we have to do it again."

Finn stared at me, his fingertips caressing my face. "You look exhausted, pale, and thin."

"Ouch."

"It's not an insult. It's an observation. I'd be a piece of shit if I take advantage of you when you're not feeling well." He traced a line down my throat to my chest, which I realized ached from the inside out. "You're bruised, and your breathing is shallow." He rested his palm on my forehead. "You're a little warm, too. Fever? Can fae get pneumonia?"

"Probably not. But I'm only half anyway. The wolf was right."

"About what?"

"Humans are weak. It's why the fae hated the rise of the new court. They are all meant to be half fae. Part human, or something like that. Spring was the first, born in the mortal realm, though never truly human. The previous sovereigns tried to kill him, and when they couldn't, they cursed him, froze him in ice and cast a thousand mortal curses to keep him from rising."

"The fae don't sound very nice."

"If you live forever watching others die every sixty or so years, you let all that go or find yourself maddened by the loss."

"Humanity? Or emotion?"

"Both? I don't know. The fae were never human."

Finn held me in silence for a few minutes, then asked, "The statues the wolf has in the sanctuary, were they all people Autumn lost?"

"I think they represent memories. Sebastian is alive. He left the cake at the cabin."

"I forgot about the cake. Do you think that would help him find you?"

"Maybe. Autumn's barrier is pretty strong, but Summer has always been a rival only to Winter."

"Hmm," Finn said. "Can you walk if you lean on me?"

"Can't I nap?" I asked sleepily staring up at him. He looked bigger again. Which meant I was back in the fawn form. The heat would rise soon.

"I can carry you for a while." He glanced around. "I was never a gym bro. But this smaller form isn't that heavy."

"You could fuck me and recharge."

"Tempting as you are... will you be good if I carry you?"

"Define good?"

"Not tempt me to throw you on the ground and fuck you till we both see stars."

"That sounds really nice."

"Not when you might have broken ribs and a fever."

I sighed.

"What?"

"Last chivalrous man on earth, and I get stuck with him as a mate."

"You want me to act more like the wolf? He's an asshole."

He was and wasn't. His demand instinct rather than emotion. Was that the difference? Animals could feel emotion. I never questioned that. Not only because I could become the Stag, but I'd seen my fair share of animals reacting to everything from harm to loss to affection. Did the wolf think he was immune to emotion if he buried it deep enough or cast it to his human half? Or maybe Winter froze that part of him.

He knelt down. "Climb on."

"The mark has gotten bigger."

"I'm trying not to drain you. Get on."

I draped myself over his back and wrapped my legs around his waist to ease some of my weight, and he rested a careful hand on my thigh when I'd rather have it on my bare ass. "You're thinking very hard," Finn said.

"I'm getting very hard, too," I grumbled as my cock pressed against his stomach.

He groaned. "I can tell. Behave. Rest. The sun is coming up and I think I know where we are."

"Okay," I agreed. The heat emanating off him soothing even while my groin ached. "Really sucks being witchborn," I grumbled into his shoulder. How could he still smell good after several days out in the woods without a bath? Was he using some sort of glamour? I licked his shoulder.

"Don't do that."

"You taste good."

"Okay." He hesitated. "Do I want to know what witchborn is?"

"It's what everyone calls those who are part fae."

"An insult, you mean?"

"Depends on the person speaking."

"Usually does," Finn said. He carried us away from the clover field and past the little creek. I longed for a bath as the sweet sound of running water trickled by, and hadn't realized how tired I was until Finn was shaking me awake.

"Huh? I'm awake." I coughed hard, lungs screaming for air. After a few rounds of coughing and wheezing, I sucked in air, though craved more.

"You're burning up." Finn leaned over me. "And still shivering. Fuck. We need to get you out of here."

"Never been sick before," I said.

"I was sick a lot as a kid." He lifted me to sit upright against a solid surface. "I can see the cake. But can't reach it."

"Cake?"

He pointed and I realized we'd found our way back to the cabin. The rubble a sprawl of charred wood. We sat near the edge of where the door had been, and a narrow tunnel glowed with light. The slice of cake sitting untouched on the plate inside.

I stared at it, half dreaming I could reach it, but must have fallen asleep again because Finn shook me awake. "Wesley, please."

Tears dripped down his face, and I reached up to trace my fingers through his warm tears. "Why are you crying?"

"You said it's okay that I cry."

"I mean, are you hurt?" My lungs ached. I stared at him with a sleepy gaze thinking he was handsome in a lot of ways, and very young in others. "Your face kind of grows on a person."

"Uh, thanks, I think. I like yours, too."

I wiped at his tears. "Did the wolf hurt you?" Had I missed another attack?

"Not me. You. I need you to get to the cake, Wesley. Can you do that for me?"

"Are you hungry?" I asked wondering why I wasn't.

"Starving."

"Oh."

"Can you get the cake for me, Wes? Please, love."

Love. That was nice. No one had ever called me that. I hauled myself over to lie on my stomach and stare at the slice of cake buried beneath some miniscule protective barrier less than two meters away. Finn leaned over me and kissed my shoulder blades one at a time and then down my back.

"That's right, love. You can do it."

"Keep that up and there will be ass instead of cake," I grumbled at him.

Finn laughed, his lips brushing my skin. "Get the cake and I'll spend days making you come in a thousand ways."

"And kisses. I like your kisses."

"I like your kisses, too. We can kiss and cuddle all you want."

I worm crawled toward the cake. "Better not be lying to me."

"Never," Finn said.

"This useless form should be for something other than sex."

"And fitting through narrow spaces," Finn said. "I don't think it's useless. You're adorable. Like a spicy kitten."

I glanced back to glare at him, but wound up looking over my bare ass, which he had full moon glory of, to see he was still crying, despite the teasing. "Finn?"

"Get the cake, please," he begged.

I turned back, crawled a few more inches and had to pause. A low hanging beam left too little space, I stretched for the plate. It sat just at the edge of my fingertips. "I can't reach it."

"Please try, baby. You can do it," Finn said. "I believe in you."

I wriggled and ended up on my back, pulling myself through an opening so narrow I got stuck for a half second, fearing my ass was too big to fit. But I slipped into a tiny dome between broken and burnt boards and scooped up the cake, triumphant.

"I got it!" I cried, sucking in air like breathing through a straw. I leaned down to peer through the opening, ready to shove the cake toward Finn, but a shadow overtook the light of day. Finn's sad face still sat beyond the tiny tunnel. Behind him loomed the dragon. "Finn?"

"I think I'm starting to figure all this out. It's in a protective dome of magic, right?"

"Huh?"

"The cake? The falling cabin didn't crush it or anything."

I held it up, a ripple of magic fluctuating around me to keep the cake safe, and since I was holding it, me too. "It's not burned or rotting or anything."

"Eat the cake, baby. Get the Summer king to keep you safe.

Okay?" A blotch of darkness crawled up his face. The blight taking him over as the beast loomed ready to retake control of its other half. Would anything be left of Finn? "Will you do that for me?"

"I thought you wanted the cake?" I asked, brain a mushy mess of weariness and fever.

"I want you safe more than I could ever want anything."

"Finn?" I called, reaching for him, but he kicked the edge of a beam near him and the tunnel collapsed on his end, leaving me sitting in a bubble of Sebastian's glowing energy, alone. "Finn!"

Thirty-Three

WESLEY

I held the plate in my hands, sobbing and wheezing, too weak to dig my way out or even think straight. The cake glistened with magic, the only source of light in the dark. I raised the fork to my lips and took a large bite. Lemon and strawberry popped in my mouth, flavor vivid like lavender lemonade and sweet bread. I gasped from one heartbeat to the next blinking darkness to the bright light of Sebastian's kitchen.

"Um…" A teen girl with curly hair gasped. "Dad! Sebastian! Someone help!"

I held the plate, but couldn't get the cake to go down. Instead, it forced its way up my throat like the magic wasn't meant for me. Maybe losing it would take me back to Finn. I threw up praying he was safe and I could climb back into his arms, bask in his teasing and sweet kisses. But maybe that was the fever talking.

"Wesley?" Sebastian leaned over me. His mate, Liam wrapped me in a blanket.

"He's burning up," Liam said.

"Can't exactly bring him to a hospital when he looks like this," Sebastian said. "He has tiny horns and hooves? Sort of?"

"Witchblood because I'm witchborn," I said. "This is what they call you, and what I am."

A burst of heat wrapped me in Summer magic. Sebastian's warmth filling the room like a hot summer day. I couldn't stop shivering.

"We've got your fae doctor on speed dial. Call her," Liam said.

"Send cake back to Finn," I begged.

"Finn? Who's Finn?" Sebastian asked as he dialed the phone.

A smaller version of Sebastian appeared, pretty and mid-teens, though I knew from the eerie eyes I was looking at the rebirth of Underhill given human form. Ari, the witchchild.

"Save Finn," I asked Ari, thinking they would understand.

"Autumn is strong," they said.

"Please. The wolf is broken. I don't know if it understands that killing Finn is suicide."

"The doctor is on her way, but it will take her an hour since she's close to the city," Sebastian said as he reappeared at my side and wrapped his arms around me. "Wesley?"

At least I was no longer hard, the heat of my fawn form vanishing without the magic madness of Autumn's realm. "Don't let him die."

"We won't," Sebastian said, his omega presence curling around me in a soothing wave. I found myself sinking into his embrace, eyes growing heavy. He pressed his ear to my chest. "His breathing is really shallow."

"I didn't think fae could get sick," Liam said.

I gazed at Ari, pleading as consciousness faded. They nodded. Agreement to help? Or simple acknowledgment. Did they understand? "Please," I whispered, strength vanishing beneath the intensity of Seb's power. "Save Finn."

Finn

Thirty-Four

FINN

The beast's drool dripped down my back with icy bite as I stared at the remains of the cabin praying Wesley escaped the realm. The shadows pressed in around me with a suffocating weight that made every breath feel like I was wading through thick, dark water. The shadow wolf, its eyes gleaming with malice and contempt, snarled at me for letting Wesley go.

The connection to Wesley grew faint, a dim, flickering light in the back of my mind. My heart clung to it like it was the last ray of sunshine I'd ever see. The curse slid up my body, cold and clammy, like the icy fingers of death. Pain branched out in waves of stinging through my nerves, followed by numbness. My lungs ached as the air chilled, and I closed my eyes.

"Thank you," I said. "For letting him go."

"Mine," the wolf growled.

"Yeah, I guess. Now what? You kill me and we both die. What's the plan here?" I expected this nightmare remnant of the Autumn king could snap me in half, but trusted Wesley's instinct and knowledge. The beast was broken, too far gone to be saved or could I fix this?

The wolf's gaze narrowed as it breathed icy breath over the

back of my neck and shoulder. The shadows slid up around me, climbing my throat until I could feel them inching over my face like a million tiny maggots of ice. The weight of the darkness a suffocating blend of terror and numbness.

"Weak," the wolf snarled.

"Because I'm human or because I still feel emotions?"

It huffed, and for a half second I feared it would rip out my throat, but the shadows swelled as if called, coating me in a rising layer of suffocating cold and darkness. I couldn't breathe, but focused on hope that Wesley was free and safe. The Summer king would protect him. The icy stretch of shadows crawled inside my nose and mouth, forcing me to gasp and draw in splintered waves of chilled nightmares inside my lungs. I gasped and gagged, darkness walloping me hard into unconsciousness.

It passed in one blink to the next without the chance to dream. I opened my eyes back to the sanctuary of statues, standing in the center of the sentinel of memories, the faces all contorted in pain, and staring at me. That was new and creepy. The water had vanished, leaving everything as though it had never been touched by the wave the wolf used to wash us from its sanctuary.

I took a step toward the Summer king, wondering if I could find shelter and warmth there, but banged into an invisible barrier face-first. I gasped and rubbed my nose, surprised to find myself dressed in the same clothes I'd vanished in. Was this a dream?

I stared at my hands, the dark blemish of the shadow curse staining them with a colorful spread of purples and blues. Wesley said it looked like a bruise. My fingers tingled with a numbing spread of needles. I reached out to rest my hand on the barrier, a slight ripple of color the only indication of where it started and stopped. Were all the statues protected? Why now? Did the wolf fear I'd harm them?

My stomach rumbled with hunger making me wonder how much of this was reality. But there were berries everywhere. Not the most balanced meal, but I stumbled my way to a nearby bush of blackberries, checking for invisible walls, and dropped to my knees to gorge myself on the fruit. A juice pop of flavor in my mouth, I devoured several handfuls before feeling full and tempted to lie down and nap.

I couldn't remember ever being hungry or full in a dream.

"Can you give me a clue?" I shouted realizing all the statues stared at me, a strange imperceptible movement as I was easily ten meters from where I'd started. The only one who didn't focus its creepy gaze on me, was the Summer king.

"Take care of Wesley, okay? He's prickly, but that's armor. He's a marshmallow inside in need of hugs and warm snuggles." Like an old cat rescued from a long and terrible life on the street.

I climbed to my feet, holding my hands in front of me to test for barriers, banging into another three. The space to walk between, a narrow spread of berry bushes, some with thorns, but all blooming with endless fruit, and not a bug or bird to be seen. I followed the path studying the faces, their eyes moving with me, gaze focused, though half lidded in most cases.

Beyond creepy. The handful of ghosts or *other*, as now I thought maybe it was fae or magic of some kind that I'd caught on video, had nothing on the unnerving trail of statues. At one end stood the scariest, the carving a contorted not quite human face frozen in a snarl of pain and rage. Bat-like wings and elongated talons grafted into the tree as though the wood were its final resting place by sheer force.

Maybe they weren't statues at all, but rather those the Autumn king captured? "I am not going to end up as a tree, you bastard," I shouted at nothing. The warped statue's barrier kept me a good dozen meters away. The base of the tree surrounded by a dark pulsing pool of crystalized black shadows. Keeping the curse out? Or in?

I turned and headed the other way, following a defined trail of jagged stones, pausing at each junction, which led down a short path to two or three closely clumped statues, before moving on.

The further from the bat-like one I ventured, the smaller the barriers became. Some only a few steps from the tree, though I kept moving until I reached the end, or perhaps the beginning of the path.

Two statues, one male and one female took up a lighted end of the path. The male towered, display more of that of a bear about to attack than a person. The woman serene, almost like that of the Summer king, her eyes closed, and she swaddled a child.

My gut flipped over as anxiety slid down my spine. The numbness not so far spread that it could alleviate the fear of what they might be. Were they my parents? And why did my mind immediately connect with her as if I could remember her from a dream?

I stood a heartbeat away from her statue, realizing she had no barrier.

"Hello," I said. "I'm Finn." She wouldn't know me anymore than I knew her, would she? Whatever I was now, some sort of split creation from the wolf. I studied her face, memorizing the soft expression. "Were you my mom? I mean I had moms who took really good care of me. But no one could ever figure out where I came from."

She said nothing.

I reached up, hesitating before touching her as I recalled the brief moment I'd been sucked into the dark memory of a statue before Wesley had yanked me out. The Summer king's youth, and the curse of Winter. Would her memory remain carved into the tree? How terrible would it be?

Statistically humans remembered the negative more than the positive. A survival mechanism to keep a fragile species from offing itself by accidentally repeating the same stupid thing that hurt over and over again. Fear another mechanism of survival, meant to make us hesitate. At least the three semesters at Uni had been good for something. Psychology had bored the hell out of me, but my therapist said it was because I was highly self-aware when most of the population lived in a fog.

How self-aware could I be if I had no idea I was the torn soul of some supernatural being? "Don't give me nightmares, okay?" I asked the statue as I rested my palm on her face, the tree warmed beneath my touch as though she were real.

I sucked in a deep breath as a swirl of color distorted my vision, and I knew I was being sucked into her memory. All I could do was pray it gave me some sense of a way out of the realm, and maybe back to Wesley.

Thirty-Five

FINN

She packed up a small wagon made of wood, tucking items around me wrapped in scraps of cloth. Her smile, sweet and patient, as she patted me on the head and handed me a piece of bread to nibble.

A flutter of rainbow-winged butterflies hovered around her as she packed up small leather pouches and bottles. The markets, as autumn closed in, always a rush of trading to prepare for the oncoming winter.

She placed a carefully packed basket in my lap. "Hold this for apa," she said, giving me a little kiss on my forehead. Since I only got to glimpse him a few times a year, excitement grew in my tummy and I couldn't help but smile and grip the basket tight. The thought of toys and sweet baked treats left on the wayside as I wondered if I'd get to finally meet him, or only observe from a distance.

"Mama," I said.

"Yes, baby?" She asked as she hummed and tucked a basket of dried flowers behind me.

"Will apa play with me?"

"Not yet, baby. You're very little. But you can set the treats for him." She finished packing the wagon. A large doe lingered near

the trees, eating clover. "Ready, Lena?" Mama asked in a gentle voice.

The doe perked up and trotted over to allow for a harness to pull the wagon. She paused to nuzzle my hair, making me giggle with her snuffles. She let mama harness her to the wagon, and off we went. I spent the first half of the ride chatting with passing squirrels and birds about the best spots for nuts and berries. Then dozed through the late afternoon knowing we wouldn't reach apa's space or town until closer to nightfall. And it was the chill of dusk that woke me from a cozy nap.

An uneasy sensation of being watched made me sit up and stare into the settling darkness. The trees loomed with a stretch of gnarled branches, like skeletal hands reaching out to snatch us. Shadows danced between the trunks, flickering and fluctuating in the dim light, making it hard to tell what was real and what was merely a trick of the eyes. Fallen leaves crinkled and crunched like a thousand footsteps surrounding us with unseen observers.

Sometimes I dreamt of the cave, and woke with nightmares, others the dark had lifted and I could crawl in beside my apa and he'd wrap me up in his snuggles.

The wagon stopped at the edge of a veil of mist, surrounded by trees and endless dark edges, the center of which stood a cave mouth, dark and ominous. The trees around the cave with twisted bark contorted as though faces of people were locked within their trunks, but too shadowed to define.

A stump sat off to the side, a good distance from the entrance of the cave, with a thick layer of animal hide over it. I crawled out of the wagon and gripped the basket in a trembling grasp.

"Leave it on the stump and we'll go," Mama instructed softly. "Let him rest."

Apa needed a lot of rest. Or at least that's how I understood mama's instructions every time we visited him. I nodded, clutching the basket and tiptoeing toward the stump. With each step, the feeling of being watched grew. The shadows followed me, closing in.

I struggled to breathe as I placed the basket on the stump, heart pounding in my chest.

I hesitated for a half a heartbeat as a pair of glowing eyes watched from the cave entrance surrounded by nothing but darkness. Was it apa? I let go of the basket and turned to run, my heart racing, and fear slammed into me like a wave of ice, trying to freeze me in place.

A terrifying growl thundered from the cave. The glowing eyes emerged as something fearsome, bearlike, eyes shining with a fire and half human limbs coated in fur and unnatural claws. His jaw opened wide with a ferocious snarl, and he landed flat on four paws, shaking the ground beneath us.

He lunged towards me; jaws wide open to deliver a deadly bite. But mama hurled herself between us, her form morphing into a majestic dragon. Her wings unfurled like vast, golden, orange, and pink burnished sails that shimmered with the light of the setting sun. Her scales glowed with an iridescent beauty, casting a warm, golden radiance around her. Spikes adorned her spine like a regal crest, and atop her head, horns gleamed like beams of sunlight, projecting an aura of divine protection.

I blinked in awe, marveling at her beauty and reaching for her in a half second of fear thinking that apa would hurt her. He hesitated, eyes narrowing at the sight of the enormous glittering figure before him. Her light near blinding as it reflected down on him, easing the spread of shadows and revealing a tired man hidden beneath, not fur, but a thousand wriggling bits of darkness. He sucked in air, as though it were the first time he'd caught his breath in a long while, blinking at her, gaze soft.

"Sleep, love," whispered through the wind. "He's not strong enough yet to bear your mantle."

Apa gazed at her, transfixed and focused, his human form a beautiful mix of man, tall and broad, though undefined beyond the bright ray of light projected on him. He backed away slowly, mama keeping the glow cast over him until he reached the entrance of the cave and disappeared inside.

Mama reappeared in her human form and stalked to my side.

"I'm sorry," I whispered. "I didn't mean to wake him."

She kissed my cheek and wiped away my tears. "You didn't, baby. Winter is close, and it makes him moody." She patted Lena's back and we moved away, mama keeping at my side, her gaze focused ahead while I couldn't help but glance back. The forest closed in around the cave, swallowing any remnants of its existence as we made our way to town.

"Why is he dark momma?"

"We all have a darkness in us. We have to find our light."

Birds and crickets sang, stars pricked the sky overhead, and mama hummed a gentle tune as night fell, the eeriness of the woods dripping away.

I blinked and realized I was still standing with my hand to her face, staring at the statue as tears dripped down my face.

"Was that supposed to be a good memory?" I asked. Her love had been unmistakable, both for me and for *apa* despite how confusing it all was. I dropped down at her feet, needing a moment to breathe and analyzing the millions of questions dancing through my head. How would Wesley have interpreted all that? Curling up to cradle my knees to my chest and rest my head on their tops, I let myself feel, no matter how complicated the emotions. Years of therapy had to be good for something. Understanding that love and pain were not two sides of one coin, but intrinsically woven inside every person, helped me see why the memory both hurt and made my heart dance at the same time.

My birth mom. Not that my adoptive moms hadn't been amazing. I'd spent my entire life wondering why she hadn't wanted me. Who left their kid in a forest? Rejection eating at me no matter how hard I tried to overcome it.

"You didn't leave me on purpose, did you?" I asked her as I

glanced up, finding her serene gaze comforting. The garden of statues glared my way as if daring to touch her added to their rage. "Memories," I said to myself as I stared out at the long path filled with answers to my questions, but I hesitated to stand and touch *apa*.

Good and bad, love and pain, hope and fear, all intertwined. I just had to survive it with my sanity intact.

Thirty-Six

FINN

I paced for a while, gearing up to touch my father, and freaking myself out at the same time. The vision of him, a strange mess of darkness, not unlike the curse the wolf and I bore. Was that part of being the Autumn king? Did it mean there was no way to break free of Winter's curse? Or perhaps it wasn't related to Winter at all.

The whole fae thing made me miss my college friend, Cassidy, who had a strange obsession for serial killer documentaries and missing persons cases. She could pick details out of things and tie it together in dizzying ways.

I stared up at the man/beast thing, heart pounding, but beyond the garden of statues, and the walkway of berries, no one came or went, not even the wolf. Why had it cast me into this place? To torture me with memories? Why keep these memories? Were they the key to our broken state?

"I could use your sarcasm," I said out loud as though Wesley could somehow hear me. "Or insight." I took a long breath. "I hope you're okay. The Summer king better take good care of you."

The Summer king's statue remained unchanged in the distance, quiet and serene, though I knew the memory of it had been a dark terror of drowning in shadows. I took a step toward my father's statue and clenched my fists.

"You can do this. Whatever you see, it's already over," I reminded myself. "Like a bad movie or a scene in a book that rips out your heart but you know will have a good ending." I hesitated, and realized that I didn't know that. "I will have a good ending," I said. "My life and my actions are my choice. I carve my own path." Wesley cursed the fates as though they were real people. Did that mean I didn't really have a choice? They made us mates, if that were the case.

"Okay," I acknowledged. "Some things are set, right? I can work with that." I reached up to set my palm on my father's arm. "Let's do this."

The world shifted to a small market, and I must have been older as I sold my mother's tinctures and pouches of herbs at a table while she wandered through the other booths. No one haggled with me, as they were all grateful to receive the goddess's blessing for everything from fertility to health through the coming winter.

Our route had changed over the years, my mind suddenly recalling a dozen towns and a several week trek changing into only a handful, making winters harsher with the lessened availability of supplies. Why?

I couldn't yet grasp that memory as a young woman approached the table with her hands clutched to her chest. "Do you have something to help me hold a child? Auntie says the goddess is best to ask. The priest says only prayer can help, but that hasn't worked."

A new wave of a strange religion had popped up across the area. Mother and I had no interest in it, and avoided it when possible, their control over the small towns and their people, frightening.

"Yes," I said, and gathered a basket of supplies. "It's a simple tea," I gave her the instructions and filled a small cloth bag.

The woman continued to glance behind her, watching the

*market with worry as she handed over a few coins. "Thank you,"
she said as she darted away like she was afraid to be seen at our
stand. The traffic had been unusually quiet, though the market
area thrived with folks haggling for eggs and other delights like the
sweet jams my mother often traded her teas and soaps to keep me in
the delicacy all winter.*

Mother approached; her expression guarded.

"Everything okay?" I asked.

*"I'm going to pack a basket for you to bring to your apa," she
answered instead of acknowledging my question.*

"Alright. But don't you need help with the market?"

*She gave me a careful smile and leaned in to kiss me on the
cheek. "I'll meet you at home."*

*"I could trade labor for a few more supplies," I offered. "I'm
strong."*

*"You are, baby. But no, bring this to apa and head home. Lena
will meet you halfway."*

"That means you'll have to pull the cart yourself."

"Do you think your mama isn't strong?"

I snorted, knowing better than most how strong she was.

*A group of men wandered through the crowd, their gazes exam-
ining each booth. I couldn't recall ever seeing men as heavily armed
in the market before. Mother stiffened. They paused at the edge of
our display.*

"What is this?" The first male demanded.

*"Soaps, teas, and scents," Mother said, her gaze focused on me.
Many of the soaps and teas had specific uses like fertility, pain
relief, or even to calm the mind.*

"Why is your boy not serving the church?"

*"We are from far away," Mother said. "Trading for supplies
for the winter."*

"Where is your husband?" The man said.

"He's working. My boy is about to take supplies to him."

It was the oddest conversation I could ever recall her having with anyone. They dug through the basket for apa, which was dried meats, mushrooms, and a handful of root vegetables, a variable feast for most. Mother added two jars of preserves to the basket, ignoring the men as they examined everything. She never gave apa preserves.

"You should go before it gets too late," Mother said to me. "You know how chilly the nights are getting."

My heart raced as I gathered up my pack, not wanting to leave with a sense of dread building in my gut. But mother took my place in our booth and shooed me away, her gaze at the men pleasantly bland. I headed away from the market feeling their eyes on me and wondering if I should hide the route to apa's. It would take me longer, meaning I'd arrive well after dark, but I didn't want them to follow.

Tension finally left my shoulders once night fell and I was several hours walk from the small town and their strange market. I'd convince mother to avoid that one next time. The religious obsession spreading across the land in an odd shift of control. Some markets completely closed or run by religious officials who demanded control of supplies. I recalled an argument mother had with a particular pair of them who demanded her entire stock as a donation. Months' worth of gathering supplies and creating items for trade, which would have left us starving during the winter. We had left that town and never returned. What would happen if they all followed suit? Would we have anywhere left to go?

Apa's cave, nested in shadows, sat untouched and quiet as usual. I stalked to the stump, set down the basket, and waited, no longer afraid of the surly beast.

A set of eerie eyes glowed from the opening of the cave, hesitant.

"Come on then," I said, setting out the display of treats I'd brought, but pausing over the jams. Had mother meant them for apa? I couldn't recall him ever eating them. I tossed a large hunk of dried meat his way.

After a few long moments of wariness, he crawled from the cave on all fours, more beast than man, and devoured the meat. I threw a few more and after a time he sat at my feet like an affectionate dog rather than a bear infected with darkness, his breath labored. Mother said the blight would eventually take him from this world and it was a kindness to give him aid until the earth took him back.

Any glimpse of the man he'd been had vanished several years prior as if the soul beneath had been suffocated by the writhing darkness. I petted his head, fur matted and coarse, but the shadows couldn't cling to me.

"Mother doesn't know of a way to remove the blight. She's not sure how it started," I said as I opened a jar of preserves and offered him a taste. He snuffled it, then licked my hand, something I'd have not braved when I was younger. "She misses you." Mother spoke of apa often, reciting memories of their youth, and the wild love that brought them together. The blight had appeared after one particularly harsh winter when mother arrived at his cave to present me, his newborn son. The madness took several years to really dig into him, and even less time to eat away at what remained of the man beneath the bear's fur.

Lost in the dark, perhaps? I didn't understand and he couldn't tell me.

"I would have liked to know you," I said and got up. "I should go." The stretch of moonlight overhead would guide my path. "Mother is waiting."

Thirty-Seven

FINN

That the dream didn't end meant something, though the memory shifted ahead to me standing in a familiar clover field, surrounded by moonlight and trees stretching up into the sky. Lena's favorite grazing spot. Yet there was no sign of her.

Maybe I'd arrived before her?

I sat down beside a tree, exhausted from the trek, and thought to wait for a time. A nuzzle of something to my cheek woke me before I realized I'd fallen asleep, and I opened my eyes expecting Lena, but finding her new fawn. The baby barely had his legs, stumbling about in that ungainly way of the newborns. Mother had hoped he and I would bond, but he was far too little to understand me as Lena could.

"Where's your mama," I asked the baby, petting his brow and ears, while I scanned the area. He snuffled me again. "Yes, you're hungry, I know. Let's find your mama."

With the sun rising, sky colored far overhead in a wash of pinks and oranges, I searched for any sign of Lena. The forest sat in strange stillness. The absence of birds at first light made me wonder if a bear or some large predator had wandered into our area.

I paused to listen, straining to hear any movement as I clutched the fawn close to me. Beyond his snuffles, the silence stretched. Where was Lena?

"Let's head home, little one. My mama will know how to find yours," I told him. He trailed along as I headed toward home, wary, and quiet as possible. A sense of doom grew in my gut with each step. The forest was never this quiet.

We approached the furthest perimeter, and I noticed the chimes cut from the trees. In the wind, their sound a gentle and soothing tinkle, but a lot of movement in the forest would stir them up as a warning. I bent to retrieve the first fallen strands. The woven vines used to hang the dried bones, pine cones, hallowed bark, and varied light rocks, had been cut. None of the deer were tall enough to reach them, and the smaller inhabitants of the trees, while occasionally stealing a piece of wood or small stone for a nest, usually left them alone.

I gazed along the tree line searching for the rest of the markers, and finding them all gone from the trees. Why?

The local townsfolk rarely hunted this deep. Mother said it was part legend of my sire's madness, and part the sensation of the woods. But this forest thrived with energy and life, sometimes to our frustration, as we'd plant a small garden, and the heart of the woods would send every woodland creature to eat it all. Usually, the mood of the forest was playful, but now I suspected the doom came from deep within the roots of the ground. The thrumming in my chest intensified with each step home.

I grabbed up the fawn, and wrapped him up in a blanket to tie around my chest, then ran. The closer I got, the more my mind screamed, while a lock remained on my jaw, keeping me silent. The forest covered any sound of my tracks, or I'd grown deaf in those few seconds of fear, as I moved like a ghost, appearing at the edge of our tiny cabin to an array of heavily armed men.

The men from the market.

I hesitated behind a tree, searching for any sign of mother. She could have made it back before me as I'd visited my father. But why were these men here?

They hauled things out of our cabin in satchels. Why were they taking our stuff? I approached with growing rage, our entire life of working to live in harmony with the forest and survive being stripped from our home. How dare they?

The fawn made a small noise, and I realized I was growling, but couldn't stop. My heart hammered in my chest; darkness wriggled at the edge of my vision. I unwrapped the baby and let it down, giving it a small push away from the chaos I could feel rising inside me. The baby didn't move, but I stalked toward the men, my hands clenched and long tendril claws dripping blood as they erupted from my fingertips. The bright beauty of my other form feeling an overwhelming sense of dread that cast a shadow over my light.

One of the men turned, his gaze flipping past me and then drawn back, eyes going wide. It was then I saw the carcass of Lena, cut wide and being carved open by another man on the opposite side of the house. My heart flipped over with rage and grief.

"Witchborn!" The first man shouted. The other looked up, but it didn't matter. I flew toward them, heart in my throat and bloodlust driving my rage. The first two died in a spray of blood. Others flooded out of the cabin, swords and arrows raised.

They all died.

The moment passed from one heartbeat to the next, and I stood among a wash of pink and red chunks of meat. Vile bits of the dead men washing me in their tainted blood. I gazed at Lena and then the open door to the cabin.

Changing from beast to man again took a few seconds of concentration. Tears ran down my face as I approached the open door. The inside of the cabin small. It had only been mama and me. I felt like the baby in the wagon again, fearing my apa's madness, as I stepped inside our home. The destruction barely registering my notice as all I could see was mama stretched out on the bed, unmoving.

I silently willed her to get up, breathe, smile and welcome me home, but her gaze cast open and blank at the ceiling. My heart pulsed in my ears, deafening me to everything as I stood over her logging a list of the things they'd done to her, from her nude body covered in blotches of blood and burns, to the discoloration around her throat.

Monsters. I tugged the blanket up over her, left the cabin, and carried Lena's remains inside, then closed the door to keep them safe from the elements as I stalked through the woods, searching for any other sign of life. I passed the fawn, tiny little thing still on shaky legs, and cursed the humans for the plague they were.

The trees withered with each step, land shriveling beneath my feet.

I ran into another group of armed men coming from the north. Had they somehow followed me? The group froze upon seeing me.

"Why's the boy covered in blood?" One asked.

"He's the babe of that witch," another said.

"She was a goddess," I said, rage rising again at their disrespect.

One of them threw a pouch at my feet, the tea bag supplies I'd given to the woman in the market. "Like this isn't witchcraft? The boy is witchborn, best to rid him of this blight before it infects us all." He raised his sword, but that's all I saw. From one moment to the next, again I stood in their shredded remains rage over the bag of tea soaking up blood at my feet.

I took to the sky, a transition as easy as breathing as long as it was fueled by rage and pain. The flight to the village, folks moving about for their day startled by the drip of blood as I hovered over them. It was only the beginning as I dove at the first armed man I saw and didn't stop until the entire town blazed behind me, covered in blood and gore.

The trip to apa's took most of the day, but my heart was too heavy to go home and give mother and Lena a proper burial yet. Turning them back to the soil would take a few days of work and the forest crumbled in waves, like my rage was killing the land. I couldn't swallow it down. Between grief and rage, I found every waking moment a drowning wave of emotions.

The shadows around the cave had seeped away, and trees lay in ruined piles, uprooted and lifeless. Had the soldiers been here too? The basket of supplies still on the table, second jar of preserves unopened. No movement from the cave.

Had he hidden away while those monsters killed mother? I stalked forward, never having entered the cave before, but held out a hand to create a light as I stepped into the dark expecting glowing eyes and a snarl to meet me.

A few dozen steps inside lay a man. At first I thought he was one of the armed men, but without blood or a sign of a struggle, he was unmoving, broad back to me. I approached and knelt beside him, no sign of life as his heart had stopped. His long hair covered his face, matted and unkempt, and when I brushed it away, I found my apa, the rare glimpse of his human self before he'd leave the cave and find himself lost in the shadows.

The dark twitching blight had vanished. I rolled him over and searched for signs of a fight. Finding him unmarred, as if he'd finally succumbed to the curse. The cave around me glittered with a thousand trinkets my mother and I had gifted him over the years. Proof he hadn't always been lost to his beast.

I rose to my feet and exited the cave, every part of me screaming, inside and out, while I swallowed the sound, fearing that I'd draw humans to us. But as I dropped to my knees and finally sank to the ground, wrapped around my knees and sobbing, I cursed the forest for not protecting mama, apa, or even Lena. Rage spawned something inside that latched on, and began to grow.

Thirty-Eight

WESLEY

"Wesley?"

I jolted out of the dream, gasping for air, surprised to find Sebastian beside me, the realm gone, and the Summer king's home surrounding me in waves of warm energy, scents of wolves and baked goods. His omega presence adding a heavy sense of calm that I knew wasn't mine.

"No!" I tried to sit up, weaker than I could ever recall having been and flailed, half falling out of bed. Seb caught me and set me back carefully.

"You've been sick for days. You need rest."

"Sick? I don't get sick. I'm fae."

"Okay," Seb didn't argue. "If I have food brought for you, will you eat?"

"I have to save Finn."

"Do you know how?"

"Isn't your mate supposed to be the rational one?" I snapped.

"I could ask a lot more questions, but I'd rather you rest."

"I'm not tired." I was. Exhausted, sweaty, starving, and heart-broken. The nightmare of Finn's childhood lingering like a thorn in my heart.

The door to the room opened and Ari entered with a tray of food. Any childlike display of the rebirth of Underhill gone, as they appeared older than Seb, and very masculine, but the magic pulse of their energy told me it was the witchchild before they entered the room.

"Did you find Finn?" I asked them.

"We can't get in," Seb said. "Ari's tried."

"Xiao catches glimpses," Ari said. "But Autumn is keeping him out." They set the tray on the table.

"Liam made the hummus," Seb said. "We have a ton of cans of beans to use. Ari said you're mostly vegan?"

I wouldn't admit to the bloodlust unless I had to. "Yes."

Seb adjusted the tray to sit over my lap. A giant bowl of freshly made hummus and homemade pita crisps making me salivate. I scooped up the first chip, loaded with dip, hand shaking, but popped it in my mouth and nearly died of joy in that half second. The room blanked out; my focus lost on eating as I hadn't realized how hungry I'd been.

I came back to myself while scraping the edges of the bowl with the last pita crisp. "Sorry," I said more out of habit than actual apology.

"What can you tell me about Finn?" Sebastian asked. He picked up the tray and handed it to Ari as the food filling my gut made me sleepy. Ari left with the empty dishes and I wished they'd magically refill it as I could eat endless bowls of that if I weren't struggling to keep my eyes open.

"You put something in the food?"

"Like?"

"Something to make me sleep."

"Did you sense magic?"

"You're being evasive. Didn't anyone tell you not to answer a question with a question?"

"I thought that was the fae way?" Seb said.

I grunted. He'd been guileless most of his youth. Cynicism

only growing after he'd become lovers with the wolf king's son. If I'd known early in their relationship, I'd have interfered. Not that the options I could have thrown his way were any better. Were the kings meant to bathe in trauma? What a shitty way to obtain a monarchy.

"I can't help if I don't know," Seb said after a few minutes of waiting on my silence.

"I can't tell you what I don't know."

"About Finn? Who he is? What he is? Why he's important?"

What did I know? More than I thought I had now. "He's the torn human soul of the Autumn king. Split from the wolf, Xander, your sire. I'm not certain when or how it happened, but the wolf took the human soul, gave it mortal form, and a new life."

"Wouldn't I have sensed *apa* was another king?"

I snorted. "And he's been broken. I'm pretty certain it happened when you were very young. You and Finn are close in age. You're a baby in fae terms. And only half. Witchblood, remember? More human than fae."

Seb stared at the distant window. "I don't think that word means what you think it means."

"Inconceivable," I muttered.

He laughed. "You do have a sense of humor. Good. I was worried *apa* would be stuck with a conceited prick."

"I'm that, too," I said.

"Hmm," Seb said, copying his mate's reply to a comment he didn't agree with, without agreeing at all. "Witchborn," Seb continued, "Kiran says it's really those who are mixed with fae."

"More fae than human, yes."

"Which means *apa* is some sort of fae, too?"

"Humans gave us that label. Not fae. We mean nothing to the fae."

"But *I* am the fae now," Seb said. His gaze sharp and firm. "I never asked to be this Summer king thing. Yet here I am."

And that was the crux of things, wasn't it? End of everything? Or beginning of something new?

"Tell me about your vision."

"You already know I can't see your future," I said in a half panic. Would he get angry? Lock me up? What about Finn? What if he died in the Autumn realm? A new king might be born, but that meant chaos for the rest. And I couldn't lose him, my heart would shatter.

"I don't mean that. The end of everything. You muttered it while you were feverish."

Had I had a vision beyond seeing Finn's dreams? Wait, was I still connected to Finn? I searched for any tie of magic linking us together that I could follow, and found nothing. My magic stores, still depleted, were slowly recharging. My hands were human, and when I reached up to check my head for any sign of nubs, their absence made me hope I wasn't at all fawn anymore. Though Seb would have seen that, wouldn't he?

Heat burned my cheeks in embarrassment. He would know how weak and useless I was. Fuck.

"Wesley," Seb prodded.

"Your birth heralded the end of everything. Didn't I tell you that a long time ago?"

He sighed. "That's what you told the fae."

"You just said you are fae."

He got up and paced the room, radiating annoyance rather than calm. "Why can't you be straight with me, Wesley? I'm trying to help."

Because *help* always warranted me punishment. I said nothing.

"Would you talk to Liam? Or Ari? You don't trust me because I'm fae, but is there anyone you do trust?"

"I just... need to find Finn." Before it's too late and he drowned in the horrors of his past.

The door opened again and Ari reappeared, this time with a slice of cake. I flinched, remembering the last bite that had taken me out of the realm. Would this one put me back. They handed me the plate, a huge slice of juicy carrot cake this time, spices wafting to my nose and I practically drooled. Had I ever had carrot cake made by the Summer king?

"Can you send me back?" I asked, slicing off a piece of cake and sliding it into my mouth. Heaven. How did an annoying kitsune like Sebastian become not only the Summer king, but design recipes that brought a Stag to his knees. "Fuck, you've been holding out on me," I said as I devoured the cake. It wasn't until I got to the last bite that I tasted the gentle fold of magic in the sweetness. "You drugged me."

"Hmm," Seb said again. "You need rest."

"I need to get back to Finn," I slurred, plate sliding from my grip. Ari took it and gave me a comforting smile. "And save him."

"I ask again, do you know how?"

"Keep him from drowning in pain," I said instinctively, sleep dragging me with an iron fist into the dark. "Please don't let him die. He's mine. Nothing has ever been mine before."

Thirty-Nine

FINN

The dream shifted in and out in waves. Vague memories of burying my family, then setting the forest ablaze. Darkness taking over for a time, the world only coming back into focus while I stood among the blowing wind and raging heat of the flames. The death of the trees and grass needed the ash to repopulate anyway. The screams of the dying plants bothered me more than the memories of the humans I'd slaughtered.

I retreated to apa's cave to wait out the fire and watch it devour the countryside, occasionally stirred by the sound of human voices which would drive the dark side of me to awaken and stray from the confines of stone and shadow to rain blood over the flames. Their bodies would add life to the regrowth of the forest. Darker in some places where the trees would gnarl and crouch with the weight of my rage.

Winter approached twice, and I cast her out with flames, the sky smoldering with ash and heat rather than snow.

The smoke drifted away with the voices. Silence creating an unusual stillness over the land. Humans decided the forest was cursed, and I was fine with that. Sometimes I'd sit at apa's stump, starving, exhausted, eyes burning with tears and ash, straining for sounds of life, a single bird or bee to remind me of joy, barely holding my human form, as much as I hated it. If I let the shift take over, I'd wake up to more destruction and no memory of what I'd done.

"Witchborn!" They screamed at me as they died. "Monster! Cursed!"

Heartbroken, grief-stricken, and alone, meant nothing to them.

I fell asleep there, and woke to snuffles, surprised to open my eyes and find Lena's fawn tickling my face with its kisses. My heart thumped in joy and fear all at once. I'd forgotten the babe, and somehow it survived.

His legs had grown steady, and he tugged at my hair, playful, though as I gazed at him, I wondered not only how he'd survived, but if it were best to chase him away.

"I'm not safe," I said, my voice rough from disuse in this form.

He made a tiny noise, and I got the vaguest image of me holding him before I'd gone mad with anger. His view of me as strong and safe coming through the delicate bond despite the monstrous form his baby gaze couldn't define.

"I'm not safe," I repeated, but reached out to pet him, heart slowing its race to finally let me breathe. Exhaustion warred with my need to stay resilient and keep the humans out of the woods. My stomach growled with hunger.

The fawn made another pleading noise and tiptoed to the forest's edge beyond the cave. The smoke faded, leaving a trail of mushrooms and moss peppering the trees. It nibbled at the moss, then looked at me.

A startled laugh burst from me, and I blinked, surprised at the sound, and the sensation of emotions rising beyond the grief. "I don't eat moss, little one."

Creatures like the fawn were food as I was some sort of beast. The thought brought back the sadness. Mother had been beautiful, a true goddess. Perhaps I'd inherited more of my father than my mother. Her death had ripped the last traces of light from me.

I turned away from the fawn and headed into the cave. I'd emptied it of memories, setting flame to the trinkets in a fit of rage after I'd removed apa's body to bury it in the soil with my mother and Lena, regrowth from the final death.

All that remained was a pile of straw for a bed, hard and musty, fit for a beast. I lay down, letting my resolve to stay alert go, and closed my eyes. The fawn hesitated at the entrance of the cave. I could sense him there, gaze peering through the dark at me, and willed him to run before I destroyed him too, as accidental as that might be.

But a few slow heartbeats later, he settled down beside me, little body curled up for added warmth.

"I'm not safe," I whispered again. The babe, too young to understand, as he snuffled my hair again and lay down for a nap as if it were normal for the beast to rest with the prey. But his quiet breathing and gentle heartbeat lulled me to the first real sleep since the death of my mother and transition to the life of a monster.

When I opened my eyes, it was back to the wolf's sanctuary, lying at my father's feet. I stared out at the long path of memories. Not a sanctuary at all, but hell. A place of nightmares, horrors of the past, inescapable.

I curled into a ball, not wanting to see the rest, body aching with spreading numbness. A chill curled down my spine as something shifted in the atmosphere, though I knew instantly what it was this time.

"Weak," the wolf growled from behind me.

I didn't get up.

"Useless."

I jolted to my feet and faced it. "Fuck you!"

"Weak," it snarled.

"They all died! We would really have to be a monster not to grieve!" I clenched my fists, but with the blackening of my hands to the blight I couldn't feel more than a tingle in them.

"If you hate me so much, and believe I'm so weak, why bring me back? Why drag me through this nightmare? I had a good life. My moms were good to me. I have friends. More than this madness." I waved at the path realizing what was missing from it.

Hope.

"You took Wesley from me. Hurt him. If anyone is weak, it's you! Afraid of light and love and goodness." I met its gaze unflinching, angry and filled with grief from returning memories of my previous existence. One chunk of many thousands still unfilled. "If all of this is to turn me into you, into a monster without a soul, I refuse."

Wesley cursed fate as unchangeable. Everything? No. I wouldn't become the heartless beast standing before me. "You let everyone die, I *saw* what kind of monster we could become. It's not the blight. It's part of what we are, still you let them die, and *I'm* the weak one?"

It snarled, jaws gaping wide as if to swallow me whole. I folded my arms across my chest. "You kill me and we both die. Right?"

It glared at me, eyes a swirl of black with hints of red. Rage. My beast, a gift from my sire, perhaps, touched with my mother, as the memories had been filled with a dozen shifts of form, a wolf, a bear, a dragon, and something much darker. This thing I stared at was part of me. A nightmare I'd unleashed a thousand times and this place was a graveyard of those memories.

Was I supposed to defeat the wolf or become it?

I dropped down to sit at the base of my father's statue, refusing to advance through the gauntlet of blood and pain. "You offer me no hope, what is the point of continuing?"

"Grow strong."

"Speech not your strong point, eh? Grow strong how? By remembering all the terrible things in our past? Where are the good things? It can't be all bad." I wrapped my arms around my knees and stared out at the path, the only hint of light glowing around the Summer king's statue, but his memory had been pain, too. "What's the point if all you offer is pain?"

The wolf crouched over me, looming and shifting into the dragon, shadows dripping dark ooze which sizzled and destroyed the growing plants. Each drop that touched my skin turned my nerves to needles of pain, but I wasn't backing down. "Give me a reason."

It huffed and a wave of wind swept through the sanctuary with an icy blast I feared would lead to some movie-quality arrival of the ice queen to end us. But the blast slammed into the end of the path and blew away a curtain of ivy, revealing a statue of Wesley. I gasped and got to my feet. An aura of shielding pulsed in visible waves of rippling magic around him locking him behind a barrier a dozen meters deep. Mushrooms and moss curling around the base of his statue. His expression serene as I'd never seen it while he was awake, but he stared down, not at me, and the foliage overhead gave way, illuminating him in sunlight.

"Is this some sort of game to you?" I asked the wolf. "A gauntlet of horrors to reach the princess in the castle?" Wesley would snap at me for calling him a princess, but I figured him for a high maintenance sort of guy. If I ever got out of this nightmare, I'd show him how good I could be at taking care of him.

"Mate," the wolf growled.

"Yeah, yeah. Why did you send him away then?"

"Safe."

"From what? Who? Us?" I glared at the beast and realized that was exactly it. The ground around us sizzled, dying beneath our feet. My mother's and father's statues expressions had changed to one of fear and horror, as the ooze began to coat the bases of their carving. "Fuck! Stop it! You're hurting them!"

The wolf vanished in a plume of smoke and ash, leaving me standing in the silent grove, watching the ground to see if it would regrow. I was some sort of fae king, right? Shouldn't I have power?

Nothing happened. The sizzling stopped, but the ground at

the base of the first two carvings remained dry and cracked, dead earth. Needles of numb pain ran up and down my body adding a Gumby-like sensation of unstable mobility to my movement. The fawn had lived. Had that been Wesley? He never mentioned us meeting before. Would he have known?

I took a hesitant step away from my parents, gaze focused on the vague wriggle of magic shielding. The next statue open was down a path to the left, a stag.

"Fuck," I cursed, dreading whatever nightmare it would bring. "Wait for me, Wesley," I told the statue at the end and wondered if he could hear me at all. "Pray that I don't come out of this some batshit crazy human version of the wolf." I could almost hear Wesley commenting that I was already there, and since I was imagining his voice and talking to myself, maybe I was.

I paced the room more like a caged cat than the Stag I was. Magic crackled around me, the full weight of it returning after a forced nap that had me growling at Seb, and brought his mate upstairs to tell me off. Upsetting the omega turned the whole pack against me as the tension in the house raged until Seb soothed them with cookies and sweet words. That his mate could easily refocus him from ready to turn me inside out to the Martha Stewart of werewolf omegas, made me worry about Finn.

Sally Homemaker I was not. He was so screwed with me as a mate.

Ari appeared with a plate of cookies and a huge glass of oat milk.

"I'm not hungry," I snapped, eyeing the plate for signs of magic. Robin slipped through the door behind them, disdain and irritation clearly displayed on his cat face. The Cheshire cat guise was only slightly less disturbing than his creepy kid form. Pucks were wild magic and chaos wrapped into one. "No," I told the cat.

"Robin's trying to help Xiao get in."

"Who's Xiao again?" I waved my hands banishing answers I

didn't need to clarify, "I mean I know he's that cat you sent, but he's fae?"

"Part fae, like most of us," Ari agreed.

Strong for part fae if he could breech the realm of a king who wanted no one in but himself. I met Ari's gaze, though they said nothing more about Xiao.

"He didn't seem to like Finn much."

"Xiao could sense Finn was part of the Autumn king. I asked Xiao to protect *you*. I didn't know you were mated to the Autumn king."

"Surprise for all of us then." I struggled to parse how they were related. Finn, with his steel resolve and sweet kisses, and the shadow beast dripping ooze, maddened with Winter's curse and madness.

Seb had dropped off a picture of Xander, but they looked nothing alike. Glamour? Or something else? Finn's memories of himself left no physical impression, and using Google to search for cursed forests and a time frame left me with too many options to narrow. "Sebastian gets the king of calm, and I get the monster broken and distorted." The comment bit deep, and felt like a half lie. Finn was Xander, Xander was Finn. But were they really? How much was the cursed wolf and how much the mortal soul along for the ride?

Ari shifted, their form morphing into one similar to Seb, not a mirror, but an obvious relation, smaller, long red hair, resting bitch face on tap. "Would it help to be angry with me like this?"

"That's almost as creepy as the puck."

"You made daddy cry." Ari folded their arms across their chest, expression cold.

"He's Summer king. With a strong link to Autumn. *He* should be able to break through the barrier and reach Finn."

"But Finn is the Autumn king."

"Right now, he's human," I continued to pace. "Is it normal

for the kings to have the power to tear their soul apart and give it new life?"

"Autumn has always been a transition. Life and death, hot and cold, light and dark," Ari said. "Never considered the strongest. Summer and Winter receive those titles due to the extreme shift, but we've already seen how incredibly powerful Spring is. Autumn would at least be his match."

And Spring had accidentally called a dozen hurricanes to fruition when Winter dared harm his mates, then ripped his lovers from the jaws of death, and resurrected them as if they were flowers to rebloom. If Summer and Winter had power to match that, I hadn't seen it yet, and it scared the shit out of me. Then there was Autumn, who was meant to be mine. A curse of fate, or something else?

"Witchchild, don't play with me. I saw Finn's dreams. The first nightmares of his parents' deaths. He became something, I don't know what it was. A bane over the land, some sort of night-mare to keep the humans out. Is that Winter's curse?"

"No. Autumn is like daddy... part elemental chaos. Winter's curse feeds on energy, that's why she took you. With the rise of each new king, her power lessens and she drains anyone she can to hold on to it."

She'd kept me chained to the floor and drained me dry over and over like a refillable juice bag. The biting memory of cold made my nerves ache, though it had all healed thanks to my heat and Finn's intervention. Now I couldn't get the idea of Finn sliding into me out of my head. Had a heat ever been that good? No one previous focused on giving me pleasure during a heat. A thousand times more satisfying than my dozen of encounters with Zephyr at Winter's command.

Of all my visions I hadn't a single one of the new rise of Winter. The last round had been queens, this time all kings. Which I thought was a dumb idea of the fates since men thought with their dicks more than their brains sometimes, myself as proof since

I could still taste Finn's kiss. But maybe that's why they were all gay so far and mated? Who was Winter and his mate? "That hag needs to die already. Where's the new fucking Winter king?"

Ari flinched, but made his way to a small table in the room, in which a teapot sat. The strawberry blend wafting with warmth and magic. Seb trying to soothe me with his baked goods, sweet teas, and omega magic. Bastard, I cursed him silently.

A tiny fox appeared on the chair beside the table, white in color, with a small red patch over one eye and his right ear. Ari set the tray of cookies on the table and the fox swiped two, peering over the tabletop at me.

"Xiao, I presume?" A dozen puzzle pieces falling into place as the fox morphed into the kitten I'd had in the Autumn realm, and then the white leopard. Free of Autumn's influence I could sense his power, and my gut flipped over with instant worry. I met Ari's gaze, their expression giving a silent warning to not overstep, but here before us was the Winter king, or at least the one meant to step into the role. And his mate. Ari reached over and scratched Xiao's ears, the cat returning to his fox form and cooing at Ari.

Did Seb know?

"Fuck," I muttered.

Xiao tilted his head in my direction, studying me. How old was this king? Kiran had been the first of the courts to be reborn after Spring passed centuries ago, then Autumn, though I hadn't known it was Finn or Xander, broken as he might be. Summer passed shortly before Seb was born, and Winter still lived. How many other young Winters had she killed to keep her choke hold on power?

"What can I do to help you protect Finn?" I asked Xiao instead.

Xiao stuffed the cookies in his mouth, and leapt off the chair, shifting with insanely fast magic to a young man, maybe mid-teens with white hair and the icy gray eyes. He looked more like a true kitsune of story than any of the other kings had, even Seb, who often cursed how much his fox bled through to his human form.

"Bond," Xiao said, touching his forehead. He still had fox ears, which I had to fight the sudden urge to touch. I took a step back, his magnetic pull as king muddling my thoughts. Holy fuck, this baby king was powerful. No wonder he was mated to the Witchchild.

I shook my head to clear out the waves of magic rippling through him like chaos. If Sebastian's hadn't been suppressed as a teen, he would have been as wild with power as this fox. "We fucked, but if there's a bond, I can't seem to find it."

"A bond is more than sex," Ari said.

The last thing I wanted to do was talk about sex with the Witchchild. I'd end up on the wrong side of the werewolf alpha wizard and his grumpy mate. "Explain to me how it works? How to get back to Finn, or find our bond or whatever? I may be a seer, but right now I'm as blind as the rest of you."

"He won't be able to complete the bond until restored," Robin said, appearing in his creepy kid form and taking a single cookie from the plate, to which Xiao looked on with sadness at the loss.

"I have more downstairs," Ari assured him.

"If I can only find him through the bond, and we can't complete it until he's *restored*, which I'm assuming you mean not torn from his wolf half, whatever that might mean, then we are screwed."

Someone knocked on the door. I continued to pace thinking it would be Seb or Liam, but it was Toby, Spring's wolf. He held out a bottle filled with a clear fluid. "This is the best I can do without testing him for side effects." He glanced my way.

"What?" I asked.

"It's a sleeping potion," Toby said. "Meant to get you deep into your subconscious, which should help you connect with Xander."

"I know nothing about Xander," I grumbled, irritated that they seemed to know the mate I was mated to more than I did. How much alike were Finn and Xander? A thousand stories of the king of werewolves and Sebastian's youth hardly led to a clear picture. Many painted Xander as a monster to be feared, which I could see especially when the wolf ruled, but also benevolent and protective, as he did everything he could to keep from slaughtering the wolves who lost themselves to their beasts. The first dreams of Finn's parents lead me to believe he hated humans, yet there were dozens living amongst his wolves which he cared for as fiercely as he had any of his pack.

"Xiao will try to slip through when you dream. Robin will amplify his link through you." Ari said. Their gaze lingered on Xiao, worry defined on their young face, though now the pair looked close in age. I wondered which was worse, fated to a broken Autumn king known for terrorizing shifters, fae, and mortals alike, or the reincarnation of Underhill itself.

I took the bottle from Toby, uncapping it to smell it, found it with a mild bite of alcohol.

"Sip it," Toby said. "Don't chug it all down, I'm not certain if you will wake up from that." He bit his lip, staring at the potion. "It's from one of Seb's forbidden books. Remember the old adage that if you die in a dream, you die in reality? Try to follow that if you can, 'cause it might actually happen with this. Strong magic mixed with alchemy and part science. I didn't tell Seb. He won't ask. Liam knows, but they are leaving the choice to you."

I put the cap back on it without drinking. The Summer court's benevolence made me sigh. Choices weren't my strong suit, not without a vision to guide me and I hadn't had one since I'd left Finn's side. "This sounds like a bad idea. Maybe we should find Finn's moms."

"And do what? Tell them he's the torn soul of the fae Autumn king reborn? Witchborn, and cursed by Winter?" Toby folded his arms across his chest. "Do you want to know what the cards say?"

I pointed at myself. "I'm the seer."

"Who's blind to his own future. I got the hanged man and the lovers card."

"Which, let me guess, means we're doomed?"

"It means there will be a sacrifice for love. It's not a bad reading, or a good one really. It could go either way. The choice is yours."

"I'm fated to the man, how is that a choice?"

"You could walk away right now," Toby said.

I couldn't. The idea knocked the breath out of me. I assumed it was fate tying us together. A few days with him and I'd begun to feel something for Finn, a need to be closer. Sure, the sex had been good, but I wanted to know more about him. What if all he had left to show me was the trauma of his past that made him the Volkov, werewolf king of nightmares?

"Could you have walked away when you met Kiran?"

"I did. My wolf and I fought over it for months, the wolf tied us to Nick until the next step had to be Kiran. If I hadn't been broken, there would have been no fight. He's mine as much as Nick is. We are stronger together."

And all a little crazy from the glimpses I'd caught into the Spring realm. Kiran refused to hold back and built a kingdom with his magic that would rival the courts of old, while Seb hesitated, layering his magic more gently over the mortal overlap between his realm and the earthen one.

I turned away to sit on the edge of the bed, dry-washed my face with my hands and wished the constant headache I'd had since I'd first woken up in Seb's realm, would go away. "I don't know Xander at all. He doesn't know me either."

"But you aren't looking for Xander," Ari said. "You're looking for Finn."

I held up the bottle for Toby to see. "A sip? How fast does it work?"

"Fast," Toby said.

"I'll have food ready each time you wake up," Ari said. "Xiao is going to try to get in, but it may take more than once." They glanced at the pretty fox boy, heart in their eyes. If Seb didn't know yet, he was either blind, or purposefully ignoring their relationship. "If it's not safe for Xiao, I won't let him enter the realm either."

"Can you do that?" Toby asked.

"I would do a lot for Xiao," Ari said.

"Creepy. You talk to your dads about all this? Get the birds and bees talk and all that?" I got under the blankets, uncapped the bottle and took a tiny sip, then set the bottle on the table beside the bed, expecting a one-two knockout punch. "Tastes like vodka and lemon?"

"I improvised," Toby said.

"Birds and bees?" Xiao asked, gazing up at Ari.

"Sex," Ari amended.

Xiao flushed, "Oh."

"*Apa* and daddy understand," Ari said, their voice fading as the room wobbled.

"Not a kid," I grumbled. "Witchchild or not." I couldn't keep my eyes open, but that was okay as long as a dream brought me back to Finn.

Forty-One

FINN

I stared at the statue of the stag, heart pounding as behind it, a half dozen yards, creeped a wolf. Not the shadow wolf, or even a living wolf, but the carving of one. It hid in the shadow of the stag's statue, larger than I knew regular wolves to be. Did they used to be larger in however many hundreds of years ago created this memory?

Was I about to watch the stag die?

I pressed my hand to my chest as if I could keep my heart from beating out of it. It wasn't Wesley. The shape of the antlers, the height of his neck, different. Nothing compared to the majesty of Wesley's Stag. Or his adorable fawn form.

"Fuck, fuck, fuck," I chanted, hating whatever pain was to come. How was reliving all this trauma meant to make me stronger? Each memory landed like a knife in my gut, lodging in an unmovable ache to make my soul bleed. If I worked my way through the sanctuary, I'd be pierced by a hundred blades, seeping blood as well as heartbreak.

I glanced in the direction of Wesley's statue again. His eyes were closed, face down as if resting. "I hope the Summer king helped," I said. "Please be safe."

I reached the stag and set my hand on his leg, the wave of dizziness instant.

We stood in a field on the shore of a hillside overlooking the ocean. A span of ships peppered the horizon and stirred my rage. The trip south meant greener pastures, more food for Hector, while I kept to the shadows, prodded to leave only at his insistence.

The woods to the north, a place I no longer considered home but rather where I'd come from, remained a shadow realm of darkness, heavy air, and little growth. The few trees that rooted after the fire gnarled and bent as if the atmosphere itself were too heavy to exist. Legends traveled far and wide, keeping people south, for which I was grateful.

"We could explore," Hector told me in a mind-to-mind communication.

"It's not normal for a stag to want to explore," I told him.

He snorted.

"Well... until you find a mate." Another thing for which I was the blame. We hadn't encountered a doe in years.

"And you," Hector said as if that were the course of things.

I sighed and glared out at the sea. "People bring hate and death."

Hector nudged me, but didn't answer. I brought hate and death, too.

"Maybe I should head back home. You go south, find a mate, I'll wait for you."

Hector sighed, a funny expression for a stag, my influence for certain. "Stay close?" He gave me a memory of me in the cave, him curled up beside me as his fawn, feeling safe and protected from everything, even if what most feared was me.

"Okay. The humans have weapons, stay out of their line of sight." Or else I'd be slaughtering more of them.

Hector agreed, nuzzling my cheek and heading down the hillside. I hoped he found a mate. Perhaps she'd distract him from me and whatever unfortunate end remaining close to me would cause him.

I followed Hector down the hillside, keeping to the shadows of the trees, but finding myself growling as the swell of human dwellings peppered the valley below.

A soft touch, like a ghost caress, made me pause. What was that? I peered around looking for anyone, but the trees grew thick up the hillside, giving me cover, and the birds a place to rest. My physical body continued onward as if nothing happened. I had forgotten for a few seconds this was a memory, and likely a traumatic one.

"Maybe," A voice whispered through my mind.

"Who?" Not Hector as his presence in my head was more of a battering ram of images, inelegant as my teaching him had likely been. "Wesley?"

"Careful, our tie is fragile," he whispered.

I gasped and wished to break free of the memory if only to talk to him for a moment, but the scene continued, me as an unwilling participant in whatever puppet tale the wolf decided I needed to remember. We approached the town with caution, keeping to the trees until the only real way in was through someone's yard on the edge of town, or the road. I waited until dark, straining to hear anything beyond the murmur of humans. All their bluster and stink made me hesitate as I studied the growing firelight as night fell.

I stopped at a well, pulling up the bucket to drink deep as no one was around, and staring at the ripple of my reflection in the water. Who was that creepy thing? I looked like a starved version of my apa before he'd lost complete control of his sanity beneath the stain of shadows: hollow, thin, and hairy.

"I've always been into bears," Wesley's thought murmured as I glared at my reflection knowing it would scare the townspeople and trying to decide if I wanted to do that or not.

"Not sure this type of bear is what you mean," I muttered

through our connection, but as I glared into the water, my form changed, the disheveled man fading and shifting into more of a young man, not all that unlike what I recalled seeing in the mirror most of my life.

"Glamour," Wesley said.

I'd done it without thinking. Or the memory version of me had. I could walk through the town unnoticed, perhaps, but touched my face anyway, surprised that it felt the way it looked. "I thought glamour was an illusion?"

"Only for the lowest of fae. You are a king."

I didn't feel like one. But I let the bucket go and stepped away from the well, turning to head toward town and met the gaze of a small boy. We both froze. I'd never seen a human with skin painted as dark as mine could be when I let the rage overwhelm me, but this boy was exactly that. Any other time I'd have launched myself at him to silence what he saw, not caring that he was a child, but I hesitated, curiosity getting the best of me.

The boy turned and ran off. I watched him go, thoughts filled with questions about where he'd come from and if he were like me. I followed the trail into town, the bluster of the day dying down as night took over. The scent of food drawing me as I caught the wafting draw of cooked bird. One of the rare treats of human creation, cooked food. Raw would do in a pinch, but I'd ravaged many a camp in my day, eating up whatever they left behind after I sent them back to the earth.

A handful of scents drifted through the town. Humans, the worst, but a sweet fragrance led me toward the far hillside. It tickled a memory of something from before my mother had passed. What was it?

"Sweet bread," Wesley said.

The scent gave rise to a half dozen memories, though the dream vision continued. I had a pouch full of coin taken from many long dead humans as they valued these strange bits of metal for trade rather than items. The smell wafted from a rowdy building illumi-

nated with torches on the exterior, and human males staggering out stinking of alcohol. I hesitated, but decided the idea of tasting that sweet warmth of a treat I'd recalled from my early childhood was worth the trouble of humans.

Inside the building, packed tables and a long dark counter stretched with men, all drinking. It wasn't the booze I wanted. As I entered, I felt eyes on me and headed to the counter. It was only then I realized I hadn't spoken out loud in years. What language would they speak? Could I form the words?

The man at the bar raised a brow in my direction, something dark wavering through his aura, which I found strange and fascinating all at once. "What can I get you?"

Whatever language he spoke translated in my mind and I simply said, "Bread?"

The man chuckled and gave me a half smile. "Draws everyone, my Sari's cooking. Stew too, or only the bread?"

"Both?" I laid coins on the counter, the man studying them, accepting a few and sliding the rest back.

"That's a lot of money, best not flaunt it around here," the man said. He turned and headed to the back where the delicious smell came from, and I glanced around to find another dozen pairs of eyes on me. Their auras shifted with something strange and unfamiliar, too. Had something happened among the humans?

The man returned with a big bowl of stew and an even bigger basket of bread wrapped in a cloth. He waved at an empty chair, and I sat, taking the food, and devouring it before I could even contemplate what I was eating. As I sopped up the last dregs of soup with my bread, I contemplated eating more. Hector would like the sweet bread, the hint of honey beneath the willowy warmth that melted on my tongue had been unlike anything I could recall ever experiencing.

"Bread?" I asked the man as he passed again. I waved at the door.

"To take with you? Alright."

I held out my coins again, he took a few, and vanished into the back again to retrieve a wrapped bundle of bread. Once he passed the bundle, I bowed my head and took it, turning to leave. Again, everyone's eyes followed me. Did I look strange? I felt like I'd copied their style easily enough. But I wandered out of the building and followed the trail out of town, wanting to be away from the humans, clutching the bundle of delicious bread.

The moon overhead glowed bright and nearly full, illuminating the forest with a familiar glow. The late eve and distance from town quieted my anxiety as the sounds of human life faded away. I found a stream and followed it north, wondering if Hector would catch the scent of bread and follow it. I bent to drink the water, but froze as the birds and bugs went silent. Not Hector.

I glanced back, expecting a predator of some kind, but finding the young dark-skinned boy. He hid along the tree line, nearly blending into the bushes. Had he followed me the whole way? How had I missed it? He met my gaze, but ducked behind a tree. His stomach grumbled. I opened the pouch of bread and broke off a piece, tossing it in his direction. He hesitated only a few seconds before snapping it up and gobbling it down as if he hadn't eaten in years. I broke off a few more pieces of it, tossing it out as though he were a baby bird to be lured close.

I held a piece out for him, and he lingered a few steps away, face gaunt and eyes focused, studying me for signs of danger. He touched his face. Had I kept the glamour up? I couldn't recall, but tossed the piece to him. He caught it and took a few steps back, watching for indication I'd chase, but I remained crouched beside the creek. He turned and ran, vanishing into the woods, and I sighed, mourning the loss of half of my bread, though still hopeful to share a bite with Hector.

FINN

"I wonder," Wesley's thought drifted through my mind.

"What?" I asked.

"Nothing yet," he said as we wandered along the creek deeper into the woods. Exhaustion led me to find a place to nap beneath the canopy of trees. The scent of the bread made my stomach growl to eat more, but I was determined to save some for Hector. The vision version of me closed his eyes and seconds later we reopened them to find the sun rising and Hector nibbling at my hair.

I laughed, the sound strange coming from my lips as I couldn't recall the last time I'd let Hector's silliness bring me joy. He tugged at my hair and nuzzled my cheek, his thoughts charging through my head in a confusing array of images. He'd met a few does, but had yet to catch their attention and wondered if he were strong enough to actually be of interest to them.

"You are," I told him as I sat up and unwrapped the remaining bread to tear off a piece.

Hector eyed the bread warily as I held it out.

"It's tasty," I said, taking a small bite. "Like honey."

Hector liked honey. He nibbled the edge of the bread, giving me images of an overripe mushroom doused in honey.

"I suppose to you, that's about how it feels."

"Rather eat clover," Hector shared as he wandered a half dozen yards away to do exactly that.

I snorted at him and ate the bread, finding the pillowy freshness had hardened overnight. The array of colors painting the sky in grays and blues meant rain on the horizon, even if I couldn't see it. I'd have to find shelter for the day, but hoped Hector would return to find the does he'd been interested in.

"Did any of the does in particular attract your attention?" I asked as I stood and took a step in his direction. He froze, head stretched up, gaze in the distance, and silence cascaded over the area, birds flying off with a flap of wings leaving us in an echo of faint wind. My heart leapt into my throat as I caught the slight movement of something in the bushes only a few steps from him.

I lunged, half flying to intercept, claws dug into me where they had been meant to latch onto Hector. I snarled and slammed a fist into the side of the beast's head, catching a glimpse of a wolf's muzzle, though the monster was easily three times the size of any other wolf I'd encountered.

"Run!" I screamed at Hector sensing a half dozen other wolves slinking through the brush. He jolted away, racing off in the opposite direction as I fought with the first wolf. The rest appeared a half breath later to give chase, but I rolled and flipped the first off me and into the rest, knocking them askew and into each other with a flail of claws.

They snarled, one continuing after Hector. I picked up a rock and chucked it, smashing the beast in the head hard enough to explode its skull. The wolves flinched and took a step back in surprise, like they hadn't thought I could hurt their kind. I released the control on my magic, changing into the shadow monster that had created horrors to keep the humans out of the north. Two of the wolves backed away, the others snarled and growled, holding their ground, likely thinking their numbers would out rule my lone beast.

We all lunged at the same time, me leaping into the fray with talons swiping, them with fangs and claws. Blood and flesh sprayed, four of their number dead in a few heartbeats, but I bled too. The beasts who had been about to turn tail and run latching on to me to try to save their packmates. They ripped at me from two sides, and I howled as flesh gave way, strength waning as blood poured from me.

A small dark form dove from the canopy, another wolf. How had I missed that one? But the new wolf dropped on the back of one of the attacking wolves, jaw clamping around its neck and shaking until the beast's bone broke with an audible snap. It fell away with dead eyes, landing beside its friends and I lashed out at the last attacking wolf, talons sliding through its belly, spilling its insides, and it breathed only twice more.

The small dark wolf backed away as I sank to the ground, my dark form slinking away with the loss of blood. Then the dead wolves began to change, from nightmare beasts to human men, all vaguely familiar. I'd seen them in the village where I'd gotten the bread. Had they followed me?

The little wolf shifted too. My gaze blurred as I laid my head down in the blood-smeared grass, thinking the tiny thing could probably end me right there. A heat erupted beneath my skin, as if the claws of the wolves contained some sort of venom. I gasped for air, the pain causing me to writhe as the little dark-skinned boy leaned in close. Tears dripped from his little face, and he said something, though I couldn't understand the words. He bounded away for a half heartbeat, and the black void of unconsciousness threatened to take me, but he returned with water, and a thick piece of leather. He shoved the leather between my lips and doused my forehead in water, which cooled the heat enough to catch a breath.

I wanted to crawl toward the water and soak myself in the spring, but my limbs trembled and spasmed refusing to obey and leaving me little more than a fish on land dying a horribly slow death.

The boy continued to murmur, soft words, followed by a small drenching of cool water. He went to and from the creek a few dozen times, and I fought to keep from biting my own tongue off as the trembling worked its way through my entire body. That's why he'd shoved the leather piece between my lips. I gnawed at the leather as control evaporated completely, only death could feel this awful, though the boy remained at my side, and I caught a brief glimpse of Hector near the creek, watching, careful, and worried.

Whatever my friend had to say, the fever and change stripped it all away as every bone in my body broke and reformed in a gut wrenchingly slow torture that wouldn't let me drop into the forgiveness of unconsciousness. A garbled scream rose from my lips and birds squawked as they flew away in terror as I felt as though my soul itself ripped into two.

Forty-Three

FINN

I gasped for air and jolted awake to find myself in the sanctuary rather than the vision. Spasms racked my body in a thousand excruciating grips as though my muscles were trying to tear themselves apart. My throat closed up, scream garbled, as I gasped for air. I'd never had a seizure before, but that's what it felt like, only every part of my mind present to experience the nightmare of pain and lack of control.

A small, cool hand ran over my forehead and I wondered if the vision had brought the dark-skinned boy into the sanctuary. When I opened my eyes, gazing with half-blurred vision, it was a teen with white hair leaning over me. He traced his fingers over my throat, careful, but spreading a calming wave of ice over the heat soothing the muscle pain.

A scream ripped from my lips as the lock on my throat released and I sucked in air. The boy flinched but remained close, letting the cooling wave of his touch ease muscle after muscle. The pain seemed to last hours, and I reached for the teen with trembling fingers. He held my hand with his spare one, continuing his calming touch and giving me comfort with soft words I barely understood.

Consciousness came and went a dozen times. When darkness fell, I searched for a tie to Wesley or any sense of my former life before I'd been dragged into the nightmare garden, but found myself back in the sanctuary time and again.

The teen remained, even when the seizures stopped and I lay curled up in a ball sobbing from the echoing ache. All that pain and I'd never changed. I understood why as the wolf arrived, his rage sucking the last dregs of joy out of the area. My heart flipped over in terror that he'd hurt the teen. But I couldn't move, everything hurt too much and I could barely breathe without feeling like every muscle in my body had torn itself apart, breaking bones and reforming. Was this what it meant to be a werewolf? I expected to open my eyes and find myself the wolf, but was still human.

The wolf snarled at the teen, black ooze dripping over both of us as the young man turned his head away, offering no challenge, but also not backing down.

"Get up," the wolf uttered.

I stared into the distance, ignoring it, in too much pain to do more than breathe.

"Weak," the wolf snarled.

"Fuck you!" I screamed at the wolf wishing I had the strength to kick the fucker. My grip on the teen's hand tightened as I feared he'd either leave or be forced out of the realm by the wolf. He closed his eyes as a drop of the dark ooze touched him. It sizzled, then froze into a chunk of ice and fell away.

A blast of icy air slammed into the wolf, turning the dripping shadows to crystals, a threat to freeze it in place, perhaps? It snarled and vanished, the shift of it leaving the sanctuary creating a pop in the atmosphere that made me nauseous. I gagged and choked, but there was nothing in my stomach to come up.

Snow fell from the sky in giant flakes, drifting down as light as feathers. I breathed deep, rolling onto my back to stare up at the beauty of the light catching the flakes, refracting in colors as they dropped. Each one landing on my skin in a gentle touch of cooling calm. Tears froze on my face and I sucked in air while the chill brought a shiver to my skin.

"Sorry, sorry," the teen murmured and the snow stopped.

I lay unmoving, the ache radiating soul deep.

A coarse tongue licked the tears from my face, and a big furry body landed on top of me as my shivering got worse. The white leopard that had tried to protect Wesley before bathed my face. Was this the teen? I blinked at him, the sandpaper tongue on my face grounding me as his big furry body eased the chill.

"Did Wesley send you?" I asked.

The cat chuffed and continued to groom my hair. I reached up and ran my fingers through his soft fur, breathing deep as the pain slowly faded. It felt like hours passed, the big cat warming, me petting him to keep myself from falling into the dark oblivion of unconsciousness, and my gaze focused on the distant statue of Wesley, whose eyes were open and gazing my way.

The barrier around his tribute in this garden of nightmares wriggled with an oil-spill array of colorful magic. A dozen paths to other terrors lay in silent brooding, waiting for me to touch them and be dragged into each horror, a gauntlet to be passed.

It's okay, a soft voice trickled through my mind. A ghost-like energy reminding me of Wesley's kiss. We barely knew each other, was it too soon to feel like he was the raft in a storm of my chaotic past?

Wesley? I thought, heart pounding as I closed my eyes and prayed to sink into the sensation of him there with me.

It's okay to rest. Wesley said.

It's too much. I admitted, overwhelmed by the prospect of facing whatever trauma the wolf thought I needed to become stronger.

Not all bad, Wesley remarked. *The boy from the last dream? I know him. He's a good friend of yours.*

What? The dark-skinned boy who could turn to a werewolf was still alive?

Yes.

I let that thought process for a few minutes as my kitty friend nuzzled my ear. The pain vanished, my body feeling overworked, rather than the throbbing wound it had been. Was there more to all this than just pain?

Can you find it? Wesley's statue closed its eyes, expression turning serene as his presence vanished in my head.

I jolted up, unseating the cat who huffed at me, and shifted into a fluffy white kitten that padded his way over to a plate of macarons. The colorful array sitting on a plate in the middle of the overgrown path made me wonder if it was a way out. I reached for the plate as the kitten gave a pitiful meow.

"Want some?" I offered the cat, surprised when I could not only pick up the plate, but also a cookie. I brought one to my lips, the scent of it fruity. It tasted like a cookie, the melt in your mouth kind that people paid bakeries a lot of money for. "Do I have to eat them all to get out of here?"

I polished them off like the starving man I was, but the garden of memories remained. "Fuck."

The kitten meowed again.

"I'm the Autumn king, right? Does that mean the Summer king's magic doesn't work on me? Double fuck."

Forty-Four

WESLEY

I woke up to Sebastian sitting beside me on the bed, e-reader in hand. My gasp at being back alone brought his attention to me.

"We can't pull him out like we did you," Seb said. "It's his realm."

"But he's split," I said, heart pounding at the idea that Finn was trapped in a reality of his own making, or at least half of him. "The wolf has taken control."

Seb sighed. The door opened and Liam came in with a tray. More food. Super. I groaned, wanting to curl up and sleep to find Finn again.

"You should eat," Liam said, his gaze falling on the bottle of the sleeping potion Toby had given me. "Too much of that will make you sick."

"You understand wolves. How can we convince Finn's wolf... Xander's other half, to not torture him?" I asked.

"Trauma sucks," Liam said. "As much as I wish we could rip away the memories from those we love, it is part of what created them." He said it as he sat down beside Seb, and slid the tray over my lap. He leaned over to kiss Seb's cheek. The trauma he wanted to strip away, was Sebastian's, and I wondered how angry at me he was for letting any of that happen. "We have to accept it as part of their past as much as they do. Burying it only causes everyone pain."

"The wolf split his soul to give him a life without all that pain. Why drag him back now?" I demanded.

"Because in order to stabilize the realm, he needs to be whole," Liam answered. "You have visions of the end of the realm, right?"

"Not only the realm, the world. Darkness overwhelming everything."

"Winter's curse," Seb said. "Kiran and I have felt it trying to gain a hold in our realms. She's devouring power. Draining anything she can get her grip into. If she has *apa*..."

Ice coated Finn's wolf half, and it dripped ooze. What if Finn restored his soul only to suffocate in Winter's curse? "I need to talk to Oberon," I said.

Seb put the reader down. "He's been managing all the packs, but couldn't help locate *apa* when I asked."

The dark-skinned boy Finn dreamt of I was certain was Oberon. Which meant Oberon had been a werewolf before Xander. Xander had been something else, and not immune to what made werewolves, werewolves. My knowledge spanned fae and the kitsune like Seb, not wolves. "Did you know Oberon has been a werewolf longer than Xander?"

"No," Seb said.

"Yes," Liam said.

Seb looked at his mate. "What?"

"Oberon is one of the oldest among all wolves," Liam said. "Xander took the lead when colonialism spread across the globe to keep Oberon safe. But those of us who are older always knew Xander was something else, not all wolf, and not as old as Oberon."

"Xander was witchborn," I said.

"Yeah, yeah, you keep saying that. So far it seems a pretty broad phrase. Mixed with fae? Or what?"

I shrugged as that was what I'd always interpreted it to mean, but Finn's memory had given it origin during the witch trials. Maybe I should have studied more of mortal history.

"Supernatural beings aren't limited to the fae," Liam said. "Elementals have been around a lot longer, spanning realms, and spreading power." He squeezed Seb's arm gently. "You are part elemental, as was Kiran, I can only assume the other kings will be as well." Liam's gaze fell on me. "Wesley is part elemental."

"The cursed part," I agreed. As my mix of Stag and Fawn came from my elemental sire.

"Is that why you claimed we are brothers?" Seb asked. "Do we have the same sire?"

"No."

Seb stared at me, waiting for me to continue, but I didn't want to talk about how the pretty little fox boy got to be king and a predator, and I got to be someone's fuck bunny.

He sighed. "I really wish you'd let me in."

"You don't even like me," I said.

"You make yourself hard to like," Seb snapped back. Liam sighed, making Seb frown. "I don't dislike you. I think you're a shady bastard who makes it hard to trust you. I'm bitter that you're mated to *apa* and that somehow you get to know him better than I ever did."

"Someone's been in therapy," I grumbled.

"And someone should be in therapy," Seb said.

"You realize the trauma you're working through was caused by the very man I'm mated to?"

"The wolf," Seb said.

"It doesn't absolve him," Liam added. "The wolf had centuries observing mortal lives tied to Xander. To say he did his best and that his best was terrible, is too kind. Forgiving him outright gives him too much power. He needs to understand his mistakes. And I think to do so, he needs the part of his soul that is Finn, returned."

"And yet I'm mated to him," I said.

"We all have a little bit of monster inside us," Seb said softly, his gaze at the floor rather than his mate.

Liam hugged Seb. "It's okay to love Xander. He was your father. You work hard to be a good father to Ari, but neither of us will ever be perfect."

"Would Finn have made different choices?" Seb asked me.

"I barely know him." But the little I knew; he'd have been a careful and loving father. Hell, the man had nearly unraveled himself waiting for my consent to fuck me while I was begging him in heat.

"Why don't you walk away?" Seb asked.

"I know you understand fated mates," I said. "You left Liam for a year after you met him. How'd that go for you?" The work tracking him and covering up his trail of misdeeds in that year had nearly undone my sanity. None ran faster toward disaster than kitsunes. I might be witchborn, but I wasn't kitsune, chaos given form.

"I felt lost, but might have kept running."

"Always pulled in my direction," Liam reminded him.

Running is what the Stag did best. Could I outrun fate? I'd been trying my whole life and failed as something always dragged me back, usually a fae of incredible power. This time my heart ached at the idea of leaving Finn. Why did he have to be nice to me? Why couldn't he just fuck me like the warm hole everyone else had and walked away? Would reuniting him with his wolf make him a monster? The memories Finn relived weren't black and white. He could rip apart towns and slaughter people, or nurture a baby deer or feed a little boy he'd just met.

"I'd really like to speak to Oberon," I said.

"He can be really scary," Seb said.

"You're the fucking Summer king, Sebastian," I said. "You could crush Oberon with a breath."

"Ha, sure," Seb said, obviously not convinced. "Making plants grow is super powerful."

"Or roasting someone like an oven set to broil," I pointed out.

He blinked, a half dozen emotions crossing his face. "Can I do that?" He asked his mate.

"Probably," Liam agreed. "Would you want to?"

"Carl..."

"No," Liam said.

"But he gave Ari—"

"A book on the birds and bees, I am aware," Liam said.

"Ari's just a baby."

"Ari isn't a baby. Ari is the rebirth of a chaotic world trying to fit everything they know and don't know into something that makes sense for the mortal skin they wear to appease us," Liam said.

Seb gaped like a fish.

"He's not wrong," I agreed with Liam. Was treating the witchchild like a child, good or bad?

"Protecting Ari, teaching them our values and critical thinking, is the best we can do to create something less..." Liam thought for a few seconds. "Traumatic and chaotic. Was Underhill crafted by someone, or did it grow wild on its own?" he asked me.

"I have no idea. Underhill outdated every fae I ever met." I glanced around the room searching for a sign of Ari, Xiao, or even Robin. "Xiao got through." A thought occurred to me. "That's why Carl gave Ari a book about sex. He's seen Ari and Xiao together."

Seb's cheeks turned red and he buried his face in his hands. "That's my baby you're talking about."

Liam met my gaze, his slight nod answering my unasked question. He knew Xiao was meant to be Winter and mate to the witchchild.

"They'll always be our baby, even while they were never really our baby." He got up. "Let me give Oberon a call. He could use an update on Xander anyway." Liam pointed at the bottle of sleeping potion. "Do not take that again until you eat and go outside for a walk. You're fae and an elemental of the earth variety, you need sunlight, grass, and food." His no-nonsense alpha command made me sigh.

"Yes, sir. Your mate is bossy," I scowled at Seb.

"I know, right? He's so sexy."

"Not what I meant, and gross."

Forty-Five

FINN

I paced for a while, then laid down beneath a tree without a statue and tried to sleep, hoping to reach Wesley in a dream. While I dozed for a time, I didn't dream at all. When I woke I stretched, the ache having vanished, and my clothes were restored. I tugged on the hoodie, sniffing it for any lingering scent of Wesley, sad to find none.

Was this glamour? It felt real.

The kitten, back to its small and fluffy pocket-size, prowled the path like a silent guard. "You should go," I told it. "Before the wolf hurts you."

The kitten glanced my way and gave me a half-hearted breathy meow.

"I appreciate your help." Even if eating the cookies hadn't released me from the realm. My heart raced with the new knowledge that the Summer king couldn't help me. I was supposed to be king of this realm, insanely powerful with magic to build an entire world. "I guess it makes sense why I was drawn to the paranormal ghost stuff." A couple dozen more statues littered the path to Wesley at the end. Each time I completed one, the barrier around the next dropped. How many nightmares did I have to survive to get through this gauntlet?

Wesley mentioned the boy, and that he still lived. I got up and wandered the path, studying the statues for a sign of him. How could all these memories exist, and yet that one wasn't featured? Because he lived? Were these unfamiliar faces all deaths I had to recall? Horrors I'd visited upon the world?

I stopped to gaze at Hector's statue, the wolf half hidden in shadows behind it. Hector hadn't died. The wolf carving wasn't the boy, rather one of the attackers. Perhaps the one who had poisoned my blood and turned me into a werewolf.

"I'm a werewolf now, right? That's what that dream was?" I asked my little fluffy friend. "A transition, which is a type of death, even if not a true death."

The kitten gave me another meow. Was that a yes?

The pain had been my body trying to shift, but the wolf had broken free from me, so did that mean I couldn't change? "Fuck."

I glanced back to my parent's statues. Both looked at peace, sleeping, as if my experience with their memory had stripped away any last discomfort they might have had. I'd never really been human, that's what their memory taught me. Perhaps my father and mother had been part human, and a thousand questions trickled through my mind, unanswered, the memories not yet returned to fill out the puzzle.

"I think she loved me," I said. "I wish I remembered more of my father."

Hector's thread unraveled in my mind and I could recall he had mated, and had a handful of fawns, whom I'd watched grow. Always from a distance as I feared I'd hurt them. From time-to-time Hector and I would meet, his sadness over our separation fading over the years, while mine grew. I convinced myself it was for the best. Not only was I a beast from birth, now a curse tainted my blood, forcing me to shift when the moon glowed full overhead.

Keeping those I loved at arm's length was safer. Both from me and the world that seemed to hate what I was.

I stared down at my hands, the dark blotch of bruise-like coloring and tingle of needles reminding me of the blight. "Do you know what this is? Is it from the wolf? How do I stop it?"

The kitten's ears drooped. I scooped him up and held him, his fur a fluffy touch-stone that triggered a handful of memories of other wolves I'd met in my life, and a quick flash of a small red fox.

"I think I remember more of Sebastian," I told the kitten as I wandered the path and petted him, cradling him like a baby. "I hope I didn't really fuck him up. I always thought I'd be a good dad, but I guess the other part of me is sort of crazy."

I set the kitten on the path near the Summer king's tree.

"Can you get back?" I asked him. "I want you to be safe." From me, I added, but didn't speak the words. Wesley cursed fate, and all of this sanctuary stood as a gauntlet of fate's attempts to control my life. Did they want me to become a raving beast?

The kitten wandered up to the statue of Sebastian, walking through the barrier as though it weren't there at all. I gaped at it, and knew I couldn't do the same as the rippling oil-spill half rainbow color told me it sizzled with magical energy.

"Can you get to Wesley's statue, too?" I asked.

The kitten peered down the path, but sat down at the base of the Summer king's carving.

"Right, this nightmare is meant for me and me alone." I sighed. "If I survive all this, mentally, I mean, then I need to have a very brutal discussion with the wolf on personal accountability, post-traumatic stress, and getting a fucking clue." I headed to the next open set of statues; a path filled with a handful of ordinary looking people. Were they friends? Family? People I'd slaughtered?

The last thought made me pause. How easily could I become that monster?

I clenched my hands into fists and closed my eyes, breathing deep and trying to pull forward whatever that beast was. My mother hadn't been a nightmare unless someone directly hurt her, and I recalled my years before her death, in which she taught me the same. Control.

Her death shattered my control. Did I ever find it again or continue killing indiscriminately? Hector's memory led me to think that I'd regained some semblance of balance. From time-to-time humans came and went, and I even wandered among them. Gentler beings never had to fear me, as I nurtured the forest back to health and kept the humans out with legends of spooky events and an occasional scare.

Not unlike a thousand ghost stories I'd heard in this lifetime.

"I could have slaughtered all of Europe," I said to no one. "But I didn't. That means I'm not all bad, right?" I glanced back at the kitten who stared at me from a little loaf position at the base of Sebastian's tree. "Every memory I complete triggers the awakening of a thousand more," I said. "The first acts as a hammer of emotion, the rest a trickle of pieces falling into place."

I nodded to myself, understanding some of what this sanctuary meant. "I have to face my past to have a chance at my future. I get that. My therapist is going to have a field day if I get out of here." The path was a battleground of choices, good and bad. Things the wolf thought I needed to grow stronger, or turning points that led it to ripping us in half?

For the first time since I'd entered this terrible realm, I got an aching sense in my heart of a gaping hole. A wound which throbbed like an old injury. Soul pain? Emptiness? The sense of something missing inside. I thought for half a heartbeat that it was Wesley, but that wasn't right either. My heart longed for him, a strange attraction that made me want to wrap him up and protect him unlike I'd ever felt before.

The soul wound dug deeper, as though it oozed blood and kept anything else from finding a connection to me, including Wesley.

"Fuck," I cursed again pressing my hand to my chest.

"Becoming a werewolf tore my soul, made it two instead of one." And now I was missing the other half of my soul, which was the wolf. It tried to give me a normal human life, without all this trauma, but injured both of us further. "Fuck," I said. "This is a disaster."

The kitten gave me another breathy meow that sounded like agreement.

Forty-Six

FINN

"Do you suppose this will be a good memory or a bad one? They look normal enough, but old me doesn't have a record of being nice to humans," I said as I approached the carving of people. "At least not after they killed my mom."

I stood a few steps away studying their clothes and expressions, though nothing stood out. The kitten relaxed in his loaf form, watching me. "You sticking close in case I do that seizure thing again?"

He let out a breathy meow.

"Thanks," I said and touched the statue.

I sank into the memory of running.

The cool night air, filled the earthy scent of the forest and the sharp tang of approaching rain, rustled my fur. I ran in my wolf form, loping through the woods in tandem with my wolf half, the two of us filled with joy and freedom as we wove around trees, bushes, and over fallen logs beneath the glowing moon. The rustle of leaves above was a symphony of nature's whispers, and I could hear the heartbeat of another wolf nearby.

He teased me from time to time, nipping at my heels or darting out from a tree ahead of me. Faster, yet playful, we'd run this game a thousand times. Odion and I played this way for years, roaming the continent. We traveled far north, where large cats ruled rather than the wolves spreading across the south, but this time we raced along the coast near my old lands. The whispers of the curse keeping people out of the north had faded, and humans spread villages, built roads, and wandered freely through spaces meant for wild earth.

As long as they stayed out of my path, I let them live. And when the full moon rose, Odion and I ran through the thick spread of forest, stretching our muscles, and soaking up the weight of our change as the coming winter would leave us chilled. Odion hated the cold, though his fur grew as thick as mine.

I raced filled with surging primal instincts of the full moon. The wind brushed against my face, cool and invigorating, filling my lungs with the scent of damp earth and pine. The air, pregnant with the promise of rain, adding a thrilling sense of adventure. Cold could drop and add a layer of snow thick and dangerous by morning rather than rain, and I longed for it as the humans huddled from the chill.

A flash of movement caught my eye, not Odion this time. A rabbit darted out from the underbrush, its white tail a stark contrast against the darkness. My heart pounded with excitement as I gave chase, Odion on my heels. His wolf grin teasing as if to say he would catch it before I could.

The rabbit zigzagged through the trees, trying to lose me, but I matched its weave, Odion keeping pace. The ground blurred beneath my paws, and I heard the rapid heartbeat of the rabbit. The scent of its fear smell fueling its desperate flight adding to the excitement of the chase. I leapt over fallen logs and twisted through dense foliage; the forest embraced our wild spirit as though it was made for us.

Odion snapped at me, and I leapt out of his way, using the force of the jump to close the distance between the rabbit and me. My *jaws snapping shut inches from the rabbit's tail. It veered sharply to the left, vanishing into the overgrowth, and I let it go.*

Odion behind me, matched my pace and gave me a teasing yip.

Yeah, yeah, I'd lost it, but we'd already eaten anyway. The chase had been enough to satisfy the desire of the wolf to be a wolf. The first drops of rain fell, cool and refreshing. I lifted my head to the sky, basking in the feeling of the chill turning the rain to tiny flakes.

Odion lifted his head, tilting it, ears turned and I froze, listening hard. Beyond the patter of half rain half snowflakes, the woods had gone silent. Odion slid himself in front of me as a handful of wolves slunk from the underbrush to surround us. The alpha of the pack, a massive wolf with fur, thick and gray, with white swatches showing his age, stepped forward. His lips curled back in a snarl, and a low growl rumbled from his chest. We were outsiders and had stumbled into his territory.

I took a step back, ready to run rather than give myself over to their destruction, but Odion stood his ground. His yellow gaze raised and challenging. The forest spanned a near endless distance, why did this small pack think it belonged to them alone? Tension tightened his stance, and I readied myself to fight.

The alpha snarled and lunged at Odion. The two wolves clashed in a flurry of fur and fangs, the sound of snapping jaws and snarls echoing through the forest. The other wolves surrounded me as though daring me to interfere. I sneered at them, snapping at the one closest to me. He swiped with sharp claws and I smacked his snout hard enough to send him flipping over the others and into unconsciousness, not dead, but a clear warning.

Odion held his own, the alpha breathing hard and bringing every ounce of rage to the fight. Two other wolves leapt out of the brush and landed on Odion's back. The surprise gave the alpha the advantage and he lunged for Odion's throat. Odion veered at the last second, the alpha's bite landing on his shoulder, where it dug deep, and he shook Odion, the other two digging claws into his back.

I surged into the fight, a growl erupting from deep within me, landing between them as if I had wings, with a fury of claws larger than any normal wolf. I collided with the alpha, smacking into him like a boulder, and sending us both spinning away from Odion. The alpha hesitated, but I latched my claws into him, digging until he bled and yelped. I growled in warning, stop this or I'd end him, a challenge to the alpha's authority.

The other two wolves and their friends, joined the fight against Odion behind me, but he'd been play fighting with me for decades, and he battled like he fought a dragon as sometimes he had.

The alpha's eyes blazed with fury. He tried to break free from my claws, but I held tight, grip digging bone deep. He snarled, unwilling to back down. I leapt away, baring my teeth in warning as Odion smashed his way free of the others and slunk to my side.

The rain intensified, soaking our fur and mingling with the scent of blood and earth as we glared at each other, a challenge. The pack circled us, nearly a dozen strong, but all bleeding, while Odion and I were barely winded. I held onto the threads of my control with a firm grip, knowing I could change and destroy them all.

Odion yipped at the alpha, a warning.

The alpha growled and snapped his jaws around Odion's front leg in a move nearly too fast to see, trying to cripple him. I twisted, gliding between them, and clamped my jaws around his neck, jaws closing, and blood flowing. A final chance to submit, or die. He let go of Odion's leg, and the others slunk away.

I waited, the alpha relaxing into my hold, his exhaustion and blood loss getting the better of him. Once he dropped to his belly, I let him go and stepped away. A moment later he began to change, a long painful process not nearly as fast or beautiful as what either Odion or I could do. The others followed suit, changing, their whines of pain filling the evening air with grunts and groans.

I waited until they stood around us in human skins to make my change, one form to the next in a heartbeat. Odion's taking only a touch longer. They all stared at us in awe and horror.

"What are you?" The alpha demanded. "You are not wolves."

I snarled at him with my human teeth. "This was my land before your curse fell upon it."

The alpha met my gaze, confusion in his eyes. "I've been a wolf for nearly a hundred years."

Odion stepped to my side. "And he is the terror of the northern woods that your ancestors have whispered about for centuries." He spent more time among the humans than I ever dared, learning their languages and ways, finding things to trade, and listening to their stories. Without Odion I'd have lost myself in the shadows much like my sire had. Perhaps become a raging monster hunted by all. And I didn't understand their ideas of time. The sun rose and set each day giving way to the moon, endlessly. Why count them?

"The beast?" The alpha whispered, his gaze turning to his pack.

I shifted again, wings expanding and towering over them as the demon things I was. Odion unphased by the change, the others dropped to the ground in fear and submission.

The alpha met my gaze but dropped to his knees. "We didn't know this was your land."

"You attack any who enter?" Odion demanded.

The alpha flinched.

"And the humans that the nearby village claim are missing?"

"We sought to expand our pack, adding strong males to our number. Not all of them survived the change."

I snarled, which sent them all into quivering puddles huddling on the ground, but shifted to my human form. "You forced them to change?"

My anger over being cursed by one of their number never truly ended despite my years of learning to control it. Something about the blood curse flowing in my veins disrupted my control over my other half. Twice I'd lost myself in the dark, waking weeks later to Odion's prodding and begging me to return to myself. The after-

math of whatever destruction I delivered often meant smoldering forests and blood.

"Humans hunt us," the alpha said.

"And you hunt them," Odion growled. Even as a human male, his size outmatched mine. He towered over me and the other wolves, glare filled with rage. "No more."

"We need to eat."

Humans. They were eating humans. Even my other form didn't do that.

"There isn't enough food in the forest to sustain us," the alpha said.

"And yet you sought to forcibly expand your pack," Odion reminded him.

Something dark flipped through the alpha's gaze, a wriggle of power and lust for control. I'd seen that same expression a thousand times in the faces of men dying beneath my fangs as they'd tried to kill me. He lunged, wolf talons where human fingers should be, swiping for my throat, and midsection as the human form was fragile.

The pack gasped, half holding their breath, likely waiting for me to die, but I deftly evaded the attack, caught the alpha in mortal hands and snapped his neck, dropping his lifeless corpse to the ground. His partially changed hands returned to their human form. Bloodied, as I realized he'd caught me, tearing thin gouges in my flesh.

I turned toward the others, scratches on my stomach seeping with blood as they resealed and healed in a few heartbeats. The other wolves bowed.

"We do as you bid, Alpha," one of the wolves said.

"Yes, Alpha," the others followed.

A surge of energy flowed through me, the pack becoming mine as I could sense them all, hear their thoughts, filled with fear and worry. Would I kill them, too? Their strength added to mine, allowing my grip on my power to tighten.

Odion met my gaze. "No more killing humans."

"No changing anyone," I said, voice low and harsh. My pack, my rules. Odion and I had never infected any with our curse, and I wanted to stop its spread, even if it meant the wolves would die out. I stared at my new pack and decided any wolf crossing our path would obey or find its end. The nightmare stories trickling through the countryside from town to town would fade much as mine had, and we'd remain in the shadows until none remained to cast the world in flame.

Forty-Seven

❧

FINN

I gasped awake as a charge of energy circulated through me. "What the..." my question cut off as the world erupted in overwhelming power. A ribbon of energy spread outward, seeking a link. The first it touched was my wolf, who paced outside the sanctuary, close, but unwilling to enter.

He snapped at me, and I flinched away. His emotions and memories battered me in a chaotic mess of tangled thoughts. More human than I expected a wolf to be, but we'd run together as one for centuries. He snarled at the idea of letting our bond reunite, reminding me how weak he thought I was, and I recoiled away from him, following the magic instead.

The power dug deep, forming a link that flew beyond the sanctuary and even the realm, carrying my mind with it as though we'd flown the route a thousand times, and wrapped up each nearby wolf, one by one. As though, if I couldn't have my wolf, all the rest would be mine. A connected weave of consciousness and power surged through the line, their packs filling a vacuum of unfamiliar silence inside my head with an overwhelming weight of emotion, magic, and noise.

I felt a sudden, overpowering kinship to the packs, their

thoughts and feelings surging through me like a tidal wave. It was disorienting, the sheer volume of their collective consciousness threatening to crush my own. Each linked wolf reminded me of a name, a human face, their wolf presence and a dozen specific memories of them. The wave began as a trickle, but quickly became a screaming tsunami of too much power all at once.

A scream broke through my lips as the world flipped from bright waves to darkness and back, not a seizure of the body like before, but of the mind. I begged my wolf for help and he growled and snarled, slamming a barrier down between us.

Blood dripped from my nose and I dropped to my knees, my vision exploding in an array of lights and stars. I sought to escape the pain which verged on euphoria. The packs linking to me one by one across not only the continent, but the entire globe. I gasped for air, struggling with the sheer volume of the power. No single being could control this. No wonder the wolf had split me off. Was there a way to survive becoming supernova?

I latched on to the last thread of hope floating through my memory, and that was Wesley. He said we were linked, and I hoped my explosion wouldn't drag him down with me. His bond floated above the rest in a delicate ribbon that anchored me to my soul. I reached out and grabbed the tie, fearing breaking it with my touch, but it pulsed warm and solid in my grasp.

I blinked and found myself standing in an unfamiliar room, heart slowing as the power continued to grow, but I'd distanced myself from it. Wesley lay on the bed, looking better, beautiful with his delicate expression of sleep. I crossed the room in a handful of strides, desperate to touch him, and shocked to find him solid and warm beneath my fingers.

He opened his eyes, confused for a half second then they went wide as he sat up and pressed his lips to mine. My heart racing as I silently begged him to help me, even while I wanted to bask in his lips forever and couldn't find the words to voice my desperate need.

Forty-Eight

WESLEY

I opened my eyes to Finn standing over me, my gasp cut off as I sat up and pressed my lips to his, desperate to feel him. His touch heated near burning with its intensity, I flinched but refused to let go. A vibration echoed beneath his skin, magic spreading outward too fast to pull back, and his lips on mine demanded more.

"Finn," I whispered, unwilling to break away, though his touch hurt, first with a raging fire, then a crisp chill that sucked energy from me. For a half second, his lips to mine, tasting him, staring into those beautiful sorrow-filled eyes, I thought it was Finn feeding on my energy as he should as my mate. But my breath puffed between us a visible icy array and that wasn't Autumn, it was Winter.

He swallowed hard, and I pressed my forehead to his to try to give him strength as the Winter queen sucked away his magic through the curse and bloomed in dark blotches like bruises across his skin. Finn trembled.

"I'm sorry," he whispered. "I don't know what's happening to me."

I silenced him with another kiss, this one long and deep, as if to show him I wanted to taste his soul through his lips. He could take as much as he needed from me, and he did, feeding at my lips, and sucking down power like a starving man.

He gasped, stealing small breaths in our kiss, and half gasps that sounded near pain. Was I hurting him?

I pulled away and watched a charge of electricity jolt him. "Finn?"

The room around us unraveled into a weave of finely tuned magic layered over the real world. The threads turned to wriggling snakes of magical energy to attack Finn.

"What the hell?"

Finn backed away, breaking our touch and the wavering of the room stopped, though I watched him wince in pain a dozen more times as the realm continued to attack. Winter's curse climbed up his neck and spread from his feet in a crystalizing layer of ice.

The door to the room burst open and Seb filled the doorway, his mate behind him. I threw myself at Finn, afraid for him. "Please don't hurt him."

"He can't stay here," Seb said, his expression filled with tension. "Winter is using him to invade my realm."

"Fuck," I cursed and turned to face Finn. "Baby, you gotta break Winter's curse."

"How?" He asked his eyes filled with pain, and through our bond I could feel him attacked in three different ways, his realm pulling him back, Winter's curse draining him, and Seb's realm trying to push him out. The rise of energy inside him continued to grow until he smoldered with the heat, his tremor scaring me more than the battle of fae magic as I worried he'd have a seizure.

Ice spread from around where he touched the floor, while his skin raged with a burning heat that sizzled against my touch. I bit back pain, trying to hold onto him and give him comfort.

"I don't know what's happening to me," Finn whispered, as the ooze of the curse climbed to cover half his face. "I feel wolves. So many wolves. Wesley?"

"I'm here," I whispered, my skin burning against his, and tears leaking from my eyes.

"Let him go, Wesley," Seb said, "he's hurting you."

Finn flinched. "I'm sorry. I didn't..." he tried to step away and his face flashed from his youthful handsomeness to a dark wave of something inhuman.

"The beast," Seb whispered. "Wesley, get back. He's dangerous."

A sense of doom trickled from Finn with an expansion of the shadows around him. He met my gaze, fear in his eyes. "Wes..."

The energy in the room shifted as a portal tore open in the room, the fabric of reality itself splitting with a sharp, echoing crack. The wolf emerged, dripping shadows, its eyes blazing.

"Weak," the wolf snarled as it dug its claws into Finn and dragged him backward. Finn screamed and the magic burning through him transferred to the wolf, as though the wolf were taking control.

Liam let out a cry of pain, and Seb turned to him as I reached for Finn. The crackling of ice dug into the floor and crawled up Liam's body as if to take him over. Seb put himself in front of Liam, his eyes meeting mine as Winter's curse slammed into him and fire erupted from Seb fighting back.

A giant of a man burst through the doorway, his gaze taking in the room for a half second before he wrapped his arms around Liam and Seb.

"Oberon," Seb said.

I'd only ever seen the man from a distance, knew of him from stories of the Volkov's right hand, and now from glimpses into Finn's memory, Odion full grown and filled with strength as only the oldest of wolves could have.

His gaze met mine and he murmured, "I'm sorry." Something snapped, doom evaporated as the overwhelming noise echoing in the back of my brain vanished and with it, Finn's terror. The fire smoldering beneath Finn's skin, the only thing keeping him from being lost beneath Winter's curse, vanished. His face morphed back to the frightened young man I needed to save. The crackling power of the Summer realm jolted waves of lightning bolts at the wolf and the portal.

Wards dragged Finn and the wolf into the portal. The magic gone, left with nothing but the curse, Finn bled, tears dripped from his eyes and sorrow etched across his face. He balled his hands into fists, holding them to his chest as though to keep from reaching for me, though his gaze never left mine.

Liam panted as the ice receded and Seb's heat cracked the slither of Winter's curse into his realm. Seb reached for me, but I shook my head, unwilling to leave Finn to this nightmare alone. He was meant to be mine, even if I had to put the bastard back together again.

The wolf ripped him through the portal, the opening closing around them, and I dove after him, hearing Seb call for me, his face stricken with fear and worry as I plunged into the dark after the man my heart ached for.

The world lurched and twisted until I feared it would spit me back on Seb's floor, but I landed in a walloping heap on the hard forest floor, breathing heavily and swallowing back bile. Nausea roiled through my gut as I lay there trying to stop my senses from spinning and staring at the grass, heart pounding.

I turned my head and found a carved statue of myself. His gaze outward, over my head and behind him a wall of nothing but green, impassable. I studied it for a few seconds until I was certain I could roll over and not throw up my soul in an attempt to purge the rot of Winter's touch.

A small sound of pain, like a muffled sob, echoed from somewhere nearby, and I turned my head to face away from the statue and found the sanctuary of statues stretched along the path I recalled from Finn's dream, and Finn lying on the ground, face down, arms curled beneath his head, face hidden.

"Finn?" I whispered.

He glanced up, eyes rimmed in red, face blotched in darkness. He gasped and jolted to his feet, running toward me. I gasped a half second before he hit the barrier, seeing it ripple as he got close and watching in horror as he slammed into it and then was airborne, the magic casting him away. He landed with a thud, hard enough I feared he'd cracked his skull.

I got to my feet, stomach still in chaos, heart racing, and carefully approached the barrier. It crackled and snapped as I raised a hand to it, but I couldn't pass through. "Finn?"

He lay on his back, breathing hard, but otherwise unmoving, too far away to see clearly. Silence stretched over the realm, the only thing I could hear beyond the low hum of the barrier around me was the sound of Finn's sobs.

"Finn," I called again, desperate for him to hear me. "Are you hurt?"

He said nothing for a long minute, then finally, "The wolf is right."

"About what?" I asked.

"I'm weak."

"You're still here."

"I don't want to be."

Forty-Nine

WESLEY

I swallowed hard. "Don't leave me," I whispered, tears filling my eyes that I fought to keep from falling.

Wherever the wolf had gone, I knew it wasn't far. What if it cast me out and left Finn here to die? Or even ripped out his soul again and forced it to relive another mortal life? Would there be anything left of the man I was coming to love?

I gasped, heart flipping over in a rise of unfamiliar terror. It was too soon. We barely knew each other. Hell, Finn barely knew himself. And yet I couldn't imagine going forward into whatever the bitches of fate had woven for me without him.

"I wish I could touch you," Finn said, staring up at the sky through the trees, still lying motionless. "But you should go back to Summer. He'll keep you safe."

"I don't want to go back to Seb. I want to be here with you."

He sat up, the darkness covering his face. "I don't want to hurt you."

"Leaving me here alone would hurt me," I huffed.

He looked away from me, toward another statue. "The kitten is gone." He let out a long sigh. "I was hoping he could help get you out so you were safe."

"Are you listening to me at all?"

"I don't know what to do," Finn said.

"Get up," I demanded.

He grimaced, but got to his feet.

"Come here."

He hesitated, but slowly approached until I said, "Stop." He stood outside the barrier, about a half meter from being jolted again. I stood on the other side wishing I could reach through it and kiss him, hold him, offer him comfort even while he looked like the darkness was eating him.

"I had power for like two seconds," he said. "I thought I could control it. I needed to see you and it happened, the magic brought me there. I hoped it could fix whatever's wrong with me. But the other wolf severed my tie to the packs."

"Oberon. You remember him, right? Odion? Winter's curse was spreading to the wolves. He had to cut your tie to them to save them."

Finn flinched and looked away. "I didn't mean to hurt them."

"I know, baby."

He paced away from me, down the path and back, his heart racing loud enough for my sensitive ears to catch. "I know I'm supposed to be this," he waved his hands in the air, "powerful fae king with a crazy past. The memories feel like a dream of something I once saw on television." He pressed his palm to his chest. "Like it's not me."

"It is, and it isn't," I said. "You and the wolf are one. It split your mortal soul free to try to give you a normal life free of all the sorrow that built the..." I hesitated to say it.

"Beast. You can say it. I know what it is. It's a monster. I have vivid memories of the blood I shed, even if it's distant."

"But that's the point," I said. A kindness from the wolf, though like most things planned by fate, it always came back to bite us in the ass in the end. "He wanted you to have a chance to live and experience love without all the pain." The wolf took the beast half and the curse, leaving Finn as little more than an ordinary young man.

"Then why drag me back?" Finn demanded. He turned and scanned the sanctuary. "I can feel you watching me. Why torture me? Why give me hope only to rip it away?"

"Because the curse is overwhelming him and if he dies, so do you." My heart ached at the thought. "You are one soul split into two beings. It weakens you both." His gaze met mine and the sadness in his eyes made me wish I could wrap my arms around him. "He could have let himself die, which would have dragged you with him. An abrupt ending to your normal life."

"But then you and I wouldn't have met, right?"

"Maybe that would have been better?"

He flinched.

"I don't mean for me," I corrected. "For you. If you didn't have to know you were bound to me? Why choose a guy like me? I'm not exactly the ideal mate. Liam is. His strength is nearly unmatched among wolves, as is his heart. And his power as a wizard focuses their power and helps his mate secure their realm. I'm really only good at running away. And can't even help warn you of coming trouble because the closer I am to you, the less likely I am to have a vision with you in it. I'm useless."

"No," he said. "This mate thing is intense. I can feel you wrapped around my heart. I've spent my whole life wondering what it really felt like. Reading books and watching movies and trying a handful of relationships but feeling empty, until you. It's this weight of something in my soul..."

Weight. I sighed, hating the idea of being a burden to anyone.

"An anchor," he said after a pause, his gaze lifting to meet mine again. "To keep me grounded, and remind me of the way home." He stalked to the barrier and I sucked in a breath fearing he'd hurt himself, but he lifted his hands and held them just beyond the rippling color of it. Electricity snapped at him in warning, but he didn't break away. "I have to defeat the final boss to get to you."

He motioned to the path and all the statues surrounded by barriers. "Each memory is a level up until the final boss."

"Huh?"

"You ever play video games?"

"No. Seb does, and some of the others in the wolf pack."

"The game always ends with a final boss, then shifts to a movie cut scene that wraps up the storyline. Defeat the boss, save the princess." He gave me a sad smile. "But the final boss is me."

"The final boss is Winter. She's been unraveling the control of you and your wolf for a long time."

He shook his head. "I had a glimpse of the power. The wolves were part of it. But there's something in me that I was born with, a rage that can be terrifying and monstrous. The wolf took that half, the nightmare, even though it wasn't his to control. It's insane."

"When provoked," I agreed. "We can all be chaos when provoked." He had no idea of the beast I could be. "Witchborn comes with a lot of curses."

"And power."

I bit my tongue to keep from voicing the adage that power corrupted as obviously that madness had taken the wolf a long time ago. Could his other half be saved at all, or would re-uniting his soul destroy them both? I'd seen power rip apart realms.

"I have to face them all, right?" Finn asked, his gaze following the path of memories to be unlocked. "Remember who I was to figure out who I am?"

"Yes," I said while fearing his sweet subtle strength would be lost under the weight of his traumatic past.

"I hope you don't hate me when this is over," Finn whispered, not looking back my way. He headed down the path to a statue without a barrier. "I hate that you're mated to me and don't have a choice. What if all this is meant to make me lose control?"

"I'm your anchor, remember?"

He glanced up, a ghost of a smile touching his lips. The dark blotch of the curse slowly crept across his skin, making him ghoul-ish-looking, but he nodded. "You're safe in there, right?"

I shrugged, looking around. "It's not a five-star hotel with room service, but I've had worse."

"You're saying you'r

\e high maintenance."

"What was your first clue?"

He laughed, and the sound loosened some of the lingering sense of doom inside me. "I wish I could kiss you again."

"Incentive," I said.

"Thanks," he replied.

"For what?"

"For being you. Which is sometimes a prickly asshole, but always exactly what I need."

"Sap."

He laughed again, then sobered as he reached for the statue. "Be safe. I'll understand if you need to call Summer to pull you out again while I'm gone. Just be safe please." Finn set his hand on the statue before I could respond, and for the first time I saw it from inside the sanctuary. He turned into a solid thing as though carved to the statue, and as I closed my eyes, I could sense him opening his to another piece of the puzzle fitting together his past.

"You too," I whispered. "Be safe, Finn, and remember, no matter what you see, you made it through."

FINN

A dark forest opened around me with a heavy memory of Odion finding a mate and leaving the pack to pursue a family of his own. The weight of the loss sent me away from the pack. My wolf snarled at the separation, but my heart ached in a way I could only recall from losing my mother. The decades of friendship had given me an anchor and his strength at my side kept me focused on the pack, now one of the largest on the entire continent.

Without him, I hated how much they demanded from me. My wolf pointed out potential mates for us, citing benefits that he thought worked well for my witchborn heart too, and yet, none of them appealed to me. I handed the wolves over to the mothers of the pack, to guide them, and help steer them in the right direction. Wolves didn't kill people, or anything unnecessarily. We'd built a community entirely of wolves, their mates, and their young. And I never felt so alone.

I wandered south and east, months passing with four paws to the ground rather than human flesh. Occasionally we'd join a pack, not to lead, rather to fulfill the need of my wolf for pack. My wolf chose a mate for us among the humans, I think because he knew we were lonely and thought it would help me find stability again. And for a time, they gave me focus, until age began to eat away at them. The short lifespans of mortals leaving me to watch them fade before my eyes. Twice it happened, a passing of years in seconds as the memories flipped from page to page on high speed, stopping when I woke curled around the third mate, chosen by me this time at the insistence of the wolf, from among the humans born within the wolf pack.

A hundred memories of our time together knit itself into my memory as though I'd relived it all in a handful of seconds to bring me back to this place. I stared at their sleeping beauty, mortal and delicate, and yet I'd found a home there with them, but my heart ached at what I knew was coming.

"Why are you awake?" They asked as they reached out to run gentle fingertips along my jaw.

"Thinking," I said. Always thinking. The wolf hated that I refused to submit to my instinct. It wanted to change them, feed the wolf curse into their blood and keep them with us.

"Eriony survived the transition," they said. "She'll be okay."

Sometimes those humans living among the pack chose to attempt a change. I hated it. There wasn't a blessing to the wolf splitting our souls. It was filled with pain, and often death. The wolf ached with sadness at my rage toward it. Unfair, I knew, as it hadn't asked to rest within me either. Only when we ran with four paws to the ground, free of the obligation of mortals did we finally feel united, and I worked to keep us from bonding further.

Self-hatred, Odion often reminded me, would lead to self-destruction. We'd seen it a dozen times among the wolves. Those wolves would go mad and have to be put down, often in a bloody and vicious battle that resulted in more than one dead wolf. I had never cursed another, even those injured in battle. Perhaps because I had been other *before the wolf settled inside my soul?*

"I'd like to change," my mate said.

"I would rather you didn't."

"But I will grow old and die."

"We all die. Some live longer than others. Wouldn't you rather have children and watch them grow, than die beneath teeth and claw?"

"I want to stay with you."

The words tugged at my heart, but I shook my head. "I want you to stay with me, too. Safe. Not cursed to try to survive in this violent world." The mortals who lived among us were protected from the violence that sometimes erupted. A few wolves would live decades and suddenly become flesh hungry, as though fueled by blood lust instead of the instinct of the wolf. Neither Odion nor I understood it, and the handful of pack alphas I encountered over the years had stories of those lost to the eventual corruption. Like the longer a wolf lived, the more likely chaos overtook their sanity.

My mate sighed and snuggled down with me, and I closed my eyes to rest, hoping the discussion was over, but when I awoke, I was alone.

Not the first time a lover had left me. But as I sat up in bed and stared at the last dregs of moonlight fading to the rising sun, a sense of dread pooled in my gut. Since I wasn't pack alpha, the draining noise of having them all linked to me and tugging at my awareness was peacefully absent.

The sense of doom intensified. I made my way to the door of our tiny house, one of a couple dozen among our pack, and stepped out to study the village, listening with a beyond human capability. Silence stretched deep. Not sleep, though I could hear a handful of human hearts resting peacefully in their dens. The absence of the faster beat of the wolves made my heart flip over.

I raced into the woods, straining for a sense of them, their scent carried on the wind with an undertone of blood, and my mate. No, no, no!

The clearing where we held pack meetings was overrun with wolves and the stink of death as I realized that Eriony, my mate's friend, lay still in the center, half wolf, half human in a horror of mid-shift turmoil. Blood and intestines stained the ground, leaving the smell of open bowels and death heavy in the air.

I took a step forward and the alpha broke my path, hand on my shoulder, though I didn't like the humans to touch me. I flinched away, but he stood firm. "They sought a change."

"No!" I said, understanding it wasn't Eriony he spoke of, but my mate.

"I had to put Eriony down..." the alpha said. "Your mate was already gone." He took a step to the side and waved his hand. A row of pack members moved to show me the remains of my mate, torn up and half blistered with bubbling masses of the change bursting beneath their skin. Even in death the curse tried to rip them from one form to the next, but they hadn't survived the first fever.

I found myself at their side, heartbroken, wolf howling inside my head, as I dropped to my knees and held their remains and wept. A tide of something dark burst from inside me, and a gasp of fear rose from the nearest packmates. I turned to snarl at anyone close to me, finding only the alpha as the rest of the wolves vanished into the woods.

The alpha stood his ground, though I could smell his fear.

"You are not a wolf," he said.

I was, and I wasn't. Just as I was human and I wasn't.

"You can't stay with us."

I growled at him, feeling the darkness slide across my body and enlarging it as though my beast would burst free at any second. The alpha trembled, but didn't back down. He was a good man, trained to care for his pack as an alpha should, never seeking power, but gifted it by gentle and protective leadership.

"Will your grief ease if you kill me?" he asked.

I knew it wouldn't. I'd killed hundreds over the years after the murder of my mother. Most I couldn't remember at all. Other wolves sought fights, and I always won, which often sent me away from the packs to wander alone. I wasn't a wolf. I wasn't a man. I was something else.

Witchborn. The memory ached as if those zealots had woven magic to span my existence.

"Let us give them a proper burial," the alpha said. "I would not have wished this on either of them. I know you wouldn't have either." I met his gaze, heard the truth in his words, though my heart bled as though sliced through the middle. "The pack has seen what you can be," he said, quietly. "It terrifies them." And him. "It's best you go."

I let out a long breath and sucked the darkness back inside, locking it deep within my soul. The wolf wept within as if my human half bled into his, making his emotions a thousand times stronger. It made sense to blend one to the other, as we shared a soul, and for some reason the wolf's heart was more delicate than mine.

I stood. The alpha took a single step back, but squared his shoulders as if ready for battle. He would die to protect his pack. I understood. He didn't have a mate. His pack was his anchor. I nodded to him and headed into the woods in the opposite direction. "Don't follow," I said in warning. Nothing would survive when I released the darkness again.

"I am sorry," the alpha said.

I left it all behind, my wolf silently weeping. We wandered for days, perhaps weeks, with unseeing eyes until we found our way into the mountains and I set free the accrued darkness. The world vanished around us, turning from summer to winter in a rush of raging winds and snow, and then back to sweltering heat. Fire latched on to the trees casting plumes of smoke into the air, raining down ash, and finally a soft blanket of snow. The forest died, trees snuffed and wildlife running from the madness.

Mortals avoided the mountains, their whispers carrying over the wind of a nightmare in the north. Once again, I was that nightmare, teetering between hot and cold, rage and silence. Decades passed before I resurfaced to try again.

Fifty-One

WESLEY

I paced the small space, catching glimpses of Finn's dream, a lover turned, the blood curse tearing them apart. His heartbreak palpable, and yet I could tell that his affection for them was rooted in the wolf's need for a pack. Finn, the original witchborn being, enjoyed the friendship of his pack, and consulting with Odion, but the relationship had stretched him in ways he didn't understand.

Was he incapable of love? No, that wasn't right. The affection and adoration had been there, just varied, as though the bond to the wolf had been greater than the bond to the human. He loved them, his memories of a dozen lovers wove themselves through our bond in memories. Each death causing a gouge in his soul that bled to this day.

As the years passed, he kept himself further and further apart from everyone. Creating packs, linking to them to keep them from changing others, adding the broken and taking their darkness as if it could stop their eventual madness, and burying his emotions in a handful of lovers that would eventually die, leaving him with another soul wound.

How many stories of a monster in the woods had been told

around human encampments? Even I, as part fae, had heard more than my fair share. Perhaps they hadn't been the Hunt as I'd thought.

I glared at the sanctuary watching for movement at the statue he'd become a part of for him to awaken. Was the other end darker than before?

The sky overhead had shifted to night, but the stars glowed bright above me, as if illuminating my space. My stomach growled, and berries grew at the base of the statue. The sensation of the wolf nearby made me want to snap at him.

"You couldn't be kinder to him?" I sighed, realizing it had tried, though failed miserably as it had given him a mortal life free from most of this trauma. "I want to save him, too. Can we work together to fix this? He needs you and I need him."

Finn rematerialized at the base of the other statue, falling to the ground in a heap and lying limp, though I could hear his heartbeat and see his chest rise and fall. He sucked in air, and the breeze wafted a hint of salt to my nose. My little king had a sensitive heart, no wonder he'd tucked it away in an iron box and split himself in half to keep from leaving it vulnerable.

"Finn?" I called.

"Have you lost people you love?" he asked softly.

"Yes."

"Does it ever stop hurting?"

I let out a long breath. "Yes, and no? Sometimes you'll be going about your day, life as usual, and everything is fine, and suddenly a memory triggers the heartbreak all over again. The more intense the love, the more agonizing the heartbreak is, even in memory."

"Hmm," Finn muttered, still lying at the base of the shadow. "Do you think it's okay to rest a little?"

"I would prefer if I could hold you. How about you ask your wolf to let me out of this barrier and we can do this together?"

He sat up and turned my way, his face overridden with the blotched darkness. Dammit. Would there be anything left of him after this fucking trip down memory lane? He flinched, catching something on my face I couldn't hide.

"I'm sorry," he said.

"Why?"

"'Cause I still feel powerless. Like the Finn I've always been, or at least that is most recent to me," he said. His words formed a mist of vapor like the temperature had dropped. Cold blanketed the sanctuary, and I knew instantly it wasn't his wolf causing it.

"Finn, honey, can you come this way please?" My gaze focused beyond him to the statues he'd already completed and the rising icy ooze that entombed them in crystals.

"My legs feel like overcooked noodles."

Fuck.

Glowing eyes materialized in the darkest corner of the sanctuary. I thought for a half second it was Finn's wolf, but as it stepped free from the shadows followed by a half dozen other beasts shaped more like Underhill's lost monsters, I knew what I was looking at, the remainder of the Hunt.

They multiplied, waiting, gaze on Finn as the ice and darkness spread.

"Finn," I called, heart racing. He swayed slightly, barely awake and I could hear his pulse slow as if on the verge of unconsciousness. "Finn, honey..."

A ghoulish smile crossed his lips. "That's nice."

"What's nice? Can you get up, please?"

"You calling me honey."

"Yeah? Okay, honey. Can you get up, please? Come here?"

"Barrier's still up." His gaze flicked down the path. The next statue open and somewhat illuminated. "Guess that's the next quest point." He fumbled to his feet, unsteady and obviously dizzy as he fell twice before limping forward.

I watched the glowing eyes with apprehension. They focused on Finn, but remained in the swell of shadows that had eaten through the first half of the sanctuary. "That's it, honey. You can do it," I said as he made his way to the newly opened statue.

He hesitated at the base of it, his face turned toward me, tears streaking his face. The darkness leeching over his skin turned them to trails of ice. "I don't want to hurt anymore, Wesley," he said, hands clenched to his chest.

I couldn't stop the pain. And that was the worst part. Even if we somehow ran away from all this, these dark memories were part of what made him, and broke him. Facing them and finding his footing would either destroy him or save him. I prayed for the latter.

The swell of shadows reached the light of this new statue and couldn't continue. I sucked in a hard breath. It was going to be a race, wasn't it? Could Finn complete the memories without losing himself to madness before Winter's curse ate through the core of his memories?

I forced myself to meet his eyes and smile while tears rolled down my cheeks. Fuck, I never cried anymore. "I believe in you."

"You'll get back to Summer if I can't do it, right?"

"You can."

"Wesley..."

"I believe in you," I repeated. "You lived through this before. It's all in the past. You have already conquered this mountain."

"At what cost?"

And that was the hardest question to answer. What would be left of Finn, the sweet boy who had adored his mother, hoped for strength to heal his father, and spent his life looking for a family, only to have them always leave him, either through death, or the path of fate.

"Fuck," I cursed. That was it, always fate fucking with people. "Remember the prize, honey." I wasn't much of one, but if it kept him moving, I wouldn't hesitate to use it. "I'll be right here waiting for you."

He stared at me, his heart in his eyes. "Everyone leaves."

"Not me," I said. "Remember fate chose me for you."

"But you can still walk away. You said so."

"I'm not going anywhere," I said and pointed at the barrier.

"Summer could get you out. He did before."

I wasn't sure I agreed as Seb had been really afraid of how Winter latched onto Liam and through Liam the wolves. His duty would be to protect his realm, and I was okay with that.

"I'm waiting right here." I sat down near the barrier, facing him, relaxed, but ready should the shadows break free. Would Finn still want me if he knew what I could become?

"The princess to rescue?" Finn asked, humor in his tone.

"Sure. Think of me as a princess. I want a castle, and jewels, and a large designer clothing collection."

He laughed and it sounded more like a cackle than anything human. The dark half of himself rising through. Strangely I found it oddly comforting. As if the pretty young man with a heart on his sleeve could never really love me, but maybe the dark monster inside him could.

"Anything you want," he agreed and reached for the statue.

"I'll be waiting," I said as the next vision slid over him. The rising well of inky slime waited too, reminding me of my vision. The world devoured by icy slime.

Fifty-Two

WESLEY

Two more statues and the memories of loss left Finn a few meters away, and the Hunt pacing the edge of Sebastian's statue. Maybe he could keep them back a little longer? I knew the worst was yet to come, though each dream Finn shared with me broke both our hearts until I paced, a fury growing beneath my skin at all the pain he'd suffered.

"Finn," I called.

He groaned, but didn't move.

"Honey," I said, softening my tone. "Please get up."

He lay face down, barely breathing, the darkness surrounding him a deep abyss that left me with little more than our bond to find him. And that bond was weak, pulsing with his pain as though he'd tried to sever it a thousand times and failed.

"I'm a monster."

"Sometimes," I agreed. His dark half took over from time to time, though it never seemed truly unwarranted. He'd destroyed entire wolf packs for forcing the change on people, killing to feed on human flesh, and enslaving humans in an attempt to breed. The memories cut like a thousand daggers, and yet he never hesitated to act. "People, of all kinds," I said, "can be corrupted. Sometimes it's better to end their madness before it spreads."

"Who am I to judge?"

I snorted. "As if a thousand less worthy don't judge every day."

"I don't want to make that decision."

"What if I help?"

"You shouldn't have that burden either."

His heart was far too soft for a fae king. "Honey," I said.

"I wish I could hold you."

"Me too. Can you make it to the next statue?" It was the final statue before Sebastian's, Felix's, and mine. An ending to the pain, or the final nail in our coffins?

"It's bad," he whispered. "I can sense it from here."

I smashed the barrier with my fists, but it was like standing in a bubble. "Fucking hell I need out of this shield. Don't suppose you can let me out?"

He rolled his head to the side to gaze my way, his face completely lost beneath the stretching veil of darkness. "Nothing's happening."

I sighed, glaring at the Hunt that paced ready to attack. What were they waiting for? "Honey, I need you to get to the next memory. I'm sorry you have to suffer like this."

Finn groaned and crawled, his form shifting and morphing like it was a bat creeping up a wall rather than the handsome young man I knew. A broken dragon, or something worse? He heaved himself across the ground until he lay at the base of the next statue of a woman whose gaze focused off into the distance. Her expression was oddly serene, not unlike Sebastian's.

"I wish I were as beautiful as my mom had been," Finn said. "You deserve that. A goddess of light and warmth."

"I'm not really into women, goddesses or otherwise. I guess you could say I'm drawn to the bad boys."

He laughed and it sounded like a cackle again, deep and echoing. "Bound to the worst then."

"Not true. You have light inside you."

"All I feel is pain, darkness, and hopelessness."

"It's okay, honey," I said. "It's almost over." The journey, our chance at a relationship, perhaps even the world, but I let him take his own meaning. The worst thing about being a seer was seeing things I couldn't change. I thought for a long time that I could stop the world from ending under the ooze of dark power, but each time I shifted the paths of those I could see, the direction of the end changed, but never slowed.

Fuck. Maybe this was all *my* fault. If I'd just left everything alone, would Finn have to suffer like this?

"No," Finn whispered.

"What?"

"I can feel you," he said. "It's not strong, but our link grows the closer I get. It's not your fault."

"You don't know that." While we'd never crossed paths, fate rippled like a pebble touching the water, a thousand tiny changes from one shift.

"Is it too soon, you think?" he asked.

"For what, honey?"

"To love you?"

I gasped and sank to my knees. "Finn..."

"It is too soon, right? But I feel it. My soul is begging to hold you. Like through all of this, you're the one thing that will calm my soul, ease the pain, and give me a touch of peace." He sucked in a large gulp of air. "Can't really see you anymore, everything is dark, shadowed." Frost grew in patches over his skin and I couldn't hold back my tears at how much it must hurt. "Not really," he said, "I'm sort of numb."

"If I could do this for you, I would," I told him.

"I know. You're sweet under all those thorns."

"Don't ruin my reputation."

He laughed, the sound half screech, half himself, which gave me hope there was enough left of him to make it through this nightmare.

"Your secret is safe with me."

Finn touched the base of the statue, and was swallowed up by the still structure. I closed my eyes, head bowed to the ground and sobbed as the memory awakened for him.

Fifty-Three

FINN

I paced outside a small house. The pack kept their distance, feeling my disquiet. I'd been cast from the room as I'd snapped at the nurses too many times. Cassa's omega energy calmed me enough to convince me to leave, but not further than outside.

"I should be with her," I told Odion who now lived as Oberon. He leaned against a tree more than two dozen yards away.

"If you weren't snarling at everyone, sure," Oberon agreed. "Can you go in there, see her in pain, and not bite everyone's head off?"

I couldn't, that's why I'd been kicked out. My wolf growled and snarled at everyone, possessive over the little omega I'd rescued more than a decade ago. A hundred alphas wandered through my pack, as we searched for her mate. I'd learned early on to keep my distance as I couldn't control the absolute nightmare I became when another alpha got close. And yet, she wasn't mine. Not fated at least, though in the end, she had chosen me.

Did she fear she'd never be free if she didn't? Or perhaps she feared the dark rage that could occasionally find a way out of my firm grasp of control?

"She must hate me," I said.

Oberon snorted. "She loves you."

"But she's not really mine."

"I think that's her choice."

If I'd left, perhaps she'd have found her true mate. Though I shuddered to think of the damaged alphas and broken wolves I'd leave behind. The darkest portions of me thought ending them might be kinder, though most had found quiet lives under my suppression of their monsters. Without me, they'd be unleashed on the world to create chaos. A burden I grew to hate more and more every day.

Now there was Cassa. The first whom my mortal soul, my wolf, and my beast agreed to let inside my heart. Love. What a complicated mess. I loved my pack, or at least the wolf did. I loved the wild ground I'd settled, the beast hidden inside my soul adored the forest's growth and madness of nature between subtle quiets. And my human side loved many, like Oberon, as family. But even the brother of my heart couldn't get close to Cassa without me snarling.

"I shouldn't have picked an omega," I grumbled. Three beings in one, yet a world of turmoil inside. Cassa soothed them all, as long as it was only her and me.

*O**beron laughed, a sound I rarely heard over the years. "You've never chosen the easy path, my friend. If you couldn't have a true mate, who would fit you better than an omega?"*

A baby cried, and I leapt to the porch, needing entrance. Oberon caught me, moving faster than any wolves should, but he wasn't any wolf. My monster snarled at him and I fought to tamp it down.

"Not until you're called," he said as he folded his arms across his chest and became a brick wall in front of the door. I could kill him if I shifted to my darkest form, but my human heart didn't want to destroy my brother. My wolf agreed with Oberon's protectiveness.

"I need to see her."

"Hmm," Oberon said.

Another ten lifetimes passed in the moments I paced waiting for approval to enter. The midwife spoke to Oberon and he stepped aside. I ran past him and into the small cabin set aside for the birth. Cassa sat up, holding a swaddled baby, her face tense with exhaustion, and the room smelled of blood and afterbirth, pain and sorrow. The last made my heart flip over. Had the baby passed? Cassa wanted it desperately, and I'd done everything I could to ensure her dream came true, even if that meant suppressing her wolf with my magic to keep the baby from being lost.

I tiptoed to her side and heard a racing heartbeat, not hers, the baby's. It lived. I sighed with relief as I sat down on the bed beside her. She opened her eyes to gaze watery eyes at me.

"Cassa, what's wrong?" I whispered, touching her carefully, fearing causing her more pain. Oberon ushered the midwife and her assistant out, whispering to them, though I couldn't hear what they said.

Cassa pulled the blanket back from the baby's face as he suckled her breast for food, and I recoiled as a ripple of dark magic briefly turned it from cute baby cheeks to a gaunt monster, not unlike my beast. I gasped and reached for him.

"No," Cassa said.

"He shouldn't be touched by the dark already."

"You were, and you're okay."

The darkness hadn't awakened in me until my mother had been murdered. Before that nightmare I'd been a glorious thing like my mother, filled with fire and light. How had it spread to the baby? My wolf breathed in the baby's scent, finding the musk of wolf strong, the curse already in his blood, but beneath the heavy aroma of the beast, something was missing. That couldn't be right.

"I need to hold him," I said, reaching for the baby again.

Cassa tightened her grip. "No."

"I won't hurt him, I promise."

Still she refused. I sat at her side as she nursed the baby, my heart hammering with worry. Oberon kept his distance, and once Cassa tired, he called for one of the packmates to come help with the baby. When Marina arrived, Cassa handed the baby off to her with strict instructions that I was not to be alone with the boy.

"That's not right, Cassa," Marina said. "The babe is his too, and he's Alpha."

I kept my distance, heartbroken by the accusations in Cassa's eyes, though I hadn't done anything other than sire the next monster. Perhaps that was enough to lose her love.

"It's all right," I said. "Cassa is just protective."

"What's his name?" Marina asked, gaze going from me to Cassa.

"Felix," Cassa answered. It was one of a handful we'd agreed on.

"Felix it is," Marina said as she rocked him. He slept and with it the touch of darkness with him buried itself deep. "Lucky, indeed. He's adorable."

Cassa curled up on her side, exhausted. I wanted desperately to hold her, but when I reached for her, she shook her head. "No."

My wolf whined inside my soul, the rejection nearly bringing me to my knees. "Cassa."

"Give her some time," Oberon said. He gently touched my shoulder, careful to not show aggression. "You can rest at my place. It's been a long day for all of us."

"Always the voice of reason," Marina said as she held Felix. "Let Cassa rest."

The effort it took to leave the cabin made my wolf howl. I knew if I changed in that moment, the darkness would rise. Would anything be left of the little pack of broken wolves I'd built?

"Xander," Oberon said.

"There's no human in that baby," I whispered, hands clenched at my sides as I followed him toward his home on our pack lands. Every step away crumbling more of my resolve to leave her with the baby. "No human soul, just a monster in human skin."

"He has a wolf soul. It will have to be enough."

"Can a wolf be taught to be human?"

Oberon met my gaze, his own too aware. "How often have you let the wolf have control?"

"Don't say that anywhere near the pack. You know I'm not a regular wolf."

"And Felix won't be either. We can teach him."

My wolf wasn't great at being human. It mimicked, and often I worried the lack of empathy he showed was because I gave him few examples. But my soul had three pieces, most wolves only had two. And none before now had ever had to suppress a beast made to thrive in the dark. "He's a baby. How will I teach him to hold back the monster?"

"You weren't a monster until your mother died," Oberon reminded me. "You could change, but the darkness didn't settle. Isn't that what you told me?"

But that wasn't what I saw in Felix's face. He wasn't the glorious dragon of my mother's lineage, rather he was touched by what ate my sire, and fought me for constant control. It was as though he'd taken the darkness I'd been drawing from the broken wolves. How was that possible?

"Fate is punishing me," I said, sinking into a chair on Oberon's porch and refusing to go inside and put another barrier between Cassa and me. Female werewolves never had children, the change made it too hard on their bodies. If Cassa had been a human untouched by the wolf taint in her blood, she might have had a child without me suppressing her wolf, but her omega would have lay dormant. "Or because I took Cassa as mine when she has a mate out there somewhere."

"I think that was her choice."

"If I'd turned her away?"

"How long do you expect your human heart to live without love?"

"I've lasted this long."

He sighed. "Xander..."

I knew he understood my loneliness like few other. His handful of chosen mates over the years lost as much as mine had been. But Oberon had always been more human than I. I was other *and without guidance, struggled to rein in the nightmare. How could I teach a baby control if I couldn't leash it myself?*

Fifty-Four

FINN

That the memory flashed forward to me in wolf form watching Felix as a toddler play at Cassa's feet, meant the bad part was yet to come. I swallowed and wished for Wesley at my side, but only felt the barest hint of him through the layers of numbing cold that made me shiver. This dream layered over me while I lay staring up at the statue without the ability to move my head, a faded remembrance rather than the detailed replay. Strange.

The feeling of the omega strength saturating the area where Felix played calmed us both, though I sat near a tree, still not allowed to get close. Cassa had cast me from her bed and her heart despite my endless promises to care for our broken child. Two years and the amount of omega strength she had to use to keep him subdued made my jaw clench. His wolf's hold was weak and fragile, but he was young.

Cassa promised over and over she'd take care of him, keep him in control. She researched endlessly, called elder pack members, witches, and any paranormal being we'd ever encountered for answers. Most were as stumped as she was. Whatever I was, which had partially passed to Felix, was a monster beyond anything of record.

I watched them play at the edge of the stream, Marina always close to help Cassa.

"He's growing so fast," Marina told me.

I nodded, though feared his wolf wouldn't gather strength fast enough to control the darkness. How Cassa kept Marina from seeing his monster was a mystery to me. But Oberon remained near to keep mine in check.

Cassa's gaze found me, accusation still in her eyes though I'd done nothing.

I sighed and got up, nodding at them before shifting to my human form and heading back to the main pack house to deal with whatever chaos the wolves brought me today. A hundred times I thought to leave and let Oberon care for the broken wolves, only the second I did, their darkness began to return. He could hold it back for a time, but he would have to destroy them eventually, and maybe it was my fault for letting them live and soak up more pain.

It didn't seem to be a guarantee of age in a wolf, as Oberon was untouched and a handful of other wolves remained mentally sound. Not proximity either as a few dominants lived among my pack with no glimpse of the beast taking them over. Why did the madness touch some and not others?

"I think we should shift the pack around. Move some of the broken ones to stable alphas," Oberon said as he followed. "It will ease the burden on you."

"But we don't know why it affects them or if it will spread to the other packs." Sometimes it did, causing an entire pack to go feral, which meant I had to destroy them all. "Could you wish possible destruction on any pack?"

"I trust a handful of alphas to take care of their people," Oberon said. "One wolf is not a heavy burden, even if it's broken. Leave it to the alpha to decide if they are too far gone. Why must it always weigh on your heart?"

The human heart was far too fragile. My wolf complained about it all the time. The beast could overwhelm it easily and I'd let myself fall into the control of the other just to ease the ache. "It should be me, shouldn't it? I'm the monster."

Oberon sighed. "Only by choice, my friend."

He wasn't wrong, but I couldn't burden anyone else with it either.

A scream echoed through the woods. I jolted into a run toward the noise, which was where we'd left Cassa. Oberon raced behind me, but the smell of blood and death reached my nose before I could exit the trees to the riverside and discover what had gone wrong. My heart pounded in fear that Cassa was hurt. A wall of doom encapsulated the area with oppression, darkness, and pain. The dark taint of magic stronger than I'd ever felt. Even my sire's cave before he died hadn't been the abyss of rage and agony this was.

But it was Marina who lay in a bloodied heap with Cassa's arms around her, protecting her with her body as the toddler Felix in a nightmare monster form snarled and clawed at her. I growled and launched myself at him, ready to kill the monster I should never have let be born.

Cassa threw herself between us, and I froze, unable to hurt her even while Felix tore into Marina's broken body giggling a terrible sound as though seeing more blood and broken skin with bone protruding made him happy.

"Cassa," I said. "Cassa, the boy is broken."

"He's mine," Cassa said. She unleashed her omega strength in a wall of calm so heavy I dropped to my knees unable to lift my head. Oberon did the same behind me, breathing heavily as if keeping upright at all were near impossible.

Felix calmed and shifted back to his toddler form, covered in blood, wide eyes staring at his mother. The wolf inside him disoriented, and I could sense it floundering for control.

Cassa wrapped her arms around him and the oppressive levels of darkness vanished. The wolf regained control and he sighed, and snuggled into her with a sweet sound of the baby he should have been.

"Cassa," I begged.

"No," she said, lifting him and walking away from us, her omega strength keeping us pinned to the ground. She vanished into the trees, leaving Marina's lifeless body, and us unable to move until she'd gotten too far away to hold her magic over us.

I stared at the empty gaze of one of my pack, horrified that I'd been unable to protect her until the omega magic vanished, and I could rise to reach her. She didn't deserve this. Marina had been one of our oldest female wolves. Never an alpha, but always protective and encouraging among the pack.

"I'll get a pyre set up," Oberon whispered.

"What do I tell the pack?"

"I don't know."

"I need to go after Cassa. Felix is dangerous."

"Could you hurt him?" Oberon asked. "He's your child, too. She's kept him from you, but your wolf adores him."

Marina's blood was still warm as I held her broken body. It would be a lie to say I didn't love Felix. He scared me, more than I scared myself, but I still loved him. He was mine as much as he was Cassa's. Two years and I'd been trying to help teach him control, and failing miserably. The wolf in him would play with the other wolves for hours without incident, and something would shift, and he'd snap at someone, drawing blood. Accidents, I thought, and Cassa pulled him away to soothe him with her omega power.

She pulled away from me because she didn't have the strength to soothe us both. Centuries I'd lived, and now relied on a single sweet omega to ensure my sanity. That said a lot of terrible things about me.

I lifted Marina and carried her toward our funeral spot, heart filled with grief. The beast wanted to break free, find Cassa and Felix, and end the nightmare. The wolf wanted to comfort his mate, and hold his pup. The human mourned. A war of three souls in one flimsy human skin.

Fifty-Five

FINN

Oberon built up the pyre. No one came. A dark wave of grief keeping them from leaving their homes. I didn't realize it was me until Oberon stopped moving, dropping to his knees, gaze turning my way.

"Let me finish," he said. "We need to set her free."

I swallowed hard, and walked her to the bed of the pyre, setting her down and leaving. It took every bit of my strength to walk away. The pack could not mourn her until I eased the oppression of my grief, but no matter how my human heart tried, the pain welled up over and over. Marina had been not only a pack mate, but a mother figure to many. Me included.

How was I to let all this go?

I stalked away from the fire, letting myself wander aimlessly into the woods. The land welcomed the release of the emotions, absorbing the grief with a spit of fire and a fizzle that left everything scorched.

How many more would I fail? Why did I keep building a pack and a family, only to lose them all?

The beast overwhelmed me for a time, and I opened my eyes to find myself on the edge of the bridge near the deepest part of the river. Felix ran about in his wolf form, alone. Which I found strange. Where was Cassa?

Smoke spiraled through the trees, more than Marina's funeral pyre. My pain having set the forest aflame, too. The beast slid away from my skin, leaving the mortal man, and Felix yipped at me, excited to see me. He raced around my feet, a rare glimpse of the child he could be when the wolf was in control. But my heart hammered as there was no sense of Cassa's omega strength to help him.

"What happened?" I asked as if the toddler could answer. His skin glowed, a pulse of magic running beneath it I'd never seen on him before. He ran to the water's edge and howled, gaze meeting mine. I dropped down at his side, running my hands over him, and finding his beast locked beneath a heavy layer of magic I couldn't explain.

"Where's momma?" I asked.

Felix turned back to human, the process faster than most full-grown wolves, but still taking a few minutes. His little toddler eyes filled with tears as he pointed toward his head and then the water.

"What?" Cassa was in the water? I hadn't seen any sign of her. I got up and leapt into the river, fearing she'd been caught by the current. Beneath the surface a glimpse of dark hair made me swim toward the bottom. My heart in my throat as I raced toward it.

Cassa's hair cascaded around her, arms floating free, gaze blank in death, expression peaceful. I screamed, air filling my lungs, and reached for her, needing to free her as though I could still save her. She didn't budge.

Darkness popped around my vision, the lack of air, and water filling my lungs threatening to add me to her grave. Strong arms yanked me from the water, dragging me to the surface. I struggled, but broke the surface, gasping for air, to find Oberon dragging me to shore.

"No!" I flailed. "Cassa is down there."

He dumped me unceremoniously on the shore, shoving me hard. "Stay there."

"Cassa..." I whispered my heart breaking.

He dove into the water and it felt like forever before he came up, Cassa in his arms, limp and lifeless. Felix curled up by my side, little face tucked against me, his wail sounding more like a wolf than a child.

Oberon carried Cassa to me. I reached for her, finding a heavy set of chains broken but linked around her waist. Oberon's hands were bloody, and he dropped down beside us, the scent of his grief wafting through the death.

"She's already gone," Oberon said as I tried to turn her over to free the water from her lungs. "Cold. Been gone awhile."

My mind spun with a thousand ideas and confusion, trying to make sense of anything. "What? How? Why?"

Oberon captured Felix's face and studied it. He gasped and looked back at Cassa. "Xander," he said after a moment.

"Help me," I begged him. How many times had I failed to save his lovers? Was this payback? I couldn't stop the wheels of time, but Cassa hadn't been at the end of hers. "Please."

"Xander," Oberon said, wrapping a firm arm around me. "She's gone. She did this to herself."

"No."

"Yes. It looks like a spell." He glanced at Felix. "To suppress the beast."

"No!" I ripped myself away from them, howling as the beast demanded control and my wolf screamed inside.

"It looks like some sort of sacrifice spell to control Felix's dark side, but I'll have to search her belongings to see if there are notes. She's gone."

I snarled and reached for the baby monster I'd created. Oberon put himself between us, the claws of my beast going into his gut. He grunted but didn't back down.

"*If you need my death to alleviate your grief, my brother, then so be it.*"

I screamed, fighting the beast and the wolf with the fragile remains of my broken human heart, demanding they not destroy my brother, too. Something splintered, a snap into darkness and I floated away into an icy dream of water, blood, and tears.

Fifty-Six

WESLEY

I felt Finn's soul splinter and realized that was the moment Finn, as I knew him, had been created. Darkness flooded the area with a dense layer of suffocating fog, and the Hunt attacked, leaping at Finn.

The bubble of protection around the tree shattered, as if the tearing of his soul released the last of his strength to protect the memories.

"No!" I screamed, finally free, I raced to Finn's side, but even I couldn't face the Hunt alone. The first icy beast tore into Finn's leg, dragging him backward, as he gasped but remained otherwise motionless. Broken, I realized, the heartbreak destroying his will to live. But he was mine, and nothing had ever been mine before. I wasn't ready to let him go yet.

I could count on one hand the times in my life I'd released my hold on the dark side of my Stag, a berserkers rage. "Get to the next statue, Finn!" I yelled.

The next was Sebastian's, which I realized hadn't been the Winter's curse as I thought, but the breaking of whatever spell Cassa had used to bind Felix's dark side. "You can do this. Honey, please, you have to." This quest through his past trauma was his and his alone. The choice his, to reunite the three pieces of his soul, or destroy himself in the process. I prayed he could do it, even if my heart ached at the thought of his agony.

I shifted to my Stag, and it towered over the Hunt, deadly horns at the ready. Blood filled my mouth, foam dripped pink as I leapt into their number spearing the first on my rack, the pain and blood adding to my rage. The monsters' focus swung my way, all snarling as the ice tried to grab hold of my feet.

Finn crawled toward the next statue, little more than a blob of dark ooze, bleeding, covered in ice crystals and emanating physical and emotional pain. He'd already suffered a hundred lifetimes of trauma.

I love you, Finn, I thought, hoping he'd hear. *I believe in you.* I set free the last grip on my blood curse. All witchborn had them, even if they presented in different ways. Mine turned to a raging monster nearly as large as the forest itself, antlers dripping blood and poison, as I speared the Hunt and they dug claws and teeth into my hide, finding it tough, but not impossible to tear.

I charged the Hunt, my antlers slashing through their bodies, sending shards of ice and blood spraying. One beast would crumble and another three would take its place. How were so many of these monsters left? Hadn't Spring taken them all? Or had the Winter witch been stealing more wolves?

The Hunt circled, unable to get past my antlers as Finn crept away. Their chilling howls vibrating through the forest, and ice slinking through the sanctuary, freezing everything it touched, solid. My hooves ached, the cold burning as it slid up my limbs. But I wouldn't stop.

Finn was *mine.*

The agonizingly slow crawl towards Sebastian's statue left a trail of blood behind Finn. The ice followed, using his fading energy to break through the glowing light of Summer's statue. The protective aura of Sebastian's control popped, sending magic in a rush that threatened to flatten me to the ground, but shoved the wolves back a few feet. The Hunt rushed me, one slipping beneath my hooves to attack Finn now that he had no barrier of protection. The beast tore into his thigh, dragging him backward as if to prevent him from reaching the next memory.

Finn howled in pain, too weak to fight back, and I snarled, sweeping my antlers in a huge arc to spear as many of the beasts that I could. I kicked another three, hitting them with my hooves, hard enough to cave skulls. But these beasts were long dead and kept coming.

Fuck.

Two more tore into my side, digging claws and teeth until they drew blood. I bucked, trying to throw them off, but they clung like the bloodsucking ticks they were.

Finn trembled, scrabbling for purchase to stop the beast from pulling him away. "Wesley," he whispered, his resolve hanging by a thread. But I fought at least three dozen wolves and was losing terribly.

Another wolf lunged at my flank, teeth bared and ice shards crackling as it moved. I twisted, driving an antler through its chest. It howled, but refused to die, its blood showering down over me in a frozen rain of blinding red. A beast snapped at my legs, claws raking deep gouges into my hide. Relentless fury drowned out the pain as I thrashed and fought, my vision completely red and focused on nothing but a need for blood and their death.

I bled. Finn bled. I could smell it pouring from him.

The shadow wolf burst from the gloominess, a ghostly reflection of Finn himself, its spectral form gleaming with an eerie light, dripping darkness and flashing from wolf to dragon and back, as though it couldn't control the transition.

The wolf launched itself into the fight, jaws snapping, tearing into the Hunt with a savagery matching Finn's nightmare beast more than any wolf. It shared a soul with the monster for a long time, understood its fury. I echoed that rage on any beast that dove for Finn.

Fifty-Seven

FINN

My wolf leapt into the fray taking a half second to pummel my numb and cold body into the air. A few seconds of weightlessness slowed time to the unfolding chaos of the distant battle of Wesley becoming some sort of giant Stag, with glowing red eyes, and dripping red foam. Reality slammed me into the base of the next statue—the Summer king.

His figure loomed over me, unmoving. His presence, a crushing weight of judgment to pierce through me. I had failed him. My first vision had been Felix's attack, but Wesley interrupted it.

I knew the Summer king lived, but how many times had I let him down? How much more would this memory show?

Fear gripped me, tightening like an icy vise around my throat, but I reached to touch the statue anyway, fingers trembling. I prayed for strength, salvation, or perhaps for the Summer king's mercy. If I could awaken him and he could see the battle ravaging our world, maybe he could help. Or at least save Wesley from the nightmare I was becoming.

The darkness came first, creeping over me like a lover's caress, wrapping me in a suffocating embrace. The numbing cold coated my body while my mind turned molten and unstable. Rage—an unfathomable, primal fury—surged through me. A thousand times worse than when my mother died, or I'd lost a dozen loved ones to the wolf curse. This anger felt alien, as if a demon had slipped into my skin, digging for control and demanding to consume everything in its path.

I clung to the only thing that could keep me tethered—Wesley, the pulse of his life force echoed through the storm of emotions, a small sliver of light, flickering like a candle's flame against the black. His glow drew me like a moth to fire, fearing the burn, but needing the guidance.

The rage that had threatened to devour me retreated, smothered by an unexpected warmth. I opened my eyes, hoping for a path back to the present, but finding myself in another unfurling past. Curled beside me, was a baby fox, its bright red fur vivid and soft, delicate and yet filled with an incredible well of magic. Warmth radiated in gentle waves, soothing and sweet. I sucked in air, struggling to stay awake, the wolf at ease from the touch. The dragon, a demon who grew from every ounce of added pain, vanished. The heartache seeped away and I could breathe.

Magic lapped at my soul like a gentle tide, washing away the grief, rage, pain, and the madness that had twisted inside me for so long. Peace swept through me to extinguish the warring will of the dragon—the demon of flame and fury that had plagued me as if a thorn were still buried in its paw a thousand years after its awakening. The magic soothed it into slumber and the monster vanished into the shadows, leaving the gentle warmth of the fox. A peace I hadn't felt in a lifetime.

My soul ached, throbbing with a new kind of pain—a sense of loss. Something severed. A wound gaped within my heart and soul. Torn. I remembered, the wolf had broken us apart, my pain overwhelming his instinct. He tried to make us stronger, but failed miserably. The baby's presence eased the worst of the pain and the wolf understood he'd made a mistake. Weakened us with his need to protect, and now the dark had begun to take over. This baby quieted the nightmare to a dull shadow of what it had been. Had the wolf known this would be the Summer king?

No. He thought only of protecting what was his. His control, his family, and his pack. Was this small, fragile magical being, the key to everything? To Felix's insanity and perhaps to healing the darkness inside me? The wolf's thoughts bled into mine, and together we wondered—had we severed ourselves too soon?

Another omega. The realization crashed into me, brutal and unforgiving. We had already failed once. Fuck.

Mine. The wolf snarled, his possessiveness snapping through our connection. Rage giving him back control as he stared at Oberon. He stood in the doorway watching, ever the silent sentinel, strong as the wolf had always wished to be.

"He's not yours," Oberon said, his voice calm but firm.

Mine. The wolf's snarl tore through my mind, a vicious growl that reverberated through my chest. I snarled too, feeling the raw need to protect. The fox stirred beside me, the fragile peace fracturing, and before I could soothe him, he shifted. In the blink of an eye, the fox was gone, replaced by a mortal child. His soulful brown eyes blinked up at me, wide with fear and confusion, his red hair a shock of color like the drying blood I'd soaked in for centuries. Was he meant to be a reminder for all the times I'd lost control?

The child's wail pierced the air, a sound so full of fear and heartbreak. My wolf shuddered, uncertain what to do, wolf cubs didn't wail like this and my human half had always taken over before. Only now I couldn't.

The wolf shifted into a human form, and lifted the child, cradling him to his chest, looking stiff and uncomfortable, and making small sounds he recalled from the human form. "Change back now, cub," the wolf pleaded. It would be easier to raise a fox than a human. But the boy clung to the wolf, tiny fingers tangling in the hair of the wolf's human form, unkempt as it was from locking the mortal half of his soul away.

"I feel a pull to the north," Oberon said, "when I hold him. He has a mate. We need to find them."

"No," the wolf snapped.

Oberon sighed, the frustration heavy in his tone. "Xander, I can't help you if you don't let me. Don't curse this child with your destruction."

"I raised Felix," I growled. "He's fine."

"He's not." Oberon's words cut deep. "Cassa's spell holds his dark side for now, but it's weakening. Let me find a pack matriarch to care for Sebastian while we search for his mate."

Sebastian. The name felt foreign on my tongue, but it belonged to the small child in my arms. The Summer king? My mind reeled, and I wondered if the wolf had known. If he had sensed the magic, the power coiled inside this tiny being. Power beyond comprehension, and yet the wolf cared only for the peace it brought—the calm that kept the darkness at bay. I dropped back down into the chair, clinging to the baby as if it were a life raft rather than a child. Before the fox child had been presented to us, the wolf rampaged through the camp twice, destroying any who got in his way.

Only Oberon still faced him. The wolf recognized his brother and fought his way free of the dark before he could destroy what was left of his family. And now there was this baby. Filled with magic and power beyond what we'd ever experienced.

"Can you tell me where your human half is?" Oberon asked carefully, voice barely above a whisper.

We glared at him, daring him to utter the words where others could hear and we'd be forced to end him. "You know not what you speak."

But Oberon knew. "You are part of one soul. A sundered soul is unstable. You have buried the human part of your soul so deep he is suffocating. If he dies, you die. Don't you understand?"

"Silence. He is weak." The wolf snarled at him, causing the

baby to cry again. "Shhh, cub, all is well," Xander whispered to the baby.

Oberon remained frozen in the doorway, his knees buckling under the weight of the Alpha's command as he sank to the ground. Sweat dripped down his brow, his fists clenched so tight his knuckles turned white. He fought it—fought with everything he had—but the magic rooted him in place, rendering him silent.

The wolf rose from the chair, eyes cold and unreadable, and began packing a bag with methodical precision. Oberon's glare could have killed him a thousand times over, but the wolf didn't even flinch.

"I will leave the pack and train the cub."

Oberon growled, unable to speak, the Alpha's command locking his voice deep within his chest. The room thrummed with energy; the magic so thick it almost hummed in the air. The baby reached for it, as if he could still the storm with a mere touch, giggling and cooing at the waves of color he wrapped around his fingers.

The wolf stepped closer, eyes flashing. "You will not tell anyone what you know." His voice was ice, the threat clear as he brushed past Oberon, the baby held protectively against him. "I will teach him to use his magic. I will master the darkness. And if you follow me, I swear by the blood we share, I will end our brotherhood with my claws."

Oberon struggled, every muscle screaming against the magic that bound him. But the wolf didn't wait. He slipped into the shadows of the forest, disappearing into the night with the cub in his arms.

And with him, the last of his humanity vanished.

Fifty-Eight

FINN

"You're the weak one," I growled through clenched teeth, feeling the wolf thrash inside me, clawing against the magic that wanted to pull us back together. The bond frayed and snapped as we neared each other again, but I refused to let him in. "You couldn't survive without the help of a child to suppress the dark, while I held it back for centuries—alone."

He howled and the world around us blurred, hurling us into the memory—the fight. Felix's curse shattered, unleashing the beast within him, twisted by the dark. The wolf's plan had been madness —bind Sebastian to gain control of the darkness—and it backfired. The light had seared him, rejecting what he'd become without his human side.

Oberon had saved the boy, pulling him from the fight, but it wasn't enough. I could still feel the wolf's anger as he watched Oberon cradle the baby, stealing away what the wolf could never claim. Felix had fled, the spell meant to contain his madness shattered, leaving destruction in its wake.

"We should have killed him," I said. Thinking of the nightmare

Felix was. Nothing good could come from the darkness in human form. "How many terrible things could we have prevented?" Sometimes we had to be the bad guy. Hadn't Wesley said something like that? "Sebastian wasn't ours."

"Protect omega," the wolf demanded.

"You failed at that too," I said. Was he hearing me at all, or still living in the past?

"That's the plan. Follow or don't," Oberon had said, his grip on Sebastian tight. He hadn't known the wolf had bound the child to save him from the consuming dark. Nor did he sense Winter's claws, creeping deeper into his soul. But I could see both now, woven as intricate and ever-growing layers within the fabric of the living.

The wolf watched him go, brother of his heart, and the child he wished had been his. He turned and stalked off into the woods away from the pack, and the harm he would cause them all if he returned broken once again. And once they were out of sight, we ran. We ran north, far from Sebastian's bonded mate, though deep down the wolf knew we should have found him. Coward.

The world blurred again, trees flashing past as we ran, and I realized the wolf wasn't running to anything—he was running from himself. Days passed in a fevered haze, his breath ragged and shallow. Sometimes he lay down, barely breathing, as if willing himself to fade. But the darkness never left. We were dying—soul torn, festering, weakening his hold over the monster and over me.

"We're weak," he growled one night, curled in the shadows of an unknown forest far from the pull of the witchblood cub. I could feel the magic boiling inside, a storm waiting to be unleashed, but the wolf held it back. If he let it loose here, the death toll would be staggering. Mortals would fall like leaves in the wind, torn apart just as our families had been. The human soul within him grieved, longing for freedom, but refusing to let more innocent blood spill.

"Weak," the wolf spat the word again, gathering the magic that pulsed inside us. He centered his human soul, the one thing that kept him tethered to reason.

"You sent me away," I whispered. "Wesley thought it was mercy—giving me a chance at life without pain. But the darkness followed." It had never been about saving me, but saving himself. Keeping me alive so he could survive. I'd been sick as a child because he'd siphoned my strength, my life force. Stolen years from me to save himself. "You're the weak one. Before the wolf curse entered my blood, I was a beautiful terror. Like my mother. I could be a god and a demon. It all fell apart when that curse curdled its way inside my soul to create you. And I've had enough," I snarled, hatred bubbling in my veins.

The world around us shifted once more, the forest fading as we stood in a place between realms. The wolf stood before me, bleeding, eyes wild, and for the first time, I saw the pain in him, the exhaustion. We were both tired—broken. Beyond us, the real world raged, and I knew Wesley was still out there, fighting—needing me.

Neither of us asked for this. But the more we fought each other, the less strength we had to control the dark.

"This has to end," I said, heart pounding. "This hatred between us, the failures, the lies. We're both too weak to keep fighting like this. You used Sebastian—not just to suppress yourself, but to hide from Felix. You've avoided what needed to be done. Felix should have been stopped by our hands. He was our creation, and we let him loose. You subjected that child to his madness." The threads of Sebastian's fate fell into place in my mind, memories unlocked with the statue's pain as the wolf recalled a thousand small things gone wrong and failures to protect the little omega.

The wolf's eyes flickered, the fight draining out of him.

"Weak," he whispered, so softly I almost didn't hear it—but I did. Not just me—*we*.

"If Wesley dies because of you, I'll make sure we go down with him. A final end—for both of us. Do you understand?" My voice was hard, steel in every word. The memory began to shatter around us, pulling us back into the present. The wolf turned his head, blood dripping from a hundred wounds, and huffed— acknowledging the truth. Fighting each other was like fighting a reflection, useless and energy consuming.

The real world snapped back into place, time resuming its normal pace. Barely seconds had passed, and yet everything had changed. Wesley was still out there, fighting for his life.

"Please be okay," I begged as the cold and dark slid over me like slugs eager to suffocate the last dregs of my mortal life. Ice etched its way through my veins in a thousand shards of broken glass rising with each heartbeat. I prayed for numbness, but found only pain. "I'm trying to fix this. Please wait for me." I opened my mouth and screamed as the curse burrowed through to my core.

Fifty-Nine

The zombie Hunt, damaged and dripping guts and ooze, rose time and again, the number overwhelming. I blanked out for a few seconds, red covering my vision as the pure insanity of the berserker madness took over. The overwhelming need for blood roared through my mind, taking hold as I drove my horns through any who got near.

Finn's scream jerked me out of the blood rage, a dozen Hunt stomped beneath my hooves. Two dozen more Hunt tore into the wolf, dragging it away, slashing into it until it bled a ghostly mix of blood, black ooze, and ice.

We were losing. Finn lay at the base of Sebastian's statue, unmoving, little more than a splotch of dark shadow creeping between glowing mushrooms and dying flowers. Ice crystalizing the entire sanctuary floor in deadly jutting shards.

I bucked, smashing Hunt beasts away, crushing skulls, ribs, and breaking bones with every hit, then leapt to save the wolf. The nightmare waves of Winter's curse flowed over him, freezing him back into stone, inch by painful inch. Not unlike where we'd first begun with the former werewolf king locked in ice, a battery to slowly drain for Winter's gain.

Finn reached his fingers toward the last statue, Felix the monster, as if he could spay the distance with pure desire instead of strength. The Hunt crashed into me, the wave of ice cresting over my head, shards piercing my flank. The wolf yelped, its breathing labored as the ice overtook it, its magic yanked away to feed the heartless bitch of Winter's curse. The Hunt's fangs tore through my hide, blood splattered in the last gasp of warmth as I stumbled. Darkness closed in, my vision blurred, pain overwhelming. The world narrowed to the sound of Finn's labored breathing and fading heartbeat as I tried to force myself up.

Could he get to the next one on his own? The ice crackled as if something deep beneath the sanctuary stirred to life, a deep, and unsettling sensation shifting in the air. The last of the barriers fell and a cord snapped in the pit of my chest. The pulse of dark magic, ancient and hungry, rippled through the space. The wolf's energy vanished as it froze solid. The last of the barriers snapped as if reaching Sebastian's tree unlocked the final memories. The dark ice shards around Felix's statue jolted to life, instantly growing in size and sending splinters of piercing magic tearing across the sanctuary.

The shadows poured into Finn with a violent force, twisting his body, reshaping it. The glow from the mushrooms dimmed, and the entire sanctuary trembled and shook as though ready to fall into ruin.

Oozing shadows crawled up my hooves, spreading cold needles of pain. I staggered; my breath ragged. I sucked in icy air, gaze locked on the goo that had been Finn, which bubbled and froze and bubbled and froze, cracking as if boiling one second then freezing the next.

A cackle erupted from the mess like something out of a nightmare as I struggled to breathe. It gurgled and grew louder as the dark mass rose, the shape something out of a book of demons. It resonated with the ancient darkness that had infected him. The blackness rising, as it reabsorbed the pieces stolen by

Felix to split off another monster, becoming one inescapable nightmare.

Finn became the monster.

The icy air burned my lungs as I sucked in a last gasp of breath, the chill creeping up to my face, one eye already lost to darkness, the other fading. The acrid scent of decay filled my nostrils. The sound of cracking ice echoed in my ears, as if the very world was fracturing around me. The end of everything, I thought briefly. The vision had been both right and wrong all at once—this was the end, unstoppable as the darkness spread, but the darkness was Finn, and I would simply not live through it. Nor did I think the Finn I knew would either.

The terrifying sound of unhinged laughter boomed through the sanctuary, shaking the ground with an explosion of rage, heat, and shadows. I tried to scream, but locked in the black, I couldn't gather a breath. Ice knives cut into me, every fiber of my being screaming to run, to escape the consuming darkness that was once Finn. But how could I abandon him? How could I live with myself if I didn't try to save him, even if it meant losing everything?

The Hunt leapt at him, trying to overwhelm the new creature, but it swatted them away as if they were mere flies. Each blow sent splatters of icy ooze flying in every direction, only for the curse to reassemble and lunge again, desperate to reclaim what it had unleashed. The dark beast that Finn had become stretched to its full height, towering over me, its form shifting and dripping with unnatural movement. Its eyes burned with cold fire, a soul-shattering void behind them. This was no longer a battle of wills. It was survival.

And we were losing.

The darkness that was Finn sucked down all of the Hunt, one by one, to feed his endless hunger. The more he devoured, the faster the darkness spread.

I gasped, unable to breathe, my heart breaking as I stared at the monster set free. The dark mass that had been Finn twisted and contorted, a grotesque mockery of his former self. Within the shadows, I glimpsed flickers of amber eyes—the same eyes that once looked at me with love, now clouded with madness. The beast roared, a sound that tore through the fabric of reality, and I knew that Finn was losing his battle. He reached for the wolf, still frozen and immobile beneath Winter's curse, and I wanted to scream, fearing it would be the end of Finn if he devoured the wolf too.

Something sharp dug into my side, and I had a half second to fear Finn's beast was on me, but I was ripped free of the darkness and pain, and jolted into a light-filled room painted with the scent of wildflowers and lavender.

Sunlight blazed through the windows, heat blistering against the cold that latched onto me. My Stag form slipped away as I bled the last of my energy. Sebastian leaned over me, the little Winter at his side, looking distraught. I opened my mouth, sucked in air, and screamed, "Finn!"

Sixty

WESLEY

"Send me back!" I demanded, heart sluggish, body aching with the slash of a thousand needles.

Tears slid down Sebastian's cheeks. "He's lost."

"He isn't! Send me back."

"We barely got you out," Sebastian said. "The darkness has overtaken everything. Autumn's realm is overrun with sorrow and rage. Kiran and I have had to shut off our realms to keep him from spreading."

"No," I said. "That was Winter. She devoured everything." My vision, having experienced it a hundred times, I'd always thought it was Winter's curse, but Autumn and Winter's magic slid adjacent to each other.

"He's fighting Winter," Xiao whispered. "Devouring her spell for fuel to spread his pain. She's losing, but so is he."

I reached for him. "Help me. What would you do if it were Ari?"

Xiao's eyes filled with sadness. "I wouldn't put you back there even if I could. He'll consume you."

No. I wouldn't let them steal him from me. "Sebastian Volkov, put me back. He's your *apa*, right? Don't you want me to save him?" I glared at the Summer king.

"You don't know that he can be saved!"

"How many times have you told me, when I promised to serve you, that you'd respect my choices?"

"To die? You want me to let you die?" Sebastian demanded.

"You don't know that. He's my mate. I'm meant to be with him. What would you do if it were Liam?"

"That's not fair, Wesley."

"Fair? When is life ever fair?" I snarled and shoved him away from me. Sebastian caught himself, but stepped away from the bed. "Mine has never been fair. Not when I was cast out for being witchborn. Not when I was given to Zephyr with the command to submit or die. Not when the Winter witch bound me at her feet to drain me."

"Finn is mine. I don't want to serve you or anyone anymore. I'm so tired of the constant pain. Why can't I have the one thing that's mine?"

"He'll destroy you and not remember," Sebastian whispered. "I don't want you to die."

"Why? Why does it matter? You don't like me. No one does. I made sure of it, kept my heart locked away and stayed away from everyone."

"To protect yourself," Sebastian nodded. "I understand, but do you?"

"More than anyone ever will," I said, with a tired sigh. "Finn... he's sweet and strong, but no one should face that sort of darkness on their own. I'd rather stand by his side than cower, waiting for the beast to overwhelm all of us until there is no other choice left but to end him." I glared at Sebastian. "I want to at least try to save him."

"At the cost of your own life?"

I shrugged. "Fate is a bitch, bring it on."

Xiao paced several feet away, wringing his hands, his gaze on the door as if wishing Ari were there. Ice crystals formed in his hair like elaborate snowflakes in giant detail. A stress response or was the old Winter witch finally losing?

"I can't send you back," Seb said. "I can't breach his realm. Let me talk to Liam and see if he has any ideas to help."

"Can Ari get me in?" I asked Xiao.

He flinched. "Ari shouldn't touch Autumn's realm right now. It might infect them with this darkness."

Fuck. None of us needed the witchchild going mad.

"Let me talk to Liam," Sebastian said. "Maybe we can find a way to get you in and provide a shield? I don't want you to die if we can't save *apa*."

But I'd wanted that for years, until I met Finn and had his sweet smile directed at me, his arms around me, and his gentle kisses peppering my face. I watched Sebastian turn away from me, fists clenched, his grief over losing his adoptive father palpable. But I wasn't ready to give up on Finn yet.

I grabbed the bottle off the side table. The potion Toby had given me to help reconnect with Finn—my last hope. I uncapped it, the potent scent of the alcohol wafting up like a final warning. Sebastian turned as I brought it to my lips.

"Don't, Wesley," Seb began.

But I tipped it back, drinking down the entire bottle at once. The liquid seared down my throat, setting my veins on fire. Too much, my senses screamed. The world tilted; the light dimmed as the darkness yanked me back to where I belonged. I felt like I was falling, a sudden drop out of myself in a gut-wrenching rush.

A voice whispered in the darkness, familiar and haunting. Finn calling my name. I let his power catch me, and floated for a brief moment in weightlessness. Then the drain began, my power leeching away. The suction of my magic and life force jolting from me happened so fast I screamed, though the sound was lost in the void of blackness around us. The chill in the air, cool, but not icy, I ached to see Finn one last time.

I wouldn't fight him, or the end. If he was lost to me, then I hoped to join him in whatever beyond for a final taste of peace. The blackness rose like a viper to attack, and then, there was nothing.

Sixty-One

FINN

Darkness slid over me—thick, suffocating, and endless. I gasped for air, clawing at the void that swallowed me whole. My mind, splintered by memories that flashed like shards of glass, each one cutting deeper than the last, screamed as if a thousand nerves bled the agony of the past. Every failure, every loss, amplified, dragging me further into the abyss, as if there was no light to be found.

I raged as the monster, cycling between hot and cold, screaming into the emptiness without sound. The crushing weight of sadness threatened to shred my soul. Faces, fleeting and twisted by my guilt—a thousand lives I'd destroyed, leaving nothing but more weeping wounds of soul deep pain.

I snarled, raging as though somehow it could stop the assault. The icy bite of Winter dug her talons into me, tearing the wolf back into the dark each time it reached for me, leaving only the beast and I, helpless to find control. Her curse weakened us. The Autumn realm, dying around me, consumed by the blackness that was me, and yet not.

My father had lost himself to the dark. I never understood why. Then my mother died, and he passed as though the last breath of light had vanished from his soul. This nightmare took over, and devoured him from the inside out.

Help me, I begged, uncertain who I was even asking, heart breaking in loneliness and fear. I hated being alone. The beast wallowed in the sadness of isolation. Memories fit into place inside my mind, dozens of lifetimes of trying to find light, family, and love, each loss tearing down the boundaries between the monster inside and me. I'd been unable to find the beautiful creature my mother's side gifted me after her death. A lack of control? A curse of the dark? Or something else?

I caught a glimpse of Wesley, a snapshot picture of him staring at me with his head tilted, curiosity and irritation on his face. One of the first moments after we'd met. I longed to stare at the brightness of his face, and his glowing gold aura, which illuminated him like a halo. He'd have snapped that he was no angel, but he was my light.

I gasped as the darkness paused for a half second. I realized a thousand things at once. My father died because my mother had. Her light had been all that held him to the living world.

Wesley! My soul screamed for him, though I caught no more than a glimpse of a dozen other memories of him. They tumbled over one another, a chaotic tide pulling me under. I saw Wesley again, his eyes full of fear and sorrow as he called my name. I couldn't reach him. Each time I reached for another image of him it shattered to dust, slipping through my fingers, sucked away from me by the biting cold.

Unworthy. Weak. Not the wolf's words this time, but the Winter witch who infected us with self-doubt. She suctioned away my control and any glimpses of joy we'd clung to of the past. The wolf and I snarled and snapped, enraged by the witch stealing him from me and let loose a wave of what could only be described as *death*, as it felt like the end of everything. A cascade of power, rage, and pain blasted everything I touched. Without Wesley there to temper me, I let it all go. The endless rage that the wolf had been trying to lock in the dark, the wild chaos of magic that blazed beneath our skin, and the suffocating pain of failing over and over. We were weak, but I'd take experiencing love over being *strong* any day. We poured it all into her, using her words echoing in our minds as the link to drive the darkness into her core. She wanted the monster? So be it.

She screamed, the darkness overwhelming even her fading shrieks as her hold on us burst, and she vanished with a pop. Escaped or dead, I wondered? Not that it mattered as the darkness slid back into place, the third part of our broken soul, reuniting.

The cold slipped away even as the darkness whispered, its voice seductive and cruel, demanding the spread of the soul suctioning ooze to end everything. It offered a dark quiet place to rest, and tried to hide the aching loneliness that lingered there, impenetrable by any light.

The beast roared its insatiable hunger. Fury boundless. It wanted to consume, to destroy, and I was powerless to stop it. The wolf, free of Winter's curse, but weak, exhausted, and heartbroken, wrapped itself around the mortal half of my soul. It, too, had lived a dozen lives of lost loves, families, and darkness. How easy would it be to give ourselves to the pain and let the beast free, sinking into rest as it rained terror on the world.

We were weak because we were divided. Did he understand? Even the monster would die if any part of us faded. The wolf sank into my touch, heartbeat sluggish, mind shattered as the sadness overwhelmed us both. We needed family, pack, and love, while we were also pure destruction. The monster had grown over the decades to an insane weight of magical darkness, reabsorbing what it lost from Felix's birth and destruction and now offered the end of everything as it shoved the wolf and I apart. Hadn't that been what Wesley's dream predicted? Not Winter as he'd thought, but me, us. The wolf, the beast, and I were the obliteration of life. Separated, none of us were strong enough to suppress the demon.

Wesley. My heart ached, as I felt my mortal soul stuttering its last breath under the weight of the darkness. I floated untethered, searching for the wolf, but drowning in the black.

I'm sorry I wasn't strong enough. I'm not worthy of you. Or any love really, that's why it was always ripped away. Ever since I'd lost my mother I'd been cursed because I was weak. Too weak to save her, too dark to save my father, too broken to save Cassa, or Felix, or even Sebastian. The memories of him and how my wolf had tried and failed added to the weight of my guilt. Fuck, how worthless was I?

Finn...

The thought was so faint, I wasn't certain I heard it or if it been a wishful dream.

Honey...

I gasped, my heart lurching to pump when I only wanted to end the pain.

Don't leave me.

Wesley?

Everything is really dark. Can you find me?

I'm not worthy of you.

You are, honey. Please, find me.

A flicker, faint and distant, burst to life like a tiny candle flame lit in the depths of the darkest cave. I latched onto the glimmer of hope, pulling myself toward it with desperation. The light intensified, cutting through the darkness like a blade. It was warm and familiar as I drew closer. But it burned.

Too hot. I flinched, hesitating in the dark with the barest touch of the brightness against my skin blistering as though it burned like a furnace.

Honey?

I trembled, crawling a few more inches toward the light, mind screaming as it burned away the dark. I had to stop again, the pain too much.

It's okay, honey.

Wesley. I clung to the memory of him with every last ounce of strength I had. *It hurts.* The pain blacked out the clarity for a few seconds as the beast forced me to retreat back into the dark.

Love, Wesley whispered, his voice faint. *Don't go.*

The beast snarled and fought, dragging me back into the dark, its rage clawing at my sanity. Common sense would have the wolf and I hiding in the dark to ease the pain, but that's what the beast wanted. It thrived in the dark, demanded control.

No. I growled at it, forcing myself to inch toward the light again. The beast basked in pain, grew in strength as the darkness overrode everything. I hated it.

It's part of you, my mind reminded me. I'd been born with this nightmare. *Witchborn.*

It's only as dark as you let it be. Wesley whispered. But there was nothing but darkness. How could he see anything beyond it?

Please, help me. I thought, the word a cry from the depths of my soul.

I'm right here, waiting for you.

Tired. I desperately wanted to hold him, bask in his strength, but feared he'd be ripped from me as well.

I'm no damsel to be saved, Finn. You saw what I could become.

The shift to his Stag during the battle echoed in my memory, a rage I'd never expected from the majestic beast, and yet he'd grown as large as the forest, his hooves and antlers deadly.

You are so fucking beautiful. I thought, hoping Wesley would catch it.

Then why are you hiding in the dark?

Because the light hurt.

Why are you letting the past keep us apart?

I stared at the light, so close, and yet so far away.

Wesley.

Yes, honey. I'm right here.

I'm not perfect.

I could sense his snort. *No kidding.*

Was it still okay to love him?

Yes.

I crept forward, my beast raging, the wolf and I finding a rare moment of commonality as we both knew what lay beyond that glow and the pain. Love. Family. Hope.

Please. I begged, needing him like I needed air.

Waiting for you. Remember who the final boss is.

Me. It had always been me. Torn into three parts of one soul, all battling for one mundane life force.

Stronger together. Wesley reminded me.

Even if that means embracing the monster?

We can all be monsters sometimes.

The wolf and I crept into the light though it blistered our flesh. I understood as the wolf did. We sank our souls together, resealing the tear. It ached from the scar left behind, but having him wrapped around me added to our strength. The beast fought us, refusing to slide into the last gaping hole between the wolf and me.

The wolf shared a thousand memories of his years alone with the dark, and I gave him the time as a mortal, not all bright, but filled with bits of love and friendship. The beast seemed to hesitate inside, observing perhaps, learning. The wolf and I settled into each other, the force of our will expanding tenfold as we crawled toward the light, hoping for a chance to bask in Wesley's brightness.

Mate. The wolf said. *Wesley.* I agreed. *We're coming.*

Sixty-Two

WESLEY

My heart beat slowly, the potion yanking me into the shadows multiple times until I wasn't certain I could climb out again. But Finn's desperation settled into my soul, our bond fragile and stretching into the darkness as I blinked open my eyes to a shimmering barrier dome surrounding me. Light illuminated the space overhead, blazing bright, but gentle and warm.

I reached up and my hand hit the barrier, snapping and fizzling with magic to keep me in. Outside the barrier the darkness pooled in an oppressive swirling ooze, wavering shadows dancing inches from the end of the ray of light, as though waiting for it to fade and the magic shield to break. The world beyond the light, nothing but a void of inky darkness, as if nothing remained of the Autumn realm but where I lay protected by some delicate energy.

Finn?

Our tie surged for a half second, his mind grasping for mine, then he'd vanish in a wave of madness for a few seconds, images flashing through our bond of all his terrible memories. I turned onto my side, unable to sit up in the small space, and stared in the direction I thought he might be, though the overwhelming blackness curled in on every side.

Honey? Could he hear me at all?

Wesley...

His voice was weak and distant, pain lacing the words, and I caught a thousand underlying whispers that sounded like him, only not. *Worthless. Unworthy. Useless. Monster.*

Was that the darkness? Was Finn already gone—lost and twisted by his monster until there was nothing of his delicate heart that remained?

It's okay, honey. I thought, hoping he heard me. Time curled around me, and I half dozed until I caught a glimpse of something moving in the dark, creeping its way toward the light. Was it Finn?

The thing was massive, a beast draped in darkness, its form twisting and warping as it struggled to maintain its shape. My stomach knotted as I recognized the dragon-like beast that Finn had become, dripping with ooze, shifting into something gaunt and bat-like, then back to the wolf. The more it touched the light, the more it howled. But I couldn't look away. This was still Finn— somewhere inside that monstrous form was the man I loved.

I closed my eyes and when I opened them again, some time had passed and the beast had vanished into the swirling shadows again. *Finn?*

Our bond stretched thin and near the point of snapping. The beast drained my strength despite the strong barrier around me. I glared up into the light like it was some link to beyond, angry that the fates hadn't chosen a stronger mate for Finn.

Love, don't go. I begged, staring at the fading movement of darkness.

The beast reappeared; glowing eyes fixed on me. It recoiled from the light as though the brightness was too much to bear. Finn's broken thoughts left me with a handful of words, self-deprecation, and sadness. He blamed himself for not being strong enough and letting the dark rule. But there was so much brightness inside him, hidden in layers of protective magic as though he feared letting any of it free would cause him more pain.

It's only as dark as you let it be. I told him, trying to give him glimpses of happy moments in his past. His mortal life had been filled with them, and the entire reason the wolf had split them. The wolf knew to save them both, he'd have to give them something to cling to.

I tried to stir memories of his moms and his friends, what little I knew of them so far, but our link faltered.

Please, help me. His whisper nearly lost in the rage of the beast.

If I couldn't share bright memories, I'd have to become one. *I'm right here, waiting for you.*

Tired.

I got the impression that he thought he needed to save me, and it made me mad. *I'm no damsel to be saved, Finn. You saw what I could become.*

You are so fucking beautiful.

Then why are you hiding in the dark? The beast crept forward and then roared, smoke rising from its skin, but beneath, as the ooze blistered away, was mortal flesh. Finn inside, fighting for freedom. I understood, though I hated it. He sank into the dark and used the beast as a shield.

Why are you letting the past keep us apart?

Wesley.

Yes, honey. I'm right here.

I fell under again for a while. My heart slowing, the drain competing with the fire in my veins and I realized it was the burn of the potion, trying to keep me asleep, but far too strong for the mortal half of me. Could I coax Finn into the light before there was nothing left for him to find? Toby said there would be a sacrifice for love, and if it meant my life, that was okay. *I want to love you,* I thought faintly.

I'm not perfect.

I snorted and rolled over, my strength fading as I said. *No kidding.*

Time vanished again. I blinked my eyes open, too weak to do

much more than breathe. He lingered in the edge of the light, so close and yet too far away. I tried to reach for him, but my hand fell, strength waning from the constant drain, the spell keeping me under and killing me all at once. My hand dropped like a stone, lying to the side of where I rested, and I longed for him to reach me. If only he could hold me one last time. His sweet kisses meant more than anything I'd ever experienced in my life.

Okay to love you?

The whisper was so faint, I thought I'd misheard, but he crept forward, skin writhing and burning, healing and sizzling, only to repeat the cycle with every advance he took. The pain had to be excruciating. Tears dripped down my cheeks as I struggled to breathe, offering him every ounce of my quickly waning strength.

Yes. Love. I love you, too. Come to me, please. Let me hold you. Could he hear me?

Please. Finn reached for me, his amber eyes glowing bright, though the beast slid its dark ooze over him to pull him back again. The darkness peeled away from its body, but he fought his way forward. Dragged two inches back, only to crawl another foot forward, reaching for me.

Waiting for you. My eyes closed again, heart slowing as if I bled more than power. Perhaps the beast needed my life force to survive as well as my magic. I would have hoped to give Finn more. More time, more love, maybe something to cling to, but all I could do was pray that he'd find his way out of the dark and lean on those among the living, like Oberon, who had been his best friend for centuries, and Sebastian, who was the child of his heart.

The beast snarled, the entire sanctuary shaking from the roar, which turned from a monstrous scream to Finn's human voice, crying and calling for me. I couldn't open my eyes, and my lungs fought for each breath. Maybe it was a dumb idea to have taken all of that potion to keep Summer from yanking me out of Autumn's grasp.

A soft snout nuzzled the tips of my fingers, followed by a wet tongue licking them carefully. I cracked a single eyelid to find the wolf, still half covered in dark ooze, rubbing his head on my hand which lay in the most faded edge of the light, just beyond the shield.

"Love you," I whispered, unable to pet him, or reach for the man I loved. My breath vanished and I slipped into the dark, painless, floating, with only a lingering sense of sadness etched through my soul that I couldn't hold him one last time.

Sixty-Three

FINN

The darkness gnawed at my resolve, trying to pull me back into its cold, merciless embrace. Each step toward Wesley felt like walking on broken glass, the light searing away the darkness that had embedded itself into my soul, blistering my skin and burning deep until my screams echoed from inside out.

The wolf and I fought our way forward together, the pain making us black out a handful of times and lose ground to the darkness. My heart stuttered, then raced, a maddening cycle that had me fearing it would burst. Wesley floated a half dozen yards away, the glow of light surrounding him like the final prize in a video game I'd been playing my entire life.

His chest rose slightly with labored breaths, his face pale and strained. The flavor of his power lingered on the back of my tongue as I unintentionally drained him to fuel the beast. I desperately reached for him even though it hurt.

But the darkness clawed at my mind, whispering insidious lies, trying to convince me that I wasn't strong enough, that I would only hurt him if I got too close. The fear of losing control gripped me like a vise. The darkness fought to drag me back into the abyss where it thrived.

I suddenly understood my father's hesitation to approach my mother's light. Not that he feared her, rather he knew the pain of the darkness raking invisible claws over his soul to regain control.

Wesley reminded me the darkness had always been there, but it hadn't always had control. My mother's light kept me stable when I was young, but I'd crumbled from the weight of losing my family, setting free the monster. The wolf was right, I was weak.

Stronger together, the wolf told me as my human skin blistered from the touch of the light and his power healed it. The agonizing pain replaced by a warmth that I hadn't felt in what seemed like an eternity.

I silently sank into the embrace of the wolf, his strength bolstering mine, and for the first time, I felt like I could finally shove back the darkness. We'd been fighting a long time, both believing we knew what was best. Both lacking the power necessary until we stood together united for one purpose:

Mate. The wolf said his tone filled with both possessiveness and affection.

Ours. I agreed. *You can't be an asshole to him.*

The wolf thought Wesley was an asshole, which made me hesitate. Not because I worried my wolf would hurt him, but because I caught the hint of humor in his tone and his grudging respect for Wesley.

He is kind of an asshole. I thought, but knew it was armor and grateful he had something to protect himself with for all these years. But that was okay—Wesley was our asshole, and we would protect him with everything we had.

Wesley was on his side. Hand fallen away from him, limp but near the faint glow of the surrounding shield. His eyes closed, his breath a stuttering beat, and the flow of his energy between us faded to a trickle.

Drained.

Was hurting him all I could do?

Mate, the wolf reminded me. *Ours.*

I reached the edge of the wriggling barrier, and feared for a split second that I'd be rejected and blasted away from him. My heart raced with worry and need to hold him again as my fingers touched the magic, and the shield shattered. Magic blasted through the sanctuary, slicing away the shadows and giving definition and life to an early morning glow. I held my hand out in front of me, surprised to see it tinged with gold. The gold dragon like my mother, perhaps? But I wore my human form, the light casting dancing rainbows into the abyss around us.

The beast quieted. The magic sinking into it like a wave of soothing music lulled it into rest, but the melody came from the soft song of birds, bugs, and a gentle breeze. A thousand times I'd fought to shove it back into the dark, and this was the first time it went willingly as I gathered Wesley into my arms. Calm radiated from the beast, as if it were well fed, and finally under control. The light soaked into my skin, gentle and warm, the sense of home settling with the wolf inside my soul.

"Wesley?" I whispered, clutching him to my chest as panic clawed at my throat as he didn't move. I couldn't lose him. "Love?"

A sense of icy dread filling my gut with the realization that I couldn't feel his magic anymore. His body was still, breathing shallow, and his golden aura flickered like a dying ember. I shook him gently, desperate to bring him back from the brink.

The wolf howled, a deep, resonant power unfurling in my core, setting the realm around us writhing with swells of magic. Electricity roared through my veins, pulsing at the tips of my fingers and adding waves of shadows to the darkest corners of the sanctuary.

My entire life I'd tried to suppress the dark monster inside, but within it, a massive charge of power that now, reunited with the wolf and calmed by the light, I understood. Everyone called me the Autumn king, and that strength pooled inside a well of endless depths, ready to be used. It could be destruction or creation, heat or cold, life or death. And if I couldn't save Wesley with it, I didn't want it at all.

I held him in my arms, cycling the darkness to warmth, and vibrance; a hot late summer breeze. It coursed through my veins, expanding to every corner of the area, blasting through the shadows to reform the sketchy edges of the realm. The wolf joined his strength with mine, shaping the fabric of reality and directing it to a balance of light and dark rather than the horror of monstrous night it longed to be.

Wesley was my light, and I held him tight, warming him with my touch and begging his soul to stay with me while I willed the magic to fill the void of his depleted power.

Nothing happened, Wesley remained limp, his aura dim and weak, cold in my arms. I screamed, heart breaking at the idea that he'd be stolen from me again. The darkness wove around him, knitting together the frayed edges of our soul bond, and allowing the heat of my heart to rekindle the spark of life that had been nearly extinguished. The golden waves of light began to fill his aura, snaking through him to his core and yanking a thousand micro drops of some unknown liquid from his body. I gathered them into a ball of floating fluid, studying it a moment to find someone else's magic woven through alcohol. Some sort of sleeping potion? Was that why he wasn't waking? I cast it away into the depths of the void.

The warmth continued to seep from my skin into him, and his breath deepened, chest rising and falling with renewed strength. The flickering glow of his aura steadied, growing brighter, until it shone with a golden light that encased our bond and filled my soul.

Tears pricked at my eyes as his magic returned, his blazing aura filling like a lightbulb turned to blinding. The wolf growled softly, flinching from the pain as he'd been in the dark a long time, but he approved and remained strong at my side.

The beast's strength flickered through the sanctuary. A hint of shadows, darkness, and fear touching the edges of everything, and where the light touched it, a golden beauty rippled beneath. The Autumn realm was a battleground where the darkness would forever linger, and as much as it was now a part of me, I had to learn to better control it before Wesley would be safe.

I leaned in to kiss him, a gentle press of lips to lips, heart in my throat as he opened his eyes like I'd lifted some spell on Sleeping Beauty. "I love you, Wesley. Be safe, okay?"

He blinked sleepy, "Finn?" He asked, "You're glowing gold. So beautiful," he whispered while his confused eyes gazed at me as my power shifted. The realm responded to my will and crafted a portal to a place of hot summer days and the scent of sweet baked goods —Summer's realm.

"Finn?" Wesley whispered, reaching up to run his fingertips over my cheek and capture the tears I didn't realize I was crying until that moment.

"I'll find you, love. I promise."

"The monster…"

"He's still here. Always," I said, heart breaking that I'd never be all he deserved.

"But he's you."

"He's me when I wallow in the pain, and I can't always hold him back," I said. He deserved so much better than the broken monster fate had tied him too.

"Wait…" Wesley said, but my power slid over him, carrying him out of the Autumn realm and into the safety of the Summer realm. He vanished from my arms, leaving me alone in the middle of the sanctuary which rippled with shadows of warning. I had two choices, learn to control the beast with the help of my wolf and bask in the light, or let it overwhelm me completely. The wolf and I agreed to face it, and prayed Wesley would be there on the other side.

The realm reformed around us, much as it had been when I'd first stumbled across thinking I was Finley, ghost hunting enthusiast, with no real purpose in life. The rainbow of changing colors and cool breeze settled something inside me, and the sun shifted overhead, from the pulsing heat of summer to a cool fall evening.

The wolf bumped my fingers with his head, and I scratched his ears as we watched the shadows slither around. They no longer frightened me. I knew they were a part of me and all the memories that wanted desperately to force me to sink into the dark. As I stepped closer, and the sun trickled through the trees to illuminate the path, they ceased to cut as deep. I absorbed the first handful, putting them back into place. The monster rippled through me, and the wolf beside me, neither of us acknowledging the flicker. But there were thousands more. How long would it take to tame them all, accept them for what they were, my past, and step forward into the future? Would Wesley still be waiting?

Sixty-Four

WESLEY

I wandered the woods with a golden dragon flying overhead. As I was in my Stag form in the dream, I knew it was a dream, and couldn't call to him, but followed at a run from below, chasing, and begging him to come down. When he vanished into the distant tree tops, I wandered that way, slowing my pace as the dark rose up around me.

The shadows never touched me, though from time to time, the normal trees would morph into things with faces. A clear path of glowing mushrooms and spider webs glistening in the light trickling through the trees guided me through the darker sections. I expected to find the wolf pacing as he often did, or the glowing, but sleepy, eyes of something lingering at the mouth of a cave. This time it was a golden dragon, curled up nose to tail. The creature almost as big as a hillside, it snoozed, opening an amber colored eye to gaze my way.

I hesitated, fearing my Stag form would trigger a chase. Many times I'd chased the golden dragon, but never found him, until now. We both waited in breathless stillness, until he huffed and closed his eye and nestled his snout within the nest of his tail. Time ticked away slowly, feeling like days until I crept forward, fearing he'd snap, change, or even fly away. But I needed to sit with him. I missed him so much.

I tiptoed forward, finding a soft spot of grass near where his tail and neck met, laying across each other like a big cat. He radiated the heat of a warm fall afternoon, and I sank down beside him, feeling like I could rest for the first time in a while. He moved, and I stilled, fearing he'd attack or run, but his tail slipped around me, curling me in against him in a gentle embrace. I closed my eyes and laid my head down to bask in the rare moment of peace.

Ripped from the dream by my phone alarm, I cursed and nearly hurled the device at the wall. But I silenced it, reminding myself it was only a dream, and got up to get ready for work. Mundane life serving the Summer king, could have been worse than rising to *work* a mortal job. I hurried through my routine, threw on my shoes and headed for the door.

The intensifying of the cool mornings, and crumple of fallen leaves beneath my feet brought a wave of sadness to slow my step. The trip to town, usually a quiet time to reflect, made me clutch my jacket and wonder why I'd agreed to live in this small nowhere town where snow fell and everyone knew my name.

Okay, it wasn't nowhere. It was growing. From a tiny blip on the map with a single road through town and no stoplights, to new housing developments, several greenhouse farms, orchards, and the most popular bakery in two hundred miles. I'd like to think the latter was all me and my brilliant marketing, but Sebastian and Liam's baking did most of the work.

A black SUV slowed beside me, passenger window rolling down.

"Want a ride?" Sebastian asked.

I shook my head, though the brisk chill stung my cheeks. At any other court I would have been afraid to turn down the ruler. But Sebastian, as king, was an enigma. Approachable and calm, gentle, yet firm, and rarely, though completely possible, terrifying.

All the kings had an inner darkness. Out of all of them, Seb, with the help of his mate, Liam, controlled his best.

Spring never left his realm without his two paramours. They were anchors to keep him balanced. And if either lost their mates, disaster. I didn't need to be a seer to know that. But the thought made me worry about Finn. He would always be Finn to me. Even if he and Xander, the werewolf king, were one and the same, two sides of a cursed coin.

"I'd like to walk until it snows." Once the leaves finally fell from the trees, their vibrant colors fading to brown, then I'd give up hope for the year. For now, I clung to it, as if walking through the depths of fall could bring him back to me.

"I'll have a cup of tea waiting for you," Seb said and the window went back up.

The SUV drove a few blocks up to park behind the bakery and teashop duo. The parking lot out front was full with customers streaming in and out at the early hour as they made their way to work. The town carved a few more roads and a handful of small shops drew crowds. Wolves and fae, side by side with humans, like some supernatural utopia or some bullshit.

I sighed. Not my utopia.

A kitten wiggled his way up out of the collar of my coat to *merow* in my face. I scratched his head understanding more than any other.

"You're probably not cold, are you?" I asked. Whatever this little king's darkness was, I had yet to encounter it.

He licked my chin, then ducked back inside the coat. Xiao would stay out of sight until I reached my office. The witchchild didn't always accompany Sebastian and Liam to the bakery, but often enough that I was careful with my little guardian.

Winter had yet to fall, but no one had heard from her. Ari raged over her attacking Xiao when she'd slithered her way into Sebastian's realm. But Xiao was fine. Ari struggled with their temper, a trait I was certain they inherited from Sebastian, which meant their power went a little wild. Seb and Liam scrambled to contain it, and teach Ari better control. But the tension in the pack house became unbearable, so when I'd left, Xiao had asked to stay with me.

I suspected the discomfort under Sebastian's roof had been a careful ruse to get me to accept a companion to watch over me. Not that Xiao talked to me much. He was a fluffy white kitten who slept on the pillow beside my head and kept me from descending into broken hearted loneliness. I preferred the cool calm touch of the little Winter over the creepy puck watching Sebastian, any day.

Autumn stabilized. No one left the realm or had been allowed in. Nearly a year passed without a word. Sebastian and Kiran agreed the realm seemed solid to them, but neither knew what went on inside of it. Was Finn reliving the horrors of his past over and over? Had the monster taken control?

Oberon sat with me sometimes. At first it scared the fuck out of me. He had a *don't fuck with me* aura like none I'd ever met. But he'd also moved my things to storage when I'd gone missing, and taken care of all my accounts, even the stash of funds I kept locked away for a rainy day, returning everything better off than when I left.

I didn't thank him. Old rules were hard to break, and while he wasn't fae, his power eclipsed a lot of the remaining fae. If anyone should have been a werewolf king, it was him, mostly because he has no interest in leading.

From time-to-time he'd tell me a story about Finn. Another lifetime and a glimpse more lighthearted than most of the memories I'd seen. The Finn Oberon knew, while a little too serious, was clumsy and curious. He was well liked, despite many fearing the dark side of him, and had adored all of his children and lovers over the years. The last part made Sebastian cry.

Would my Finn remember him? Would my Finn ever come home? Or would all that remain be Xander, the werewolf king, who kept everyone in line with brute strength, practicality, and doom?

I made my way into the shop, accepting the tea from Sebastian as I headed to my office trying to shrug off the lingering chill and the melancholy.

"Do you need help?" Liam asked.

"Can I bring you something to eat?" Seb added.

I stared at them both for a beat, trying to guess intentions they likely didn't have. "I'm fine."

As the marketing and project manager, I took over the logistics of the growing appeal of a bakery located in the middle of a fae realm. Seb and Liam crafted the world with layers of wards to protect the locals, while others traveled through. I'd never met a ruler willing to let others traverse their realm, but the magic led travelers to the shops and out, no one stayed, or at least not beyond those accepted by the pack.

"Can I bring you a sandwich?" Seb asked. "Or a muffin? I have some carrot cake ones. They are vegetarian." He wrung his hands. "Not vegan, but that's okay, right?"

I swallowed my sigh and nodded. "Sure. Bring me a muffin." Xiao wiggled in my coat, and I added. "Maybe some macarons, too?"

"I'll be right in with that stuff," Liam said, tugging Sebastian away. Neither would be fooled by Xiao hiding in my jacket, but they didn't bring him up either. I hoped to protect the little king from any future trauma. Was it moot? Probably. But I was already too close to him to see his future. No one asked either, for which I was grateful. Mostly they fussed over me like mother hens until I snapped at them, and then they left me alone to grieve in peace.

I entered my office, set down my laptop bag and opened it while I pulled out my planner and sipped my tea. Events from the beginning of October through Christmas kept the bakery and tea shop hopping. Liam had mentioned wanting to expand into catering next year, and I was trying to find a way that could work without tripling their staff and space. One of the pack began wedding planning, building a beautiful location that could be rented for the event with the option of enjoying the changing weather, and an indoor pavilion. Catering weddings seemed like the best place to start, and I knew Sebastian's cake recipes would draw more business.

Xiao crawled out of my coat, but I didn't take it off. I was always cold these days. He made his way to a set of crafted wood paper organizers and curled up on the top one. "You could talk to them," I said. He curled himself nose to tail and closed his eyes, not acknowledging my comment. Lately he'd been avoiding the witchchild when possible. I didn't know why they were fighting, or even if they were, but I wouldn't throw him to the curb either. Most days I appreciated the company, even if it felt like I always had a babysitter.

Liam came in and set a sandwich and a muffin on the corner of the desk, and two cookies beside Xiao on the paper tray. "Ari's home today. The sandwich is a vegan avocado, tomato, and grilled mushroom on sourdough."

"Alright," I said.

"My offer still stands. If the holiday planning is too much..."

"It's fine." Busy was better than endless hours of thinking. "You can put the order forms out. I've got everything entered into the system for a seamless process. We'll need to look at either expanding the bakery early next year, or buying a bigger building if you continue to grow like this." If he hadn't turned the other half into a tea shop, he would have had enough space.

"None of us expected the shop to be this popular. Either of them," Liam said.

"Sebastian's omega aura combined with his power as Summer king draws them," I said. Twice I'd left the area, only to be drawn back by the subtle warmth of his realm. Not that I'd ever gotten a distance that the sensation faded. "The excellent food helps," I added, as not to disparage Liam's magic with sweet bread, sourdough, and the dozens of pastries the shop now offered.

Liam snorted. "Thanks." Unlike fae of the past, no ripples of magic came from his words. Not even a flicker of obligation. How did they do that? "Eat something, please." He stared at me a few moments longer before leaving the office and letting me work. I had calls to make, meetings to plan, advertisements to design.

Toby popped his head in to get approval for some art he was taking to the printer, but the day flew by. Xiao vanished after lunch, likely portaling himself back home. Sebastian and Liam looked in on me, or threw occasional questions my way. I added a dozen more things to my ever-growing list, but kept working, scheduling interviews from nearby towns in papers and online media for Sebastian and Liam, food reviews, and even a handful of small party events that would draw more business and need an increase of staff.

I nibbled at the muffin, eating only half of it, and picked apart the sandwich. Not really hungry, I got up to stretch. The front of the store sounded busy. Voices loud and grating, I was ready to go home. The idea of socializing, pretending to be a normal functioning person made me nauseous.

Liam stopped in for the fifth time, frowning over the food still on my plate.

"I'm fine," I said, again.

"Maybe you should go home and rest?"

Because I looked like I hadn't slept? I knew how big the bags under my eyes were and was too tired to use glamour. The lack of sleep made it hard to recharge, and sometimes when I closed my eyes, I dreamed of him. When I didn't, I lay there heartbroken, unable to sleep at all.

Toby refused to give me more sleeping potion. Only after pushing myself to the brink, would I finally drop into a restless sleep for a few hours, then wake and start all over. I'd shifted overnight when I couldn't sleep and ran a dozen miles through the forest to try to calm my racing mind. Liam understood how maddening it was to be separated from a fated mate.

"I don't know if I'll sleep if I go home," I told him honestly. I'd like to dream of him, as that often gave me a few days of reprieve, heart semi-calming and mind easing. I struggled to focus on work most days, but did my best.

Liam sat on the corner of the desk; his gaze concerned.

"Heartbreak won't kill me." I repeated the mantra to myself as if it could become a spell by willpower alone.

"I'm going to have Dylan drive you home." He waved at the computer. "It's not like you can't work from home if you need to."

I stared at the laptop for a minute before shutting it down and packing it up, silently agreeing. The noise from the front of the shop and the mixers in the back had been grating all day. Not their fault as they were the normal sounds of a functioning business. It was me who was broken.

"Xiao should really talk to Ari," I said as I stuffed my laptop in my bag and swung it over my shoulder. "He seems pretty lonely."

"It's fine," Liam said. "Ari is learning a lot, and Xiao is giving them some space. I'm grateful you're taking care of him."

"Small favors to not be a magic world crafted into a pseudo-human being."

Liam sighed and followed me out of the office. "We all work with what we have."

I wasn't surprised to see Dylan waiting for me by the door. But Sebastian thrust a large hot cup of tea and a box of food at me. "Take it with you. Eat something," he commanded.

And because I served him and he demanded it, I would eat, even if it meant choking it down. I took the boxes and silently followed Dylan to his truck. He drove me home, the mile going by fast as the red and orange glow of the autumn leaves made my heart heavy. He pulled into a little gravel road leading through some trees to a tiny house, and put the car in park.

"You need anything?" Dylan asked.

"No," I said as I got out. He waited until I opened the door to the house before steering the car back around and out. I put the food and the computer on the kitchen counter inside the door. The whole house was less than five hundred square feet. Not a castle by any definition. But the wide-open lower level, which was all kitchen, a small bathroom with an all-in-one washer and dryer, and fluffy sofa facing a television I used for background noise, made it feel big. The upper loft hosted a queen-sized mattress surrounded by windows looking out into the woods. And after living here for nearly nine months, it felt like home for the first time in my entire life.

"Xiao?" I called, not seeing him on the sofa and wondering if he was upstairs. But I couldn't hear his breathing either. Maybe he'd gone back to the big house. I sent a text to Liam just in case, worried about the little would-be king.

I'll keep an eye out for him. Liam replied. *Get some rest.*

I sighed and headed up to the loft, crawling into bed and lying there, tired and cold, but anxious. The realization made me roll over and stare off into the distance as though I could sense where the feeling was coming from. It wasn't mine as I couldn't identify a source for the apprehension. How odd.

I lay there a while. Closed my eyes, and even dozed for a time. The sound of a car pulling up outside and a door closing roused me from a groggy half sleep. Were they dropping Xiao off? He never traveled by car. I hoped they weren't bringing me more food. Sebastian already raided my house twice a week to clean out my fridge and restock it with ready to eat meals even if I rarely touched the ones from the week before. His compulsion from earlier lingered, but without a set time, I could push it off until it became unbearable to comply.

The scent of cinnamon wafted through my open windows, unfamiliar but warming, like a hot cup of apple cider laced with the spicy bite. The car drove away, though I'd only ever heard one door close. Strange.

A soft knock sounded on my door. Sebastian and Liam had a key and entered all the time. Xiao could just pop in whenever he wanted. No one else visited. Who could it be?

I rolled out of bed, tired and exhausted, fumbling my way down the stairs. The left side of the house was a wall of windows behind the sofa peering out into the woods, but the door stood as a solid barrier of wood without a peephole. On warded land within Summer's territory, I had never had cause to worry, yet the anxiety in my gut grew as I approached the door, as did the scent of cinnamon and apple.

I braced myself to open it, chiding myself for being a scared idiot. But when I cracked the door, the man standing on my tiny porch made me gasp. "Finn?"

Sixty-Five

WESLEY

He looked as I remembered, young, with his dude-bro attire of a college hoodie and short on the sides, long on top, haircut, no hint of shadow in his face. The kind of guy who could be any college kid, and I'd feared had only been a glamour of the man I'd been mated to.

"Hey," he said, seeming nervous. He thrust a small box at me, but since it was from the Sweet Tooth, Liam and Seb's bakery, I knew it was pastry. "Sebastian said he has been working on perfecting this for a while." He looked really uncomfortable for a few seconds. "He didn't recognize me. But I understand from my wolf's memories, how bad we fucked up. I was going to say something but the Alpha wolf showed up and Oberon ran interference before dropping me off. He said they want to interrogate me, but I had to see you." He let out a long breath. "It hurt to see him and he didn't recognize me, and yet I knew him and all the terrible things I did..."

I took the box, our hands brushing and my heart fluttering in my chest. He was really here, in front of me. Had I fallen asleep? Was this some sort of dream? Most of the time, when I dreamed of him as Finn, we sat down together and I dreamt of him holding me. I always woke up from them crying and alone.

"I'm sorry," Finn whispered.

I stood in the doorway, uncertain what to say, wanting to throw myself at him, and fearing I'd shatter our dream.

"I'm not a dream, baby. I'm sorry I took so long to get control of everything." He leaned against the side of the house, his heartbeat racing to my sensitive hearing. "I got my shit together, and had to talk to my moms. Was gone a long time and they were worried, but they look forward to meeting you, and then I called Oberon to figure out how to get here and not have Summer put me in an oven..." he rambled as if uncertain where to stop.

It hurt to breathe. He couldn't be real.

"I am. Wesley, please."

I blinked at him, a lock on my jaw as a thousand thoughts ricocheted through my mind.

"Wes," Finn said. He caught my arm, holding my elbow as he settled into the bubble of my personal space, amber eyes meeting mine.

He didn't look like some werewolf king. He looked like *my* Finn.

"I am, baby. Love... say something. Please."

Tears blurred my gaze as I feared this was some final goodbye. Probably necessary as he'd spent the last year not needing me at all.

"That's not true," Finn cupped my cheek in his palm. "I've missed you desperately. I tried to stay out of your dreams at first, but sometimes it just happened and then you didn't run away or scream at me. So sometimes I found you. Even if it was to sit with you, or watch you wander through my realm. And since the kitten watched us a lot, and I let him in, I thought it was okay, that maybe you knew and Summer knew..."

"Then where the fuck have you been? Why did you..." I couldn't repeat that he'd sent me to Sebastian like some used up toy.

"He kept you safe, right?"

"I keep myself safe."

"Always prickly."

I opened my mouth to berate him for the comment, but he said, "Love, I'm sorry. The darkness needed to be tamed. I needed to learn control and build a safe place for you."

"What?" I asked.

"You said something about jewels and castles..."

I would have rather had *him* for the last year than any amount of material wealth. How many times had I thought about shifting and taking off into the woods? I could run a long time. Maybe to the other side of the continent or until my heart gave out.

He sucked in a pained breath. "Could you outrun us?" Finn asked as he pressed his forehead to mine. My breath hitched at his touch. The bond between us flared to life with a jolt, and his emotions poured into me—regret, longing, love. The anxiety I'd felt was his at the thought of me walking away from him.

"I never wanted to leave you," Finn whispered, his voice thick with emotion. "But I had to control the dark. It was eating me alive, and drained you nearly to death."

My heart ached. The agony of the past year, overwhelming. I wanted to scream and push him away for the hurt he'd caused. But the warmth of his touch, the way his thumb gently brushed my cheek, melted the anger, leaving only the raw ache of how much I'd missed him. He looked uncertain and sad, but hope radiated off him.

"I'm sorry I wasn't faster. The wolf and I had a lot to learn."

Were they still at war with each other?

Finn's eyes shifted, the wolf suddenly staring back at me, not with anger or even disdain, but affection. He leaned in close to nuzzle my cheek and whispered a guttural, "Mate." Which made me shiver with the need to be alone with him. "He likes you," Finn said. "Even if he thinks you're a bit of an asshole."

"I think he's an asshole, too," I said.

His eyes returned to the pretty amber youthful gaze that I knew as Finn. "I am Finn," he said. "I will always be Finn. Even when the wolf has control."

"Won't it be weird for everyone else for you not to be Xander?" I wondered.

"I'm still Xander," Finn said. "Oberon reminded me that this is closer to how he remembers me from our early years together. It's how I feel most natural, maybe because I spent the most recent years in this human skin?" His gaze searched mine. "Unless you want something else?"

"I just want you."

Finn's his fingers threading through my hair as he pulled me closer. "I'm here," he said.

What if he left again? What if they needed him to be the king of wolves? I was just a Stag, a seer unable to see his future because I was too close.

"Wesley," Finn said as he pressed our foreheads together again. "I'm not going anywhere. You are mine and I am yours."

"Caveman bullshit," I grumbled.

He chuckled, the sound sweet and light, touching something in my soul. "As long as you're with me, I will be whatever you need." The bond between us pulsed with renewed strength. "Please, Wes, give us a chance." Finn closed the distance between us, his lips pressed to mine, and I sank into his touch. The loneliness, fear, desperate longing—crashed into me with the force of a tidal wave as I threw myself into his arms.

He caught me, wrapping my legs around his waist and pressing me against the side of the house. The box of pastry tumbled from my grasp and I didn't care as I clutched his shirt, needing to feel every inch of him against me, and I opened for him, letting his tongue slip inside and sucked on it. I moaned into the kiss, Finn swallowing the sound, his lips firm and demanding.

I wanted to stay lost in him, existing in a world where nothing else mattered but the two of us. But eventually, we had to come up for air, and Finn pulled back just enough to rest his forehead against mine once more.

"I'm so sorry," he whispered, his voice thick with emotion. "For everything. Every time grief took over in the past, I let the dark gain a stronger hold. Sometimes something awakes a memory and I just want to sink into the dark to cry. The wolf and I have been working on it, but Oberon has suggested I try human therapy, too."

Tears slipped down my cheeks, and he brushed them away with his thumb, his touch as gentle as it was reverent. "Seems to be helping Sebastian," I said.

Finn's lips curved into a smile. "I've got a lot of relationships to mend," he said. "But I need to start with you. Nothing works without you. Will you give us a chance?"

I nodded, unable to speak as the weight of his words settled over me. Even after all this mess, and knowing that I would always be the proverbial weak link in his armor, he still wanted me.

"I do," he said. "But it has to be your choice."

"Promise me," I demanded, "Promise me you won't leave again. That you won't cast me away, or give me to someone. Promise that I am yours and yours alone."

Finn leaned in, pressing a tender kiss to my lips. "I promise," he murmured against my mouth. "You're mine, and I'm yours, Wesley. Always."

I rutted against him, grinding my hips into his, my cock desperate to be touched as he dove into another deep kiss with me. My heart pounded with a need to have him, to feel him inside me, around me, and strengthen our soul bond.

"Are you using magic on me?" I asked, breathing hard and gazing into his eyes for any sign of a lie.

He snorted. "No. Not unless me being horny automatically makes that happen. It's not something the wolf and I thought we'd need. Do you feel magic coming off of me? I have it tamped down as much as I can. I wanted to be as much me as possible for you, but sometimes the wolf bleeds through."

"All I feel is you," I said. "Anxiety and hope." Not magic. But really needy. "Fuck, I need you."

He hummed as he kissed down my jaw and over my neck, the vibration of his kiss on my throat making me desperate to go inside and strip. "Your house is warded by the Summer king," Finn said. "His magic and his mate's."

"Huh?" I knew about the wards, but my lust filled brain wondered why they would keep him out.

"It has to be your choice," Finn said. He peppered small kisses over my face and neck, hands on my hips firm to keep me still else I'd have been rutting against him again. "You have to invite me in. Oberon warned me that if I tried to force anything on you Sebastian would blast me into the next county. Even if that means stepping inside your house without an official invite."

"Oh," I said. "You can come in. I mean, I want you to." The magic of the wards rippled around us, pressure at my back easing, though the hum of them lingered.

Finn lifted me away from the wall and carried me through the open door, then nudged it closed with his foot. He turned me to press me into the door and devour my lips with his again. I sunk into his kiss, desperate for his touch, and his flesh on mine.

"My magic is limited inside the house," Finn said. "Can't zap away the clothes," he grumbled as he leaned back to yank off his hoodie, and the white undershirt beneath, tossing them aside. "Can I?" He tugged at my shirt.

"Yes," I agreed, and lifted the sweater, struggling to get it off while pressed against the door, but not wanting to let go of him either. If it was a dream, I planned to savor it.

"I'm not a dream, baby." Finn pulled the sweater away and pressed himself against me, his skin warm and soothing.

"Prove it," I demanded. I had thought the scent of cinnamon and apple had been the pastry he brought, but the box was abandoned outside on the porch. The smell was him. His skin radiated the warm crisp of an autumn day.

He wrapped his hand around the back of my neck and dragged me into another long kiss. Could a dream feel this real? No one kissed like Finn, like he wanted to worship and devour me all at once.

"I do, baby," he breathed between us. His eyes glowed with brightness, part him and part wolf. "The darkness will always be there," he said. "It's part of me."

"I'm not afraid of it, or of you. I'm dangerous too, you know."

He smiled. "You're kind of terrifying, and I fucking love it."

"Then why aren't we both naked?" I asked.

He grunted, and unwrapped my legs from his, then shoved his pants down, kicking them, his boxers, and his shoes all to the side. His cock jutted upward, a fine thing I asked for in a dozen ways. Memories of our encounter during my heat returned and how careful he'd been despite the raging lust.

"This okay?" he asked. "You're not in your fawn form…"

I unbuttoned my pants and shoved them off, leaving myself bare to his gaze, worried it wouldn't be enough without glamour.

He blew out a breath, eyes smokey with desire, gaze flicking down and back up. I waited for rejection, but he dropped to his knees and took my cock down the back of his throat in one long stroke. I cried out and wound my fingers through his hair, his gaze meeting mine as he sucked hard, sliding off to tease the tip of me with his tongue and then swallowing me back down until I bumped the back of his throat.

"Fuck, you're good at this," I cursed, hips moving of their own accord to thrust into him. He hummed around me, holding me deep until I thought he'd choke before pulling back to a teasing glide. Not fast, though I was desperate to come as the heat pooled in the base of my spine and trickled upward like an inferno ready to erupt.

He bobbed on my dick, my heart pounding as I struggled to maintain control.

"I don't want to come until you're inside of me," I said. His cock leaked against his stomach, the drops decorating his belly button. I longed to lick them up and savor the taste of him.

Finn popped off my cock, teasing the foreskin with his tongue and warm breath. "Couch okay, or would you rather go upstairs? I'd like you to ride me."

The idea of sinking down on his cock nearly undid my resolve. "Couch."

He tugged me a few steps to the cushy sofa, and I'd never been so grateful for a small space when he lay down on his back and slid me over him, placing a handful of kisses over my hips and inner thighs. "I promised to eat your ass before," he reminded me.

"Don't you dare. I need you to fuck me." I scrambled over him, determined to line him up and shove that fine cock as deep as I could take it.

"Lube," Finn said as I wrapped my hand around his dick to press it against my hole. "Magic limited in your house," he said.

"Fuck." I cursed and reached for the side table drawer and the unopened tube of lube that had appeared after one of Sebastian's raids. I never asked, but at least now it was useful. It took a few precious seconds to open, and I clumsily dumped a giant amount over him.

He helped coat himself and held my hips in a firm grip as I guided him to enter. We both hissed as he slid in, his cock stretching me as it burrowed deep. It ached for only a few seconds before the divine heat of him pulsing inside made me nearly come undone.

"Go at your own pace," Finn said, his breathing strained with his infinite control.

I *was* going at my own pace, and that meant taking him to the root where I ground into his hips and threw back my head, licking my lips as he rubbed things inside of me that whittled away my resolve. I bounced on him, only rising an inch or two before slamming back down and grinding into his hips until his cock tickled my prostate drawing small gasps from me.

Finn steadied my hips, meeting my downward thrust with his up, the both of us breathing hard, gaze locked as if we looked away, the moment would be broken. I leaned forward to catch his lips, desperate to have every ounce of him inside me, coating me with his come and his soul.

"Yes," Finn murmured against my lips, tongue meeting mine for a duel as we ground together. "Won't come until you do," he said, releasing my right hip to wrap his hand around my cock. His heated touch made me growl and speed up. He matched my rhythm, drawing me to the edge of maddening waves of desire.

If this was a dream, it was the best I'd ever had.

"Not a dream, baby," Finn said.

I couldn't hold back any longer, and came hard, the ribbon painting his chest and coating his hand. He gasped as my body squeezed him tight and his heat filled me.

"Fuck," I said, stars sparkling across my vision as his cock seemed to grow.

"A knot," he said, as our bodies locked together, dragging another orgasm from me, and more waves of come from him to fill the inside of me. Had that happened during my heat? I couldn't recall it. "No," he said. "Never before." He threw his head back, his magic popping around us and the house wards sizzled and snapped in warning. "Sorry."

I worried a half second about the rising sensation being too much, but my cock hardened again, taking only a half dozen more grinding thrusts of his hard knot inside of me to make me come again. He followed, filling me until I was certain there couldn't be room for more of his spend, and the magic sizzling around us would cause some sort of explosion. His power sank into my skin. Our auras expanding until they overlapped with wriggling rainbow colors to combine and solidify our soul bond.

"Finn," I whispered against his lips, the waves of lust rising again. Even my heat had never rewarded me with this many orgasms and continued desire.

"Right here, Wes. Fuck, you feel amazing." He gazed at me with adoration and lust. "I love you so much, Wes. Please stay with me."

I groaned, his words making my heart skip a beat. "I love you, honey. Thank you for coming back. If you ever leave me again, I'll track you down and rip your guts out through your nose."

He laughed. "So romantic."

"It's my fae half, what can I say? There are some perks to being witchborn."

"I'll say," he agreed as we slid together and came again, cries pressed to each other's lips. "This is better than the heat," he said.

"Yeah? My other form is made for this." The human body didn't make its own lube or fit as nicely against him as my fawn form.

"Yes," Finn said. "I love this, and you, in all your forms. Even the scary as fuck giant Stag with bloodred eyes and razor-sharp hooves."

"Saw that, did you?"

"Mhmm."

"And you're still here fucking me."

"Oh yes," he groaned. "Not sure I'll ever get enough of this."

I dove in to claim his lips again and pin him to the back of the sofa as I rode him through another dozen orgasms, and we were both dripping sweat, come, and magic. I was pretty sure I'd never get enough either.

Sixty-Six

WESLEY

Night had long since fallen, leaving moonlight and the cool breeze of the evening streaming through my windows as the knot finally released and we both laid on the couch, spent. I'd never felt as thoroughly loved or filthy as I did in that moment, sweat and dried come all over me. A hundred tiny red marks decorated my skin from Finn rolling me over to taste me. I wanted to climb up into the loft and sleep with him curled around me in my bed, but neither of us seemed to have the energy.

I was draped over him on the couch as if I were a Wesley shaped blanket made only for him. The sound of a car pulling up outside made me scramble off as I knew instantly who it was because the wards had been going crazy the entire time we'd made love.

"Fuck, it's Sebastian," I said.

Finn rose slowly, groaning as the wards continued to snap at him, but his shape changed to the larger male the wolf favored. He shoved me behind him, not bothering to dress as he ripped the door open.

Seb stood on the porch with Liam behind him, his face immediately turning pink, and he put his back to us. "Holy fuck!"

"I'll say," I muttered.

Finn snorted. "Don't suppose the two of you can hand the wards over to me so they'll stop tickling me?"

"Is that what Wesley wants?" Seb asked, his back to us, gaze focused on his mate. He wrung his hands and stared at his mate.

"Yes, please," I said.

"I do not need to know if Wesley is naked and gross, too," Seb said.

Since Finn blocked my body from view, I hoped all they were rewarded with was the overwhelming smell of sex.

Liam put his hand to the side of the house, his other reaching for Seb, and the wards shifted, soothing from a raging miniature electric storm to a quiet fall day.

"Thank you," Finn said. And like Liam and Seb's gratitude, it held no magic. Maybe this new world really would be free of obligation.

Liam tugged Sebastian off the porch. "We expect to see you both at the bakery tomorrow." The threat clear.

"Uh, we could use some time," I said.

"Not negotiable," Liam said. "The fact that the Autumn king walked through our territory without raising alarm is worrisome for everyone. Especially since no one knows where Winter is."

"About that," Finn said, "I sort of have her imprisoned in my realm."

"What?" Seb stuttered a few words of protest I couldn't really make out.

"The little Winter is safe, right? He visited from time to time when Wesley let me in through his dreams. But I wasn't about to let her out to hurt him," Finn said.

"He's fine," Liam said.

"Good. We'll catch up with you tomorrow, sit down and go over things," Finn said.

I groaned, was this going to be a war?

"Wesley knows to call if he needs something."

"You're still required to eat something," Seb called as he got into the SUV and covered his eyes rather than looking up at his naked *apa* standing in front of me in the doorway. "I'm glad you don't look like I remember because this memory is going to be burned in my brain forever."

"This isn't his normal form either," I called.

"I don't want to know," Seb grumbled.

Finn took a step back as the SUV turned around, making its way out of my yard. He closed the door and instantly returned to *my* Finn. "I will always be your Finn."

I sighed. "I still have to eat something. I vowed to serve their court..." Would he be mad.

"The box I brought is on the counter." He pointed and I blinked at it, thinking it was strange that it had made its way inside. But a lump of white fur curled itself up in the cat tower near the far window. Had the baby Winter gotten an eyeful?

"Aw, there is little Winter. Good," Finn said as he tugged me to the kitchen counter and opened the box to reveal a slice of cake, still perfect and smelling like divine sugar sweetness. "Let's get you fed."

"Food and a shower," I agreed, feeling crusty.

"Then bed," Finn said. "I promised to eat your ass and plan to make it good."

I swallowed hard, cock rising again, and groaned. "Not in front of the little King."

"That's why I said upstairs," Finn lifted the cake out of the container and held it to my lips. I took a bite and licked the frosting off his finger.

"That's delicious."

"The cake, or me coated in frosting?" Finn wanted to know.

"Both."

"I'll have to see how you taste with frosting, too." He groaned as his cock jutted toward his stomach again. "Not sure we should bother with the shower. I'm just going to make you messy again. If that's okay with you?"

Anyone else I'd have complained, but with Finn, I didn't care as long as he kissed me.

Epilogue

FINN

Thick decay lingered in the scent of wet leaves left to rot after a fall rain. Shadows twisted between gnarled trees clawing toward the darkening sky. Spirits whispered all around, little more than wisps of energy. The path wove us through lit jack-o'-lantern faces hanging from trees as if grown rather than hung. The glow of the moon in full glory crowning the sky far overhead.

This deep into the Autumn realm, my darkest side found comfort.

"Macabre," Kiran said, his mates at his side.

"I love it," Toby said.

"Of course you would. It's like Halloween on steroids," Nick added.

"Not a vacation spot I'd choose," Seb said, Liam at his back.

"You like spooky," Liam said. "I bet you could make cookies like those lanterns."

"Oh, pumpkin flavored filling would be delicious," Seb agreed.

I led them through the chaos with ease. I had debated on bringing Wesley, but wanted to show him the entire realm at my pace, and the Winter bitch needed to be gone before I'd trust it was safe for him.

After sitting down with Sebastian and Liam in the bakery, I understood why the wolf had tried to avoid the pull toward Liam, knowing the man was Sebastian's mate. The two were paired perfectly. But Sebastian stared at me a long time, asking to see *Finn*. And Finn was who I was at the core, even while Xander would always be a part of me. A hundred lifetimes and we either learned to evolve, or let it destroy us. Liam had been better at that too. I could flip between a dozen personas recognized by a handful of people who still lived, but I lived in Finn's skin now, and felt at home there, mostly because Wesley stared at me like I mattered.

Wandering through a maze of withering vines and deadfall, the crunch of leaves beneath our feet, I let the shadows gather to me. The ripple of the beast trickled over my skin, though none of the others paused. I'd promised them I had control, much as they did. Sometimes the beast would need to roam free, but the wolf and I worked in tandem with it now, giving small tastes of freedom to the dark to build things like this spooky area of the Autumn realm.

"What's the plan?" Nick asked. "I'm not sure any of us should absorb the power of the Winter queen, and Xiao's not ready."

The Winter realm would wait as there wasn't much remaining of it beyond fractured ice puddles. I didn't think the little king needed the trauma of killing the former ruler, as none of us had. Spring, Summer, and Autumn gone long before we were born with the witchcurse in our blood. That Xiao was meant to be Winter, meant he, too, was witchborn of some kind. But we all hoped to spare him the brutal trial by fire we'd all experienced to obtain our realms.

"Can we release her power, like let the weave of magic reabsorb it naturally?" Sebastian asked. "Did you guys find anything in the library?"

"No. But it might have been lost when Underhill passed," Toby added.

"I'm okay killing her," Kiran said. "Absorbing her power."

"Didn't she raise you?" Seb asked.

"And beat me, and cursed me, and locked me in ice for a few centuries. No love lost. Summer was my mother and I don't remember her at all," Kiran said. "Why would I care for the witch who lived to drive a dagger into my gut at every turn?"

"He's still a bit feral, eh?" I asked.

Seb snorted. "You have no idea."

"Doesn't play well with others," Toby chuckled.

"I play well enough with you and Nick," Kiran defended.

"Gross," Seb said. "Don't make things gross."

I let them banter knowing it eased their anxiety. The Winter queen had cursed us all, drained magic and crafted a thousand ways to make each of us miserable. My beast still echoed her nasty words as if they belonged to it.

A ripple of magic tugged at something inside my gut, as if something or someone had crossed into my realm. "What the hell?" I said pausing to analyze the sensation.

"What?" Seb asked.

"I felt it too," Liam added. "Someone entered the realm. Did you call Wesley?"

"No." As far as I knew he was tucked away in his little office at the bakery, Oberon on guard without my mate knowing it, as my friend sat at a table, eating pastries and drinking coffee, while using their wi-fi to *work*. If Wesley knew I'd asked Oberon to look after him while I was away, he'd have laid into me. And while his scowl turned me on in a lot of masochistic ways, I didn't really want to be sleeping on the sofa when I could be wrapped around him.

"The queen can't break out, right?" Toby asked.

"Not possible," I said, but raced through the array of trees toward the central gnarl of my magic meant to keep her locked away. The prison came into view, a giant section of earth with braided ropes of trees and magic pulsing like an otherworldly birdcage. But a section split wide, like ribs peeled open to release a wayward heart.

The magic wards and wriggling array of spells flickered,

shredded and partially dissolved, leaving wisps of energy floating like fireflies. Someone had broken through the magic in one small section. Had she escaped? Had I somehow underestimated the strength she had left? Her power drained, and without a tether to any remaining living fae, as I'd already hunted them down and severed any bonds, it seemed an impossible feat.

"I thought you said she was contained," Kiran said.

"Someone broke her out," Seb said as Liam approached the open area. "Was it a spell or something?"

Liam shook his head. "Power." He glanced my way. "Can you ease back on the wards so I can examine the break?"

I loosed my grip on the wild array of power locking down the space and the crackling lights of the broken magic faded. Leaves crunched beneath my boots as I moved around Liam to examine the spot myself. The cold energy of her fight to get free clung to the insides of the cage as though she'd been there seconds before. The signs of her power fading away. Not from an escape, but as if it were gone altogether, but that wasn't possible.

"How?" I muttered examining the area as the last touches of ice and frost melted. "There's no way she could have escaped." The shadows squirmed and gathered as I felt the monster rise up inside, fearing she'd gotten away and needing to go after her to protect everyone, Wesley, Sebastian, and even the little king who found solace in Wesley's tiny cabin.

I held back the change but stalked beyond the cage and into the waiting swell of overwhelming darkness tinged with tiny traces of icicles. The others followed close behind, and while a chill rose in the air, Sebastian poured heat over the group to warm us as we emerged from the thickest remnants of swollen and gnarled trees to a tiny clearing of glowing mushrooms.

A small figure lay curled in on themselves in the center, and for a few seconds I feared it was Xiao, and that the little king had taken the curse of the fae queen and wouldn't survive it. But the tiny being in the clearing pulsed with wild waves of magic.

"Ari," Seb cried and stepped forward, but Liam grabbed him around his waist and held him back.

"Wait."

Splintered crystals of ice formed and shattered around them, darkness sliding over them in pools of shadows that rippled with color and pops of fire, then ice. I recalled how much my own transition had hurt, burning away the worst of the shadows. Was that what Ari was experiencing after taking the Winter queen's power?

"Baby, what have you done?" Seb called, pleading for an answer from the unmoving being in the middle of the clearing. They didn't answer, but sucked in a deep breath that we all could see and slowly stood.

They looked like a teen version of Sebastian, though in their eyes power radiated as shadows crossed them as if something dark lived inside. They raised their hands and ice formed in one, fire in the other. They snuffed the fire and focused on the ice, which sculpted itself into a delicate snowflake shape and then into a familiar face, which I recognized as the human form of Xiao.

"He's mine," Ari said. "She tried to hurt him."

"Ari," Liam said, "We were going to take care of it. We would never let her hurt you or Xiao."

"He's mine," Ari said, voice firm. "Mine to protect. Mine and mine alone."

Silence stretched through the clearing and we all studied the supernatural being before us. Had a realm ever been made cognizant before? Perhaps it was how all gods of mortal mythology formed as I couldn't imagine a being more powerful. But Wesley mentioned Xiao hadn't wanted Ari infected with my darkness. I could only imagine how bad the witchchild would be now that they had absorbed the nightmare queen.

"Ari," Sebastian said, hesitating as though he didn't know what to say.

"Do you hate me?" Ari asked in a childlike voice, their gaze focused on Sebastian's face, and then darting to Liam's.

"No, never," Sebastian said and rushed to wrap his arms around Ari. Liam did the same while Kiran and I shared a cautious glance. Would love be enough to save Ari from becoming a nightmare?

I put my hand over my heart and stepped forward to offer my help to keep this baby superpower from becoming supernova and let my magic surge, creating a bond that I knew would have Wesley screaming at me later, but it had to be done. "I vow to protect Xiao until he fully embraces his Winter powers, so long as you keep your grip on the magic within you."

Kiran did the same, offering himself as another barrier. "Seconded."

Sebastian gaped at us. "Ari would never..." But they could. Ari could easily overwhelm all of us and bring the entire universe into chaos.

Liam added, "Summer agrees," his gaze met Sebastian's. "We protect Winter as long as you continue to learn control and keep a tight grip on your magic." He narrowed his eyes at Ari. "This is the first and last time you will have disobeyed us. We told you to stay home and watch over the pack. We would have handled this."

Another wave of shadows flickered through Ari's eyes, as if demons were waiting inside, ready to break free. But just as quickly, the darkness receded, and Ari clutched the frozen statue of Xiao to their chest. "I accept. Help me protect Xiao and be the mate he needs."

We all nodded, adding magic promises to help bind the witchchild to humanity. Would it work? Only time would tell, but I couldn't wait to get home to Wesley, and maybe check on a small white kitten that often seemed to hide in his pocket.

Fin

Grave Beginnings

Subscribe to check out the **exclusive** to **Ream** new series:

Grave Beginnings: A Beyond the Veil Mystery

https://reamstories.com/page/ljblawxnty/story/m1cn90xzyd
Cover Image temporary place holding and created by Lissa Kasey

Night with the Morningstar

Join the newsletter and get Night with the Morningstar free, and read about Star and Yuri's night together as the world explodes around them:

https://BookHip.com/FZBTZMT

Letter from Lissa

Want to read before everyone else? Join my <u>Ream</u> <u>Subscription:</u>
https://reamstories.com/lissakasey .

Thank you so much for reading *WitchBorn: A Kitsune Chronicle story*! Read a Kitsune Short (Seb goes to Costco) on Ream: https://reamstories.com/page/ljblawxnty/story/ltu5zs6lac

Lissa Kasey specializes in Urban Fantasy contemporary romance with magic, witches, vampires, fae, shifters, and even a few ghost hunters thrown in.

Be sure to join my <u>Facebook group</u> Lissa Kasey's Mystical Men, for fun daily polls, writing snippets, and updates on new releases to this series and others. Also check out my website at Lissa Kasey.com for new information, visiting authors, and novel shorts.

If you enjoyed the book, please take a moment to leave a review!

Thank you so much for reading!

About the Author

Lissa Kasey is more than just romance. Lissa specializes in in-depth characters, detailed world building, and twisting plots to keep you clinging to the page. All stories have a side of romance, emotionally messed up protagonists and feature LGBTQA spectrum characters facing real world problems no matter how fictional the story.

Buy Direct from Lissa Kasey at:
Lissakasey.com

bookbub.com/authors/lissa-kasey
amazon.com/Lissa-Kasey/e/B008FTIBOK

Also by Lissa Kasey

Also, if you like Lissa Kasey's writing, check out her other works:

Rise of the Fallen:

Touched by the Morningstar

Scion of the Morningstar

Sword of the Morningstar

Simply Crafty Paranormal Mystery Series:

Stalked by Shadows

Marked by Shadows

Conventional Shadows

Possessed by Shadows

Touched by Shadows (Novella)

Sky's Shadow (Novella)

Kitsune Chronicles:

Witchblood

WitchMinion

WitchBond

WitchBane

WitchWolf (Novella)

WitchCurse

WitchBorn

Pillars of Magic: Dominion Chapter:

Inheritance (Pillars of Magic: Dominion Chapter 1)

Reclamation (Pillars of Magic: Dominion Chapter 2)

Conviction (Pillars of Magic: Dominion Chapter 3)

Ascendance (Pillars of Magic: Dominion Chapter 4)

Absolution (Pillars of Magic: Dominion Chapter 5)

Raising Kaine (Novella)

Pillars of Magic: Dark Awakening

Resurrection (Pillars of Magic: Dark Awakening 1)

Transfiguration (Pillars of Magic: Dark Awakening 2)

Romance a Curse:

Heir to a Curse

Recipe for a Curse

Reflection of a Curse

Hidden Gem Series:

Hidden Gem (Hidden Gem 1)

Cardinal Sins (Hidden Gem 2)

Candy Land (Hidden Gem 3)

Benny's Carnival (Hidden Gem 3.5)

Haven Investigations Series:

Model Citizen (Haven Investigations 1)

Model Bodyguard (Haven Investigations 2)

Model Investigator (Haven Investigations 3)

Model Exposure (Haven Investigations 4)

Survivors Find Love:

Painting with Fire

An Arresting Ride

Range of Emotion

Evolution: Genesis

Boys Next Door Omnibus